MY PROMISE

GREG KUJALA

DORRANCE
PUBLISHING CO
EST. 1920
PITTSBURGH, PENNSYLVANIA 15238

The contents of this work, including, but not limited to, the accuracy of events, people, and places depicted; opinions expressed; permission to use previously published materials included; and any advice given or actions advocated are solely the responsibility of the author, who assumes all liability for said work and indemnifies the publisher against any claims stemming from publication of the work.

Dorrance Publishing Co
585 Alpha Drive
Suite 103
Pittsburgh, PA 15238
Visit our website at www.dorrancebookstore.com

ISBN: 979-8-88683-492-5
eISBN: 979-8-88683-580-9

MY PROMISE
GREG KUJALA

Acknowledgements

First and foremost, I thank my wife Eileen for her valuable editorial comments, especially dealing with voice and transitions. I take full responsibility for any deficiencies with this tale and ascribe the fleshing out of the characters to her efforts.

Sam Quinone's excellent book Dreamland revealed a world of which I knew nothing before reading about the opioid epidemic that swept our country while I was in school.

My classmates and teachers at Jefferson and Wilmington Medical Center provided me with excellent opportunities to learn the art of medicine and I am thankful for the time and wisdom they graciously gave to me.

And finally, my great appreciation for my high school English teachers Maryann Galloway and Gary Boom, who did their level best to teach me the skills of critical thinking, composition, and writing.

CHAPTER ONE

Monday, Day One of the Four Years at Jefferson Medical College

David walked into the auditorium and took a seat with the other students for their first day orientation. The room was in the Curtis Building facing Walnut Street and probably one of the original school buildings that Jefferson Medical College had occupied. The ceilings were ornate with dark brown wooden beams. Between heavy, walnut bookcases hung pictures, presumably of Jefferson professors from past years. David recalled that Jefferson Medical College was established in 1824 by George McClellan who was Thomas Jefferson's personal physician. Pennsylvania Hospital of the University of Pennsylvania was established in 1765 and located a few blocks from Jefferson. He wondered if students at Penn and Temple were starting with similar orientations. "There must be a couple hundred people in this class," David thought. He later found out there were 225 students.

Professor Martin was first up for the day. "Welcome to Jefferson Medical College. I am Professor Martin of the Anatomy Department. We will meet again in the dissection lab. Today you will complete several forms, which are being passed out now. Each is important despite seeming trivial. There are a few important items that you must pay attention to and complete correctly. We are Jefferson Medical College for the purposes of these forms, not Thomas Jefferson University. Completely fill in the circles with a number 2 pencil. Use a green not red eraser and be sure to remove all traces of the pencil marks if you change an answer. Red erasers can leave a trace of darkness, thus confusing the scanner and possibly leading to an incorrect answer, whether on these forms or on your exam forms. Use a green eraser. At Jefferson, we strive for the best grades possible not just for the individual students receiving the correct grade, but also because Jefferson receives state and federal money based on student performance in the aggregate.

David leaned over to the attractive, blond woman to his left, later introduced as Amanda and asked, "Are we in grade school? I have a Master's in Marine Biology and somehow made it through undergrad and grad school without that pearl of eraser information."

Amanda shifted in her seat to face David and replied, "I suspect more of this sort of instruction is coming today and during our four years at Jefferson. By the way I'm Amanda Jackson."

"David Coleman. Glad to have this seat next to a lovely and wise woman. Where did you go to school?" He darkened a few more circles, completing his first questionnaire.

"Catholic University in D.C. I majored in English, minored in Music."

"Instrument?"

"Flute."

David replied, "I bought a Gemeinhardt while in college for a hundred bucks and can play a few tunes but am really a rank amateur. I'm also equally poor on clarinet and tenor sax. I want to try cello and piano but have this four-year commitment to deal with."

"More likely at least 8 years."

"Oh yeah, you're right."

"Where are you living?"

"An apartment in a brownstone at 854 Spruce. You?"

"I was lazy and arranged for the Orlowitz dorm from the burgeoning metropolis of Orono, Maine. My roomie, Don, is a Penn Stater, five-year man-boy. Never yet cooked a hot dog, can you believe that? Nor has he thrown a frisbee, but he told me he can make bread."

"Mr. Phelps, should you choose to accept this mission, you will boil, grill, and chop slices of hot dogs into baked beans to save this poor lad. This tape will self-destruct in two minutes."

David chuckled quietly, fearing the wrath of Dr. Martin who was pacing up and down the aisles observing the students, most of whom were quietly completing their forms.

Next up was Dr. Prince, Medical Examiner, City of Philadelphia. His schtick was Shock and Awe. Dr. Prince showed graphic pictures of decapitation by telephone pole. He explained that an intoxicated co-ed had been hanging out of the passenger window while her boyfriend took the corner a little too tightly. Dozens of people with horrible burns and the resulting scars were even more shocking. Victims of gunshots and stabbings were splayed on autopsy tables, more graphicly than in any cop show David had ever watched. Dr. Prince described a woman ejected from a car involved in a motor vehicle accident. The unusual outcome was that the woman was naked, her clothes scattered around the car. The man's body was partially naked as well. Dr. Prince said he still does not know how the force of the impact could have blown clothing off their bodies.

Amanda leaned over toward David and said, "I suspect the answer to that question is that the woman had taken her clothing off while in the car and perhaps the two had been involved in sexual activities while driving."

"So, you think it was not the crash that blew the clothes off." David chuckled and continued, "I certainly have no experience in this area."

The cold, pale faces of previously attractive men and women looked out at the students. They were more than just asleep from drug overdoses. Close up shots of heroin needle tracks on their arms told the tale.

"What would be the purpose of showing us these?" asked Amanda, "Disgust us, toughen us up for upcoming lectures?"

"Seems an odd choice for our first day," replied David, "It's not likely they'll scare us off at this late stage."

The final speaker was Dean Ollman who described the process of farming out the third year and fourth year students to area hospitals for clinical experiences. David had already decided to do most if not all of his clinicals in the Wilmington, Delaware Hospital system and live at home.

"I'm going to try to do some at Lankenau and Chestnut Hill Hospitals," said Amanda. "I was born at Lankenau."

"Ah, local girl comes home to roost. Where do your parents live?"

"Radnor. I'm a girl from the suburbs. Attended Archbishop Carroll High, loved it. You?"

"Equally suburban, North Wilmington, Delaware. And I loved being able to ride my bike to the river to go hiking and fishing. Concord High School was once rated the most innovative school in the nation, mostly due to our Principal, Bill Bailey. Great guy."

"Where'd you do your undergrad?"

"University of Delaware. Great school for me. Had everything I needed and wanted. Also, Delaware has this great program with Jefferson College called DIMER that reserves twenty seats for qualified Delaware residents, so I probably got a break on the admission process."

"I'm sure you are well qualified," said Amanda. "I think we better be quiet. Here comes Dr. Martin prowling for talkers."

Two hours later the orientation wrapped up, having extracted sufficient demographic, family, and undergraduate information for the next four years. Nauseating the group had evidently been an added bonus for Dr. Prince. David extended his hand.

Amanda, a bit surprised, took it and they shook hands.

"Great to have met you, Amanda. I'm going to a Guinness world record event tonight. There is a barber on Fifth and Locust trying to cut hair for 100 hours straight. He gets to nap fifteen minutes every two hours. I'm his midnight head of hair. Interested?"

"That gives me time to grab a nap. It is raining, I'll need an umbrella. I'll meet you in front of my house at 11:30," replied Amanda. "Tricky way getting my address without really asking."

"I really did set up the barber appointment yesterday. It was on the radio. MMR is great. I listened to it when I lived in Wilmington and attended University of Delaware. A big contrast to Maine, which was and is a rock and roll wasteland."

"You poor man, how did you ever survive?"

"I have a reel to reel tape recorder, Sony 3 head, great sound, and I recorded 24/7 for weeks before leaving for the great northern woods."

"Commercials and all?"

"They were as much a breath of fresh air as Bruce Springsteen at the Main Point."

"You have live Springsteen?"

"Bonnie Raitt and a few others, just dumb luck."

"I might be interested in an auditory appraisal if you are willing to share."

"Almost any time but given the load of work we've just been assigned it may be a while."

"A person has to eat well. Rock music is food for the soul," replied Amanda.

"A true believer! Bring it on. 11:30 in front of 854 Spruce. Need me to walk you home?"

"Thanks, but I'm ok."

"The Orlowitz dorm is across the Quad," said David.

Amanda walked with him to Orlowitz, then crossed Ninth Street and took Spruce home. They separated, smiles on each of their faces. David did not fail to notice Amanda's curvaceous butt in her tightly fitting jeans.

CHAPTER TWO

Haircut for the Guinness Record

It was drizzling at 11:30. Amanda wore yellow rain boots and a yellow raincoat. A yellow umbrella with Dalmatians on it that caught the porch light as she stood waiting for David. David wore the blue windbreaker he had worn while riding his bike ride from Orono to Wilmington, a bit ratty for the wear, bearing multiple patches and sewing repair jobs.

"David, the legs of your jeans and Adidas are already soaked."

"I'm ok. You win the outfit prize tonight, Amanda. Are you warm enough?"

"Yes, thank you, just something I threw on," she replied with a broad smile, "An interesting jacket. The blue is showing its age."

"Oh, this thing," indicating his jacket, "I rode 1,000 miles in this windbreaker and every mile took its toll, I know. I've had to patch it up a few times. You like this one?" he asked pointing to the sunflower patch on his right elbow. "I had to sew this one on after I was knocked off my bike and tore a big hole in the jacket. It keeps me dry, except my legs of course. Shall we?" asked David indicating going to the right.

"We shall." The pair walked down Spruce Street.

"So how was your nap?"

"Wonderful, I have come to appreciate a good nap. My house and room are very quiet, just Mrs. Hopkins and me."

"Did you have to sign out and give a time of return."

"No, but I did tell her what I would be doing to be polite and not to cause her to be afraid when I opened the door at who knows when later tonight."

"I told Don I would be back late. I'm not in practice for being polite in my comings and goings. I spent a long year alone in an Orono basement room in a suburban house. I'll tell you the sordid tale someday if you're interested."

"Tonight, it's all about hair and hopefully MMR broadcasting live."

"I hope Michael Tearson, one of the best disc jockeys, is there."

"That may be too much to ask. Look at all the water in the gutter. Every street dumping its contents into the Delaware on its way to the Atlantic."

The barber shop, complete with barber pole turning in the pale light was on the corner of Fifth and Locust. Lights were on inside the shop and a black man was in the chair. David wondered why Amanda had agreed to accompany him on this crazy, midnight barber shop excursion. She must be pretty adventurous having just met me and confident that I would be pretty safe to be with.

"Ten 'til midnight, I'm up next." David held the door. Three men turned to see the woman in yellow enter.

Amanda and David were greeted at the door by the powerful smell of hair products. A hand printed sign explaining the Guinness Challenge was against the rear wall: "Help me break the Guinness Book of World Records for longest continuous hair cutting."

The days for haircuts were listed on the door and two were crossed out. Amanda took a seat on the stainless-steel chair with its red plastic cushions. David walked over to introduce himself, careful not to startle the tall and lanky barber, who after 48 hours on the job might have cut off an ear. A black comb poked out of his left coat pocket. Four pairs of scissors were immersed in a jar filled with blue fluid on the shelf behind him. The mandatory can of talcum powder stood at attention and a hand mirror rested against the wall. Advertisements for Brylcreme and Aqua Velva were between wall mirrors, and photos of crew cuts for children and various haircuts for men lined the walls as well.

"Be with you in a minute, almost done here. What do you think, Harold?" asked the barber as he unsnapped and removed the black cape from Harold's shoulders. He shook the contents of the cape onto the floor, adding to the pile of black, brown, and reddish hairs.

"Great job Roland."

"Grab one of the albums from the box over by the DJ. MMR brought them, they're free."

David waited for Harold to get out of the chair.

Roland took a swig from a mug of what smelled like strong coffee.

"They allow me as much coffee as I want, and I want a lot of coffee," explained Roland without looking up.

David whispered, "Who's the DJ tonight?" asked David grabbing the arms and sitting in the barber chair.

"The guy on the graveyard shift, Ed Sciaky."

"Wow, so that's him. I've listened for years."

"You can go over and say 'Hi' when he has a break. Ed's a professional. Nice guy. So how do you want it?"

"Can you shorten it in the back to collar line and shorten up the mess on top? "

"You want bangs?" Roland spun the chair around and chuckled, "Just kiddin'."

"Mid-length all the way around, please."

"Why the major hair cut change?"

"New place, new people don't know me. Trying to start fresh and, well not reinvent myself, but try out things I've learned," David replied, "That make any sense?"

"I dig it, man. You got a lot to work with here. A new look coming up."

"Thanks. I guess I don't really know exactly what I want from you."

"No problem. Got to be who you are, or in your case who you want to be. So, where you from?" asked Roland as he ran his hand through David's hair and made his first cut.

"Wilmington Delaware. Amanda over there and I are starting med school at Jeff."

"Girlfriend?"

"We just met at orientation." Amanda was flipping the pages of a magazine.

"Great looking and very trusting of you to be out this late at night to watch me cut your hair. I can't do women this time, just men for the record book."

"I'm just as amazed as you that she came along. She grew up in Radnor. You can hear Philly in the way she says a few words: back stoop."

"Man, you gotta hold onto that lady. Philly women are the best! Now sit back and relax while Roland does his magic."

"One more thing. Where are you from?"

"Born and raised in the City of Brotherly Love, my man."

15 minutes later another young man entered the shop, took a seat across from Amanda and waited for Roland to finish up with David.

"I'm Gary. I'm next for the chair," he said addressing Amanda.

"I'm Amanda and that's David who is looking a hundred percent better. Roland's the man with the scissors and comb," replied Amanda.

"Is that ok?" Roland asked David.

"Better than great Roland. Can I tip you ten bucks? I know you have coffee expenses."

"That would be great, my man," replied Roland reaching under his counter producing a coffee can stuffed with bills. David pushed his ten-dollar bill into the can and got up.

"You're next Gary," said Amanda.

"Not so fast." Roland stated. "I need to donate some coffee to the mayor."

"David motioned for Amanda to come over and they introduced themselves to Mr. Sciaky who seemed truly interested in meeting people especially Amanda.

"I've been a fan of yours and WMMR for years, Mr. Sciaky, " said David.

"Ed, please."

"I am a fan, too," said Amanda.

"Well, you each grab an LP from the MMR stash and remember this momentous night each time you crank up the tunes. I've got to get back to work. Nice meeting you Amanda and you too David."

Amanda chose Joni Mitchell's 'Court and Spark' album, which was in mint condition. David pulled out Bob Seger and the Silver Bullet Band's 'Night Moves' that showed a little wear. "A good sign," thought David, hoping for a future of night moves.

"Joni Mitchell, I don't know many of her songs," admitted David.

"I'll have to begin your education post haste. I equally have heard only a few of Seger's, but 'Night Moves' is all over the air waves."

The pair thanked Roland who had emerged from the back. "Nice to have met you, David, enjoy."

They walked out into the dark night, glad that it was not raining.

"He did a nice job. You are still recognizable but cleaned up a bit."

"It will grow back if I don't like it. Feels a lot lighter. I've got, we've got, a chance to change, maybe re-invent parts of ourselves, try things out where no one knows our back stories."

"Maybe we should stick with changing haircuts first," Amanda chuckled. "I'm just getting to know you. How about we try to make changes slowly, so we can adapt."

"Absolutely."

They walked in silence, thinking forward to the next four years, both feeling tired after a very long day.

"Here's 854 and the hall light is still on. Mrs. Hopkins seems thoughtful."

"See you tomorrow in the lecture hall. Thanks for an interesting time. I'd invite you in for tea, but I need to sleep."

"Thanks, I am exhausted as well. Proverbial rain check, your place or mine."

This time Amanda extended her hand and David shook it looking at the woman decked out in yellow thinking how fortunate he'd been to meet her.

"An exceptionally nice outfit, Amanda. Good night." Amanda ascended her eight stairs and David watched, considering more than her clothing. Amanda turned to say thanks for an interesting first night in Philly. "We just may get through this," and entered her new home.

David's mind would have worked on the possibilities had he not been so sleepy. "I'll remember these as the good old days. Time to ponder all that tomorrow," he thought as he walked to Orlowitz.

"Anticipation," Carly Simon

CHAPTER THREE

Breakfast with Mrs. Hopkins

When Amanda came down for breakfast the next morning, Mrs. Hopkins had already boiled the tea water and had placed some blueberry muffins on a plate.

"So how was your first Philadelphia date, Amanda?"

"I guess it was a date. An unusual first foray, by very enjoyable and informative overall," replied Amanda, taking a bite of a muffin.

Mrs. Hopkins poured water into two floral porcelain teacups. "What is your choice for tea?"

"I would like Lady Earl Gray if you have it. If not, I will buy some today and contribute to our supply," offered Amanda.

"Oh, I have Lady Gray, don't you worry. Do you take sugar or honey?"

"I enjoy a little bit of honey."

Mrs. Hopkins took the box of tea bags and the honey from the cabinet. Does this man from last night's date have a name?" She smiled.

"David Coleman. He lives in the Orlowitz dorm. Recently from University of Maine where he earned a Masters in Zoology, studied the tiny guppy fish. Not sure how that worked. I'm sure I'll learn more about that thesis in due time."

"Was he a gentleman?"

"Very much so: on time, held the door, introduced me to the barber and WMMR Dee Jay. Very relaxed and sure of himself. He placed me at ease. We had a nice time."

"And the purpose of getting a haircut at midnight?"

"The barber, Roland, was attempting to break the Guinness record for continuous hair cutting, only men this time."

"A quirky first date, but I imagine it says something about him, this David."

"I believe it said something about my degree of comfort being with him to traipse around Philadelphia in the rain at midnight with an almost total stranger. Granted he is a classmate with whom I conversed for two hours during orientation."

"Will you be seeing more of David, other than in the Jefferson lecture hall?"

"I think so. He appeared more than a little interested in me and I am certainly going to check him out. After the haircut, he looked more like a city guy and less like a wild man from the Maine woods," Amanda chuckled, "He must have had Roland remove half of the hair on his head. The result was appealing." Amanda reached for a second muffin as she sipped her tea.

"So, did he comment on your outfit since you had coordinated boots, raincoat, and umbrella? Was he entertaining? It seems that he was pleasant and gracious. I'd say you and he have a good start. I wondered whom you would meet among the couple hundred students. You've told me only a few things about you time at Catholic University, but your choice of clothes and your demeanor tells me you are confident and meet people easily. I know you are a very talented and bright young woman, Amanda."

"Thank you for all the compliments. I hope to live up to them, and yes, I will be seeing more of David, and I hope not just in the lecture hall." Amanda finished her tea and pushed back from the table. "Thank you for the tea and muffins. Breakfast was a treat as was our wonderful conversation."

"We can do this as often as you care to. I am an early riser and would very much enjoy getting to know more about you, Amanda."

"Then it's a date for tomorrow. I'll pick up some danish and make eggs if that's what you enjoy for breakfast."

"It has been a long time since my husband, Richard, died and I always said that breakfast is always better when shared."

"Well, I appreciate being your house guest and look forward to learning more about you, too, Mrs. Hopkins," said Amanda placing her teacup in the sink as she prepared to leave for class.

"I'll wash the cups and silverware, Amanda. You scoot along to class. Will I see you for lunch?"

"I hope the lecture schedule will allow for an hour break to return her for something to eat. Could I impose on your pantry to look for a few lunch items for today? I'll go shopping for both of us this evening, if you tell me where to shop, that is," replied Amanda, "Got to go. See you after noon."

"I plan to be here."

With that Amanda picked up her book bag and opened the front door.

CHAPTER FOUR

Studying Together

David walked down the concrete steps into the lecture hall. He took a seat in the middle section ten rows back, which was in his comfort zone. He scanned the room and noted the typical groups and cliques in the back and one in the lower right. He later learned the lower right students were the twenty who were placed at Jefferson with the assistance of a federal grant. Money for the Jefferson medical school machine. Rumor had it these twenty students were not of the same caliber, academically, as the other 200 students. Unfortunately, this group all but disappeared by third year. David saw Amanda come in and take a seat third row, center section on the left.

"Damn," thought David, "Not sitting with me."

As David would learn, Amanda dressed up for lectures. Today she was in a blue skirt with a white blouse adorned with blue beagles. He couldn't see her shoes, but guessed they were not sneakers.

"I'll have to step up my game and buy some new shirts and jeans," thought David.

"Hello class of 81," called out the lecturer as he stood up from one of the front row seats. He wore a white shirt, a maroon and gold checked bow tie, and a white lab coat. The blackboard behind him dominated the front of the lecture hall. The professor was illuminated by ceiling lights, while the rest of the lecture hall was in dimmer light.

"I am Dr. Shep of the Anatomy department. You met Dr. Martin at orientation, and you will meet us again, as well as other Anatomy faculty members in this hall for lectures and in the lab while you learn to dissect the cadavers. Anatomy is a fascinating discipline and I hope all of you take it very seriously, as it will provide the basis for much of your medical training."

Dr. Shep walked back and forth as he addressed the students. "Diagnosis and treatment of illness must stand on knowledge of anatomy. As important as physiology, lab tests, and medications are, none play as critical a role in the detective work of diagnosis. I will share with you a tremendous amount of information, which you will need to incorporate, not simply memorize, into your daily lives. You will learn over a hundred thousand new words in the next two years, many will be anatomical terms. This will be a new language that will allow you entry into the fellowship of Physicians. Do not take this lightly if you have your eyes set on a discipline that you now believe will not involve anatomy," Dr. Shep said as he emphasized his remarks with an extended index finger. "Anatomy is not simply for Surgeons or Pathologists. The medical specialties rely heavily on a solid grasp of anatomy. I suspect a few of you are thinking Psychiatry will be exempt, but you will be rethinking that in the weeks to come. So enough of this introduction. Let us now define the axes of the body. Anterior, posterior, dorsal, caudal, proximal, distal . . ."

David blanked out for a moment, gazing at the third row before him and considering Amanda's anatomy.

" . . . location, size, and relationships to other structures all define the organ or the lesion. You will find all these terms defined in your textbook. Read it every night to reinforce what we discuss here and keep up."

Dr. Shep went on to describe the structures of the head: skull bones, muscles, nerves, and blood vessels.

"You will find all these structures in your Clemente text. I recommend you read over the chapters before you get to the dissection lab to have the terms in your heads."

David waited for Amanda to pass him as she walked up the stairs after the lecture.

"Would you like to come to my apartment for dessert and then study together?"

"What are you offering for sweets?"

"Other than me?" David chuckled, "My mom sent me off with a tin of home baked sugar cookies and I can make tea or coffee."

"Sounds good. What time works for you?"

"Is six thirty too early?"

"Perfect. Where's your apartment?"

"1002 Orlowitz. Don is my roommate. He may grab a few cookies."

"See you then."

That evening, David had arranged a plateful of sugar cookies that his mother sent in a care package to assist him to adjust to his first week at Jefferson. He had a few choices of tea: Earl Grey, Lipton, White Rose, and Orange Pekoe. There were no delicate teacups available, just coffee mugs, but the sugar bowl and four small plates were English porcelain he picked up at a from a yard sale years ago.

"I'll get the door," said Don answering Amanda's knocking.

"Hello, I'm Don, David's roommate."

"Glad to meet you, Don. So, you men are having a tea party? Interesting beverage choice for young men."

"First of its kind."

"Come on in. David is arranging the cookies and boiling water. Please take a seat at our modest table."

"Oh, hi David," said Amanda.

Amanda looked around at the sparsely furnished room. She doubted the men had added anything to the basics that Orlowitz provided: the table and four chairs, dark wood, functional, but not attractive. The two living room chairs faced the television in the corner. One small, black bookcase had a few textbooks on its shelves, but no novels. The door to the bedroom was open and Amanda noticed a long, blue banner on the bedroom wall.

"What's the blue banner for?" she asked.

"David and I are going to document the changes we will go through using paper cutouts glued to the blue material," answered Don.

"I got a bolt of the blue, cotton cloth from an old fabric mill in Wilmington. I was one of a crew hired to gut the old, quarter mile long building along the Brandywine River. Sledgehammers, gloves, and hardhats all summer long. I was the only one to have a valid driver's license, so I got to drive the dump truck. Didn't know how to double clutch but eventually learned. A great experience. A bonus was that there were bolts of discarded fabric up for grabs. Don and I each put one work of art on our banner so far, like to see them? The room is reasonably neat."

Amanda looked at the two paper cutouts on the wall above the beds and pointed to the caterpillar on the left crawling toward the skyline of a city, emerging to the right as a butterfly. "Who did this one?"

"Don."

"I like it, delivers the message in color. And you made this one?" she added indicating the cutout of music notes flying out of a flute only to drop to the ground as seeds and grow into a new flute.

"Life cycle of a flute," David replied.

"I like this one as well, being a flautist myself."

"We both have more ideas, but this thing called studying is getting in the way of our creative energies," David chuckled.

"I see that these apartments have a kitchen. Do you plan to cook much?"

David chuckled, "Well that or starve."

"I am not the greatest cook, but I do know how to make bread," offered Don.

"And you, David, can you cook?"

"My mom taught me well. My greatest achievement, other than baking a mean banana bread was the twenty-five- pound turkey I cooked at Delaware."

"What? For Thanksgiving? And why? Did you have many people to feed?" asked Amanda.

"Just my two roommates and me. We ate well. By the way, the twenty-five pounder was on sale, so I just went ahead and bought it. The thing was huge and just barely fit into our oven. Took hours to cook. Amanda, help yourself to the sugar cookies. I'll get the hot water; you select the tea. I hope we have one you like."

"I'm an Earl Grey fan, David."

"Good, because so am I. What about you, Don, Earl Grey okay with you?"

"Never had it, but it's tea, right?"

"So, Don, David tells me you are in the five-year Penn State program. What exactly is that?"

"I went to Penn State as a freshman undergraduate during the summer after my junior high school year and will graduate from Jefferson and Penn State at the same time. I won't get any time off during the summers at Jeff."

David chimed in, "The problem is that Don here does not yet know some college essentials, like how to throw a frisbee! He's been totally busy with the books."

"Yeah, yeah. A valuable skill for sure," replied Don, leaning forward to grab two cookies. "I plan to join Jefferson's ultimate frisbee team. Let me ask you, Amanda, do you know how to throw a frisbee?"

"No, I do not, and I do not plan to join the team," she replied then took a sip of tea.

"Now see, David, I'm not the only one to lack frisbee flight skills," said Don.

Amanda jumped into the roommates' apparently longstanding debate and asked, "May I have another cookie?"

David passed the plate, “Of course. My mom makes a mean Toll House cookie as well.”

“Now there is a skill you will surely be glad to have, Don,” laughed Amanda, “I love Toll House cookies. A classic.”

Don stood up and said, “Nice to meet you, Amanda. Watch this guy,” said Don patting David on the shoulder as he stood to walk back to his desk, his tea mug in his hand. “He’s an odd fellow. Did you know he disappears at midnight only to return all sweaty an hour later? What is he doing out there?”

“Perhaps he’s saving lives, battling crime, picking up litter on Broad Street. I just know whatever he is doing it is for some possible greater good.” Amanda smiled and touched David’s arm.

“Yeah, whatever. I can see the third wheel should be over there studying,” Don said with a broad smile.

“More hot water? A new tea bag, Amanda? Please forgive Don, he’s just intensely jealous that I am hanging out with you.”

“So, what do you do at midnight?”

“I run to the Vet Stadium and back.”

“Is that safe?”

“I run mostly up Eighth Street, because it is safe. I guess anything could happen, maybe around the stadium, but I’ve never been hassled.”

“And you run at midnight for exercise?”

“And to relax after six hours of studying. I can’t just go to sleep, so I run first.”

“I prefer a good book and some Vivaldi in the background before shut eye.”

“I had you pegged for enjoying Tchaikovsky, Amanda. Vivaldi, huh?”

“The Four Seasons was one of the pieces I played for my final exam, I really like it.”

“I vaguely recall the Four Seasons; can’t say I can call up any flute in it.”

"You and I should get together and play some time. Do you have your Gemeinhardt here?"

"Sure do, but I will tell you I'm not the best at reading sheet music. It's been a long time since I was in the orchestra playing my saxophone. Do you know a tenor sax can play baritone horn bass clef music as treble clef and it sounds good? I've never read flute music, but I'll bet most of the notes are way up there above the 'Every Good Boy Does Fine' lines. I play by ear."

"Well, we can work on reading music, but I'd still like to play a song or two with you."

"I like how you were sure to insert "a song or two."

Amanda blushed, took a sip of her tea, and reached for another cookie.

"What?" asked David with a smile. "Any other composers you appreciate, Amanda?"

"I like the clean lines of Mozart, I enjoy Beethoven, and really would like to be able to play Shostakovich."

"I don't have a clue who Shostakovich is or was."

"Good. Another lesson on the list. We could start with a song you can play by ear."

"Rhymin' Simon, Elton John, James Taylor, Joni Mitchell, maybe some Mozart, Beethoven, Copeland, Stravinsky, but minimal."

That's doable. Hey, it's getting late, and we have an anatomy chapter to read."

David walked over to the bookcase, grabbed some paper and a pen. He brought the anatomy text to the table. "I'll read first. You take notes."

After an hour, they decided to call it quits.

"Thank you for the study time and tea. Tell your mom her cookies are wonderful."

"Thanks. I'll walk you home. No refusals this time, Amanda."

"Ok. Do you remember the address?"

"854 Locust. Let me get the door," said David draining the remaining tea from his mug and grabbing a cookie for the road. "Glad that you came over, Amanda. I really enjoy spending time with you. Are we on for tomorrow after class?

"Yep. After dinner with Mrs. Hopkins. I'll call you."

CHAPTER FIVE

The Freedom Trail Talk

It was Friday and Amanda and David studied briefly, but both were tired after a long week of classes. They decided to meet early on Saturday at David's apartment to study. He hoped they would finish up by noon and could go out for lunch and a beer. He was looking forward to learning more about Amanda and discovering more of Philadelphia such as walking in the historic district.

On Saturday, Amanda arrived uncharacteristically dressed in blue jeans and a gray sweatshirt with the Cardinal logo of Catholic University emblazoned on the left chest. Amanda and David spent the morning studying. After a while, David asked, "What would you like to do tomorrow?" He put his anatomy text down and reached over to touch Amanda's shoulder.

"I try to go to Mass every Sunday, probably just habit from my Archbishop Carroll High School days. But I really do enjoy the hour of solitude within a familiar, structured environment." Amanda stated.

They continued to review the anatomy lecture material and compared notes about their last couple dissection labs. David was really getting into the delicate process of dissecting nerves and blood vessels of the cadaver of a man. Specifically, he liked learning details about the head and neck. He noticed that Amanda had taken more notes, rather than completing the dissections over the prior couple days. She was equally enjoying the time examining her cadaver, a woman. They finished studying just before noon and agreed to walk to a soup and sandwich shop on Walnut Street, then decided they would walk on the "Freedom Trail." They started their tour with the Betsy Ross House and were approaching the Liberty Bell when Amanda asked David, "So, would you like to come to seven o'clock Mass tomorrow with me?"

"Which church do you attend?"

"Old Saint Mary's Church which is located between Locust and Walnut Street in Society Hill. It has beautiful stained-glass windows and they have a great organ that fills the sanctuary with sound."

"You sold me. Tie and sports coat type of place? Admittedly, I'd go just to see you in a dress, Amanda."

"Letcher! They may not let you in," Amanda laughed.

"Oh, they'll let me in if I'm with you. You are the walking, stained-glass window woman. Do you want me to coordinate the color of my shirt and tie with your outfit?"

"Listen to you! Blue jeans and torn tee shirt is your signature uniform. Now, you are talking about coordinating a shirt and tie. I'll look my selection over and let you know about the color scheme."

"So, which part of the Mass do you like the most?"

"I like the Epistle and Gospel readings," replied Amanda. "Sometimes they seem overly simplistic. The old chestnuts of mustard seeds cast on rocks not growing, the rich man who can't get into heaven any more than a camel fitting through the eye of a needle, or turning water to wine can't be beat."

"I do recall those. I like the one about Lazarus and the leper healed by their faith. Just touched the edge of Jesus' coat and poof! He starts walking and no leprosy. Imagine how different medicine would be if it acknowledged the contributions of faith-based therapy."

"I actually believe medicine as it was practiced a hundred years ago and some of how it is practiced today has a huge faith-based component."

"Are you referring to the placebo effect? By the way I read it's a real consideration in almost all double-blind studies," asked David.

"I'm referring to the trust between patient and physician, trust in the FDA to ensure medications are as safe as they can be, and overall trust in diagnostic tests, the whole experience."

"So, a portion of our medical school training should be to cultivate and polish our skills at relating to patients and instilling that mutual trust, . . ."

"And recognizing when certain patients need different types of reassurances, and perhaps less data to make their decisions," added Amanda.

"I wonder if such concepts are included in our curriculum?" pondered David, "Probably as important as knowing where the fifth cranial nerve is."

They were walking up the stairs into Independence Hall when Amanda asked, "Which portion of the Mass most appeals to you?"

"I have several memories of attending church. I can remember in middle school feeling a strong sense of security and familiarity while attending Mass, whether at St. Bridget's in Glassboro, New Jersey, where I received my First Holy Communion and Confirmation, or at Mass with my Boy Scout Troop near French Creek, Pennsylvania. I recall explaining what was going on at the altar to a couple fellow scouts who had never been to church. They were especially amused when the altar boys rang the bells and the priest took a sip of wine, then rang the bells again, took another sip. Quite a ritual. I like the intimacy of receiving the Host. I like standing up to show I'm going to receive the Host, getting in line in the aisle, hands folded, eyes down in contemplation of what is about to transpire, then kneeling at the railing. I like the moment when the priest places it on my tongue."

"So, you are not a 'put the host in my hand and I'll place in my own mouth-person?' Neither am I. This will be interesting to see how you like the service at Saint Mary's. It has some Latin prayers and responses and there is no guitar music."

"I'll bet I will be able to join in with the prayers when I hear the beginnings spoken by the priest. I was a big fan of the ten o'clock Latin Mass when I was a kid. I tried to memorize the words to the prayers and responses, but really was only reciting fragments when I heard the priest prompt us."

"Okay. It takes me fifteen minutes to walk from my place. How about you come by at six thirty tomorrow morning? We could get breakfast after Mass. Then we can decide what to do for fun later in the day."

"I haven't been to Mass since one time as an undergraduate student in Newark, Delaware. It will be interesting to see if the Mass has changed since I last went."

"Now let's get back to my place to go over some pharmacology notes. I'll read."

CHAPTER SIX

Sunday Mass

David walked up the stairs and knocked quietly on Amanda's door at six twenty-five.

"Look at you, all dressed up for church in a blue blazer, light blue shirt, and a blue and yellow striped tie. I've never seen you in gray slacks and dress shoes. Very nice. How you'd know I'd pick a blue dress?"

"Lucky guess. You look good in everything you wear Amanda, I thought yellow and blue would go well with your blonde hair."

"Come on, I like to sit up front behind the nuns."

They walked in the crisp July morning air to Old Saint Mary's Church without having to hurry. The townhomes were all darkened, and the streetlights still lit the sidewalk.

"Were you ever an altar boy, David?"

"No, I was intimidated by having to remember all the duties and being in the spotlight. I was the ring bearer for my cousin's wedding when I was eight years old. I dropped the pillow with the rings, picked it up and kept on walking. I never forgot all the eyes on me and my performance."

"And you're still bothered about that? You were a kid! You still bear the shame of dropping the pillow?"

"Yeah, it's a bit silly. Funny how things stick around in my memory."

"Well, I hope you've got some good memories as well."

"Of course, I do, lots of them. My childhood was special. I thought my parents were the best. I thought I lived in the best neighborhood in a great town. I now recall walking the entire route with Mr. Johnson, the Mailman, being treated as a special kid. Mr. Johnson was a black man. No one spoke about his skin color, but my parents and my friends were very envious of my special bond with him. What about you? Did you consider your parents the best in the neighborhood?"

"Yes, I did. I'm not a Child Psychologist, but I'll bet thinking your parents were perfect is a good sign of a happy child in a healthy, loving family. That naivete is good for a child as there's plenty of time for imperfections to creep in to taint those impressions."

David pointed to the church standing between large trees. "Is that Saint Mary's? You were right, it's a beautiful building in a peaceful setting. I'll bet it is even more impressive in full daylight."

David held the door and Amanda walked in, dipped her fingers in the basin of Holy Water, and made the sing of the cross. David followed suit. Amanda led David to the second center row, knelt and crossed herself again before sliding across the wooden pew. She waited for David to sit down before easing the kneeler down. She made the sign of the cross a third time, folded her hands and bowed her head in silent prayer.

David looked up at the altar and was impressed by the understated crucifix in front of stained-glass windows. The ceiling was composed of dark brown, wooden planks. Statues of Mary and Joseph flanked the altar as in most Catholic churches. The eternal flame flickered atop the huge candle to the right of the altar. The altar was on a massive block of white marble.

The priest entered from the right, following a single altar boy, already reciting the Introit. David felt the calm reassurance of the Mass descend on him as the priest led the congregation through the sign of the cross, the opening prayers of the Kyrie, Gloria, and penitent's prayer, which David recited without having to refer to the order of the Mass. He recalled how devoted his mother was in church. Amanda made the cross on her forehead, over her lips, then over her heart. He saw that Amanda was reciting the prayers without prompting, as well. She reached for his hand when they sat for the Epistle reading. The reading was not familiar to David. Equally unfamiliar was the Gospel from Matthew about sewing good wheat seeds contaminated with darnel weeds, burned at the harvest, sewing mustard seeds that produced plants as big as a tree, and a woman who mixed yeast with flour to leaven the entire amount to make her bread. David could have sworn he knew most of the Gospels, but these were new to him. David pondered the Gospel's message while listening to the homily.

The priest, Father Joseph, delivered a short sermon, emphasizing the relevance of the Gospel in modern times. Amanda surprised David with a kiss for their exchange of the Sign of Peace. David shook hands with as many nuns as he could reach. As there were no songs, Communion followed soon thereafter. The nuns received the Host first. David stepped into the aisle to allow Amanda to lead to the communion rail where they both knelt and allowed the priest to place the Host on their tongues. They again crossed themselves and returned to their pew. The priest made eye contact with all present before delivering his final blessing and exiting. David had not previously noticed how many times one made the sign of the cross at Mass. There was no formal passing of the collection plate, so David took a crisp twenty bill out of his wallet and put it in the charity box.

Once outside Amanda said, "That was nice of you. How about we alternate donating twenty dollars each Sunday? So, was Mass somewhat familiar, enjoyable? I like Father Joseph. His homilies make the message of the centuries old Gospels relevant to our current lives."

"I once went to Mass in Worchester, Massachusetts with my mom and I could swear the priest come out of the side door ready to read the Epistle. It was a six A.M. service in the basement of Saint Casmir's, same church where my cousin was married in the Cathedral above. I suppose people had to get to work."

"Speaking of six A.M., I'm famished. What would you like for breakfast?"

"I saw a Greek mom and pop place a couple blocks back. Would that be ok?"

"Lead on and thanks for coming with me, Mass is so much richer when shared."

"I never thought about Mass that way, but I've almost always have gone with my family. Maybe a few times went to the early Mass when I was a paper boy to get it done before the Sunday Bulletin arrived. There were no Saturday Masses back then. My mom was a strict enforcer of weekly Mass."

"There's your Greek diner," noted Amanda, "Smells good from here. How about I treat today?"

While he was enjoying his waffles, seated in a booth, David said to Amanda, "You've not told me about your family. Do you have brothers and sisters?"

"My sister is sixteen years old and goes to Archbishop Carroll High. She's a good student and a gorgeous young woman. I miss her already. We used to talk almost every night when I was in college. My brother is seventeen, a less than stellar student, but a great lacrosse midfielder. He will probably get a college scholarship, that is if he wants to go to college."

"And mom and dad?"

"Mom graduated from college, majoring in Chemistry, but elected to be a stay-at-home mom. I think she is considering returning to work now but is afraid she is not up to date."

"Did she ever think about taking a few community college classes and see what's changed?" asked David.

"I think she has considered that, we'll see. Dad is a partner in a law firm, mainly doing corporate tax law."

"Does he enjoy it?"

"Very much so. He thought I may want to be an Attorney but was not too disappointed when I chose medicine."

"And you?"

"Well, you've met Ben, my bigger, younger brother."

"Ben is a big man, in the Navy, right?"

"He's a great guy, do anything for you. I think he's looking to get out before the Iran hostage thing heats up. That's why he took on a side job with the ambulance service. He's a corpsman at the Philly Naval Hospital."

"I'll bet he has a few stories to tell."

"The best one is about the time he was sent, without a partner, to a home in West Philadelphia. The dispatcher didn't have much to tell him, just that a child needed transportation to the Emergency Room. Ben shows up and it's an infant baby boy with a fever and was probably dehydrated. Ben's vehicle does not have an incubator, so he wraps the child in a blanket, puts him against his chest in the coat he's wearing, and drives like hell to the ER. The baby recovered!"

"What about your mom and dad?"

"Mom's been an Elementary School Teacher for twenty-five years. Went through the desegregation of her school district, was reassigned to an inner-city school and is surviving. The kids were significantly behind the proverbial eight ball in terms of real knowledge, but she got them up to speed."

"My dad is a chemical engineer with DuPont and is vice president of the computer division involved in running the supercomputer they have. I visited it back in Boy Scout days. The thing takes up an entire floor of the building. Of course, computers now are more compact, but that monster, with all its tubes, is still doing work crunching the numbers to predict costs and availability of cotton cloth and blue dye, locations with the least expensive labor to make the blue jeans, and the cost to transport them to the U.S."

"We both come from highly educated families, David."

"But different occupations."

"So, it seems that you and I might bring different perspectives to our relationship, David."

"I agree, and that's probably a good thing. What do you want to do today before we have to hit the books?"

"I'd like to do a bit of shopping at John Wanamaker downtown."

"No problem there, I love that store. I think the giant eagle in the lobby is so cool."

"Do you have something specific in mind to look for, David?"

"I can see buying some pants and shirts after asking for your advice. Wanamaker has an excellent selection for men, casual and dress. But, Amanda, really, you must have an entire room in Mrs. Hopkin's place just for your clothes." David smiled at Amanda.

"How do you think I keep it fresh? Anyway, I'll need to change before we go."

"And I need to get out of this monkey suit."

"You look great. Let's see if we can't find you some fashionable jeans and a nice shirt."

David reached for his wallet, but Amanda said, "I said I'd treat for breakfast today."

When they reached Amanda's home, David asked, "When do you want me to come by for our walk to go shopping?"

"Give me thirty minutes."

David hustled back to Orlowitz, changed into jeans and a short-sleeved shirt, and grabbed some more money.

"I'm going shopping Don. Be back in few hours."

"Let me guess. Amanda suggested an upgrade to your wardrobe and you're only too eager to oblige," smiled Don.

"Requiem for a Friend," Elton John

CHAPTER SEVEN

Shopping

David walked to Amanda's house. She had changed into jeans and a white blouse and was waiting on the steps.

"I've got to tell you, the only thing I like more than shopping, is shopping at a sale," remarked Amanda.

"I don't know if there is a sale, but I enjoy the quality and selection at John Wanamaker stores," replied David.

They walked up Ninth Street, then turned onto Chestnut Street.

"It's been years since I came shopping here with my mother. She's the family shopper who knows ahead of time what she wants and can go in and get it without spending time to browse."

They headed up the escalator to Women's Fashions. Do you have a favorite brand, Amanda?"

"I don't search for a specific brand. I'm more interested in quality clothes."

David stopped at a rack of dress shirts. "Do you have any favorite colors? Do you like prints and stripes or solids?"

"This shirt is my style," said Amanda, holding a light blue blouse with red pin stripes against her chest, "Do these colors look okay?"

"It's a nice shirt, Amanda. Looks like cotton, right? Do you have any silk shirts?" David asked holding up a blue silk shirt with red and yellow flowers on it.

"I like the colors. What size is it?"

"Eight petite."

"Perfect."

"Let me hold your shirts so that you will have both hands free."

Amanda went over to a rack with women's pants. She held up a straight legged, light gray pair.

"Size eight," said Amanda. I'll take the shirts and pants into the fitting room," she said reaching for the blouses, "I'll be back in a couple of minutes."

Amanda reappeared dressed in the gray pants and the silk, flower print shirt. "What do you think?"

"You look beautiful, Amanda. The pants fit very well, and the shirt is nicely tapered to your waist." Amanda disappeared into the fitting room to change back into her clothes. "Okay, now over to the Men's Department."

"My shirt size is a sixteen neck and thirty-three arm length."

Amanda held up a blue and violet checked, short sleeved shirt. "This pattern is sharp. Now you need a pair of tailored jeans."

"Tailored? I usually go with Wrangler's, but I suspect those are too basic and you're leaning towards the ones over in that section. What do they cost?"

"Sixty-five Dollars."

"I've never paid that much for a pair of jeans in my life! Oh well, let me try them on."

David reappeared out of the fitting room dressed in the new shirt and jeans. "What do you think? They fit well."

"I think they are fine. Do you want another shirt?"

"How about a collared tee shirt, like a rugby shirt?"

"How about this one? You've got a nice broad chest and long legs. Hmm . . . , just what I'm looking for in a man.

"I like blue pin stripes. I'll try this one on as well," he said heading for the dressing rooms. He reemerged a few minutes later in the new jeans and the rugby shirt.

"They fit well, David. We'll pay for them over there."

Twenty minutes later Amanda and David were on the down escalator.

"Want to grab some lunch?" David asked.

"Sure. I'm thinking I would like a Cobb salad," Amanda replied.

"I'm leaning toward having a cheese steak with fries. Not as healthy as you, Amanda."

"But I'll be eyeing your fries and snatching a few."

"Didn't we pass a steak place back there? This will be my treat."

They backtracked a half block and crossed the street.

David held the door open for Amanda and she walked over and slid into a booth. David sat across from her and reached for the menus. I'm still looking for a steak sub. Cobb salad for you? What do you want to drink?"

"Diet Coke please."

A young waitress came to their table, "Have you made up your minds?"

"Yes, thank you. She'll have the Cobb salad with a diet coke and I would like a cheese steak with onions and banana peppers. Oh, and a 7-UP, please. Thanks."

"I am so glad you helped me step up my clothing game Amanda. I think I heard you say that you liked my chest and legs."

"Not the first time either that I noticed!" Amanda shifted in her seat.

David wanted to hear more. "So, Amanda have you been studying my anatomy?"

Amanda blushed and added, "David, I do like the way you look. You are quite appealing, and I am attracted to you. But I don't want to talk about here. Can we change the subject?"

David replied, "Sure, as long as we can talk later. I want to know more about what looks good."

Amanda pressed on to change topics. "So, David, how did you decide on medical school? Just couldn't stop learning new things, was that it?"

"That was part of it, but I also didn't have a real plan other than spending a year in Israel after graduate school. It was my friend, Mary, who suggested I think about medical school. She was in med tech school. I said what have I got to lose? And then I just applied to Jefferson," replied David.

"Only to Jefferson? That was a bit bold. Why Jefferson?"

"My college roommate's brother is a Jeff graduate, an Obstetrician. I met him once while in my junior year at U of D. I asked him if he enjoyed it and was Jefferson as good as any med school? He said he was having a blast in his fourth year. So, I remembered that and before I left for Israel, I heard I was accepted at Jeff."

"Couldn't just take some time off and relax, could you? I get the feeling that you are always thinking about the next goal or task." Amanda laughed.

"Well, what about you? What's your story?"

"I didn't go to graduate school and my biology Professor suggested I think about medicine. I looked up the pre-requirements to apply and somehow, I'd taken most of the courses. Jefferson was close to home, so I applied to Jefferson, University of Pennsylvania, and University of Maryland. I was happy Jefferson accepted me."

"So am I. Did you take the science and math classes while you were majoring in English and practicing flute every day?"

"The flute classes were more of a time to relax and enjoy the music, and I received credit for having fun!"

"I felt that way about my geology classes. We took field trips, learned surveying, stumbled across rattlesnakes, . . ."

"Snakes! No snakes in my classes."

"I didn't mind the snakes because I felt that we were prepared. Often there were snakes sunning on the rocks we explored and if you left them alone, they left you alone. We had snake bite kits and walkie talkies in case we needed rescuing. Never happened and we were a class of twenty-two. Are you about done your lunch? I was thinking of searching out an ice cream shop for a milkshake."

"David how can you still think of eating after all you had here?"

"Milkshakes don't count as part of a meal. They are a stand-alone treat," David chuckled, "I'll get the check."

"Thanks. One more thing, what's your milkshake flavor of choice? I may be enticed to take a sip or two if you order wisely," Amanda grinned.

"Chocolate. Think of it as brain food for the studying."

"Lead on, but I promised Karen I'd study with her tonight, I hope you won't be devastated having to study with Don."

"I'll manage to survive the separation, but I won't be happy, Amanda. I'm growing used to us being attached at the hip."

"Will holding hands be enough to keep you going for now, David?"

"With promises for more contact down the road, Amanda?"

"You have more designs on me?"

"Absolutely. Every waking minute and probably in my dreams which, sadly, I don't always remember in the morning," replied David, leaning in to give her a kiss.

"Oh, you are smooth. I'll have to be more prepared for your advances."

"Forewarned is forearmed and I'm hoping both of your arms are ready to wrap around this chest you were so attracted to."

Amanda released her grip on David's hand and ran up the street, laughing.

David laughed in turn and took off after her. He wrapped her up before the next intersection, kissing her lips, first tentatively, then more firmly for a long time.

Amanda drew back only slightly and took a deep breath. "I think you took all the air out of my chest!"

"Your chest looks just great, Amanda, but a closer inspection is needed if you continue to have symptoms."

"We are on a public street!" But Amanda returned his kiss with passion. They walked on holding hands. Amanda said, "Oh good, here's Locust Street. Thanks for a delightful afternoon. I'll see you in Jefferson Hall tomorrow," said Amanda giving David a light, sweet kiss on the cheek, then walking up the sandstone stairs to 854. David waved as she opened the door and slipped inside.

"What a great day," thought David with a broad smile on his face as he walked to Orlowitz.

CHAPTER EIGHT

Drinks at Watson's Pub. First Meeting of the 10th Floor Social Committee

Later that evening David and Don were studying when Don asked, "How about knocking off for an hour and going for a beer at Watson's Pub?"

"Sure. I'll go across the hall and invite Lisa and Cindi," replied David halfway to the door. "I think they might enjoy the company."

The two women indicated to David that they were definitely up for a break. They seemed most interested in being with their hall mates.

"Can you give us a sec?" asked Lisa, who reappeared in a pair of ironed, tight-fitting jeans, and a white blouse. Cindi grabbed their coats and the four took the elevator down. They walked across the Quad to Doc Watson's Pub, the local watering hole.

"Table or bar stools?" asked David, holding the door. The smell of beer and whiskey hit David in the face but was not unpleasant. He looked forward to something different than Earl Grey tea.

"Table," replied Lisa, taking a seat facing the door. "A little dark in here. You guys come here often?"

"First time," replied Don holding her chair. "Lisa, are you positioning yourself to see what prospects walk in?"

"Am I that obvious, Don?" Lisa laughed and added, "The answer is yes. I love to see who is out there."

David walked to the bar with its huge central mirror and shelves of liquor bottles on either side. He returned to the table with a pitcher of Coors and four glasses.

"I see you went all out to impress us," laughed Cindi.

David seemed puzzled, "I just ordered what was on tap."

"Oh, come on. I was just pulling your chain. Pour the beer David."

Don stood, beer in hand and said, "Let me be the first to welcome you to the inaugural meeting of the Tenth Floor Social Committee. Cheers."

"Cheers," replied three voices, taking sips of the watery brew.

"So, how's it going with your nursing classes, Cindi?"

"Anatomy and physiology are gonna break my metaphorical balls for sure, but since I don't have any, I'll do okay," she laughed.

"And how are your classes shaping up in the world of Med Tech, Lisa?" asked David, refilling her glass, "Will you be needing more of my serum for your Proteus OX-19 project?"

"What are you talking about David?" asked Don.

"When I was in Israel, I was bitten by fleas living in a borrowed sleeping bag. I contracted scrub Typhus, a nasty illness, let me tell you. I had huge lymph nodes in my neck and when I got back to Delaware the docs thought I had Hodgkin's Lymphoma. Thank God one of them ordered a Torch panel, which is a series of viral tests. He picked up the Proteus OX-19 in my blood. There is no cure, so I just waited it out. Lisa has been harvesting my serum for those antibodies to use in testing at the hospital lab."

"Lisa, you're second year, correct?"

"Yep. We covered the easy and boring stuff last year. I start in the hematology lab tomorrow. Can't wait to get my hands on the Coulter counter."

"That's Tech speak for the CBC autoanalyzer, Don," offered David.

"I'll have you know I spent a whole day on that machine last summer," replied Don, "Pipette the blood into plastic cups, push a button, insert the lab request, pull out the slip with the results. A monkey can do it."

"Careful med student," cautioned Lisa, "The real work comes when the platelets are clumped, the white count is abnormally elevated, and the differential skewed calling for a hand count. That's when I can make a preliminary diagnosis of Leukemia, then call some handsome, I hope, medical resident and pass on my differential diagnosis."

"Are you always on the prowl, Lisa?" asked David.

"You had your chance."

"One shot and out? That's cold, Lisa. I thought our tete-a-tete at T.J. Fridays was enjoyable."

"Enjoyable was half the anticipated outcome."

"You've got to give me a second chance, Lisa, but I'm not willing to beg."

"Not this early in the semester," Cindi chuckled.

"Hello. There is another eligible man sitting inches away," called out Don.

"When I see him, I'll let you know, Don." Lisa retorted.

"Lisa, you're colder than the beer, which is running low. I'll get a refill," said Don pushing the heavy wooden chair away from the table.

"You're a gentle-boy, Don, thanks," said Lisa.

"Anyone interested in going to the Rolling Stones concert on Saturday? It's three weeks from now at the Army-Navy Stadium." asked David.

"The Stones? I would love to see them," exclaimed Lisa.

"Me too," said Cindi, "I haven't been to a concert in years. Last band I heard was Renaissance at the Robinhood Dell West."

"Well, the Stones will deliver a very different experience," said David, "Don are you in?"

"I don't know The Stones from any other rock group, but I'm willing to give them a try," replied Don as he walked to the bar to refill the pitcher.

"Anyone else you want to invite? I was thinking that I'd invite Amanda Jackson, a classmate I met during orientation. I'll get the tickets for all of us," said David.

"So, is your eye focused only on this classmate, Amanda, David?"

"You've got me all wrong, Cindi, I'm here to study and learn."

"You can pack that brain of yours with anatomical structures and pharmacology only so much, David, you must come up for air and glance around for other real- life prospects."

"If you were in the row in front of me, Lisa, I'd for sure be unable to concentrate on the lecture. Come to think about it, and this is in confidence, we four being now in executive session of the newly formed Tenth Floor Social Committee, Amanda is a very bright and attractive young woman who may have responded to my charms sufficiently to go to the concert."

"A burgeoning infatuation?" asked Lisa.

"No, too early in what will be, I'm certain, a wonderful friendship."

"Friendship, my ass," chimed in Don, returning to the table, pitcher in hand, "I saw you leave Monday's very boring orientation with her."

"Platonic, intellectual discussions, an exchange of views."

"And addresses, I would hope," chuckled Cindi.

"1002 Orlowitz, Cindi," smiled Don, "Always available for dinner and dancing."

"Maybe someday Don." They all finished their beers.

"Look, this has been great, but I've got another chapter to read for tomorrow. Either of you manly men willing to provide an escort?"

"I say we'll travel together for safety's sake."

"I'm quite certain Cindi can look after you, Don."

And with that the group adjourned to their respective apartments, promising to do it again.

"It'll be our Sunday ritual," said Don.

"One gathering at a bar is hardly a ritual, Don, but you organize it for next Sunday and I'll be there," replied David, reaching for his anatomy text that was calling to him from his desk.

CHAPTER NINE

Dissection Lab

David entered the dissection laboratory and was greeted by the strong smell of formalin. The floor was spotlessly white, the windows were closed, and the walls were devoid of pictures. On each of the forty or so stainless-steel tables was a white plastic bag containing a cadaver. Amanda was not a student in his group, so David could focus entirely on the task at hand. He knew they would compare their experiences later that night when they studied together.

"Ladies and gentlemen please move to your respective dissection tables. I am Dr. Arwell. Dr. Martin, Dr. Shep and I will be here to aid you in your delicate dissection of these cadavers. My greatest hope is for you all to learn the mysteries that anatomy can teach you. My second hope is that you will respect the tremendous gift you have been given by these deceased on your tables. You will never know who they were or the reasons for the altruism that drove them to donate their bodies for your education. Through their gifts you will learn the human body in all its amazing intricacies, connections, and systems. Please unzip the bags carefully, as you will be restoring the bodies to the bags after each dissection session. I see some of you are repelled by the odor. This will be minimized by you moistening the bodies with saline after each session. If the experience gets the better of any of you, please feel free to step outside to refresh yourselves. Please assign one person in your group to be the archivist and hold Clemente as reference for the ones doing the dissections. I know there will be a few who love to dissect and become adept, others may prefer to draw and take written notes to share with the others. Please share the time with the bodies."

David decided he would be one of those to dissect and had purchased a dissection kit at the bookstore. He had been a terrible artist when taking paleontology.

"Thankfully Maureen was a tremendous artist and all too eager to draw the fossils as I identified them," recalled David.

David and the others all commented on the advanced age but apparent fitness of their man.

David started to wonder, "Why and how did this man die? Was he in pain? Was he at home or in a hospital?" Each of the five students had different questions about the man and his body, none of which were to be answered unless his mortal illness manifested during the course of their dissection. They worked on the head that first day. The brain had already been removed for the Neuroscientists to study, but there were plenty of cranial and superficial nerves and blood vessels to isolate and tag. The tissues were stiff and brittle, but the team took care to be gentle and were able to dissect the tissues.

"Barry, please write down white, elderly man with blue eyes, balding, with a good set of teeth, and no obvious trauma to the head," asked David.

"We should ask Dr. Arwell his age, weight, and height," added Susan.

David looked around the room and located Amanda in her white lab coat. He tried to catch her eye, but Amanda was intent on writing in her notebook.

"Is that the greater occipital nerve that are you dissecting, Brad?" Amanda asked her partner, "Where does it originate?"

"I can follow it to the second cervical nerve, maybe the third. I have not sufficiently dissected that area of the neck yet."

"Can you lift the nerve a little, so I can draw it?" asked Amanda. "Thanks. Got it."

Dr. Arwell and Dr. Shep buzzed around the dissection lab exuding energy and obviously enjoyed teaching the students. No question seemed too trivial for them, and their answers and patience were reassuring.

"I'm just concerned I may tear a nerve,"" David confided to Dr. Arwell.

"It happens but do your best to minimize the damage. You will become more delicate as time goes on. The fact that you asked means you care." Dr. Arwell moved on to the next dissection table.

The next three hours passed quickly while the students identified and tagged muscles, nerves, and blood vessels. They applied moistened gauze strips to the tissues that had been exposed and carefully slid the cadaver into his plastic bag.

"We all seem to be treating our charge with reverence," thought David as he zipped him in. "See you tomorrow old fellow and thanks for the use of your body."

"I'm pretty sure I won't be eating chicken for a long time," remarked Bob. All heads nodded in agreement.

CHAPTER TEN

Midnight Jogging

Amanda and David met at Amanda's home to study for two hours, comparing what their dissection groups had accomplished that day.

"Did your table get to the greater occipital nerve today, David?"

"I was able to dissect the terminal branches, but we spent more time on the vasculature. Why do you ask?" replied David.

"We were able to track it to the second cervical nerve in the neck but ran out of time to completely expose the area. I drew this, but it is incomplete, and I thought you would have a better illustration from your group."

David turned a few pages in the dissection text. "Clemente's picture is clear, and your sketch looks good. We will get to that area tomorrow and I'm sure your group will complete the dissection as well."

A while later Amanda begged off, saying she needed to get some sleep. David thanked her for the tea and cookies, kissed her and headed home. Once at his desk he realized he was not ready to call it quits for the night and took out his pharmacology notes. He spent three more hours at his desk, studying, his Koss Pro 4-A headphones covering his ears to block out the street noise. He was listening to the reel-to-reel tape he had made of Elton John albums. He stood up and walked to the open window. The summer night in South Philly was quiet and the air lay heavily. The smells of car exhaust and the Delaware River were oppressive.

"My eyes are really tired tonight and my hand hurts from copying so many notes from the biostats text," thought David, "I need to run."

David had been in the habit of running late at night just to relax, often at midnight after studying. He stood up and stretched, turned his desk lamp off and walked over to his dresser to grab socks, blue tee shirt and shorts.

"May be a bit cool," thought David, "I'll grab the yellow windbreaker."

David ran a block down Tenth Street crossed onto South then turned down Eighth. His favorite part of the run was always through the Italian Market. The cheeses and meats hanging in the windows were fascinating. The colorful awnings were barely visible in the midnight darkness. Once past the restaurants and storefronts the townhomes were repetitious and boring, but he wondered who lived there. Cars lined both sides of Eighth Street and trashcans blocked the sidewalks, so David ran in the street.

"Not a single car out tonight," he said out loud.

Tonight, he had Paul Simon's 'Kodachrome' playing in his head and it kept him going the entire run. David usually had one or two songs in his head to set his pace. Another favorite was 'Amerita/Sense of Direction' by Climax Blues Band.

David had to walk a few blocks every once in a while. He knew he was relatively out of shape because he had done more bicycle riding than running while in graduate school up in Orono, Maine. Eventually he reached the wide sidewalk approaching Vet Stadium along Eleventh Street. He ran to Pattison Street walked a block, then turned around and headed back. The brick row homes were dark and quiet. There were no dogs barking at his heels. Other than the occasional police car there was no traffic this time of night. At Packer Street, he cut back over to Ninth Street. David was amazed at how similar all the townhomes were with their four concrete steps and metal bars across the doors and first floor windows. Some homes had a few plants in pots on the top stoop. Even fewer had plastic flowers poking through the metal work that guarded the windows. Each home was about four strides wide and for the most part the sidewalks were in good shape. The rare tree poked out of the concrete between the sidewalk and the curb. Sometimes David had to duck under a branch, but he had an uneventful run back to the Quad where he walked around catching his breath and stripping off his jacket and sweatshirt before entering Orlowitz.

"Man, I feel good. I wish I had been able to do the whole thing without walking, but I'll get there," he thought as he unlocked his apartment door.

He hung up his running gear, took a shower, and got into bed. He slept well, but morning came all too early. The good news was that his legs were not tight nor sore in the morning. He was very hungry and had a couple pancakes and orange juice.

"Must be getting back into shape," he thought. "I wonder if Amanda would enjoy running at night, but it is late when I run, and I would guess she goes to sleep earlier. I'll have to ask her. I really don't know those kinds of details about her lifestyle."

David grabbed his notepad and pens, walked out of the apartment, and pushed the elevator button for the lobby. "Anatomy first, then Cell Biology, shouldn't be a difficult morning. He was a biology major and took quite a few 400 level courses, and the cell biology curriculum at Jeff was no tougher than at Delaware," he thought, "Both entail a lot of lists to memorize, which I can do." David stepped into the elevator while his mind wandered back to the shopping trip with Amanda. "Funny how it works when you fall for someone," he thought as he rode the elevator down, "The attraction is way out front of the reality of knowing about the person."

The elevator stopped at the Eighth floor. David said good morning to two women he did not recognize. "I'm David Coleman, recently from Wilmington, Delaware, now a denizen of the City of Brotherly Love."

"Jennifer Strawderman from Reading, PA."

"Brittany Jones from Wilkes Barre, PA. Glad to meet you, David. Are you a first-year medical student? We are. We have not bumped into you before. Two hundred people is a lot to get to know in a few days, isn't it?"

"I suppose we will learn our dissection group first, then branch out from there."

They reached the Orlowitz lobby. David stood back while the two women left the elevator. He followed them out and across the Quad to Jeff Hall. They walked up the stairs and he held the door for the two women to enter the building. They got on the escalator and David continued his musings about his attraction to Amanda.

"I don't think the attraction is purely physical, although there is that aspect. Beauty is the lure, the eye catcher. The details of someone's personality will become apparent later. My task is to make sure there is a later in our beginning relationship. Hell, I've got time, at least I hope she will give me time to learn all about her, she is definitely the one I want to be with."

"Amerita/Sense of Direction," Climax Blues Band

CHAPTER ELEVEN

Vascular Disease

Dr. Powers lectured on peripheral vascular disease and its relationships with hyperlipidemia, diabetes, and tobacco abuse.

David told Amanda that night, "Those intraoperative photos of gangrenous feet and the resulting below the leg amputations were so very sad"

Amanda replied that she hoped the patients saw the light and got on board with medications and lifestyle changes to prevent further limb loss. They walked through red and brown leaves to Amanda's house in a somber mood. Lunch with Rocky and Bullwinkle was not the usual relaxing and happy time.

"The routine of learning body system diseases is becoming less esoteric and more authentic," observed David, "I'm finding it more difficult to distance myself from the human side of the consequences of illness and necessary medical care."

They reviewed lecture notes as well as the notes each of them had taken down. As usual, both Amanda and David picked up on details the other had not.

"I wonder if my mind was wandering when Dr. Powers said that," he confided to Amanda, "I don't recall drifting off, but it's obvious you heard it, felt it was significant, and wrote it down. Do you recall ever consciously omitting some things from your note because you thought them insignificant?"

"I think it's as you mentioned, David. Often it is difficult to listen to a lecture, process the information, and take verbatim notes. More often than not I decide to write it all down knowing I can make sense of it later at home."

"It's either that or skip writing comprehensive notes and simply listen and take it in. That's why our hybrid system is useful, Amanda. You may be listening for the central themes while I'm nose down, taking verbatim notes without really hearing what is being discussed."

"I couldn't write notes without hearing some of what's being said, David. I need to pay attention, but in a different way than you."

"One thing I do pay particular attention to is how well you coordinate your clothes. You are a rainbow of colors. Your blouses compliment your slacks and your shoes whether heels or sneakers enhance your outfits. I imagine you put a tremendous amount of effort into your ensembles. Now take me, as representative of most men. I throw on a shirt, stripes, print, checks, no matter, because I'm going with the neutral and universal blue-jeans. Sneakers or loafers are not going to make or break the look," admitted David.

Amanda looked David up and down. "You are very observant of my outfits, and I guess expend some of your attire capital pleasing me, knowing you will pass muster with your clothes as long as they are clean, never mind pressed," she chuckled. "Now your attempt to distract us from the issues at hand having worked, its back to the notes."

After another hour of studying, Amanda closed her books, kissed David good night and announced she had to get home to shower and sleep.

"I'll walk you home Amanda," offered David.

"It's raining out there and only one of us needs to get wet but thank you for offering. Meet you on the corner at seven-thirty. I'll bring the coffee tomorrow," she said before shutting the front door.

As Amanda closed the door David closed his notebook and put it in his canvas Boy Scout backpack.

"I've had this for years," he thought to himself, "Made it through the four years at Delaware, the trip to Maine, Israel, and now Philly. He recalled how the Israeli border personnel inspected it with a fine-tooth comb after finding a postcard of the Dome of the Rock inside. "Must have thought I was a terrorist," recalled David. It took a call to Hillel Gordin, the Yotvata kibbutz president and incidentally, was also the Israeli Minister of Fisheries to get David off the hook. Hillel told the guard that David was a good Zionist and to let him board the plane to Elat.

"Good to have friends in high places," smiled David reliving the memory.

Despite the pleasant memory he did not enjoy his climb up the wooden hill to his bedroom this night any more than any other. He decided not to run to the Vet, because of the rain. As he lay on his back listening to the street traffic and the raindrops striking the windows, he reviewed the day that had passed and made a mental list of the things he could anticipate for tomorrow. Sleep did not easily come most nights. More and more of David's nights were intruded, quite pleasantly, by visions of making love with Amanda, sometimes causing an hour of insomnia, cutting into his much-needed sleep.

David thought to himself, "I never fantasize about love making with Amanda while running. Probably a good thing. I'd likely wander into traffic and get run over."

"She's a Rainbow," Rolling Stones

CHAPTER TWELVE

Dissection Lab

The days and weeks wore on with the dissections moving to examining the torso. Some of the students showed their stress and became a bit weird and inappropriate. David was dissecting the stomach from the pancreas while Bob was separating the liver from the overlying diaphragm. Over in the corner there was a commotion that caused everyone to look up from their careful work. Two of the students were playing football with a liver! After the pass was almost dropped and the hardened liver was saved by a diving catch, they tried to run a second play, but Dr. Shep was on the two in a flash. A few of the other students thought it was humorous, but Dr. Shep did not. They of course apologized and returned to work identifying nerves and vessels. However, a week later, after the class had dissected the shoulder joint and in doing so essentially removed one arm from the bodies. One of the same football players stuck the arm up inside his lab coat and hunched over, dragging the dead arm along the floor chanting, "Master, what is your command for Igor today?" It seemed funny for a minute, but Dr. Martin was on them like white on rice and the arm was returned to the dissection table and apologies were made. David and Bob returned to their tasks and the group made notes about the various blood vessels that were revealed once the larger muscles were mobilized.

Betty was an excellent artist. She later made copies and shared her drawings with the rest of the dissection group. That night while reviewing the dissections and reading in the anatomy text, David thought the drawings communicated the anatomy better than the textbook or written descriptions that Hank had shared with the others. Amanda had the same feeling that the pictures were more helpful than the text. They both had been to the library and had consulted the drawings by the amazing Frank Netter.

"I looked into purchasing a set of Netter texts," said David, "But they were way out of my price range. I like the green manual."

"Clemente's "Anatomy" is not a bad choice for us at this level of expertise," said Amanda. "I'll wager that you and I will read these pages so many times we'll have them all but memorized. I already see some of the head and neck drawings in my sleep."

"I wonder if our education will entail a series of compromises over cost, time, versus need to know, and in what detail," David wondered out loud.

"If it's an issue about money, I'm willing to go without a few extras, but if it's about time, then we're stuck," replied Amanda. "I'll put in the hours when I need to, but there's only so many hours in a day. I need to shower and change outfits now and then."

"You're right. I hope you take the time to look so amazing. But for me, forget about a relaxed meal, I've got to sleep sometime," laughed David.

"Hey, how was the concert? Did Mick Jagger deliver the great show you hoped for?" asked Amanda.

"Oh yeah. Jagger pranced across the stage and sang his heart out while Keith Richards and the gang backed him up in typical Stones fashion. Don and I went with the two women across the hall from our apartment. There was one odd fellow in the audience, however. I first saw him way across the stadium and couldn't tell exactly what he was doing. He made his way towards where we were sitting and then proceeded to urinate into a red Solo cup."

"EW! A bit rude, don't you think?"

"It gets worse. This tall, skinny man spoke with the people next to him and one handed this guy some money. He then proceeded to drink his urine."

"No way!"

"Oh yes, to the last drop as far as I could see. The people near the person who gave him the money were clapping and laughing as the man walked up the stairs and repeated his performance."

"Pretty weird." said Amanda.

"Otherwise just good Stones music. I really liked 'Sympathy for the Devil.' They also did a great job with 'Its Only Rock and Roll, But I Like It' and 'Hot Stuff.' Oh, and I bought a black tee shirt with the iconic Stones tongue. I think it will become my go-to running shirt. How was dinner with Brad?"

Amanda's mood darkened. "The dinner was okay, a little place in Chinatown. The food was fresh and tasty, at least the Chow Mein that I had."

"And the Troc show? What did you two see?"

"It was a burlesque. Having never seen a show like that, I have no way to compare whether it was a good show or not."

"Did you and Brad have a good time together?" asked David.

"To tell you the truth . . ."

"Always a good thing."

"That was a problem. Brad's wasn't the most gracious person I've ever been with."

"How so?"

"Let's just say his sense of humor and his appreciation of women was more than a bit coarse, perhaps bordering on rude. I think he should have gone to the show with his buddies, so they could hoot and holler at the scantily dressed women."

"Oh, that's not good, Amanda."

"Live and learn. I may try burlesque again someday, but I'll be sure to select a more appropriate companion. Take you for example, always polite and respectful of my delicate sensitivities," chuckled Amanda.

"Well I will think twice before suggesting we go to a cabaret."

"I wonder if a guy like Brad would ever go to a show that included male strippers?"

"I would bet Brad wouldn't be caught dead in such a place, he's too macho."

"How much more do we have to study tonight?"

"I'd like to finish the rotator cuff and then knock off. I'm tired."

"I'll read, you try to stay awake enough to follow the illustrations."

"I'd like to know how to examine someone with a rotator cuff tear."

"I have DeGowen's text on physical examination. I'll get it and read the chapter to you, then you can go through the exam on me, but I'm pretty sure my shoulder is intact," replied David.

"I believe I have to examine you to understand the textbook," laughed Amanda.

David shucked his shirt and handed Amanda his DeGowen.

"Wow, eager for an examination?"

"My aim is to please."

"Now hold still while I find the page on shoulders. Here it is. So, I place my hand here…"

"Nice warm fingers, Amanda."

"Hush. You're the subject. Okay, push out with your elbow. That's strong. Now push out with your wrist. Equally intact. Pull in with your wrist. No problem. Let me test the deltoid, arm up and push up with your elbow."

"Oh, sorry, my arm appears to have fallen. I think that there is a spasm in my adductor muscle."

"Okay with the spasm," said Amanda returning the hug and they kissed for a long time. Amanda finally pulled back and said, "We have work to do."

"Well it was worth a try," thought David.

CHAPTER THIRTEEN

Florence's Birthday

Florence and Amanda had been dissection partners. One day while walking out of the lab Florence confided to Amanda that she was struggling with Pharmacology. Passing it was required to move to third year and Florence was not sure she was going to pass. Amanda told David about it that night. Florence's apartment was up the hall from David's in Orlowitz. Amanda had done some investigating and told David that tomorrow was Florence's birthday.

"Amanda, do you think I could invite Florence out for a nice Italian dinner. Remember Ralph's Restaurant? We both thought the ravioli were the best."

"Great idea. I won't say I'll not be a little jealous, of the dinner of course."

David called Florence the next day and she accepted the invitation. David showed up an hour early with a bottle of Valpolicella and two glasses. Florence lived in a single bedroom apartment, furnished much as the one David and Don inhabited, sparsely appointed, clean and neat.

"I thought we'd have a glass of Italian wine before we trek to Ralph's."

"You are being so thoughtful, David. Did Amanda put you up to this?" she asked.

"She did tell me it was your birthday, but the rest is all me."

"Well pull the cork and pour me a glass."

David asked Florence "So where are you from and where do you want to end up after your training?"

"I grew up in the central coal producing Pennsylvania countryside. Right now, it's a one Doctor town. I attended Penn State to study Biology. I want to return as a general Internist, maybe solo practice, maybe interview to join the other physician's practice. And you?"

"I'm University of Delaware trained and went to Maine for a Masters in Zoology. I'm not sure Internal Medicine is what I want, but I'm starting with that idea. I'll wait for the clinical rotations to taste specialty care. I'll probably know which ones I do not enjoy rather rapidly. I realize this means a Fellowship and more low paying years to get there. Where to locate my practice is also up in the air. I suspect that will have more to do with access to my family and perhaps the extended family of whoever tolerates me enough to marry me."

"I'll grab some cheese and crackers to pair with this delicious wine." said Florence.

After they shared the wine they left for the walk to Ralph's, which took twenty minutes. They had a delicious dinner. Service was impeccable; the food was better than expected, and they had another bottle of wine, this time a Sangiovese.

"This wine is just as good as the one we had in my apartment." remarked Florence. "This dinner was so good, David. I won't be able to just have TV dinners anymore."

"I have not been able to buy frozen ravioli at the supermarket since I first had ravioli here," replied David. "I don't think I could ever become bored with the food here."

"I'll have to watch my weight if come here more often," said Florence.

David and Florence were comparing their feelings about the first few weeks of med school when Florence paused then said, "I am really afraid I may not pass Pharmacology and then won't move to the second year."

"Have you tried going to office hours with Dr. Jacobi. I hear he's a great guy and I'm sure he will give you time to talk about it."

"Okay, but first let me run something by you, David. I get stuck when reading the notes or the textbook and then get stuck again during the exams. To be quite honest, I have recurring, and intrusive thoughts about my brother and his drug problem."

"Oh . . . What kind of drug problem?"

"He was a superstar football player, wrecked his left shoulder, but chose to defer surgery and played while taking opioids the rest of the season. He went from taking Hydrocodone to Percocet, to Oxycontin. After the season ended he had surgery, a pretty extensive rotator cuff repair. He wanted to continue taking Oxycontin, but the Orthopedist was strict and tapered him to immediate release Oxy, then back to Hydrocodone. He had a lot of pain and started buying Oxycontin on the street."

"Did the Orthopod refer your brother to a pain clinic?"

"He did refer him to a pain clinic, but they elected to start Methadone. The dosage was not strong enough, nor did the relief last long enough."

"Couldn't they increase the dose of Methadone? I don't know much about Methadone."

"They didn't, but the weirdest thing happened. He was met outside the Methadone clinic by a guy who gave him something called black tar Heroin, which he was able to use in the evening and it did relieve his pain."

"Oh, my God, heroin! Did he start shooting up?"

"He started what was called 'skin popping' at first, but then used it intravenously and multiple times a day. The black tar Heroin was not very expensive, and the dealer delivered it to him making the whole process very easy."

"He was able to continue in school while on heroin?"

"Oh yeah, he shot up in the bathroom, kept the dose low and he said no one could tell."

"I'm so sorry, Florence. It sounds really terrible. Did something bad eventually happened?"

"One day his connection did not show up, so my baby brother went out and found something called White Horse heroin. He had no idea how strong it was, but he shot up his usual amount, overdosed and died." Florence had tears in her eyes. She paused.

"That's so sad Florence." David had never dealt with some who had lost a loved one. He reached across the table and held her hand.

"Yes. That's the story that intrudes when I think of opioids, or of Pharmacology in general. I can't get past it. When my brother died I swore to learn all I could about Pharmacology to prevent anyone else from the same terrible fate, but I can't learn anything." She began to cry softly.

"You've got to confide in Dr. Jacobi. Maybe he can refer you to a counselor to eliminate this block. You've got time before the final and if you pass that you pass the course. I could call Dr. Jacobi for you and ask him to make time, but you've got to call him and schedule office hours." David was feeling out of his comfort zone at this point, less a friend and more of a professional giving advice.

"I promise to call tomorrow."

"Good and I will call to check on you. Thanks for sharing such a tough story with me, Florence."

There was a pause in the conversation, then Florence smiled and leaned in toward David.

"Whew, two wines in one night. Can we take a long way home to clear my head?" she asked.

"We can walk thru Society Hill and up Walnut Street, should be as safe as any way back to Orlowitz."

David waved the waiter over and paid the tab over Florence's protests, "Your birthday, Florence. Maybe you pick the place next time."

The pair rose and walked out, David's arm on Florence's shoulder. They walked quietly at first given the emotion about Florence's brother.

Once they left the commercial strip the night sky was full of stars. The gentrified Society Hill townhomes were mostly dark, but the streetlights provided a sense of safety. There was comfort in just walking in the dark quiet. They walked past Washington Square and Florence asked if the Liberty Bell wasn't just a few blocks away.

"It's on the other side of the old City Hall where John Hancock wrote his name down as the first on the Declaration of Independence and started the whole thing."

"I heard that that there is a Ben Franklin home and printing press museum nearby," said Florence, "Ever been there?"

"My brother and I went there on a tour through City Hall, the Liberty Bell, and lunch at Bookbinders years ago."

They walked past the diamond district to Tenth and Walnut Street where they made a left into the Quad toward Orlowitz.

"Thanks for a pleasant and totally unexpected night, David. You have been very sweet. Thanks for listening. I will find some equally delicious restaurant for next time. Are you sure Amanda won't become jealous?"

"Amanda and I will be fine, Florence. I had fun being out tonight. Let's do it again," David said pushing the elevator button for the tenth floor.

They were both lost in their thoughts as the elevator ascended to the tenth floor. Once in the hallway, David reminded Florence, "Let me know when you've called Dr. Jacobi."

"I will and thanks again for listening."

David held the door to Florence's apartment and said, "Good night."

"I think Amanda and I need to try out another Italian restaurant such as Dante and Luigi's," thought David walking back up the hallway to his apartment, "I want Ralph's to be for a special night out."

CHAPTER 14

Musculoskeletal System

The Chief of Rheumatology, Dr. Harrison lectured on the musculoskeletal system.

"I've had first-hand experience with shoulder and knee injuries," David said to himself, "I'd be interested in learning a bit more about the inflammatory diseases."

Dr. Harrison described joint structures, components of cartilage and some interesting associations between low back pain due to sacroiliac inflammation and ocular and aortic valve disorders due to inflammation in these three locations in ankylosing spondylitis.

"I can see how physicians put these manifestations together clinically, but to determine it was autoimmunity directed against Type II cartilage in all three sites is pretty amazing," Amanda said.

"You've got orthopedists or rheumatologists working with cardiologists and ophthalmologists, then a biochemist to figure it all out. Amazing bit of cooperation," replied David.

"And then you've got dermatologists treating psoriasis with UV light and coal tar joining with rheumatologists to treat psoriatic arthritis. Seems like that is one tough nut to crack. Long term use of prednisone doesn't seem such a great idea."

Amanda looked up from her notes and said, "I read somewhere in my path book that the Mayo Clinic was starting to use methotrexate to treat rheumatoid arthritis and psoriatic arthritis."

"Isn't methotrexate used mainly in oncology for things like renal cell and head and neck cancers? Who thought that it would be appropriate for inflammatory joint and skin disorders?"

"Pretty gutsy to take an oncologic agent for a non-malignant illness," added Amanda.

The next day Dr. Harrison was scheduled to lecture on degenerative joint conditions, but someone thought a bit of levity was in order and inserted a slide of Burt Reynolds famously lying on his left side, smiling and facing the class with a rheumatology text obscuring the critical area. Professor Harrison took the joke in stride and commented on Mr. Reynold's muscular definition and talked briefly about Burt's football career and injuries. David was impressed that he knew those details and was not affronted by the interruption. The lecture went on to describe the desiccation of cartilage leading to fissuring and tiny fractures that interfered with joint stability and further compromised normal joint function. Some of the changes were due to senescence, but trauma, whether due to work related activities or major injuries also injured joint functions.

"I'm a bit bummed at the prospect of developing arthritis later in life due to my injuries" admitted David to Amanda that night.

CHAPTER FIFTEEN

Clinical Skills

In addition to the biostatistics and anatomy lectures, the students were required to practice physical exams during the Wednesday clinical skills time. David was surprised at how intimidating it was to do a simple medical exam, having never before listened to heart or lung sounds, or pushing around on the belly. He and his partner, Ted, were both lean and it was easy to palpate their respective livers. There was no lack of borborygmi, but neither could palpate the spleen.

"Take off your shirt, Ted, I'll look for an abnormal nevus, anything that could be more interesting than perfectly normal. Take the ocular exam. Probably completely normal, or you'd know about it. Look left, look right, up and down. Follow my finger, no don't move your head."

"I almost wish one of us had some enlarged glands to palpate, David, not that I want either of us to contract anything more serious than a sore throat," said Ted, peering down David's pharynx with his pen light.

"I enjoyed moving your bones and feeling the joints. Not that I mean anything with that comment, my man," laughed David.

"Thinking of orthopedics, David?"

"Nah, I can't see myself cutting into someone. I like carpentry but building my bookcases didn't run me the risk of infections or death due to hemorrhage."

"I want to get to the library and listen to heart murmurs, gallops, and bruits," said Ted, "You've got a very boring, normal heart, David."

"You wanted me to have horrible murmurs having had Rheumatic Fever, didn't you!"

"Perhaps. We'll have to wait until third year to examine real patients with abnormal findings.

David said, "I hope I don't miss an important murmur and look foolish."

"Are you kidding? How are you going to learn? If you knew it all you'd be hanging out your shingle and making the big bucks already," laughed Ted.

"Good point, but anticipatory anxiety is a bitch."

"Why don't you ask Amanda if she needs an exam?" smirked Ted, "You could really play doctor. Who knows what may develop? She may need a specialty exam."

"Hey! Our relationship is entirely professional," smiled David.

"Perhaps offer her some fine Italian wine and see where that leads, on a purely educational basis of course."

"I think we're done here. Let's fill out the exam forms and split. I want to tape an Electric Light Orchestra album from Helen Leicht's Lunch show on WIOQ. She's gonna play 'Eldorado' start to finish."

"I really like 'Boy Blue' on that album," said Ted.

"She does albums at lunch every day, but I'm not interested in taping most of them."

"But David, you'll miss Rocky and Bullwinkle!"

"Sometimes you have to make the tough call, Ted."

"Boy Blue," ELO

CHAPTER SIXTEEN

The Note Service

After Anatomy, Clinical Med, and Biostats came the Fall weather and Pathology, Microbiology, and Pharmacology. David had taken a lot of Microbiology as an undergraduate and had little difficulty with that material. Pathology was generally considered the tallest mountain to climb, do or die. No one made it to second year if they did not pass Path. The sheer volume of information was what made it so daunting, but for David the challenge of learning so many facts and relationships challenged him like no other course he had ever taken. Amanda enjoyed the clarity of the material, but admitted to David that it was often overwhelming, having come from an undergraduate program in English and Music. David and Amanda had both been doing some after-hours work in the Pathology Department. Amanda was working on a project dealing with pharyngeal cancer and its link to Human Papilloma Viral infections. David enjoyed working with a dynamo Biochemist, Dr. Taylor, looking at antibodies from lupus patients and how they interacted with receptors on red blood cells. They both worked on their projects during the rare afternoons they had free.

Amanda and David were considered by some of their classmates as the dynamic pathology duo for their love of the subject. One night after studying, Amanda mentioned to David that she was thinking about a career as a Pathologist.

"I think it's far too early in our training to settle on a life-long discipline," replied David, "But certainly there is no problem toying with the idea."

"And I suppose you have not considered a career in research as opposed to clinical medicine, David?"

"I enjoyed doing a senior thesis in the Geology Department at Delaware, and my master's thesis was interesting, but I want to explore learning about medicine and diseases. I'm thinking I'd like to be more of a detective, ferreting out causes for illness and being able to treat diseases, rather than work in the lab all the time."

"Why do you take so much pride in taking notes and typing up such good summaries of lectures? Do you see that as a challenge, or does it satisfy some literary appeal?"

"I like interpreting not only what the lecturer says, but what is behind the facts. I try to produce notes that are accurate, but also provide insight into where the lecture was going. Hell, I could just tape the lectures and make copies for everyone paying for the note service if I wanted to be purely factual, Amanda."

"You're doing a good job and you do add something to a pure transcript. I'm sure the Group C students don't realize how much more they are receiving than simple transcripts with the note service."

"The problem for me is I get no feedback, other than your kind compliments, from consumers of the notes."

"Oh, I'll bet you will hear if you screw up."

"Maybe I will push it a bit. Remember how I wrote a poem instead of an essay to apply to Jeff? Maybe I'll rhyme the entire lecture notes."

"How that'd the poem application letter go over with the Professor that interviewed you?"

"He said he enjoyed it and as it contained all the required information and had no problem with the format. He did caution me about not pushing the Jefferson sensibilities too hard, at least early in my career."

"Probably good advice. Jefferson is set in its ways and they seem to like things their way..."

"Or the highway."

"Just try to make it to second year, will you please."

"I'll do my best. By the way are you interested in going to a small art museum over on Cherry Street, just across from City Hall?" asked David.

"Which one is that?"

"The Pennsylvania Museum of the Fine Arts."

"What kind of art do they display, abstract, modern, classic? Is there an admission fee?"

"I'm not sure, but I'll pay for the tickets and for lunch. How about Saturday morning?"

"Sure, but how do you know about it?"

"I went there once while at U of D and I recall it being a mixture of styles. I went with Connie, a friend from High School. I remember one piece hanging on the left wall in the lobby. The artist had squished a hundred tubes of paint between two big pieces of Lucite," replied David. "I recall enjoying the museum. It is the oldest art museum and art academy in the U.S. Thomas Eakins trained there."

"Didn't he paint the famous picture of The Gross Clinic that Jefferson speaks of so highly?"

"That's the one. I heard that one painting is valued at millions of dollars."

"Let's do it."

The next morning David walked over Amanda's home around ten o'clock and the two strolled up Locust Street to Broad then cut over in front of City Hall.

"There's that giant clothespin. That is an iconic sculpture that really says: Philadelphia," said Amanda, "I'd like to stop and get a picture of us next to it. Maybe we could use it for our Christmas card. What do you think?"

"I think you're intimating we are going to be an official Christmas card sending couple this winter."

"Is that a problem?"

"I love it, been waiting and hoping to hear you say something like this for a long time, Amanda."

"So, what about the Clothespin background as the setting for 'We are a couple in Philly' theme?"

"I like it. We'll have to find a time when it's not swarming with people. Perhaps someone can take the picture for us. You have that nice Nikon."

Once inside the art museum they were able to stroll around. It was not as large or impressive as the Philadelphia Art Museum with all its floors full of exhibits. The art in the Cherry Street gallery was a mixture of classics, such as painted by Thomas Eakins and his contemporaries, with a smattering of more recent art, including some pretty wild abstractionist pieces.

"What the heck is that one supposed to be? What is it trying to say?"

"Not a thing to me," replied Amanda.

"I have to give the artist credit for having the guts to put that one out there."

"Perhaps it was a period piece, you had to be there to make sense of it."

Amanda walked over to the docent in the next room. "Excuse me, can you tell us a little about that abstract work my boyfriend is looking at?"

"That one is definitely one of a kind, just a color and a dot," replied the docent, "The museum purchased it from a fairly famous student who went on to painting huge half red, half blue pieces. I believe quite a few are hanging on walls in Rittenhouse Square apartments."

"It sounds like it is hard to interpret the painting no matter who you are, not that it makes the painting irrelevant, just not our style."

"I could paint a wall with a roller half red, half blue and put a sphere along the border between the colors and call it art at a fraction of the cost," added David.

"And in two years we could paint over it and make it a green, yellow, and black composition," said Amanda.

"He got to it first and your painting would not have his signature on the right corner, would it?" replied the docent, "Makes all the difference between twenty dollars of wall paint and a ten-thousand-dollar work of art."

"We're going to move on and find something more representative of the real world," said Amanda. "Thanks for explaining it to us. I hope you are able to move around to other sections of the museum, closer to paintings that interest you."

"Amen to that."

After taking in the other paintings, David suggested they walk a block along Cherry Street and go into a couple galleries where paintings for sale hung on the walls. "Maybe we can pick up a bargain, Amanda."

They walked into one store and were overwhelmed at the diversity of all the paintings hanging on those walls. Most had very heavy, gold frames, some frames were black, but equally ornate.

"Check out this one. I think it's the Schuylkill above the spillway where the scullers practice."

"It has a certain minimalist elegance, doesn't it?"

"The price is more than elegant at $950, but that's probably the going rate for that artist."

"Someday I'll have real paintings hanging on my walls, but for now I'll stick with prints on fishing line hanging from the ceiling."

"I like your six by six Van Gogh's and Renoirs. They make a curtain of art."

"If you find a print of that size that you like, let me know and I'll make a decal of it and put it on art board so you can hang it up in your room, Amanda."

They went next door and into a gallery with sculpture, ancient lamps, and fewer paintings. David pointed one out to Amanda. The trees in the painting vaguely resembled those that Van Gogh painted, somewhat twisted, suggesting motion.

"I see what you mean about the movement, but the artist did not use the vibrant yellow, blue, and greens that Van Gogh applied so often," commented Amanda.

"I still like it," said David, "And look, only a buck fifty!" He smiled when Amanda looked at the price.

"It's a hundred and fifty dollars!"

"I'm sure in the art world that's a buck fifty, Amanda."

Having seen enough, they went looking for a lunch spot, then walked home.

"Overall, an interesting day, David. You know I have not really paid much attention to the Eakins 'Gross Clinic' before. I'll need to check it out."

CHAPTER SEVENTEEN

Renal Pathology Lectures

The Monday morning lecture by Dr. Carlos dealt with inflammatory diseases of the kidney. The class very rapidly settled into the morning marathon of renal pathology. It was all interesting and added to David's understanding of glomerulonephritis as related to his research project on lupus patients and the DNA-C3 immune complexes that accumulate and damage the glomeruli, but it was difficult to keep up. Almost all the students planned to rely on the note service to fill in gaps in their lecture notes. After Dr. Carlos finished at noon the class made the usual mad exodus to watch their favorite respite cartoon, Rocky and Bullwinkle. After lunch Dr. Siegle and Dr. Green lectured on renal physiology, but most students were still reeling from the sheer volume of information Dr. Carlos had already imparted that morning. David took to reading the pathology text early in the evening and the lecture notes later each night with Amanda. They both made some progress on retention. They both enjoyed Pathology for its clarity. Almost everything Dr. Carlos discussed was new and interesting. He was able to describe not only the pathology but did a good job of illustrating the clinical features of someone with disease.

David was not particularly concerned he would develop nephritis or suffer renal failure, but at one point he was convinced he had contracted tuberculosis based on his cough and fatigue. He mentioned it in passing to a third-year student who told him it was common for freshman to be convinced they had Leukemia, chronic infections, or a GI illness, but that it was all a manifestation of stress. David learned that keeping up with his routine of running to the Vet most nights allowed him to dump the stresses of the day and to review the masses of information so recently crammed into his head. He usually returned fatigued yet relaxed with a clear head and slept like one of the dead.

The next day was one that David had to transcribe for the note service, for those who wanted to mine every shred of lecture gold. The Path lectures were well attended, and David was able to take almost verbatim notes. There were quite a few Group C students, who routinely skipped lectures and opted to rely on a correspondence method of receiving lecture notes. David tried to give them as close to a comprehensive account of the lecture as possible, but thought they were crazy to skip lectures. He had always relied on learning with the triad of one third hearing it, one third writing it down, and one third review. It had served him well in his undergraduate years. Plus, the tuition was not trivial, and David wanted to avail himself of every opportunity to interact with the incredibly bright professors. Quite a few were interesting and friendly people as well. Dr. Carlos, the Chief of Pathology was the one that delivered the bulk of the path material and was certainly an impressive person. He commanded attention by the style of his delivery of information. When Dr. Carlos spoke on a topic, it was obvious that he knew everything about it. He had a conversational style and he did not pontificate. After listening to Dr. Carlos, David felt that he could also comprehend the information. In this way Dr. Carlos set a high bar for mastery of the pathological facts. He also wore beautiful suits, probably different ones every day. His shirt and tie collections were equally impressive.

After three hours of trying to take notes on Dr. Carlos' lecture, David's brain hurt. Dr. Carlos imparted pearls of wisdom and David found he was enjoying the challenge of keeping up.

"It's still a lot of stuff to remember," said David to himself.

He hoped to do better than his usual 84% on the final exam. Right now, David was looking forward to the relaxing nonsense of the Rocky and Bullwinkle Show during lunch. Unfortunately, there was that one student, Mike, who just had to ask a clarifying question at the end of the lecture, which delayed the exodus for television respite. David thought those questions could easily have been asked as the class exited, but Mike loved the attention.

"Maybe he's just a clueless first row jerk," he thought, but stayed in his seat until Dr. Carlos answered Mike's question, more out of respect for Dr. Carlos than for Mike.

Just before David was going to leave, he noticed Kyle talking with Amanda. At one point, Kyle looked back at David and pointed, then returned to talking with Amanda. Kyle walked up the stairs past David and said, "Hello, David," but kept walking, not really interested in a conversation. David stood up, then waited for Amanda to walk up and asked, "What was that about? I think I remember his name is Kyle."

"Kyle invited me to a party he, Jason, and Paul are having tonight at their place. I asked if I could come with you, and Kyle said sure."

David thought, "Kyle would have said sure to Amanda if she brought a trained monkey to their medical school frat house, as long as she came to his party."

"So, will you go with me?" asked Amanda.

"I don't know those guys and it's not really my style, but sure, I'll go with you. I'll just have to adapt. I want to be with you, Amanda. Thanks for thinking of me."

"Do me and us a favor, David and I'll reciprocate in turn. If this pushes you out of your comfort zone promise you'll be honest with me as we still don't each other that well. I want to get to know about you."

"And ditto for you, Amanda. It would be better if we are on the same page."

"Ok, lets step on outta here, get some studying done before the party. I'll go home and change into a party outfit. You could do the same then we could review the notes for a half hour."

"Good idea. I'll try to look half as good as I know you will. Let me walk you home."

CHAPTER SEVENTEEN

Friday Night Party

Amanda knocked on David's apartment door. David opened the door and said, "Hi, come on in."

Amanda suggested, "We have forty-five minutes before the party, I'll read the notes and you can relax and listen. Jump in if you hear something that doesn't make sense." Amanda commenced to read the physiology notes and David interrupted her only once. He felt the stress of having to switch back to studying all the information they had amassed during their classes that day and he wished he could dump the stress as he did while running at night. He confided this to Amanda and she said, "Running really seems to relax you. Do you keep track of your times?"

"Not really. I'm more interested in how the run goes, if I can make it up and back without walking, and whether I'm tight and sore the next morning," replied David.

"Doesn't it get boring running the same route each night?"

"Not really. I look forward to making it to that next intersection, looking down the cross streets to see if anything is happening, which is rare. Sometimes I recall something Dr. Carlos or Dr. Siegle had said that I didn't catch the meaning of during lecture. Its times like that I wish I had a tape recorder or another gadget to listen to the lecture while I'm running."

"Always multitasking aren't you: singing a song in your head, putting one foot in front of the other, and now you want to review lecture notes. Why not just enjoy deep breathing and the rhythm of the run?" Amanda shook her head but was smiling.

David reached over and gave Amanda a hug and kissed her cheek.

"What was that for?"

"I enjoy being with you."

"That's great, because we are going to be spending a lot of time together during Path if we want to do well."

David did not share that as soon as he finished running, he felt fully charged and amorous. Amanda was his constant companion during the initiation of sleep.

"I will just have to be patient and be willing to pay attention to Amanda's cues," he told himself. "I don't want to rush into making love, but I do want Amanda to know that I love her both for her brains and her sexy body." David reached for Amanda again and they settled into a kissing marathon side by side on the couch. Neither pulled away for a long time.

"Whew! That was intense. What brought that on?"

"Just the thought of spending a lot more time with you learning Pathology. Pathology plus you are a real turn on," David laughed, "No I'm seriously in love with you at this moment, can't get enough of you."

As it turned out, Amanda was experiencing some of the same nighttime thoughts about David and wanted to make love with him. "That will be a big step in our relationship," she told herself. "Maybe I'm not giving the proper signals. David has dropped a few hints in general conversation. I could say something about being attracted to his gentle and attentive manner. Of course, his body is difficult to resist when we are together and pressed up against each other. "Can we get back to the notes?"

"Sure. So, the kidneys can autoregulate blood pressure to a certain extent with the angiotensin-renin system? Fascinating."

"Unfortunately for the people with heart failure that system can lead to fluid overload and more symptoms."

"Seems someone needs to develop a drug to modulate the angiotensin-renin system."

"I'm sure one of the pharmaceutical companies is on it," replied Amanda. "Looks like it's time to walk over to the party."

David reached for Amanda's hand, pulled her close and kissed her again. Then they walked out of Orlowitz and down to Locust Street. He enjoyed the feel of her hand in his. Her palm was dry, and her slender fingers felt strong in his hand. The night air was cool, but the little bit of a breeze carried the smell of dinners prepared in the homes they passed

"Kyle's place is on Eleventh and Spruce," said Amanda, "Thanks again for going with me. It's nice to have you here. I didn't want to show up alone. I suspect those guys were in Kappa Alpha or some equally sexist fraternity in college."

"There was a Kappa Alpha house at Delaware. They asked me to rush. There were a lot of soccer players living there, but I decided to stay in the dorms the first year. Probably a good choice. Being on the soccer team was fun, but I nearly flunked German while I tried to play soccer and make all the practices. Do you know what the coach said when I told him about my D in German? He said I should not have taken 19 credit hours while playing soccer, and that I should just drop the class and make it up during Spring semester."

"Sounds reasonable. What did you do?"

"I quit the soccer team, got my grades up and played pickup games every Saturday with the international students. I had a great time."

"So how did you do overall?"

"Not to brag, but I got a B in Genetics. It was a B plus, plus, plus and the Prof wouldn't let me do extra work to make it an A. But I got a D in German"

"Sounds like you have issues. Still holding that grudge? For what? Did you have a 3.99 overall? What were the rest of your grades?"

"A's," replied a sheepish David, "When you take 168 credit hours it tends to dilute out the couple that were not A's. And what about your GPA?"

"I enjoyed all my classes and did well. My GPA was 3.96. Let's not talk about this anymore, especially at the party," said Amanda with a smile, "We're here. Enough talk, I'm her to relax and leave classwork behind for the next few hours."

"They've really cranked up the music. Good stuff, Led Zeppelin."

"Well, let's find Kyle to say hello. Would you get me a gin and tonic? I prefer Boodles gin if they have it, Tanqueray is my second choice."

"Well, you certainly know your way around gin. I'll also try a gin and tonic. Tanqueray sounds familiar."

Once they had their drinks in their hands, they went looking for their hosts. They ran into Jason first.

"Thanks for inviting us, Jason," said Amanda.

"Nice place," added David.

"Have some food and feel free to check out the house. I've got a few last-minute things to do, but I'm sure I'll see you later."

"Thanks," answered David, "Are you hungry Amanda?"

"I could check out the offerings. Oh, there's Sara. Do you know her? She's very nice and very bright." Amanda took a few steps toward Sara. "How are you, Sara? This is David."

"Hey, Amanda. You look great as usual. Doesn't she look great in that black and gold shirt, David?"

"I'm always impressed by Amanda's outfits. Pleased to meet you. I don't think that I have met you before."

"Oh yeah, there's only two hundred and twenty-five people to know, no big deal, David," Sara replied laughing. "My name is Sara Eriksen. I'm from New Hampshire, but now I'm a Philly chick."

"What'cha drinking Sara?" asked Amanda.

"Vodka and tonic."

"David, do you mind if I confer with Amanda alone for a few minutes?"

"Not at all," replied David, looking around the living room with its overstuffed couch, tall chairs covered in dark blue fabric, and wooden end tables. The three men had oriental rugs on their wood floors and the lamps were matching with stained glass lampshades. Overall, an attractive room to hang out in. He was more than a little surprised that he was also a bit envious of their furnishings. David looked over the group at the party and spotted Arthur, one of the guys on the Jefferson soccer team. "Hi Arthur. Will you be able to make the match this Sunday?"

"Of course. Wouldn't miss it for anything. I'm glad Paul asked me to this party on a Friday night. Saturday night would not have been very smart for a Sunday morning match."

"I agree. I was wondering, how do you get along so well with the other forwards? It must be difficult to have just met them, but you guys seem to coordinate really well."

"I think the trick is that Bill, Joe, and I are all playing the positions we are used to from college. I like being right wing."

"Don't you think it feels odd not to have a coach?"

"Yes, but so far we are working it out. You and the other backs seem to be able to be an impassable wall, which is great for guys like me that only want to stay up top, run with the ball and take shots. I hate having to come back and play defense, as I'm sure you've noticed."

"As long as you are willing to get back for corner kicks, free kicks, and if things really fall apart, I'm cool with you three staying up top and being ready for my passes."

"So far, so good. Sunday is Temple's team. I hear they are a strong team."

"We'll beat them. I'm hungry. Let's drift over to the food table."

Meanwhile Sara had linked her arm with Amanda's and pulled her over to the couch in the corner of the dining room.

"So, what's up, Sara?"

"Ok. I see that you and David are getting along fabulously. I was wondering if it puts a strain on the time you need for studying. I've had trouble fitting the dissection lab in with the lectures and then being able to study without falling asleep. How do you fit a relationship in there as well?"

"Turns out, David and I are great study partners. We have slightly different takes on what information we write down as notes, so we complement each other. Then there is the textbook stuff and the note service. We take turns reading, which saves my eyes."

"You are so fortunate to have met David and be able to work together. Do you think just studying together also counts a bit toward a relationship, I mean romantically?"

"I don't think I feel romantic while studying, but you're right, we seem to have developed a bond and it probably has grown stronger as time has passed."

"Well, tell me, what else? Have you slept with him yet?"

"Oh God no! I mean it's not that I wouldn't enjoy being close, but I don't want to rush things. I think I told you I was not very active on Catholic University's dating scene and now hanging with David seems to be filling that gap, at least so far."

"I'd say it sounds great!" replied Sara, "Well I've got my eye on Paul, who was the one that invited me for tonight. I don't want to start something with him only to make trouble with my homework and then have to back away from a relationship. But, I wouldn't mind some physical distraction!"

"I know nothing about Paul, but if you have a good feeling, go for a beer or grab dinner on South Street sometime and check it out."

"I guess I'll have to put some effort into it along with all the class work we've got to attend to."

"David and Arthur are over at the food table. Let's join them."

"Getting hungry?" David asked, "The meatball subs are good with the sauce, and the cheddar is really sharp."

"I'm up for some cheese and crackers," said Sara reaching for two plates. "Here Amanda, load up."

Amanda looked up and called out, "Hi Paul, great party."

"Thanks Amanda. Hi Sara, glad you made time to come tonight," replied Paul stepping closer to Sara. "Take advantage of the bar and the food. Jason organized the food, Kyle stocked the bar, and I arranged the tunes. Do you have any suggestions for music?"

"Everything is great." said Amanda, "I would like to hear some Humble Pie if you've got it."

"Humble Pie?" said a surprised Paul, "Amanda I am impressed. Oh yeah, I have the 'Smokin' album and it is great!"

"I really like 'Thirty Days in the Hole' best on that album," added Amanda.

"I'll grab it. Anyway enjoy. Talk to you later, Sara," said Paul moving off.

"I'll hold you to it, Paul. You're not gonna get away from me tonight"

"There's Kyle with a tray of shots. Let's try one," said Amanda.

"Want to do a couple, David?" asked Sara.

"No thanks, enjoy."

"Come on, Amanda."

"I'll talk with you Sunday, David," said Arthur.

David watched Amanda slam down a Jell-O shot. Sara handed her a plastic cup with another shot.

"I sure hope she knows her limits," thought David, munching on some grapes from his plate.

"Hi David."

David looked to his left and saw Doug, a fellow Delawarean from Wilmington. They had met on the commuter train that took them to downtown Philly. Doug was known as Bearclaws, a humorous adjustment to his last name. Doug, Steve, Henry, and David met on the Philly train, after having spent the weekend home with family. Once in Philly, they had the option of going up to street level at the iconic Clothespin, or if the weather was nasty, they could walk the tunnel to Eleventh and Walnut. It was usually a stinky tunnel, having served as a latrine for the homeless, but it was dry.

"How are things going David?"

"Can't complain, Doug, and if I wanted to it wouldn't do anyone any good," he laughed. "No really, I am enjoying life in the big city and the challenge of keeping my head above water in the classes."

"Ain't that the truth, David. I thank God for the note service. Your transcripts are especially readable. Do you spend a lot of time on them?"

"Usually an hour, but its time well spent reviewing the lectures. Sometimes typing them out forces me to research the subject so I get it right."

"I'm sure many of us are thankful you're doing such a good job, especially when we miss a lecture."

"Thanks for that, Doug. I try to make the notes as accurate as possible. I'd feel terrible if I wrote something incorrectly and caused anyone to miss an answer on the exam because of me."

"Good catching up with you, David. I'm gonna go over and talk with Kyle."

"Later, Doug."

David took a couple more shrimp and saw Paul across the room. David wanted to know some things about wine and had heard that Paul was really knowledgeable regarding wine.

"Hey Paul, thanks for inviting Amanda and me to this party. I'm glad to be out of the books. You have a nice spread of food and the music is great. You know, I like beer, but I want to get into drinking wine. I heard that you accompanied your father on his business trips to Europe to select wines for his import company. I wanted to ask you a wine question. How long ago did Montepulciano de Abruzzi make it to the states?"

"I'm not quite sure, but its been an important wine in Italy for decades. It was probably here, but not as popular a choice among those pursuing Lancers, various Chianti's, and Mateus in the early seventies. By now you can find many varietals to choose from and almost all are excellent. But this is not a wine drinking party. I may be the only one sampling the grapes. Drinking from a plastic cup doesn't really enhance the taste or the drinking experience!"

"I get it." David wanted to challenge Paul, "I heard that you can identify a wine to a region and varietal, perhaps close to the vintage with just a sip."

"Sometimes I can get close, but only with European wines. Let me try this one," he said reaching for the closest bottle. He poured a small amount and swirled the wine in a red Solo cup. "I could do this blindfolded, but red versus white is fairly simple. Paul took a sip and sloshed it in the front of his mouth, then swallowed. A red, probably Italian, medium body, I'll bet Kyle didn't spent a fortune, so it's likely a 1975 Valpolicella."

"You are the wizard of wine, the valedictorian of the vineyard, Paul. Amazing! It's a 1974 Valpolicella."

"I got lucky, David. And I know Kyle's budget. My dad and I spent a lot of time in northern Italy and that wine was really popular even back then. Listen, I promised Amanda some Humble Pie. Talk with you later."

An hour later David was ready to leave. He had spoken with as many people as he wanted to, mostly about topics he had no interest in. "I hope I didn't show people how bored I am," thought David.

He looked around to locate Amanda and Sara. They were sitting on the sofa giggling.

"I really hate to break this party up for Amanda, but I want to get to bed early tonight to be rested for the match this weekend," thought David. "I'll go over and drop a hint that I'd like to leave. I can't just leave Amanda here, she's a little toasty, and I have a responsibility to see her home."

He came up to the back of the couch and said, "Hello ladies. Having a wonderful time? Amanda, I'd like to think about leaving soon. What do you want to do?" Amanda looked relaxed and was having a good time.

"I suppose Amanda rarely gets to hang with other women and it seems she is really enjoying herself," observed David.

"Give me a few minutes more with Sara. It seems as if we just got here." Amanda had not been out with David to a party before. Still, she was a bit surprised David couldn't make small talk and find someone new and interesting spend time with. "This is a side of David that, of course, I have not realized. We spend a lot of time together, but its mostly studying together. I want to stay longer, but I know David wants to leave."

"Sara would you be able to walk me home?"

"Sure, Amanda. I'll take care of her, David, don't you worry. I heard you and Arthur talking about your soccer match, so you'll want to get a good night's sleep. Feel free to go home now. We women will hold down the fort."

David walked around to the front of the couch. Amanda stood up and they embraced and shared a short kiss. He said, "Thanks, Amanda, I know you want to stay. See you tomorrow. Nice meeting you Sara, take care of my girl," and walked across the living room and left.

Sara observed, "David's a quiet man, isn't he? Does his intensity drive you a little crazy sometimes?"

"David's a little more solitary than I am. He can be intense, but always about things that matter. I suspect big parties are not his thing," Amanda said as she sat back down on the couch and held Sara's hand.

"Does he ever just laugh?"

"David can be a riot when it suits him. He's clever and kind, never sarcastic or mean and I love that about him. I feel very safe and secure around him," said Amanda. "Not a day goes by that I don't think of how lucky I am that we sat next to each other that first day of orientation. How about this, David invited me to a barber shop at midnight after orientation. It was to support a local barber going for a Guinness record for continuous hair cutting."

"Was it fun?"

"Once in a lifetime date for sure. We hit it off right away and have been cruising along ever since."

"You certainly have someone special, Amanda."

The two women put their heads together as they giggled. "One more, Sara?" asked Amanda as Kyle walked by with his tray of shots.

"Thirty Days in the Hole," Humble Pie

CHAPTER NINETEEN

Night Running

When David got back to his place, he was ready to run. "Might be cold tonight, better go for layers," he thought and pulled his running gear over his Stones tee shirt. Keys and handkerchief went in the coat pocket. He was already becoming overheated. "Got to get outside and cool off."

Once outside he began to stretch his calves with heels in the street, toes on the curb.

"Never pleasant first few go rounds, but I gotta stretch," he thought.

He put his hands on the light pole and stretched his low back, shrugged his shoulders a couple of times and began to run down Tenth Street. There was mist in the night air which bode well for breathing. The city was quiet, there were no cars coming behind him and the homes lining Tenth Street were mostly dark. David ran through the regularly spaced circular oases of light from the tall poles above. He enjoyed running down Tenth Street to Oregon, hooking around the Vet, then back on Ninth. He alternated running on Tenth with running down Eighth Street, but preferred Eighth, as the Italian Market was well lit and interesting. After that it was a straight shot to the Vet.

Tonight, he was running effortlessly, and his mind drifted back to the party. "Why was I so bothered by Amanda doing shots? Was it because she had just had a G & T? Was it that she enjoyed the red Jell-O and vodka concoction? Makes me want to vomit at the thought of having to hide the taste of vodka with Jell-O. Perhaps I should just let that go. It's probably better to live and let live. Amanda's not the only one in the history of the world to enjoy a buzz. I'd prefer to relax with a single malt, but that's me. Am I concerned she is not who I thought she was, having seen another side of her? Who am I kidding? There'll be plenty of things to learn about her and she about me with all my quirks as our relationship goes along. I just don't like change or surprises. That's probably all it is. Jell-O shots and getting silly are for sure not deal beakers, not even close." David paused in his ruminations to look through the windows of the restaurants as he ran by. White linen on tables ready for hungry customers to enjoy a meal tomorrow. "I can see now that I will have to take a breath and consider my own hesitations. I can bring this up with Amanda at some appropriate time, vent my concerns and sit back while she reacts to my naivete."

David ran up to then across Oregon and observed, "Nothing going on at the Spectrum arena tonight. They keep the parking lot lights on all night, safer for me, but it must cost a fortune."

He was running well, no chest or leg pains. The row homes seemed to be flying by as he ran on Seventh Street. Sometimes he'd return on Ninth instead of Seventh, mixing it up to prevent late night boredom. Seventh Street seemed to be more industrial than Ninth lined with big, boarded up buildings, perhaps old factories.

"It seems a little less safe," considered David, "Maybe I'll go over to Ninth tonight."

David passed one man walking his dog, which looked like a black lab. Neither the man nor the dog acknowledged him, which was just fine. Pretty soon David could see the lights of the Italian Market and decided to run a block over toward Ninth Street. He was able to run farther each time, eventually could make it all way to Vet Stadium and back without stopping to catch his breath. Tonight, was one of those nights. He passed the darkened town homes. His footsteps producing the only noise on the street.

"I'm sure my classmates are asleep by now," he thought.

Once back to Jeff he walked around the block, past Scott Library and Doc Watson's to cool down.

"The party wasn't all that bad," he thought, "I enjoyed talking with Doug and Arthur. I know Amanda had a good time, but I had not seen that side of her. I would not have guessed she liked parties and drinking."

He took the elevator and got off at the Tenth floor. He walked up the hall trying to be quiet, put the key into the lock, and entered the apartment. Don was asleep. The kitchen had a familiar, comforting smell of dinner cooked a couple days ago, but the place on the whole was a bit sterile.

"It's a lot better than my place in Orono. Not as stylish as the home, Kyle, Paul, and Jason have, but still comfortable. I'm glad Don agreed to move to a townhome on Tenth and Pine. I think we will enjoy having our own place, especially having our own bedrooms," he thought, "Right now I've got to get to bed, Amanda and I are planning to study tomorrow and then go to the Chestnut Street Theater to see a movie. She told me which one, but I've forgotten," he thought as he showered.

Saturday morning was all blue skies, breezy, and cool. Don was already up and out of the apartment.

"Probably over at Scott Library," he thought. David noticed that Don had made cinnamon bread and left a note telling David to eat some. David sliced two pieces and put them in the toaster. He got the butter and milk from the fridge, grabbed a bowl and spoon from the dish drainer and reached up in the cabinet for the Cheerio's. He filled the kettle and put it on the stove for coffee. Taster's Choice was not his favorite, but it was quick. He spread his notes out on the kitchen table and was able to get a spoonful of cereal down before the toaster popped the bread up. Once that was buttered and the boiling water added to the instant coffee, he opened his notebook. He had not read more than a few pages before Amanda called asking if he wanted to get together to study.

"Your place or mine?"

"Here's okay, I made a Bundt cake. Interested?"

"I'm halfway there already, Amanda."

"I'll see you when you get here."

David made short work of the cinnamon toast and coffee, finished the Cheerios, and packed up his notes. They studied until noon, David enjoyed the cake with its vanilla frosting drizzle. They decided to take a break and walk to Penn's Landing and grab some lunch in Society Hill. Amanda reminded David they were going to see 'Kramer versus Kramer' that night.

"We can get more Path done this afternoon and still have time to go out for dinner before the movie," said Amanda.

They studied until five o'clock then walked up to Rittenhouse Square. While they were walking, hand in hand, David asked Amanda what had been on his mind since the party. "I don't want this to come across as critical, but do you enjoy drinking as much as you did Friday night?"

Amanda stopped and turned to face David, still holding onto his hand, which had become a bit sweaty. "I was wondering when you'd bring that up. I could tell you were not into the drinking scene. Obviously not as much as I enjoyed it last night."

"It's just that. . . ."

"No, let me finish. I don't drink to excess that often, but I felt safe and was enjoying talking with Sara. Kyle was a great host and I had never done shots before, but I thought, what the hell." Amanda turned and continued walking. "And yes, I had just finished my gin and tonic and could have waited a while and should have eaten something. I didn't become fall down drunk, mostly because I stayed on the couch with Sara. We had a great time talking about all the things that would have driven you crazy. I am not Amanda the crazy drunk, David," she laughed out loud. "I think you handled what was probably an uncomfortable situation for you very well. I hope you didn't spend too much time fretting about it. Now you."

"I'm glad you told me to go home. I ran to the Vet, thought a lot about my reaction to seeing you drinking and having a good time. And no, you were not inappropriate, at least during the time I was at the party," David jumped ahead and spun around to face Amanda, smiled at her and kissed her. He paused and let a taxi pass before crossing Broad Street. "I decided I needed to expand my comfort zone, take on new experiences, much as I did while in Israel. You would have been surprised to have seen me in Israel."

"What crazy things did you do there, my introverted friend?"

"I'll have you know that my first time wearing a dress was in Elat at the dare of Martin, my roommate. Got plenty of cat calls walking to a house party, too."

"So, remember that you're capable of getting a little bit wild and cut me some slack."

They got to the corner of Rittenhouse Square and ate dinner at a cute café. They decided to forego dessert and splurge on junk food at the theater. Kramer versus Kramer was not exactly David's cup of tea, but he enjoyed the buttery popcorn and Amanda enjoyed the interplay between Meryl Streep and Dustin Hoffman.

"So, who do you play tomorrow?"

"The match is with Temple at Temple, which is a ways uptown. I'll have to leave time to find the field. Are you interested in watching?"

"Sure. Anyone else bringing friends to the game?"

"I'll bet Henry's girlfriend, Kathy, will be there and its likely there will be others for you to sit with. I'll throw a couple lawn chairs in the back of the bug and pack you some goodies. I'll pick you up at nine. I'll throw in a blanket as well."

By this time they had reached Amanda's home. David reached for her hoping for a prolonged embrace.

"Don't get all hot and bothered, David, save it for the match tomorrow," she laughed, giving him a quick kiss and ran up the stairs.

CHAPTER TWENTY

Temple versus Jefferson

David knocked softly on the door at 854 and Amanda came out in slacks and a light jacket. "I am going to ask for a special dispensation during Mass. Something akin to the blessing of the soccer shoes," he said.

"I'm sure Our Heavenly Father will make a special note that you are attending Mass before such an important sporting event, David." Amanda smiled and pulled in close to David, who put his arm around her as they walked to St. Mary's. Mass was rather well attended for some reason and Father Joseph delivered a passionate homily about caring for the less fortunate. David felt good when he dropped his twenty-dollar bill into the poor box.

"I need to get back and change, but you look great, Amanda. Your outfit will brighten up the sideline."

"Thanks for your ongoing appreciation of my Sunday outfits, but I am going to change into something warmer and more appropriate for the soccer match, Mister."

"Okay, I'll swing by in 30 minutes to pick you up."

"That will give me sufficient time to make a thermos of coffee and wrap up some of the Bundt cake. You're going to need something to eat if you are going to run around for ninety minutes."

The drive to Temple was easy on Sunday morning without rush hour traffic. The sky was clear, the air was still and cool. David asked a security guard where the soccer field parking was located, so he didn't have to drive around in circles, which was his usual don't ask and just try to figure it out style. Most of the Jefferson squad had already arrived and were warming up. David parked the car and took the two lawn chairs and the blanket over to the side of the pitch. Amanda carried the coffee and snacks and went over to say hi to Kathy, who was already sitting, wrapped up in her blanket. A little later two more women arrived and came over to the Jefferson side. Amanda shared her extra chair and offered them coffee. She kept the blanket for her own legs, however. David stretched out, took a lap around the pitch, then joined Arthur and Henry who were passing a ball back and forth. They made a few passes and Arthur made a run down the sideline to receive David's pass, which landed at Arthur's feet. Arthur passed it back to Henry who knocked it back a few feet in front of Arthur who trapped it, spun around and passed it back. When ten o'clock arrived, the captains met at the center circle. They were fortunate to have enlisted someone to be center referee who flipped the coin. Temple won the toss and elected to kick off. The ref made a note about the kickoff time, blew his whistle, and the two Temple forwards passed the ball back to the midfielder. The Jefferson center challenged him, and the ball was sent out to the left wing who made it as far as the Jefferson midfielder who stripped it and sent it back to Henry. The game was on. The two teams were equally matched, neither gained an advantage until Bill, Jeff's left back got off a beautiful pass over the Temple center back. Arthur flew up the side and tapped it to Albert, the forward who cut back to the left and took a shot on goal. The Temple goalie was out of position, having gone after Arthur on the right. The ball hooked into the back of the Temple net and the score was one-nil. The Temple forwards in the center circle again sent the ball back to the midfielder, but Joe on left wing was ready for him, faked left and went to the center, stealing the ball. He rapidly sent it over to Arthur who then dropped it back to the right midfielder who in turn sent it back up to Joe's left foot. Joe had timed his run perfectly to stay onside, trapped the ball and crossed it to Arthur's right foot, which tapped it home. The referee blew the half time whistle and the teams retired to the sidelines to grab some water. Jefferson had only one sub and Brad replaced the center midfielder for the start of the second half.

The Jefferson forwards passed the ball to each other and got past the Temple striker and center midfielder. When challenged by the Temple back the ball was sent back and picked up by Brad at midfield who passed it to the outside midfielder. They kept control of the ball for eight consecutive passes before Henry again led Arthur with a pass to the right outside. Arthur ran the ball to the baseline, sent it across in the air to the left side and Tom, the left wing headed it in. A dejected Temple squad was looking at a three-nil deficit. They did not fold, rather had a couple runs against David down the center of the field, but David stepped up and Bill dropped in behind David to plug the gap. Jefferson's defense handled them easily and by the end of time the three-nil score held up. The two teams lined up and shook hands, promising to play again later in the season. Most of the players made a point of thanking the referee for managing the game so well.

The Jefferson players sat together for a while, shared food, drink, and the high points of the match with each other. Amanda was glad to have seen this side of David. He was fast, confident, and a clean player, as were all the players that morning. After a time, the squad and their friends said their goodbyes and promised to make it to next week's match. Amanda and David walked back to the car with their chairs and the empty basket.

"I spoke with Kathy, we agreed to team up on what to bring to the next match and to try to get more people to come to the game," she said. "By the way, great game, David. You were pretty good out there."

"Thanks. It was a good match and I think everyone had fun," replied David. "I'm glad you came. I hope you weren't too chilled."

"I saw quite a few players looking pretty tired, but its obvious your runs to the Vet have you in great shape. I know you weren't watching Kathy or me, but we spent very little time in our chairs. Did you even hear us cheering for you, Henry, and Arthur?"

"Sorry. Can't say I did, but I appreciate your support."

"I'll have to learn the other player's names, so we can do a better job of cheering everyone along."

"I'm sure everyone will appreciate the encouragement, Amanda." David opened the door for Amanda. "Hop in. Where would you like to go for brunch?"

"How about the Greek diner where we had our second, or was it our third date, if you count the first time we went to Mass?"

"I recall that as a very special day in the life of this hungry soccer player, Amanda."

CHAPTER TWENTY-ONE

Moving Day

Don and David had made plans to move out of the Orlowitz high rise dorm after a year and had signed a three-year contract on a town-home in the middle of Tenth Street below Pine. They should have inspected it more closely but were in a rush to get something close to Jefferson, plus the rent was about what they were paying at Orlowitz. David's room faced Tenth Street and unfortunately, he could stick his fingers outside between the bricks and the window casement. The summer air that leaked in was acceptable, but David made plans to cover the wall with plastic during the cold winter months. The bedroom floor was in terrible shape, but nothing that an hour with a belt sander and a couple coats of polyurethane would not fix. The place had a very tiny, bricked in back patio that could accommodate a table and a few chairs. The patio was closed in by tall walls at the back and on both sides, which was good for security, but made it dark and damp. David had read about attaching a wooden pallet to a wall and hanging plants on the rungs and thought that might brighten up the dingy back yard. They transported some furniture from their parent's homes into the living room and added a couple of chairs, a short couch, and a table picked up on sale at a close out furniture store on South Street. The rectangular oriental rug had seen better days, but it was colorful, fit the space well, and would keep the freezing floor from giving their toes frostbite in the winter. What was nice was the gas fireplace in the living room. It had a piece of dark marble separating the hearth from the pine floor boards. Don had turned on the flame on and it took the chill out of the room quite nicely.

David had a twin bed in the bedroom at his parent's home that made the trip up the spiral staircase in their Philly townhome without incident. Don, however, went out and purchased a king box spring and mattress. They were able to fold the mattress, bend it around and move it up the curved staircase, but the box spring was another matter. David had his circular saw in the basement as he was making a bookcase. He could tell that the box spring was not going to fit up the staircase. Without speaking to Don, he grabbed his circular saw and sliced every cross tie under the box spring before he could object.

"How else are we going to get it upstairs, Don?" he asked his distressed roommate, "I've got my drill and will bridge the box spring boards back together with pine 1 x 4's once it is upstairs. I know you want to entertain the ladies with your king bed. It will serve your purpose just fine once I brace it back together.

"I just bought that bed and you better make it good as new. I don't want any boards poking up through the mattress. I hope you're as good with your drill as you were with the saw."

"Don't worry about it, Don. You'll never be able to tell the difference once I'm done."

David looked around the room and said, "Nice poster. Is that Cheryl Tiegs? Could she have any less on that tanned body?"

"I want to meet a nurse who looks just as good in a bikini," replied Don. "Don't you think she has a healthy appeal?"

"Healthy. Oh yes. That was my first thought, Don, healthy. And do you think nursing students visiting your bedroom will feel the same way? At least put the poster on the inside of your closet door.

Are you up for the task of pursuing healthy Jeff nurses while studying every night?"

"I'll have to make time, David, I don't want to end up an old bachelor."

"You are insulting this old bachelor, roomie, but I admit I am doing a little work in that area with Amanda," smiled David.

Don and David celebrated moving into their townhouse with a shot of Jack Daniels on ice, then hit the books. Don liked to study in the living room, David preferred his bedroom where he had a Formica topped piece of plywood held up by a three-drawer file cabinet on the left and an oak end table on the right on which sat his Sony reel to reel. The three shelves of BASF tapes were quite the investment. David had purchased one or two tapes each week while at Delaware using the money he made washing the floors at Burger King. He actively scoured the Morris Library at U of D for Swann Lake, Rite of Spring, New World Symphony, and a complete set of Beethoven's Symphonies. He put on his headphones and started the Sony triple head tape deck listening to Beethoven's Seventh. The room had its own smell, somewhat old and dusty, very different from the Orlowitz apartment, all clean and fresh.

"I've got to get a painting or at least a Van Gogh print over the desk," thought David, "I can't stare at that white paint every night. I'll bring 'The Fields of Arles' I framed a few years ago from home. Maybe outfit the rest of the walls with the other Van Gogh prints I've got," he said to himself, "Then I can get an oriental for this room as well to keep it quiet and warm."

David let Beethoven dampen out the street sounds and he was deep into the lecture notes in no time. He really didn't follow the music while he concentrated on loading the lecture notes and textbook information into his brain. It was after midnight before he finished. He brushed his teeth and hit the bed.

"Thank God mom spent some money on this mattress," he thought. "I've only got seven hours so I gotta make them count. First night in our townhouse. I'll have to have Amanda over for dinner soon. I'm quite sure her place is much nicer, but this will do. Maybe she'll stay overnight."

He drifted into sleep thinking of Amanda sleeping in her bed.

"I wonder if she wears pajamas," was his last thought before falling into sleep.

CHAPTER TWENTY-TWO

Running Down Twelfth Street Toward Bainbridge

One night David tried running up Twelfth Street to mix it up. He was wearing his green Air Force field jacket over the black, hooded sweatshirt and of course had on his Stones T-shirt from the Army-Navy concert that he and Don had attended. The Eagles ski hat, teal green sweatpants, and white Adidas sneakers completed his ensemble. He knew he looked like a bum. The late-night denizens of the Italian Market would call out, 'Rocky,' which made him feel safe. David had run only a few blocks on Twelfth Street and was coming up on Bainbridge when he noticed a group of young men standing under the light pole ahead on the left.

One yelled out, "What you doin' here, white boy?"

This was immediately followed by what sounded like a quarter hitting the windshield of the car to David's right. Why he imagined a quarter had done the damage and not a bullet was not clear when it was obvious the impact shattered the glass. David stopped in his tracks, then was spun around and landed face down on the asphalt. Only then did he feel the pain in his right chest and shoulder.

"I've been shot," he thought.

He hadn't heard the second shot. He got to his feet, bracing himself against the car and immediately turned and started to run back toward Jefferson. Every stride jolted the pain in his shoulder. It became more difficult to breath the more he ran so he slowed down and eventually started walking. He took the time to look back to see if anyone was pursuing him. They were not. He took a right on Locust then cut left on Eleventh. By the time David reached Doc Watson's Pub, he was woozy, and his chest hurt like hell. He recognized one of his friends leaving Watson's and called out to Mark, asking for help. Mark eased David down to the stone step.

"What the hell David, what happened?"

"Someone Shot Me in my Shoulder." John Legend

"I think I've been shot and may have a right pneumothorax, possibly now a tension pneumo," David confided to Mark, who called out for help. "Bill, John, someone give me some help here. David's been shot."

One of Mark's drinking buddies was a first-year surgery resident. "What happened? You okay, David? Don't worry, I got this," Bill said, "l always carry a trochar needle for just this occasion. Really. John, run inside and grab a pitcher of water, a bottle of whiskey, a pile of napkins, and a foot of tubing."

"Where am I gonna get tubing?"

"Cut two feet of tap line and bring the stuff here. Put it on David's tab," Bill laughed.

Mark removed David's jacket, sweatshirt, and the bloody Tee-shirt. Bill cleaned the wound and the needle with whiskey after taking a swig for good luck. Bill poured whiskey on five napkins and told Mark to put on his gloves and apply pressure to the gunshot wound. He then inserted the needle into David's right chest, which hissed as air left David's chest.

"Hang in there, buddy. You feel better now? Want a shot of whiskey?"

"Hell yeah."

"Good stick Bill," said Mark. "His pulse was 180, but now is 120 after you released the pressure."

"It's what I do. Now pour some whiskey into the tubing, attach the tubing to the needle, and put the other end of the tubing under water in the pitcher."

They all knew what the bubbles in the pitcher meant. David was not paying much attention after the whiskey but felt better and decided to pass out. Bill told John to hold the pitcher close to David's chest and the group carried him to the Emergency Department, which luckily was not far away.

Once in the ER David was awakened by the jostling and was able to say very weakly, "Save my stuff, please."

"We will. Mark called Amanda. Now relax."

The Emergency Room resident asked, "Where were you? How'd you get shot? Do you know who shot you?"

David was very tired, but said, "I was running up Twelfth Street to Bainbridge and some guys at the corner just shot me."

"You probably spooked a group of drug dealers. Who knows why they shot you. Maybe for the thrill."

David was appropriately poked and prodded, blood was drawn, stethoscopes appeared in everyone's hands, and all concluded David had a pneumothorax.

"Please order a full blood count, type and cross, ABG's, chemistries, ECG, and a chest radiograph," said the ER resident to the nurse. "I think STAT is in order for this one."

David's chest radiograph did demonstrate a slight leftward shift of his heart indicating there was a lot of air in his chest. Not good. Bill's needle was removed, and a larger chest tube inserted.

"That hurt like a son of a bitch," said David rousing himself from his slumber.

"Nice job with the beer pitcher and tubing, Bill," chuckled the Emergency Room Resident, "One for the books."

David was hustled off to surgery and the bullet had passed completely through David's jacket and chest and went out the back of his shoulder not to be found. The bullet had entered the chest just above the third rib.

"The Airforce jacket and sweatshirt probably slowed it just enough," noted Dr. Slocumb, the second year TCV resident. "The bullet did not sever any large blood vessels and a few stitches closed the tear in the lung. That was still a close call, just inches from being deadly."

David was sent up to the surgical floor once he was half awake in PACU and had received a very nice dose of morphine.

"I Can't Write with My Left Hand," Bill Withers

CHAPTER TWENTY-THREE

Recovery

David awoke to see Amanda and Don asleep in chairs beside his bed. He did not rouse them for a while, but Amanda did wake on her own and jumped up to ask what happened and how he felt.

"Like a two by four was rammed into my chest," he replied, "But that terrible dyspnea and pleurisy is gone."

"You don't have to speak doctor-ese, you're a patient now," she laughed. Don was now awake and was more interested in when David would be coming home.

"I don't mean to sound cold, but now that I see you're okay I was thinking of entertaining someone special in the townhouse if you're staying put."

"No one has done rounds on me yet. I don't know who I need to thank for stitching me back together. What time is it? Did they save my coat and sweatshirt?"

"7:15, and yes the coat is here. I'll patch the hole and get it washed. The sweatshirt and tee shirt were bloody messes and won't make it. The nurses had to cut them off.

"I really liked that Stone's shirt. Can you save part of it so I can try to get the same one again?"

"You can get new clothes, David. You may have to let some things go once in a while. Look, I've just enough time to get home, take a shower, and change for lecture," replied Amanda.

"Well you two should go. Don, I have a big favor to ask of you! Thank Mark and whoever else saved my miserable life. Nice of you to sit with me, Amanda, you too Don. I'll be fine. See you tonight?" he asked of Amanda.

"Guaranteed. I'll bring lecture notes. You look in the mood for another dose of morphine."

"Good stuff," replied David.

Amanda and Don left the room and David's nurse Katelyn came in to take vitals and asked how his pain control was doing. David tried to sit up, but found the pain was waiting for him.

"Pretty bad now. Can you help me sit up and get me some morphine, maybe oral so it lasts longer?"

"Listen I'm very capable of administering the proper medications, you just say ouch and I'll deliver," said a slightly miffed Katelyn. "You don't know this yet, but we Nurses run this hospital. Do you hear what I'm saying? The docs admit patients and then disappear. And yes, I'll sit you up."

Even the chest tube didn't keep David awake once the morphine kicked in. It was an IV dose, not a pill again this time.

"Sister Morphine," Rolling Stones

Amanda walked in to find David asleep, but David woke when he heard her pull the chair close to the head of his bed. He recognized her perfume.

"So, can you explain how you managed to get shot? Did you run into the wrong neighborhood and say something inappropriate?

"No. I was just running up Twelfth Street and saw four guys at the lamppost. One of them didn't seem to like a white boy running in their neighborhood. Maybe he is just a punk with a grudge. I don't know. So, he shot me. First shot missed and cracked a windshield, second one got me."

"That's terrible, David. You've been running for months and nothing like this ever happened. Do you think Twelfth Street is just a bad location?"

"I was out for my midnight run. I picked Twelfth to see if it was more interesting than Tenth, and it obviously was."

"Stay the hell off Twelfth if you just have to do these midnight runs. It could have been a lot worse, David. Do you think you should report being shot to the police?"

"Now that I'm out of surgery I will. And I'll call my parents in a little while. You're right, Amanda. But I like to run after studying, really relaxes me."

"Stick to the Italian Market on Eighth and maybe run at eleven o'clock. You could tell me which route you are going to take in case you get into trouble again."

"All good suggestions, Amanda, But I am neglecting you. Have you had dinner?"

"Not yet. I thought I'd sample the cuisine at Chez Jefferson tonight."

"You can have my dinner, I'm not hungry yet."

"Tell you what. I'll run down and see if I can find a strawberry shake for you and I'll eat your dinner. Be back in no time. You rest."

David did. He looked around the room with green walls after he woke up. Before he opened his right eye, he smelled her perfume. Then he opened his left eye and saw Amanda sitting at the left side of his bed.

"The shake is not completely melted you sleepy head. You are so lazy. You can't even open both eyes for me, after all the effort I went through to provide you with a nourishing meal."

"Thanks Amanda, here let me have it." David could not lift his right arm.

"Here, I'll hold the chalice. Here's a straw," said Amanda.

David did have the strength to drink the milkshake and pronounced it wonderful.

"Thanks. How's the mystery meat? Thank God I didn't get green Jell-O and apple juice."

"You would have, but I asked Katelyn if she could change the order to a meal I could actually eat. She's a sweetheart. I think its roast beast, corn, and mashed potatoes. Not bad."

David smiled. "Roast beast; 'How the Grinch Stole Christmas,' right?"

"That was your mental assessment and you passed. You tell me if you're up for my lecture notes. They are not as good as the verbatim notes you take. Yes, its well-known you produce court transcripts for the Note Service. I recall you pissed off quite a few when you rhymed the entire lecture."

"And I won't be using German again. That 'um' really got Marvin angry. 'Um' means around and allowed the information to fit on the same line. Anyway, my eyes aren't focusing very well right now. Can you just read the notes to me?"

"My scribbles are usually not for popular consumption, but yes, I will translate out loud."

Amanda and David reviewed the physiology lecture dealing this time on medications having activity due to GI receptors. David fell asleep having almost made it to the end. Amanda kissed his head and slipped out.

That night, David dreamt about the time he traveled to Cyprus on his way from Tel Aviv to Venice on a trampy cruise ship. He'd booked a steerage ticket and he and nineteen others were given what would best be described as movie theatre seats bolted to the deck. They reclined, but not enough to provide for a sound sleep. Unfortunately for David and the other nineteen passengers, he had an unrelenting cough. David took it upon himself to go up to the deck and spread his scratchy, woolen prayer blanket under a metal staircase. The stairs deflected some of the cold mist and the Air force jacket was up to the task of keeping his chest dry. The painter pants got damp if not soaked by morning, but he slept between spasms of coughing. Once in port on Cyprus, David changed into his khakis and hung the painter pants to dry on his chair. He disembarked and went exploring in the village. He found bread and cheese at one shop and was told by a very pleasant merchant a fruit stand was just around the corner. David located the stand and selected two oranges and a bunch of green grapes. He asked the price and pulled out some Israeli lire. The merchant said he'd accept the money, but that David needed a few coins more. David pulled a US quarter from his pants pocket and handed it over. The merchant went ballistic and threw the quarter at David, who took the hint and high tailed it back to the ship. He could hear the merchant ranting to the other customers. He of course did not know the Cypriot language, but the word 'bastard' did come through loud and clear. David made it to the ship and asked a crew member why all the fuss over the quarter.

"Americans sold tanks to Turkey who then deployed them to Northern Cyprus to bolster the rebels. We are now in south Cyprus and your merchant-patriot doesn't appreciate Americans right now. I'm glad you got out of there fast."

David woke up in his hospital bed, slightly disoriented, with the vague recollection of being chased and the sound of metal striking a windshield still in his mind. The pain in his chest was manageable. Amanda had left her physiology text on the chair on David's left side.

He smiled. "That Amanda, she always thinks of everything."

He lifted the text onto his lap and flipped to the chapter, indicated of course by Amanda's bookmark, and started to read about GI medications. He realized he was hungry and just then his breakfast tray arrived. The scrambled, likely freeze dried, eggs and oatmeal with butter were on the cool side but were tasty.

David's new day nurse, Linda, came in to do vitals and asked how breakfast went and had he slept well.

"Had a very odd dream about being chased and had a quarter thrown at me."

"Well, you were shot."

Linda adjusted his pillows and told him he could get out to a chair. She removed the breakfast tray, so he could put the book on the bedside table if he wanted to.

"How about a pain pill that won't knock me out first?"

Lisa knocked on David's door, "Ok if we come in for a visit with our wounded friend?"

"Sure. Come in. Who are we?" asked David.

"Cindi, Florence and I," replied Lisa as she entered David's room and took a seat.

"You look good for a guy who just got shot," said Cindi.

"How do you feel, David? Are you taking medications for your pain?" asked Florence.

"My shoulder and chest are doing well. I'm still receiving an occasional dose of morphine, but I'm thinking I may try to move on down to Hydrocodone."

Florence moved closer to David. "You were just shot, had thoracic surgery and you are thinking of dropping down to a pain pill that dentists give me for root canal work? David!"

"Don't you think you might be rushing things?" asked Cindi.

"I've never been shot nor had chest surgery, but I can't imagine dropping down to a walk around pain pill so soon after being shot," exclaimed Lisa.

"I appreciate the concern you three are expressing, but its just a plan. I may find out that without morphine I'll have the screaming meanies and have to take a Percocet. I'll have to talk with Dr. Slocumb, my surgery resident. Oh, Lisa, you'd should meet him, good looking, smart, a Surgeon. Did I mention he's a good-looking thoracic surgeon? Anyway, we'll see. I want to get on with therapy to get my motion and strength back, but I also want to get back to classes with a clear head. I took Hydrocodone when I had my wisdom teeth extracted as an undergrad. I got no 'High" from them. They worked quickly and lasted six to eight hours without nausea, although constipation was a frequent, albeit, temporary visitor."

"Well we're glad to see you doing well. Cool it with the medical technicalities. Can you just be a recovering patient? We have to get back to classes," said Cindi.

"Anything you need?"

"Anything Amanda has not already thought of, David?" Lisa said with a chuckle.

"Just to see more of you three," replied David.

"Aw shucks, David, we can visit you so often you'll come to regret saying that," said Cindi.

"Gotta go, David. See you soon," said Florence heading to the door.

Amanda came by around four forty-five with some dinner for herself and a bowl of mac and cheese and a Milky Way bar for David.

"Just in case dinner is not to your liking tonight. Did you retain anything I read to you last night?"

"Enough, and things came back when I read the physio text. Thanks for that. You probably need it back."

"I went to your place and Don gave me yours, so I'm good. I have notes from today's lectures. It's Wednesday so Darla the touchy-feely Prof was up to bat. Pretty interesting stuff, I must admit. She discussed techniques to improve trust during the history interview and physical exam, and later, compliance with treatment."

"Sorry I missed that talk. This mac and cheese tastes great. My beautiful lady brings great eats and helps with my courses. I'm a lucky man."

Amanda leaned over and planted a kiss on his lips.

"Another kiss. I hope it was not under duress."

"Keep up with using beautiful and you may receive a few more. Now eat up so we can get to work. Here's yesterday's physio notes."

"When is the next test? I need to psych up for that."

"You just get healthy, and we'll talk about tests. I told all the Profs about your run in with the bullet, but news travels fast and they all knew. Dr. Green said some nice things about you before the lecture. She's such a good lecturer. She did warn everyone to stay away from Twelfth and Bainbridge, probably a drug corner."

"I spoke with a Policeman today. I think he was the Detective in charge of my shooting," said David, "He was all about the facts, not much about sympathy. No 'How're you doing.' He did say they recovered a 9 mm slug from the front seat of the car with the shattered windshield. The other slug must have passed right through me and so it was not recovered to compare to the slug found in the car seat. I was wondering if I could eventually get the slug as a memento."

"It's evidence for catching the one who shot you, and then there's the trial. That may take a couple years. You've got to be realistic. Pretty morbid stuff anyway. Eat."

They studied until ten thirty.

Amanda said, "I'm done in. David, I think we study faster together than when alone. I hope your retention is ok with the morphine in your system."

"With an attractive and accomplished Tutor, we shall make it a regular event."

That was met with another, this time long lasting kiss.

"I told you, keep up that language and your lips are all mine!"

"Threats, just idle threats."

"Don't you forget them when they aren't so idle."

"I'll be back tomorrow at lunch time in case they pull the chest tube and you get some discharge news. You do know I'm missing Rocky and Bullwinkle to be with you."

"Terribly sorry about that, priorities, priorities."

"You're on pain pills, aren't you? I'll forgive you that one. You know how crucial Bullwinkle is for overall class mental health."

"Haven't needed a shot for a day. I'll probably be fighting constipation next."

"So now you're all about the GI physiology and adverse effects of morphine, huh? Mental exam: intermediate term memory intact. I'll be going. Sleep well. I'll say a prayer for you."

"Hey, you look upset," noted David. "I'll be fine. Great Surgeon, great Nurses, and beautiful Tutor."

Amanda leaned over to give him a kiss and her tears fell onto David's cheek.

"Sorry. It's just that a few inches to the left and the bullet could have severed a pulmonary artery or torn a hole in your heart. You would have bled out right then and there on Twelfth Street. I'm not interested in attending your funeral." Amanda was crying uncontrollably.

David was also crying silently as he held Amanda.

"But I didn't and I'm well on my way to recovery thanks to you, Amanda."

David put his one good arm around her as she put her head on his left chest.

"I know this has been hard on you," he said stroking her long blond hair. "You've been storing it all up, putting on the brave face when you're here. I love you for that, but you need to know you can always be who you need to be around me."

Amanda pulled away.

"Thanks. I really need to get some rest. You sleep and heal up."

She kissed David again before leaving the room.

David slept soundly that night. He didn't remember any dreams in the morning when Linda woke him for a check of his vitals.

"Dr. Slocumb, your surgery resident will be by, maybe to pull the chest tube. I haven't seen evidence of a leak all shift. You can't walk out with a chest tube, so hope it is pulled and you get discharged. As nice a patient as you are, you're now a bit boring. I like patients that require my services. You're more a job for the food service now. Pulling the chest tube will hurt like hell for a few minutes, so I'll try to give you a pill a half hour before he's due up here if we're lucky. Oh, and you'll need to go down for a chest x-ray after it's pulled."

David cracked open the physiology text and read the next chapter about diuretics, renal insufficiency, and treatment of heart failure.

Dr. Slocumb thought the chest tube could come out. He warned David that it would be painful, but to sit still and hold his breath. Pulling the chest tube hurt more than hell, but the severe pain lasted only a few seconds. Dr. Slocumb said he would write for Hydrocodone, but that he would keep Morphine on for prn severe pain. He then asked David to see if he could take a few deep breaths. David complied but tears came to his eyes with the resurgence of pain.

"I'm now an expert on pleuritic pain," thought David, "I hope more deep breaths will eventually decrease the pain."

"Dr. Slocumb noticed David's distress and said that David should bear the pain and, take deep breaths. "You won't do any damage with deep breathing, David. Take another deep one," he asked, placing his stethoscope of David's chest.

David thought he would pass out from the pain but took the breaths.

Dr. Slocumb observed, "Good breath sounds on both sides, David. Keep it up. Linda, please give David another pain pill."

"Come on Hydrocodone," thought David," closing his eyes and concentrating on deep breathing.

He picked up the physiology text and tried to focus on the actions and adverse effects of diuretics, but he felt a little loopy so he took a short nap.

Lunch came just about when he'd had enough about furosemide and hydrochlorothiazide. He tried to wait for Amanda, but was starved, so he nibbled at the ham sandwich.

Amanda appeared, all excited that the chest tube was out.

"No pneumothorax, or at least just a tiny one," she said. "Probably, a little blood at the right lung base. Radiology said that was typical. You'll need another chest X-ray tomorrow. You eat. I don't care for ham. I'll eat ham on holidays to be pleasant, but not in sandwiches."

"Any other gastronomical issues I should know. Won't take you for a barbeque pork shoulder dinner, that's for sure."

"I don't eat scungilli. Octopi are very smart animals. Squid calamari is ok. Veggie and rice sushi are fine. Don't like lima beans or okra."

"I'll fix you some baby lima beans, not overly cooked, all soft and tasty. My mom used to boil or bake the living hell out of limas, usually big, ol' limas. Terrible. Once I was able to taste Southern style limas in bacon grease with touch of bacon from the U of D cooks I grew to appreciate them."

"Maybe you can fix some of your signature limas for dinner once you are home. So, we'll plan on you getting out Friday at 11-ish, they'll deliver you to your place by ambulance. No, you can't walk home. I'll be there to sign for you like a UPS package. You get a good night's sleep. I'll pray for a clean chest X-ray and I'll call you after lecture. It'll be good to have you home. We've got a lot to review. Path, physio, cell bio, and biochem tests are on Tuesday. Here's the cell bio and bio chem notes."

"I'll review them tonight. I haven't been to class for a week. I hope my Class C status will be sufficient to pass those tests."

"I told Professor Green that you had your own physio lesson with the morphine. Your surgeons must have known their way around the chest the way you're healing up."

"Tomorrow then."

David reached out with both arms to pull Amanda to him but gave up on the right arm because of shoulder pain. He kissed her for what seemed an eternity.

"Whew. I would say you are mostly healed."

"I'm willing to give it my all."

"See you tomorrow, here or at home."

CHAPTER TWENTY-FOUR

Discharge Day

David had another restful night. The morning chest x-ray was improved. Dr. Slocumb examined him and pronounced him good for discharge with a return to clinic on Wednesday afternoon with a follow up chest radiograph.

Linda came in with the same news a little later and went over discharge instructions, "No lifting. If pleurisy or shortness of breath return get to the emergency room ASAP. Use the hydrocodone every four to six hours as needed. Control the pain as soon as it starts. It's easier to prevent it than relieve it once it's severe. You need to take deep inspirations as often as you can. Use the incentive spirometer and keep a diary for the thoracic resident. You can also substitute two Tylenol every six hours. Follow up in Radiology is at one thirty and surgical clinic is Wednesday at two o'clock. I hope you can miss a couple hours of lecture for this, it's important. And don't play doctor with yourself. You're a patient for a few more days."

"Thanks Linda. You and Katelyn have been wonderful. Nurses do run the hospital. I've seen my docs for less than an hour all told. I'm sure they spent hours in the Operating Room. Not complaining, just saying I'm not a big priority for them now that I'm healing and stable. I'm glad."

"You stay in your gown for the ride home. Your clothes are in that bag in the corner. Pack up your books in this bag for the ambulance ride. You'll go out in a wheelchair. Show the transporters you can transfer bed to wheel chair here and they'll let you do it in your apartment."

"Again, thanks, but can't say I'll miss the hospital bed," smiled David.

"Oh, I forgot to tell you that you will need to go to physical therapy every day. It can be after your classes as late as five o'clock. Get your shoulder motion back to normal. I put a referral slip in your discharge packet. You can call and set it up. I know you will be busy with classes, but PT is very important. Get it going early so you don't lose range of motion or strength. Call me if you have trouble arranging PT."

David arrived home and Amanda was there to meet the ambulance. The drivers tested his ability to walk the stairs to his bedroom. David planned on studying at his desk, then move downstairs to the kitchen table later on. Friday classes were review sessions, so he could miss a couple hours. Amanda had informed Dr. Carlos that David would be returning next week. They studied until 9:30 then listened to 'Night Moves' and 'Court and Spark' until eleven o'clock. They spent time sitting in an embrace, kissing, then Amanda was ready to leave.

"Sleep well."

"I wish I could walk you home, Amanda."

"I think I'd have to carry you back here anyway, so keep that thought for a few days from now. Good night."

By Monday David was able to walk to lecture, leaning on Amanda's arm. He sat in the back row instead of attempting the walk down stairs to his usual tenth row. After the lectures, David waited for Amanda to walk by as she climbed the stairs of the lecture hall. She looked good in tight jeans and red and black checked shirt.

"Interested in studying together tonight? I could come to your home after dinner," offered David, "That way I can see more of you."

"Yes, let's do it. Speedy review and early to bed. They say a good night's sleep is the most important pre-test preparation."

"I say a long hug and hot good night kiss is a better pre-test preparation."

"That works for me, David, come closer." He wrapped his left arm around her and pulled her close. Amanda did not protest and returned the embrace.

"I love the feeling of your arms around me, David," she said, "I'll just have to wait for a two-armed hug."

Tuesday's exams, the next of many they would take at Jefferson were difficult, but not brutal. David thought he'd lost a step or two since his undergrad days when his brain and pencil worked on auto-pilot.

"I probably did okay," he thought.

It turned out David had earned solid 86, not the 100 percenters he was used to and had hoped for, especially in Pathology.

"It's going to require more than a mild mental readjustment," he said to himself.

After the tests, Amanda asked David as they walked home, "How you'd do on Physiology?"

"86%. How about you give me a night to mull over why my path grade was not closer to 100%. How'd you do?"

I got 92%. Sorry, David," replied Amanda.

"No need to apologize for a great pathology grade, Amanda. You'll now be my inspiration for another facet of my life. Amanda saw David was disappointed about his grades, so she did not push it about Biochemistry or Cell Biology. She did not let on how she had fared in her other exams either.

CHAPTER TWENTY-FIVE

Intimacy

"Would you like to come by and have tea tonight?"

"That'd be nice. What time were you thinking of, Amanda?"

"How about seven."

"I'll bring some Pepperidge Farm cookies."

David walked along the sidewalk with a mild wind from the south blowing leaves past his feet. They scuttled like ghost crabs on the Wildwood beach, somehow never banging into each other. David ascended the sandstone steps to the porch at 854 Locust. He lifted the big brass knocker on Ms. Hopkin's wooden door.

The door opened. "Did you bring the cookies? Then you may come in," said Amanda. "We can sit in the living room. It is my favorite in the whole house. Water's boiling, I'm having Lady Earl Gray. What's your taste running to tonight?"

"Earl Gray as well, please. This room conveys comfort and is welcoming, must have ten-foot ceilings. I like the Persian, is it a Serapi?"

Amanda called out from the kitchen, "How do you know Persian rugs?"

"I did a summer with a moving company and for a whole week we transported Persians from a warehouse to a showroom. I would ask the names of the rugs and why is a Serapi not just a variation of a Kashan or a Tabriz? I learned a lot as we unrolled the rugs, read the labels, and stacked them into piles of similar sizes. The names just stuck."

"Do you know how to identify a quality rug?"

"Some of it has to do with the knot count, 200 is way better than 40. Sometimes the rugmaker throws in silk with the wool for accents. A lot has to do with how well and tight the knotting process was accomplished. I'm certainly no expert, but I can tell a better rug from a cheap commercial one."

"So, is Ms. Hopkin's Persian a quality rug?"

"May I flip up one corner? Oh, yes, the knot count must be 300 or more and the colors are intense. The wool was dyed with exacting care. The various colors remain true all around the rug. This was, is a very expensive rug and I would suspect it is very old and in great shape."

"The tea is ready. I spread your cookies out on a plate."

"So, do you like this room?" Amanda said handing David his cup of tea.

"Oh, yes. It is very elegant without being pretentious. The ivory walls, the eight-inch baseboards and impressive crown molding hold the space. I've always liked Queen Anne chairs and the Waverly floral print goes well with the pattern in the Persian. The couch is a very nice shade of plum. The pillows are obviously each one of a kind."

"You should think of a backup career as an interior designer, David. Have a cookie."

"Who are the two men in that photo, Ms. Hopkin's sons?"

"I have assumed so. I'll have to ask her."

"What's the significance of that painting?"

"They purchased it on their honeymoon in Paris. I imagine them sipping champagne in a café while people stroll past. They may have stayed in a little hotel near the Champs-Elysees and walked everywhere. Joe died just three years ago. I think Ms. Hopkins took it pretty hard after so many years of marriage."

"I've been thinking that during our four years at Jeff, we will have relationships with teachers and our classmates, some simply professional, a few close, many fleeting."

"I would hope many will be rewarding, perhaps one even intimate."

"Intimacy is a rarity. Intimacy with its different flavors: intellectual, emotional, hopefully leading to a physical intimacy."

"Speaking of intimacy, I want to tell you I feel very safe with you, David. I would place our relationship at the intellectual stage according to your hierarchy, don't you agree?"

"You want my honest opinion?"

"Always."

"For me, intellectual with a hint of emotional, ever since we first spoke at orientation."

"You're putting some pressure on me."

"I'm a patient man, Amanda. I'm a gardener, willing to prepare the soil and nurture our relationship," he replied after taking a sip of his tea.

"Good to hear that. What cultivation plans do you have for this weekend mister green jeans?"

"Would you like to spend some time at the Philly Art Museum, perhaps take in the Rodin?"

"Good idea. I read they have a Degas exhibit."

"Ballerinas in tutus. Do you think we will need reservations?"

"I'll call. Do you want to try for an early time?"

"Early will be good, leave time to go through the Rodin and then grab lunch downtown. Thanks for the tea and conversation, Amanda. I should be going. Pick you up at seven thirty?" David said as he placed his tea cup on the tray and stood up.

"See you then," replied Amanda as they walked to the front door.

David held Amanda and kissed her before stepping out onto the front steps. "Thanks again," he called over his shoulder as he walked down the steps. Amanda stood in the doorway until David had turned onto Ninth Street. She closed the big door with a smile on her face.

"Let's Stay Together," Al Green

CHAPTER TWENTY-SIX

Second Meeting of the Tenth Floor Social Club

"David, can you get that?" Don asked.

David stood up and walked to the door. He opened it and saw Cindi and Lisa standing on the front steps. You boys up for a drink at Watson's?" asked Lisa.

"Perfect timing, Lisa. Hello Cindi. And who is that in the back? Oh, hi Florence, glad you could come along. Did Lisa tell you this will be the second meeting of the 10th Floor Social Committee?" asked David. "Please come in and see our humble home."

"You've done a nice job with this room, David. Do you and Don each have a separate bedroom upstairs? Great."

"Hey Don," he called to the kitchen, "You want to take a break and hit Watson's with the ladies?"

"I'm coming."

The five walked up the street. Leaves were swirling at their feet, but the night air was pleasant, and the sky was filled with stars.

"Don, have you met Florence? She lives in 1006 Orlowitz," said David.

"Nice to meet you, Florence."

"Thanks for inviting me along," said Florence.

"Absolutely," replied Cindi.

"You have a nice townhome and have fixed it up with the furniture and carpet," Florence said to Don.

"Don and I will have to have a house warming party soon," said David.

The group walked up Ninth Street, then across the Quad and into Watson's. David took the time to speak with Florence about her grades.

"I'm barely passing, David, despite having met with Dr. Jacobi. He was very kind to me and offered some good suggestions, but I am still having trouble focusing on the material."

"Intrusive thoughts about your bother?"

"Even more frequently than before, David. I don't get much done no matter how long I study. Nights are long, and I am not sleeping very well."

"Is there an option to see a counselor? Jefferson must have any number of psychiatrists. You can't be the only student to have run into such difficulties, Florence."

"I'll call the Psychiatry Department tomorrow. This whole thing is not only difficult, it is frightening. How well will I handle the clinical rotations if I can't deal with passing tests? It's depressing that I can't just power through it."

David heard the word depressing and mentally stiffened. "Is this the time to intervene?" he asked himself. He decided to walk to class with Florence tomorrow.

The group walked up the steps to Watson's and Don held the door open. They walked into the tavern, on its well-worn, wooden floor.

Florence took a deep breath, appreciating the smells of beer and wood. She looked around the poorly lit space, taking it all in. "The bar is pretty large for a place of this size."

"Grab a table, please, Cindi." David went to the bar and ordered a pitcher of Heineken and five glasses.

"Stepping up the brew this time, huh David," smiled Lisa taking a seat on the green leather of her chair, "Good choice."

Once the glasses were filled, Lisa stood. "Welcome, Florence, to the second meeting of the Tenth Floor Social Committee. Cheers."

"I've never had Heineken before, it's good," said Florence after taking a sip and placing her glass on the brown, wooden table.

David sat, and a group of students entered the bar, ushering in a few leaves and cold air.

Don asked, "Any agenda items for the group?"

"I want to thank everyone for the support I received in the hospital and after I returned home," said David.

"I believe Amanda did the lion's share of supporting you, probably knocked a couple days off your hospitalization," said Florence.

"And it appears you didn't lose a step with the lectures. You did great on the biochem and cell biology tests," said Don.

"Does the shoulder bother you, David?" asked Florence.

"I'm amazed it doesn't bother me more when I sleep," replied David.

"Did the police ever catch the guy that shot you?" asked Lisa.

"A Detective Cermak came to my room in the hospital and asked me about it, but I was not able to give him any names, and now I'm planning not to."

"What do you mean, David?" asked Florence.

"I am going to try to meet up with those four guys, talk to them about what one of them did to me, maybe change the trajectory of that man's life."

"Sounds dangerous, David," said Cindi, "You can't just walk up to them and tell them you want them to alter their lives."

"I know it won't be that simple. I can walk up to them because they will think I want to buy drugs. My plan is to ask Detective Cermack to drive me to the corner where they hang but stay in the car. I also thought I'd ask him to get three of his detective buddies to stake out the corner and provide some protection if I need it."

"You could get shot in a New York minute, David. Those policemen could shoot the punks, but you'd be dead. You are going to do this nutso intervention in broad daylight, I hope," added Cindi.

"Oh yeah. I have to talk it over with Cermack and if he refuses to help, well then it's not going to happen."

"Where did this idea come from, David?" asked Lisa.

"Have you seen the Star Trek episode where violence is passed from one person to another, until someone, probably Spock, suggested the Enterprise crew treat it like an infectious epidemic and start acting with peace in their hearts and actions. The infection of violence then went into remission," replied David.

"I don't watch Star Trek," said Cindi, "I'm more of a Three's Company person."

Don said, "I love Star Trek. I think I saw that episode. So, violence can be passed from one person to another like a viral fever?"

"I still don't like it. Are you a social worker trying to save the dope dealers of Twelfth Street?" asked Lisa, "Your life is more valuable than that, David."

"I agree with Lisa," said Cindi, "Drug dealers are not known for their soft and sensitive sides. They want to sell drugs and get rid of the customers as rapidly as possible to avoid attracting attention. They are not likely to be interested in having a lengthy chat about the benefits of non-violence, and especially admitting to shooting you, David."

"I'm not sure this is a good idea either, David. I don't think you'll come back to us in one piece," said Lisa.

"Well, I've nothing that rises to the level of confronting a gun toting drug dealer as an agenda item," said Don, standing up. "Again, welcome Florence. You get to pick the beer next time. The Social Club meets on Sunday nights."

"I enjoyed being included. You all seem to get along very well. I hope I can get to know you better."

"Now I've got work to do while I'm still awake," said Don. "May I escort you ladies across the Quad? David, you coming?"

"Let's go. Sorry I dominated the meeting," said David."

"You're one crazy man, but if you pull it off you may be on your way to minor legendary status," said Cindi.

As they walked to Orlowitz, David leaned into Florence and asked her to elaborate on what Dr. Jacobi told her.

"I barely passed. Office hours with Dr. Jacobi really didn't help, David, but thanks for the referral."

"So, what happened?"

"Dr. Jacobi suggested I buckle down and spend more time studying. He did not understand that I can't stay focused. My brother's death is always weighing on my mind. I drift into thinking about failing the exam and not moving on to next year. Maybe going to Med School was a mistake."

"I can see you are in a tough spot, Florence and I wish I had all the answers, but I don't. Please keep talking with me. I'm your friend. Tell you what, I'll come by tomorrow and we'll get coffee before class. Would that be ok?"

"You are very sweet, David, and yes I'd like to grab a coffee before class."

"I'll see you tomorrow. I hope you can get some sleep. How about I come by when you're ready for bed. I'll read you a story until you fall asleep.

"You don't have to do that, David."

"Not a problem. It worked for me when I was a kid. You pick the story and I'll read," replied David.

David pushed the elevator button for the tenth floor and the group got in. Lisa and Cindi said good night at their door and the men walked Florence to her apartment.

"Call me," said David.

"I will. Thanks David."

After Don and David escorted the ladies to their apartments in Orlowitz, they walked down Tenth Street toward their townhouse. There was a bit of a chill in the air. They pushed through the stiff breeze that faced them as they crossed Spruce Street.

"What was that about?"

"I'm concerned about Florence, Don," said David and proceeded to tell Don the story.

"You really are in a tight spot, David. I know you want to help, but I think you need to take Florence's use of the word depression very seriously. We're just students and friends. Who do we call if we want to notify someone with authority and the know how to help her?"

"I'm going to call Dr. Darla, first thing tomorrow" responded David, "I trust her to do the right thing for Florence."

"I think that's a good idea, David."

The next morning before the lecture began David waited for Florence to pass his apartment. They walked to the coffee shop before heading into Jeff Hall. David walked into the lecture hall. Florence always sat in the upper rows of the left side of the auditorium. "How'd you sleep last night, Florence?"

"My usual, not well."

"How about tonight? I could come over when you're ready to try to sleep. Have a book picked out and I'll come by and read a while, may help you relax and fall asleep."

"If you think it will help and is not too much trouble for you, David, maybe ten o'clock?"

"Great. See you then and make the story a relaxing one, not a mystery or anything that would make you think."

That night David knocked on Florence's door at ten and she answered it in her PJ's. "Come on in, David. This really is nice of you."

"Sure thing, Florence. What've you got for me to read?"

"How about 'Watership Down' as I've already started reading it?"

Ok. You get in bed. I assume you brushed your teeth," David chuckled. David read for a few minutes, looked over and was surprised to see Florence already asleep. "She looks so peaceful," thought David, "I'll keep reading to be sure she stays asleep." Thirty minutes later it was obvious Florence was deeply asleep, so David closed the book and placed it on her night table. "I enjoyed reading that book while I was on that train traveling through southern France," he recalled, "I enjoyed reading it again tonight." He quietly stood up and went to the front door. He paused to be sure she had not stirred, then opened the door, made sure it was locked, then stepped out into the hallway, heading for his townhome.

CHAPTER TWENTY-SEVEN

Wear a Hat Day

Lectures in the main auditorium served as a time for bonding for most of the students, granted some in their cliques, while some elected to remain alone. The months dragged on and the pressure was constantly intense, but some students took it upon themselves to lighten up the proceedings. One such event involved someone writing on the blackboard 'Wear a Hat Day Tomorrow' before the Professor appeared. David had a red Pinch Pond ballcap from a camping trip near Hershey Park. Amanda wore a green beret and coordinated her blouse, scarf, and pants with the green theme. David noticed a black ten-gallon hat on John, Ari wore his Yarmulke as he always did, a green Boy Scout's cap sat on Phillip's head, a pair of women wore colorful, woolen ski hats, and David was surprised to see Dr. Marion sporting an Irish Tam. Uncharacteristically, Ralph did not remember to wear a hat, but as it had been raining, he opened his umbrella and stuck it down the back of his shirt for his chapeau. He received a round of applause from all. Even Professor Marion was amused and shared her recollection of medical school when a number of students wore shorts, sandals, and tee shirts to class on a cold, snowy, winter day. So, it seems the clothing theme to bond a medical school class was not a new idea.

The lecture on lung physiology resumed and David had to work to keep up with Dr. Marion. He tried to sketch the bronchi, bronchioles, alveolar ducts, alveoli, with pneumocytes held in place by fibrocytes, coated by surfactant, and lying in capillary beds, the end organ for the pulmonary arteries and pulmonary veins.

"This is so much more than I ever guessed," thought David, "I always considered the lungs as bellows to transfer air to the blood stream, but it turns out the lungs are a huge immune organ both synthesizing and removing neuroendocrine moieties and transforming angiotensin I to angiotensin II with its effects on vascular flow."

He found the entire lecture complicated, not so much entertaining as thought provoking. Amanda also thought the lecture was excellent when they compared notes.

"I'm surprised that your notes reflect different topics than do mine," commented David.

"I'm so glad we can share and compare what we heard and compare our takes about the photomicrographs we saw," replied Amanda. "Do you have any of that delicious Montepulciano left from the other night?"

"Coming right up. How about some bread and cheese to go with it? Should improve the studying, don't you think?"

"Cheers. Ah, yes. This is a great wine. Pretty good provolone and the bread is just hard enough. Thanks."

"You know, Amanda, I'm thinking that the information we are learning is overly linear."

"What do you mean by linear, David?"

"We are being taught the classic presentations of illnesses. I suspect that once we get into our clinical years we will encounter variations on the themes we are studying."

"Keep going," said Amanda.

"A woman presents to the ED with exertional chest pain incompletely relieved by nitroglycerin. She's forty years old, not a smoker, not diabetic nor hypertensive, and not taking medications for hyperlipidemia. She was walking two miles three times per week and only in the last few weeks did she notice exertional chest pains and dyspnea. How would you proceed with her evaluation?"

"Assuming her electrocardiogram, chest radiograph, CPK, CBC, and electrolytes are normal I would ask her where the chest pain is first located and if it radiates to her arm. I would then consider GI causes and give her a swig of Mylanta, and palpate her costochondrals. I may consider a pulmonary angiogram if her vitals are consistent with a PE."

"Let's say she is not tachycardic, her respiratory rate is twelve, and her ABG rock solid normal. Plus, her chest pains radiate from substernal to right arm, right lateral neck, and rarely to her right scapular area and are not pleuritic."

"I'd order an abdominal ultrasound looking for gallbladder disease, perhaps run a chem 24 and order amylase and lipase on the off chance she has a pancreatic problem."

"So, you are not looking for the classic male pattern angina radiating to the left arm, are you?"

"I read something about Syndrome X presenting as chest pain in women who later have unremarkable coronary caths."

"And you may eventually question her about emotional stressors at home and work."

"I had not considered that."

"That's my point. We won't know how many of these non-linear, non-male pattern presentations are out there until we get into the ED, but just having the willingness to consider causes for atypical chest pain will serve us well."

"So where did this line of ideas come from, David?"

"You my not believe it, but I am reading a book by Stephen Jay Gould about a geologic formation called the Burgess Shale. Anyway, Dr. Gould and his students examined hundreds of Burgess fossils and took a very different approach to their interpretation. Previously, paleontologists tended to buttonhole the fossils into well-worn categories. Dr. Gould made the case that many, many fossils were actually representative of previously undescribed species, even belonging to new phyla. He was willing to allow his classifications to branch out. His hypotheses are now main stream. Paleontologists now recognize that the Cambrian Era was witness to an enormous dying off of perhaps twenty-five phyla. We are now living in the Holocene era with eleven extant phyla. I wonder if medicine will come around to expanding diagnostic categories to account for the atypical cases of illnesses now cared for without a clear understanding of their etiology."

"I often forget you were a geologist as an undergrad, David."

"I can envision reclassifications in the leukemias and lymphomas or new microorganisms being described as was Legionella, differentiated from atypical pneumonia with multi-organ involvement."

"Speaking of pneumonitis, I wonder if you will ponder some of the lung physiology we just learned about while you are running to the Vet tonight," said Amanda.

"If it helps me run a few blocks more without stopping to gasp for air, I'll let you know."

"Now that you've started getting back into shape, I've been thinking of joining a racquetball club. Are you interested?"

"Sure. I'll have to buy a racquet. Do you have one? I think there's a Modell's on Walnut or Chestnut. I had a racquet a long time ago, but it was small and aluminum. I think I lent it to someone. May be good for us to step it up to new, ultralight ones anyway."

"Plus, the balls I have from my days at Catholic are old and soft, so a package of them too. I should warn you that I played racquetball at Catholic and am willing to beat the pants off you in a fair match."

"I like the pants coming off part. However, I would prefer that to occur in my bedroom or yours," smiled David. Amanda turned away and resumed reading her notes aloud.

"Her voice is a bit shaky," thought David. "I wonder if I made a big error in bringing up the sex angle. Oh well, the cat's out of the proverbial bag, perhaps for the better. We'll see."

CHAPTER TWENTY-EIGHT

Florence's Suicide

The days passed, lectures were transcribed, and facts memorized. One day here was a knock on the door. David opened the door to see Lisa looking frantic.

"David, I just saw the EMT's go into Florence's apartment with a stretcher!"

They both ran down the hallway and looked in to see the two EMT's lifting the stretcher. There was a body under a sheet. The sheet covered the face.

"Oh my God," exclaimed Lisa, "She's... dead."

David asked the EMT if he would pause and allow them to see Florence's face one last time. The EMT flipped the sheet back revealing Florence's pale blue face. David leaned over and kissed both of her eyelids, "I'm so sorry you felt you had to do this Florence. We loved you."

He stood up and replaced the sheet over Florence's face. David surprised himself, as he was openly crying. Lisa hugged him, her tears mixing with his. The stretcher moved past them and toward the elevator.

"Did Florence leave a note?" Lisa asked of the EMT pushing the stretcher.

"Yeah, take a look."

Lisa took the note card with shaky hands and read it aloud. “Thanks for all the support you gave me. I know I was loved, but I couldn’t make it any longer. Goodbye.”

“That is so sad,” said David.

“She was all alone when she died,” added Lisa, “Why didn’t she come and talk with us?”

“I understand that overwhelming isolation often accompanies depression,” replied David, more to himself than to Lisa.”

“Could we have done more for her?” asked Lisa.

“Florence chose her own time.”

“I am just so sad. I’m not sure what to do.”

Lisa ran up the hall to catch up with the EMT pushing Florence’s stretcher. “Do you have an idea how Florence committed suicide?”

“She left a bunch of pill bottles right by her head. I packed them up and they’re under the stretcher. I’m sure the coroner will want to see them.”

Lisa and David walked back to their apartments in silence.

“Do you think we can organize a wake in honor of Florence?” asked Lisa.

“I’m sure quite a few of her friends will want to do something for her,” answered David.

“I’d like it to be outside, perhaps a picnic in Fairmont Park,” said Lisa.

“You’re a good person, Lisa. Florence was battling a real set of demons.” said David as he gave her a kiss and opened her apartment door.

“For A Dancer,” Jackson Browne

That night David woke with his pillow soaked in tears. He took a minute to recall Florence’s suicide. He felt sadness and despair descend with an incredible heaviness and tightness in his chest with each breath. He flashed back and felt that gunshot in his right shoulder. He also felt a panic that would not leave despite his best efforts to do slow, square corner breathing. After a few minutes he thought of Florence's last minutes. "She must have been terrified, all alone with her thoughts of failure. She probably recalled her brother's last minutes as well."

David got up, moved to his desk, and grabbed paper and pencil to write down his thoughts, thinking a poem could capture the sadness of her suicide and his terror of being shot.

"Perhaps I can regain some control of these emotions. This must be what PTSD is all about," he thought. Words were not coming easily. He felt himself forcing structure onto the poem.

"These feeling don't lend themselves to a rhyme, my usual style of poetry," thought David, "I've got to break free and write what comes to mind in open verse and not worry about structure or rhymes, maybe just use pace and rhythm."

Once David allowed the feelings to grab hold, the words followed. They did not flow gently, rather broke free in a torrent. David had to stop a few times and peer down which path his thoughts were leading him. He did not feel at all in control but was not particularly concerned.

Florence
I thought we were stronger together than either alone
To battle our demons and each day carry on.
You made the decision to end your fight,
To leave us tonight, alone with our struggles.
What were you feeling when you swallowed those pills,
Taking that mixture to prevent any rescue?
Your fear of failing pursued you,
But you knew enough to do this thing.
What else were you confronting?
What was so terrible that death was your only option?
Did you have a moment of terror, a time without caution.

Was there pain? Were you gasping for breath? I pray not.
So now I am here remembering your peaceful face,
Wondering if you're satisfied in your new place.
I am surrounded by people that love and care for me,
But feel some terror at the memory
Of running for safety with a bullet in my chest
Not knowing what was next,
Then to awaken, surrounded by friends such as you.
I will think of you every day and will abide.
What advice do you have for me from the other side?
I am here should you wish to converse
More deeply than this one-sided verse.

"I really wonder what contemplating suicide feels like. Some believe it involves temporary insanity, but I'm not sure I agree with that. I think Florence knew what she was doing. I hope this poem captures her last minutes and presents a view of my getting shot, then saved by surgery. I did have some control over my retreat to Doc Watson's, but Florence likely felt helpless up to the very end." David was trembling at the memory of how helpless he had been and how well his friends cared for him on the concrete steps.

"I really should throw some sort of party at the Pub for those guys, the ER and OR teams, and my two nurses."

It was two A.M. when David put down his pencil and looked over the lines that he had written.

"I'll have to revisit this, make my message clearer, my brush with death and her suicide. I'll let it percolate," he thought and returned to bed.

He awoke in the morning feeling refreshed and was ready to take on the lectures at Jeff Hall. He checked in on Lisa before walking to class.

"I didn't sleep much at all," she confided. "Cindi was pretty torn up as well. Thanks for being there last night and for stopping by today. We'll get through this somehow.

A few days later, he went over to Amanda's place hoping to walk with her to class.

"I don't know why, David, but you seem to be under a weight."

"Did you hear Florence from your dissection group committed suicide last night?"

"That's terrible."

"It's also terrible I used the term committed. So wrong of me when she was likely reaching out for help. I'm sorry, I'm more upset than I thought I'd be."

"How upset did you think you'd be, David? Florence ended her life. Was she alone in her apartment?"

"Yes. Alone, just steps away from Cindi, Lisa, and me."

"Can we talk about this later? I don't want to push you off, but we'll have time to sit and go over it after class."

"Sure. I can hold off about it for a while. There is something, a poem, that I want to share with you."

"Absolutely you can. We have not shared our poems much at all."

"Thanks. It will be better after some more work. It's the first poem I've written since arriving in Philly. Such a sorry thing to prompt a poem. I'd like to organize a wake for Florence. Lisa suggested we make it a picnic in Fairmont park and invite all who knew her."

"That's a wonderful idea. We should celebrate her life and doing it in the Park is just perfect. I want to help. The women in our class will want to be there, but I will take directions from you and Lisa."

David opened the door to Jeff Hall and they took the escalator to the top of the lecture hall. He followed Amanda down the stairs to their seats. David walked down went to Professor Marion to ask to say a few words about Florence and his idea of a wake. That done David walked back to his seat. He would've liked to have sat with Amanda as he was feeling sad but enjoyed looking at her from his seat behind her. During their walk to David's town home after class he asked Amanda, “Interested in watching the sunrise over Penn’s landing tomorrow, before class?”.

“That would be nice. Do you expect nice weather?”

“Supposed to be cool and clear. I’ll come by at six A.M. Better bring one of your signature jackets, it may be a bit brisk.”

“Sounds great. You think you can make the walk? Well ok. Thanks for thinking of it.”

CHAPTER TWENTY-NINE

Watching the Sunrise

Next morning was as the weatherman had promised, cool and clear with assurances to get to fifty degrees by noon. David climbed the sandstone stairs and was just about to knock when the door opened, and Amanda stepped out, both hands holding travel mugs.

"Coffee? Sugar, no cream, as you like it."

"Thanks, this should take the chill off," replied David reaching for a mug.

They walked down the stairs to the sidewalk and turned right, heading for the river.

"I'm so sorry that Florence died, David. You two seem to have gotten close over the past few months."

"Thanks. I am kinda surprised that it hit me so hard. There is a certain incomplete finality of a suicide. Florence shared a lot of her back story."

"And she was struggling in her classes," added Amanda, "I hope you are not assuming any responsibility for Florence's action, David. You were a supportive force in her life."

"Thanks. I'll have to take time to sort it out but now I want to be with you, enjoying this morning together."

"So, what will we see?" asked Amanda, taking a swig of her coffee.

"I hope you will enjoy seeing the two ships docked at Penn's Landing, Amanda. Brother Ben spent four years at the VA hospital as a corpsman, but he wrangled permission to live off base, on the Gazella Primeiro."

"What is the Gazella Primeiro and how did he do that?"

"The Gazella Primeiro is a tall-masted ship that has been restored by volunteers and lives a second life at the landing. Ben did some scuba diving, salvaged the running lights off a schooner wreck upstream from the Ben Franklin Bridge, polished them up and gave them to the Admiral. The Admiral appreciates naval memorabilia and gave Ben permission to live off base."

"Smart man. Has he done any tours out to sea?"

"Not yet. Did you know the Navy doesn't teach any of their people to pilot sailboats?"

"Does Ben?"

"Oh yeah. He told me he plans to start a sailing course in his spare time. He's spoken to the Admiral about it."

"Does the Navy have any sailboats?"

"Not really, but my bro is one smart dude. He got a 40-foot sloop from the Coast Guard, one that was confiscated in a marijuana bust. It will be perfect to teach the basics of sailing to the Middies."

"Not bad. Is that the Gazella over there?"

"No, that's the Moshulu It was a grain transport ship a hundred years ago. It's a restaurant now. The Gazella Primeiro is the tall-masted barkentine further down-stream. It fished for cod off the coast of Newfoundland."

"It's still too dark to see her."

"Come on. We can sit on the bollards. Sun should be up anytime now." Their faces were touched by a gentle breeze off the Delaware River.

"Look down the river. See the glow?"

"It's beautiful. Hard to believe this is Philly and Camden is across the water."

"The air is surprisingly refreshing for the Delaware River, don't you think? And the sun is huge on the horizon, isn't it?"

“I’m trying to think of something poetic to say,” replied Amanda leaning in on David’s good shoulder.

“Morning rays illumed two shadows blended to one on the cobblestones,” said David.

“Not too shabby.”

They sat in silence, watching the sun rise above the warehouses along the Delaware.

“Now I see the Gazella. That’s a beautiful ship.”

“She is. The Gazella is sea worthy, at least along the eastern coastline and staying on the intercostal waterway. She’ll participate in the Tall Ship event in New York Harbor this summer. But no trans-Atlantic voyages for the old lady.”

David put his arm around Amanda.

“I want to talk about our plans in a couple of years, Amanda.”

“About what?”

“I’m thinking I may want to do a psychiatric residency, not pathology.”

Amanda didn’t say anything. She stiffened ever so slightly, then she pulled away from David, turning to face him. “Florence’s suicide. I’m so sorry David. I know you extended yourself to her.”

“It didn’t prevent Florence from killing herself.”

“She was really terrified about her poor grade in pharmacology leading to failure at school. You couldn’t change that.”

“That’s probably part of it, but I’ve been drawn to psych for a couple years. Dr. Asher’s death really got me thinking. He was an incredibly smart man, knew that smoking could, . . . would kill him, but kept on smoking like a dragon. I cannot believe he smoked, all the time knowing about COPD and lung cancer. He was a brilliant Pulmonologist. I recall seeing him light up as soon as he stepped out of Jeff Hall.”

“A slow suicide?”

“I think so. I wonder what he was running from.”

“I didn’t have the opportunity to know him well at all.”

"Me either. When should someone intervene? Do you have to be really close to someone to bring it up?"

"Well, you spoke to Florence a lot about her depression."

"Certainly not thinking about suicide."

"But you had to think it was a possibility. You know the short form questions to ask patients. You saw the signs that she was in a bad place."

"Yeah, but I didn't really face up to the possibility of suicide."

"You were talking with a friend, not a patient. There's a big difference, a measure of distancing."

"And objectivity. If I want to be a physician, I'll need to decide when to step back and treat the situation more objectively."

"And sometimes you'll want to be just a good friend," replied Amanda. "Just be sure you're as honest with yourself as you can be while you are asking patients to be honest with you."

"I can see that with honesty comes responsibility. If I had suspected Florence was even a little suicidal, I would have had the obligation to see that she was protected, even if that meant causing bad feelings between us and possibly ruining our relationship."

"It would have changed the relationship for sure, maybe not destroyed it completely."

"I want to see if I can change the way we 'work up' depression. I have never been satisfied with the diagnostic categories that ended up with a 'chemical' cause if it wasn't situational, post-traumatic, or the other types."

"So, what's your plan?"

"I want to work up causes of depression like we will work up Fever of Unknown Origin."

"FUO?"

"Yeah. I'd like to define the extended workup of depression of unknown etiology."

"DUE, nice."

"So, what do you think of me going into psych? We are the path power team, our scopes side by side . . . ."

"Things were going to change, David. It would be a stretch to get our residencies together."

"Are you still thinking we could try for the same hospital, you in path, me psych? It could work."

"Our relationship, my love for you would be strained, but not broken by a few miles between us. Residencies are difficult and time consuming under the best of circumstances. Yeah, we should look at it like it's going to work out."

"I was really hesitant to bring it up, but I wanted to be out and honest with you, always have been."

"And I value that, and I appreciate you telling me." Amanda deftly changed the subject, "I enjoy being with you. Not a bad setting either. I've never been to Penn's Landing to watch the river before."

"Penn's landing at six, sun rising, river flows by, cool morning with you."

"Sitting on the Dock by the Bay." Otis Redding

Amanda leaned back onto David's chest, who breathed a big sigh of relief. They both gazed downstream to the sun rising in the East."

"We'd better be getting back, Amanda. I feel relieved after discussing my thoughts about Florence and my possible future plans. I know it was difficult news."

"I'll have to spend some thinking about it. In the meantime, I brought a part of a poem I'd like to share with you, David," said Amanda, turning to face him. "It was written by Gerard Manley Hopkins in 1877."

"What's the title?"

"Hurrahing in Harvest. This is the second stanza.

'I walk, I lift up, I lift up heart, eyes
Down all that glory in the heavens to glean our Saviour:
And eyes, heart, what looks, what lips yet gave you a
Rapturous love's greeting of realer, of rounder replies?'"

"Nice. Can you give me the entire poem someday? The language is a bit stilted for our time."

"But Hopkins' imagery is powerful."

"Thanks for thinking of me and for what I know lies in your heart, behind those words."

"Thanks for a lovely morning, David," said Amanda. They walked back to Tenth Street in silence, hand in hand as the sun rose and illuminated the street.

CHAPTER THIRTY

Meeting Up with the Shooter

David called the police officer who had questioned him while he was recovering in the hospital. Detective Cermak said he'd stop by the townhome in about an hour.

Once in David's place, Cermak sat down and looked intently at David who was sitting on the couch.

David said, "Do you think you could help me arrange a meeting with the man who shot me?"

Cermak thought he was crazy and told him so. "What possible reason would you have in confronting the punk who tried to murder you?"

When David hesitated to answer Cermak added, "I've got to hear this," then leaned back in the chair, a smile on his face, waiting for David's explanation.

"I want to confront him for two reasons. The first is to prove to myself that I can face him, and second to let him know I have not yet filed charges. I want him to think about what he did to me and ask him to never shoot anyone else. I want him to register his handgun and I want him to know if he does use the gun to commit a crime I will help prosecute him for my injury."

"So just how do you see this confrontation playing out, David?" asked Cermak.

"I am assuming the four hoodlums still hang out at Twelfth and Bainbridge. I thought I'd confront them in the daylight with you and maybe three other officers nearby. I'm probably naïve in believing I could just walk up to them, say my peace, and walk away without getting shot again."

Cermak interrupted David at that point. "So, I'm in the car, three other officers are stationed, unseen around the corner and you walk up and introduce yourself. Do you plan to demand an apology? Will you tell them we are surrounding them and not to try to injure you?"

"I plan to ask the guy who shot me to let me take a picture with him, then to take out his gun and drop it on the street."

"You are nuts."

"Twisted," Joni Mitchell

"I will tell him it will be registered, tested, and returned to him if it has not been involved in a crime other than shooting me. Do you think it likely he will get it back?"

"Depends on his age and prior offenses. You did not provide me with a name when we spoke in the hospital, so I don't know his rap sheet. We could require him to take a basic gun safety course to determine if he is willing to follow the law. That still does not ensure your safety. Even having four officers training their weapons on the four of them does not ensure you won't get shot again. Are you trying to be some kind of social worker, or a martyr?"

"I want to give this guy a chance to turn his life around. You think I'm crazy, I know, but I want to become a healer, perhaps preventing the disease of gun violence, not just a physician caring for someone after they are infected with murder."

"Infected with murder. Sounds like a science fiction notion."

"It was an episode on Star Trek, Next Generation. I do believe violence can be contagious, and therefore can be prevented."

"Okay, okay. Doing this in broad daylight with backup is better than at night. I would recommend not pushing it too far if this shooter looks like he could go off on you, though Lord knows getting this guy to give up his weapon is a stretch. Being willing to walk away if things turn dicey, is crazy doable. When do you see this happening?"

"We'd need to determine if they in fact hang out in the daytime on the same corner. You see if any other officers are willing to help, then let me know."

"I'll get back to you in a few days. Meanwhile you stay away from that corner and away from them."

True to his word, Cermak enlisted three other officers and had determined the four men did spend time during the day on Twelfth and Bainbridge. He suspected them of dealing drugs given the car and foot traffic they interact with.

"How's next Wednesday?" Sargent Cermack asked.

"I'm free after three o'clock."

"I'll swing by in an unmarked car and pick you up. Don't discuss this with anyone."

David decided to wear his new black sweatshirt under the green Air Force jacket. Amanda had stitched a red bull's eye patch over the bullet hole in the jacket. When Cermak arrived, David asked if the four were on their corner. Cermak said they were.

"You still want to do this?" he asked.

"Yes."

"So, let's do it." They drove up Twelfth and parked just shy of Bainbridge on the side opposite to the street light under which the four loitered.

David got out of the car and walked over to them.

"What you doin' here, white boy?"

"I would like to talk with the man who shot me a couple weeks ago."

The group instantly looked around, then back at David who had approached within ten feet.

"Say what?"

"I was the guy jogging at midnight. Same jacket as this one. First shot hit the windshield of a car over there, second shot got me in the chest, right here." David pointed to the bull's eye sewn onto his coat over his right chest.

"Don't know nuthin 'bout no shooting."

"Since you're talking to me, I'll talk to you," replied David. "A bullet went through my chest that night. I want you to know I know you shot me and that I want you to never shoot anyone else, ever."

"You crazy, white boy. What say I just pop you here and now and be done wid it?"

"I'd not do that. By the way, my name is David, not white boy. What's your name?"

"Yeah, right, I'm telling you."

"We are surrounded by police officers. Rizzo's cops have been known to shoot a man in the back."

The four again looked around, then back toward David.

One of the other three said, "Too much talking, Sly, get rid of him."

"My roommate in college was named Sylvester, also went by Sly," said David.

"Don't mean nuthin'. What you want anyway?"

"Three things. First, I want you to swear here and now you'll never shoot at anyone again. Two, I want you to replace my Rolling Stones tee shirt I got when they were at the Army-Navy field concert last year." David reached into his jacket pocket and pulled out the remnants of the shirt showing the famous tongue. "Here, get me this one. Get it legally."

"So, what's the third thing, David?" Sly dragged David's name out in derision."

"I want you to give up your gun so it can be registered."

"What?" the others exclaimed.

"I want you to take your nine mm out and put in on the street. One of the officers will take it and have it registered. You will get it back when you've completed a gun safety course, assuming the gun is not linked to a crime. I have not told them your name or pressed charges against you, yet, for shooting me, so there's nothing linking you or the gun."

"You want me to give up my piece and maybe I'll get it back?"

"Oh, and I want one of you to take our pictures together, one for you, one for me, so you don't forget."

"And if I don't do all this shit for you?"

"Well then I call my police officer pals over and we talk about pressing charges. They'll get the gun either way, Sly."

"This is fucking crazy, Sly," said the tall man next to Sly.

"I got this, Gordy. So, if I put my piece on the street we walk away?"

"I'll come back in a week for the Stone's shirt. We can take the photographs now," David said pulling out an Instamatic camera and handing it over to the tallest of the other three who went by Gordy. David walked over to Sly and put his right arm around his shoulder. "How's this for a picture? Please take two."

"Do it," said Sly to Gordy who took two pictures and handed the camera back to David.

"Thanks. Now drop the gun and back away," said David. "I'll get an officer to write out a receipt if you want."

Sly looked around and then reached inside his coat for the gun. He placed it on the sidewalk and looked hard at David. "Why you want to do all this, David?"

"In another couple years I'll graduate and be a physician. I want to start saving lives now. You'll be my first save."

"Better hope you live that long."

David took a few steps back and motioned for Cermak to come over to retrieve the Glock. "Let's not push things, David," Cermak said, picking up the gun with his pen and placing it in a plastic bag.

David extended his hand toward Sly. Sly extended a fist. David fist bumped Sly and they parted company without another word.

“Craziest thing I ever witnessed. Let’s get back to the vehicle and out of here,” said Cermak.

“I need a drink,” replied David getting into the car. “I’m buying for you and your buddies. You pick the bar.”

CHAPTER THIRTY-ONE

Amanda Starts an Expressive Writing Group

David told Amanda about his meeting with Sly while they were studying at David's kitchen. "It went as well as could be expected. Detective Cermack still thinks I'm a crazy man, but he admitted I carried it off. I'm waiting to hear from him about the gun's history and if Sly takes the gun safety course."

"This whole story would lend itself to a short story, David. Would you be interested in meeting with a few students for a writing group?"

"I think that's a great idea, Amanda. Would you invite people from all four years?"

"I was thinking even faculty."

"I wonder if you could model it after the creative salons such as Gertrude Stein and others held."

"So, you're thinking couches and overstuffed chairs, not a classroom setting. I like it," said Amanda.

"I wonder if there is an upstairs lounge at one of the bars or restaurants that would let us use their space if we promised to pony up a minimum for wine and snacks. I'll start inquiring around. What night were you thinking of?"

"Wednesday is our lightest class day. Do you think Tuesday night around seven o 'clock would work? I want to ask Karen for her input as she minored in English at Penn."

"Announce it at Jeff Hall during lectures for the first and second years and try to get a mailing list for the third- and fourth-year students."

"I'll ask Dr. Darla if this has been attempted in previous years. Maybe she'd recall the location they used."

"You know, I bet we could entice a member of Penn's literature department to attend a couple gatherings. You said Karen went to Penn."

"Won't hurt to ask her for her choice of an English Professor. She and I get along well together."

"I haven't tried to write much since I got here, but plenty has happened to me. How many students are shot and try to have a relationship with the shooter? I'd have to jazz it up, make it more universal," said David.

"I can see your wheels turning already."

"I'd like to do more writing. It's just a matter making the time and having the discipline to devoting the time on a regular basis. Water's boiling, Earl Grey good for you?"

"Yes, please. I once read that Michener wrote for four hours every morning and researched during the afternoon in preparation for the next day."

"How else could he regularly crank out those enormous tomes on such diverse topics?"

"Personally, I was thinking of poems and short stories for our group to be realistic about our time constraints."

"Would you want to ask the literature Prof to review what makes for an effective poem or short story?"

"You know, David, I have not seen much of your writing. I did like the one about Florence."

"Nor have I seen much of yours, Amanda. I'll lay good money you have a notebook with all sorts of poems in your bookcase."

"I do, and back at you for your collection of poems. Can we have a reading tonight after dinner? I would like to see how different our styles are, David. The two off the cuff Haiku's you dropped at Penn's Landing were pretty impressive."

"Thanks. I was inspired by my beautiful companion."

Amanda moved to the couch and said, "Why don't you come over here and show me how beautiful you really think I am."

David pushed his chair back so fast it almost toppled over. "Is this too close for you?" he said sitting on the couch and pushing his right thigh under her.

"No I think this is just right," Amanda said turning to face David and reaching around with her right arm to pull him closer and pressed her lips against his.

David responded instantly, returning the kiss and his left hand unbuttoned her blouse. He reached inside Amanda's shirt and stroked her right breast, pinching her nipple. Amanda leaned into his hand and David reached inside her pants and grabbed her buttock with his right hand. Amanda had not separated her lips from his as her tongue searched out his. Amanda reached down and unbuttoned his pants, sliding her hand inside his boxers. Her fingers gripped his shaft and as she moved her grasp David moved his hand from her breast to her pants. First releasing the button, then the zipper on her slacks. His fingers explored her belly, then mons, then inside, massaging her clitoris as she arched her back. David's right hand lifted her buttocks and as Amanda rubbed the tip of his penis with her thumb, David pressed back into the couch as his finger reached deeper inside. Amanda arched and moaned then she placed her hand on David's, stopping his stroking. She reached around David's back and held him tighter as her body became rigid with pleasure. David had already relaxed as Amanda leaned back into the couch and took a deep breath.

"Whew, that was wonderful."

"Intense doesn't come close, Amanda."

They both shifted to embrace each other with both arms and kissed again.

"I've got a little mess to attend to upstairs," said David.

"I'll just wash up in the sink," replied Amanda.

Neither released their hold on the other for a few more moments then David got up and went upstairs holding his pants up. Amanda giggled at that sight, as she walked to the kitchen sink to wash her hands.

"Interested in sleeping here tonight, Amanda?" asked David walking down the stairs.

"Thank you for the offer, but I need to get home, change, and get ready for tomorrow. Some other time for sure."

"Let me walk you home," David asked as he held Amanda's coat for her.

CHAPTER THIRTY-TWO

Ethics

"This is going to be so very dry," complained David as he and Amanda walked into Jeff Hall and took the escalator.

"Come on David, you are usually positive for almost all the classes. What's got you down on ethics?"

"I know it's important, but its common sense, isn't it?"

"Unless you are willing to get up front and deliver the lecture, I suggest you listen and take your usual and sometimes incisive notes."

David was impressed at Dr. Darla's opening account of a physician who withheld critical information from a patient in order to 'spare' the patient distress concerning the risks of the procedure she was to undergo.

"This well-meaning physician denied his patient the opportunity to make her own informed decision about the breast biopsy. Our resident was very fortunate the patient did not make a formal complaint about the lack of full disclosure. She was able to make her decision to not proceed with treatment after the biopsy. I was involved with this case and can tell you the patient thought she had lived a good, long life and considered the possibility of breast cancer causing her death to be part of God's plan for her. The resident delivered the results of the biopsy with sensitivity, which probably went a long way to restore trust between him and the patient. Another point, my sharing this account with you as part of your training still requires permission from both the patient and the resident. Should you wish to discuss these types of cases with your classmates, you will have to decide whether to obtain written consent to disclose information from the patient, or just get verbal permission, which is what I did for this case. Many, if not all of you will at some time discuss cases with your teachers in situations such as during morning report. These are intrinsically covered as all present are caring for the patients under review. Be very careful when discussing patients at forums like Grand Rounds or in publications. Things have a way of making their way into the public sphere and not infrequently can become known to the patients involved. Frank discussions are reasonable and very useful but can be hurtful to patients not understanding the context." Dr. Darla paused and looked around the room.

"I want each of you to write a short description of an ethical situation you have been involved in while in college, with friends, family members. If you can't recall an ethical dilemma, perhaps invent a scenario and solve the issue. I do want to read all of them and I will offer my comments. I will return them in a week, so keep them short and to the point. I will discuss another ethical issue next week."

"I've already got an issue tee'd up," David told Amanda later that night, "When I was a freshman I thought it important to offer advice to a classmate I knew in high school. I perceived she was lonely. I told her she had created distance between herself and quite a few people because she was a gossip. I believe to this day that I destroyed a lot of her self-confidence and made her very sad. We were not the best of friends, didn't have a lot of history between us to buffer such a statement on my part. I should have also had some positive things to say about her and should have offered suggestions to improve relationships, because like most people she was a complex person and I did like her."

"At least you didn't share your wisdom in a group setting, David," said Amanda, "It's probably way too late to apologize, now. You have been dealt a lesson to remember for similar situations in the future. So, write it up for Dr. Darla."

"Can you recall an example in your past, Amanda?"

"There was an incident at Catholic where my roommate purchased a term paper from a classmate, because she didn't leave sufficient time to write it herself. I heard about it when the author dropped it off and asked me to read it for typos."

"Did you edit it?"

"No. I did not want to become involved. And to answer your next question, no I did not say anything to anyone about the matter. I probably should have taken time at a later date to tell my roomie what I thought she was risking, but I'll admit I was not a little embarrassed about her cheating."

"What would you do now if you discovered someone stealing answers to a test, or something similar?"

"I'd likely run it by you, weigh the consequences for the student, our classmates, and the teacher. My decision to reveal what I knew would be greatly influenced by your take on it. You seem to have a solid backbone for honesty."

"Thanks for that. Let's get home. I have a piece of redfish and baby potatoes to make into dinner for us. I may have time to whip up some chocolate pudding for the 'Nilla Wafers' in the cabinet. If you are willing, I would be appreciative if you could read to me from the textbook while I cook. Do you mind if I invite Don to share dinner tonight?"

"I think that would be great. I don't interact much with Don. And can do about reading to you. I hate to say I told you so, but I told you it was quite possible you would enjoy and maybe learn something from the ethics lecture."

CHAPTER THIRTY-THREE

Switching Slides

As the semester slogged along there were pranks played on students and lecturers. One such episode was especially notable when someone, and Ralph was suspected, placed a Kodachrome photo of a nude woman reading the Pharmacology textbook while reclining on her left side as the first slide in the carousel. Another textbook was strategically placed to obscure her pelvis. Her breasts were lovely, and the entire photo on the big screen of the lecture board was quite distracting, at least to the men. The next day Professor Jones tried to prevent a recurrence of the prank by gluing down the top of his carousel, but a very ingenious student, whose name started with "R" brought his own carousel with a photo of a naked woman sitting cross legged eating a banana. He switched the carousels. This time a very small copy of 'Guidebook to Fruit Trees' was placed over her lap. Even Professor Jones got a kick out of that. By the time Dr. Jones had his carousel substituted and finished his lecture, the slide of the woman was all but forgotten. David had compiled seven pages of notes on the interactions between antibiotics and other medications commonly taken by many patients. David had not previously considered that diverse medications could prolong the half-lives of antibiotics, and vice versa, sometimes leading to serious effects on cardiac or pulmonary function.

"More details to remember," thought David, "When all I would want to do is prescribe the appropriate antibiotic for an infection, but that's the way it needs to be. And I'll bet things become more complicated when the person receiving the antibiotic is in the hospital, dehydrated, anemic, hypotensive and on a bucket load of other medications instead of at home with a simple sore throat."

Amanda had the same take on this when she and David reviewed their notes that evening. "It's an uphill battle for sure. Any action creates a myriad of sometimes unforeseen consequences."

"And I imagine there will be new adverse events and interactions uncovered as we progress in medicine," replied David.

"Like Dr. Jane says, 'nothing is irrelevant,'" they both said together.

"How will we be able to keep up to date?"

"Read, discuss, share with other students and attendings, and be willing to question decisions if things don't seem right."

David glanced at his watch. "Didn't we book a court for seven o'clock?"

"We'll have to hurry to get there on time," replied Amanda.

"You go home and change into a distracting outfit. I'll get us a cab to come to your townhouse," said David.

They made it with a minute to spare. Amanda won the coin toss and immediately took the lead with some nice, soft shots to the left corner. David noticed she went to the left corner eighty percent of the time.

"I need to make it harder for her to go to the left with her forearm returns," he thought, "That means putting the ball in the backcourt on the left side and make her use her backhand."

It was obvious Amanda knew what David was trying to do, but David was able to make things difficult for her. He was able to place the ball in the right corner and have it drop to the floor within inches of the wall a few times.

"At least I won't be shut out this time," he thought. "I know she has an unfair advantage over me in that skimpy red skirt and sleeveless white blouse."

The games ended with Amanda easily winning each by ten or more points.

"Smirk while you can, my love, I am a quick study and you will soon have your comeuppance."

"Bring it all on."

CHAPTER THIRTY-FOUR

Visiting Amanda's Parents

One day after classes David asked Amanda, "What would you say we visit our parents, introduce you to mine and me to yours?"

"That would be fun," replied Amanda, "When were you thinking of?"

"How about we try to visit one on Saturday and the other on Sunday, would depend on them. We need to contact them to hear if they're home and not otherwise busy."

"I'll call my mom and ask if we could visit around lunchtime on Saturday," said Amanda.

"And I'll call my mom and see about Sunday afternoon. I don't want to go at dinnertime, we'd get home too late."

"Just a meet and greet. Anything I should know about your mom and dad?" asked Amanda.

"Mom's a hugger, dad's not. Dad will likely seem to be asking a lot of questions about your future plans, but that's the way he is, how he gets to know people. Mom is also a feeder. Cookies and tea will be standard fare. She will assume you are the greatest and want to know if you are you a cook and can she share a few recipes with you, that sort of thing. What about your mom and dad?"

"I would say both are a bit standoffish at first but will really warm up once you get to know them and they you. They will want to get to know who you are and see how you treat me," replied Amanda, "Just be your charming self and I'm sure it will all go well."

David picked Amanda up Saturday at ten thirty, leaving plenty of time to enjoy the drive to Radnor in the clear sunshine.

"I see you dressed for the occasion, nice pants and shirt, and look, the dress shoes are not just for Sunday Mass anymore."

"You look lovely as always, Amanda. So which route do you take to go home?"

"Head over to 76 north then 30 West to 476 north. The Radnor exit is well marked, and I'll tell you which road to take once we're off 476."

Traffic was light compared to rush hour so they made it without incident. The Jacksons lived in a white two-story home in a quiet suburban Radnor neighborhood. David pulled the VW into the driveway and he and Amanda walked up to the front door. Amanda called out, "Mom, Dad, David and I are here. Are you busy?"

Amanda's mom called back, "Come on in. I'll go get your dad. Make yourselves comfortable. I'll be right out."

Mrs. Jackson appeared a few minutes later flanked by Mr. Jackson. They were both tall and slender, as was Amanda.

"Mom, Dad, this is David Coleman."

"We've been hearing a lot about you lately, David," said Mrs. Jackson.

"I hope some of it was positive, Mrs. Jackson," replied David with a smile.

"Certainly, David. Amanda goes on and on about you," said Mr. Jackson.

"Really, Dad." Amanda was blushing.

"Come on in and have a seat. Can I get you anything? How about ice tea?"

"That would be great Mrs. Jackson, thanks."

The living room was cozy and well-lit by the bay window facing the front of the house.

"Who likes orchids?" asked David. "They are beautiful."

Mr. Jackson smiled at the compliment. "Thank you. It has taken me many years to be able to keep orchids alive and blooming."

David settled back into the leather chair. Amanda was on the couch with her mom.

"So, Amanda told me you met and became fast friends the very first day at orientation," said Mrs. Jackson. "Seems that you have continued and strengthened a nice friendship."

"Yes, we have. Amanda supports me, and I hope I am supporting her during these very stressful days where a lot of information is thrown at us every day."

"We were told we would learn a hundred thousand new words during the four years at Jeff and we are well on our way to that goal, Mom."

"Do you have time for anything besides studying and taking more notes?"

"We try to go to the museums and out to dinner on occasion."

"We've seen a few classic movies, even some live music," replied Amanda.

"But all the fun is bracketed by more studying," added David, "The really good thing is Amanda and I study together and compare notes, which I believe gives us a leg up on either one of us going it alone."

"Glad to hear that, David," replied Mrs. Jackson as she stood up and went into the kitchen.

She returned with iced tea and a plate of cookies.

"I hope you like Toll House cookies, David. They are Amanda's favorite."

"I had not realized that, Mrs. Jackson. I learned to make a mean Toll House in college once my mom taught me to refrigerate the cookie dough overnight to let the glutens hydrate."

"Well you've got the secret to a good cookie right there, David. My advice is to make a double batch each time anticipating Amanda's consuming the first while they are still warm out of the oven. Oh, and have a gallon of milk ready as well," she chuckled.

"Really Mom, I eat a few cookies here and there, that's true, but I am not a cookie monster."

"I'll take your advice Mrs. Jackson so I'm assured to have a few for myself. I definitely am a cookie monster. Amanda told me you majored in chemistry. I once purchased a cookbook written by a chemist. The author, a woman, describes the attributes of the many different types of flour, what they are useful for and how they require different treatment. I'll try to bring it back to Philly from my parent's home."

"I'd very much like to read it, David. Thank you," replied Mrs. Jackson.

"And Mr. Jackson," said David turning to Mr. Jackson, "Amanda told me you are an attorney. Which type of law do you practice?"

"I am a corporate lawyer specializing in contract law. Thanks for asking David. Amanda tells me you are both interested in pursuing pathology residencies after medical school. Did you come to Jefferson with that goal in mind?" asked Mr. Jackson reaching for a cookie.

"No sir. I had no idea where medical school was going to take me. So far pathology appears to offer very precise answers, while providing the excitement of detective work. We have yet to go out into the clinical settings and meet real patients to uncover the causes of their illnesses, so I may switch my allegiance down the road."

"Can you tell me a little about the project you are working on?" asked Mrs. Jackson.

"I am still learning about the subject, but within the disease Lupus there is the hypothesis that certain antibodies are responsible for much of the organ damage that occurs. One such antibody is called double stranded DNA. This antibody is not normally in circulation in healthy individuals and when it combines with a series of proteins called complement, which do normally circulate, the resulting immune complexes can lodge in healthy tissues and cause damage such as to the kidney resulting in something called glomerulonephritis that can lead to kidney failure. I apologize for the jargon, but I get a bit excited by it all."

"Are you trying to get rid of these proteins?"

"At this stage, a Ph.D., Dr. Taylor, has been doing experiments to determine the way the antibodies and one type of protein, C3 complement, bind to the antibodies. Then as a new entity it binds to receptors on red blood cells called the C-1 receptor. He is also interested in how they are cleared from the circulation. My job has been to combine antibodies harvested from the blood of actual Lupus patients with purified complement in various ratios. The materials are radiolabeled and counting the resulting combinations provides some answers."

Mrs. Jackson asked, "Is the radiation dangerous?"

"No, we work with trace amounts, but of course take precautions not to get the materials on or inside our bodies."

"So, what will you do with this information, David?" asked Mr. Jackson.

"Well sir, if I stick with Dr. Taylor, we plan to inject these materials into rabbits and then remove blood samples at specific times to determine how these components are cleared from the circulation, not just interact in a tube. Later, we hope to see where the pathogenic materials end up. Our hypothesis is that the liver recognizes the red blood cells carrying the C3 and DNA combinations, and then destroys and clears them from the circulation, thus preventing damage to the kidneys, lungs, brain, skin, or other target organs. I hope I've explained this clearly enough."

"Sounds exciting. If you could develop a clearing mechanism like an external filter you could prevent people with lupus from suffering from these proteins," said Mrs. Jackson.

"That is called plasmapheresis and yes that is where all this will hopefully lead. Again, I am just a lowly technician, pipetting solutions into tiny plastic vials, but I do enjoy being part of the Taylor team. He has even put my name on a couple of publications."

"And David does this work on his time off from the regular classwork," added Amanda.

"Well, Amanda, I suppose you've explained your work with HPV infection and cancer, also during your quote, free time," chuckled David.

"Yes, and we are very proud of our Amanda."

"Do you live in a townhouse?"

"Yes, with my roommate Don."

"And you feel safe and secure?"

"Oh yes. We are just a couple blocks from the Jefferson campus and the area is well patrolled by the police," replied David, "Our place is just around the corner from Amanda's home with Mrs. Hopkins."

"Well Mom and Dad, I hate to break up this love fest, but David and I have to get back to the mundane world of cracking the books and filling our heads with orthopedics: broken bones and mangled muscles this week," said Amanda.

"Thank you for a lovely time, great cookies, and good advice about your daughter's tendency to ravage innocent platefuls of Toll House cookies. I hope we can meet again soon."

"Nice meeting you, David."

Amanda gave her mom and dad hugs and kisses. David shook Mr. Jackson's hand and received a hug from Mrs. Jackson.

"Please let us know when you wish to visit Philly and we'll show you the sights and take you to a great Italian restaurant for dinner," offered David as he and Amanda walked out of the front door.

"Well that went well," said Amanda, giving David's arm a squeeze as they walked to the car."

"I hope I didn't go overboard with the details of Dr. Taylor's research."

"Quite the opposite, you kept it in people talk, which is not easy to do. My parents would have quizzed you for more details if you hadn't laid it out so well."

"Do you want to stop for a milk shake or a sundae before heading back to the expressway. You must know of a place around here."

"Got just the place in mind. It's a mile down the road. Great suggestion, and last time I was there they had an ample supply of cookies," Amanda laughed.

"Point the way, cookie girl."

CHAPTER THIRTY-FIVE

Visiting David's Parents

The ride on Sunday to Wilmington took a little longer. David decided to avoid I-95 in favor of Route One and Route 202 taking them through the more attractive areas of southeastern Pennsylvania north of Wilmington.

"Someday this strip will all be developed," commented David. "I used to ride my bike while in high school from Wilmington to Chadds Ford and feel safe. Now I'm not so sure the traffic would be as friendly."

"Did you ever visit the Brandywine River Museum?"

"Many times. Jimmy and I would stop and do a quick look around the Museum on our way to Lenape Park, which is just past Andrew Wyeth's home. We rode the merry go round, collected a handful of brass rings, and bought a couple Tootsie Rolls. Man were they hard as rocks, but just fine for the long bike ride home."

"Do you remember N.C. Wyeth's pictures?"

"Oh yeah. Great colors on swashbuckling heroes. N.C. Wyeth and Maxfield Parrish were able to create the best blues and greens."

"What did you think of Jamie Wyeth's giant pig?"

"I remember coming around the corner in the museum for the first time, and there it was, so super real, so pink and hairy."

"You were what, fourteen years old then?"

"Twelve and we rode three speed bicycles. The hills were monsters, but we beat them. I think that's when I first caught the art bug looking at the Wyeth works. Maybe not my aspiration to be a collector, but certainly to know the artists and their works. Jimmy and I spent a lot of time looking for things to do. We didn't have much money but made our own fun."

"Was there a shopping mall near your home when you were a kid?"

"Only a department store called Almart. A great place for a kid to wander around and dream of having the money to buy things like a chemistry set. One of my first jobs was doing the store wide inventory. Perfect job for a guy like me, counting pencils and erasers all day for a buck twenty an hour. I could walk from our house across the golf course to get there. Farther across Concord Pike, which is Route 202, the land was all undeveloped and about a mile further in is the Brandywine River. We'd ride our bikes to the river and go fishing all day; never caught much, but that wasn't the point."

"We live deep in suburbia, as you saw. A bunch of housing developments. No river near my home," mentioned Amanda. "I always thought the neighborhood would have been more interesting if all the houses were not so similar."

"Where I grew up there were a few cookie-cutter homes, but the majority were unique. I had a paper route and knew almost every family for miles around. We are crossing Shipley Road on Silverside, great memories. Next left is Tarleton and my parent's home. Personally, I never liked that house, but it's my home. Can you get that?"

"I get it. Looking back, I'd rather have lived in the country in a big stone home on ten acres, maybe have a horse, definitely a big ol' golden lab. But I had a good childhood as I'm sure you did."

"I did. Here we are. I hope you're hungry. Mom will want to feed us."

"No problem, David."

David's dad was in the front yard garden. He stood up when the yellow VW passed him. He dusted off his pants. "I thought I recognized that car." He took off his gloves and walked over to greet Amanda with a handshake after David introduced them.

Mom came out of the front door, arms wide greeting them with, "Welcome Amanda," giving her a big hug. "Come in. Dave go in and clean up, then join us in the living room."

Amanda turned to me and said, "You never told me you're David junior."

Once inside, sitting on the green couch, which rested on gold wall to wall shag carpet, Amanda was peppered with questions from Vera, David's mom.

"Amanda, how do you like medical school so far? Is it what you expected? How many women are in your class? Are you keeping up? Oh, I suppose I'd better let you answer at least one of these questions, shouldn't I."

"First of all, I really enjoy the challenge of all the information we have to absorb. I was never a classroom slouch or a huge athlete, but I can imagine running a very long race, pacing myself for the hills that I'm sure will be coming. Medical school is not entirely what I expected, but how was I to know what to expect. I did expect it to be difficult. I am trying to meet all the women in my class, there aren't many of us." Amanda paused, waiting for another question, but Vera was silent.

"I think part two of your question would be, 'Are we treated with the same respect as the men?' I would say yes."

Dave jumped in with, "Do you feel safe in Philadelphia? David has told us you live around the corner from his townhouse and from what I've seen it is a reasonably nice area."

"I love my townhome and the owner, Mrs. Hopkins, who treats me very well. Of course, David and I spend a lot of time together studying. I feel very safe."

Vera said, "That's so nice. I grew up in Worcester, Massachusetts where the neighborhoods changed block by block. We referred to them as ghettos in the classic, cultural sense. There was the French ghetto, the Polish ghetto, the Italian ghetto, and of course our area, the Lithuanian ghetto. It was safe, but sometimes not as friendly as

I would have wanted. Dave grew up in Holden, a smaller and more suburban town adjacent to Worcester. It was perhaps more neighborly; wouldn't you say so Dave?"

"Worcester is a big city; Holden a bedroom and farm community."

"David told me your parents live in Radnor. I've never visited Radnor, is it a busy town?"

"Quite the opposite. From what David has shown me of Wilmington so far, I'd say Wilmington is somewhat of a busy and sprawling city. Radnor is a quiet little town."

"Excuse me for not offering you something to drink and eat earlier, Amanda. How about some tea and cookies? David told me you enjoy Toll House. I made them earlier this morning."

David gave Amanda a knowing smile. Amanda replied, "I would love tea and some of your signature cookies Ms. Coleman. May I help you in the kitchen?"

Vera stood up and replied, "Of course Amanda, glad to have your help. Will Earl Grey be good for you?"

"Yes ma'am. I suspect David has called and let out my secrets."

"Probably not all of them," she replied to Amanda. "We'll be right back," Vera said to the men.

Dave took the opportunity to quiz David on the wisdom of being in such a serious relationship while in medical school with all the stresses involved with studying. "Do you have sufficient time to devote to your classes? I remember how long and hard you studied at Delaware. Do you two spend a lot of time together?"

"Actually Dad, we study together almost every night after dinner, which we sometimes prepare together," replied David realizing where Dave was coming from, but refused to take the bait. "Amanda and I find we learn more together than apart. We have slightly different skills and where I am a detail person, taking almost verbatim notes, Amanda tends to listen for the big picture, analyzing the information during the lecture in real time." David shifted on the couch to face

Dave. "And I love Amanda very much and I know she loves me right back. It is very important to have someone you can count on for support. Med school is a very tough environment, many times more than Delaware ever was, and I value her being there for me 24/7."

"Are you living together, David?"

"No, we have the good fortune of living in separate townhomes a couple blocks apart. This gives us both breathing space. For example, I can spend time with Ben or Don without worrying that I am neglecting Amanda."

Amanda and Vera returned to the living room with a tray of cookies and another with the tall silver teapot from Grandma Jankauskas's tea service and four porcelain tea cups. Amanda set the cookies down on the coffee table and looked around the room. She commented on the bookcase covering one entire wall. "Those are a lot of books, Mr. Coleman. Have you read them all?"

"Not the Collier's, but most of the others."

"Dad's a Book of the Month man, Amanda. He has a great collection of 'The Making of the President,' Michener, Faulkner, Steinbeck, and many others."

"Impressive. Did you make the bookcase, Mr. Coleman?"

"David and I took many weeks to put it together."

"So, dad, what are you planting today?" asked David reaching for the cookies and offering one to Amanda, then Dave.

Vera poured the tea and gave each a cup. "Sugar cubes are in this bowl," she offered removing the silver lid.

"Your silver tea service is quite impressive, Mrs. Coleman."

"It was my mother's. I'm glad you like it. The silver service was made in Lithuania. My father, Walter, made that beautiful cart."

"I found some zinnia seeds from last year's flowers," said Dave, "I and wanted to see if they would come up around the boulder out front."

"My dad is a master gardener, Amanda, whether flowers or vegetables. You should have seen the ten-foot tall horseradish he grew last year. We had enough horseradish for the entire neighborhood."

"Horseradish mostly grows itself, but the plant was impressive," said Dave after sipping his tea, "Would you care for a jar of horseradish, Amanda? Don't be afraid to say no, it's an acquired taste."

"I like horseradish on hot dogs and roast beef, Mr. Coleman and I would appreciate some. Thank you."

"Here you go Amanda. Here are the sugar cubes in case you prefer your tea sweet. I hope you like the cookies, David certainly does," said Mrs. Jackson.

"These cookies are delicious, Mrs. Coleman. I like Toll House that bend ever so slightly before they break. May I try some sugar?"

"Of course, Amanda. David, you need not stand on principle, have a cookie. You too Dave."

"Do you see much of Ben these days?" asked Dave.

"Ben lives with you in the townhouse? I'll bet he's gone most of the time, knowing Ben," added Vera.

"Days at the Naval Hospital, nights running with the EMTs; he keeps busy. He stays overnight once in a while. We get to eat dinner together a couple time a week. Ben makes meatloaf and I do fish," replied David.

"Amanda, I wanted to ask you if you have any idea of what you'll do after medical school," asked Vera.

"So far pathology is most interesting."

"Doing autopsies and that sort of thing?"

"No, I am more interested in investigating cancer in cells in the subdiscipline referred to as cytopathology and some of the causes, perhaps related to viral infections."

"Amanda is doing research in her free time, mom. Really cutting-edge work. Where she finds the time I'll never know, but it could lead to strategies to prevent certain cancers, which is really exciting," added David.

"Good for you Amanda. You were an English major in college and also play the flute? You are certainly a busy person," said Dave between bites of the cookie.

"And David, are your studies to your liking?" asked Vera.

"I have not considered them to my liking, mom, they just are. I do enjoy the difficult challenge of learning so much new information."

"Amanda, David has told us you and he study together and that it seems to improve your comprehension."

"Oh, definitely, Mr. Coleman. David often has a slightly different take on the lectures than me and by comparing notes we cover the material twice, which seems to be beneficial when the exams roll around."

Mrs. Coleman passed the cookie plate to Amanda. "Do you have time to see the city, perhaps have a dinner at a nice restaurant?"

"We try to find the time for fun, Mrs. Coleman. David and I have been able to get to the Art Museum, see a couple plays, and the occasional movie."

"Speaking of time, Mom, thanks for the cookies, but we've got to get back to Philly."

"Dave stood up, "I'll run out into the garage for that jar of horseradish if you still want it, Amanda."

"Absolutely, Mr. Jackson, and thanks for the tea and cookies Mrs. Jackson."

"Vera, please, Amanda."

"Ok, thank you Vera. I hope David and I can return the favor and treat you to a day in Philly some time."

"I'd love that, Amanda."

"Here you go Amanda, don't be afraid to ask me for more if you run out," said Dave handing Amanda a quart sized bottle. David chuckled at the thought of Amanda ever running out of horseradish.

"Thank you, Mr. Coleman."

"We really have to get going," said David, "I'll give you a call later in the week."

"I wrapped up some cookies for the ride home, I know you didn't eat many."

"Thanks Mom."

David kissed his mom and dad. Amanda shook Dave's hand, Vera hugged Amanda and walked them to the front door.

"Come back any time, you two."

"Bye Mom, bye Dad."

David held the car door for Amanda. "Putting on a show for the folks, huh?" she said.

"Whatever do you mean? I hold the door for you at least once a month," David laughed.

"Can we take 95 back to save time?"

"My thought exactly. We can visit the Brandywine some other time, maybe check out the River Museum and canoe down to Thompson's Bridge. You do canoe?"

"Girl scout canoe and rowing badge certified, boy'oo."

CHAPTER THIRTY-SIX

Visit to the Barnes Foundation

One morning over coffee, David asked Amanda if she would like to visit one of the world's greatest collections of French impressionist paintings.

"I have always enjoyed going to the Philadelphia Art Museum. I also enjoy the Rodin," replied Amanda.

"I also love the Philly Art Museum and the Rodin, but I am talking about another great art collection. This one is in Merion, The Barnes Foundation. We could take a train and spend the day immersed in great art. What do you say?"

"If you say it's a great museum, then what can I say but let's go."

"I'll call for reservations. It has free admission, but because it is located within the home of Mr. Albert Barnes space is somewhat limited. I was there once before years ago. I doubt any new French masters have popped up recently. It was founded in 1922 and Dr. Barnes used his considerable fortune to acquire the paintings. He developed Argyrol, a silver compound used to treat ocular infections, still used today."

David and Amanda took the 8:00 am commuter train to Merion Station where it was a short walk to the Barnes home. The line for admission was short at that time of day and after they hung up their coats David led Amanda around the home.

"How did Barnes collect all these French masterpieces?" asked Amanda, expressing her amazement.

"Barnes was incredibly fortunate to be able to travel to France at the time that Renoir, Cezanne, Monet, Manet, Matisse, Gauguin, Seurat, Van Gogh, Picasso, and many others were essentially starving artists, producing many works of art and at the same time their work was significantly undervalued."

"So, Barnes was able to snatch up the early works of these masters before the world caught on," observed Amanda.

"Furthermore, Barnes kept the paintings in his home and was somewhat secretive about his couple hundred master works. You see he did not often loan them out to other museums, which miffed not a few powerful people in the art world."

"This sounds amazing."

"Oh, it is. You can see that Barnes also had an eye for wrought iron works such as hinges and locks, as well as furniture, and ceramics that were placed with and complemented the paintings. This room we're in is a great example of the juxtapositions of Renoir's painting of women and men in formal attire 'Leaving the Conservatoire' positioned over that elegant green, wooden trunk with a blue and grey ceramic bowl flanked by two brass figures. I also enjoy how Barnes hung smaller paintings above the larger ones to complement them both. Plus, Barnes hung iron pieces above the pairs of paintings."

"I don't think I've seen you so excited, David."

"I would love to live in a home that is as full of art as this one," he replied.

"A home filled with art of this caliber is not going to happen, David, but now I see where you got the idea of suspending those six by six inch paintings from your bedroom ceiling."

"I know I will have to make do with reproductions of the masterworks, small ones at that, but I can dream, can't I?"

Amanda and David spent the better part of Saturday walking through the rooms on the first and second floors.

"I took two semesters of Art History at Delaware," said David,

"Even then I tended to favor the Impressionists for their color and soft styles."

"I must admit I am more than a little overwhelmed at this point, David. Do you think you could tear yourself away and take me to lunch?" asked Amanda.

"It was not my intent to overload you, especially on your first visit. Yes, let's go grab lunch. We can come back someday soon."

Back on the train Amanda asked David which painting he liked the most.

"That's a difficult one, so many different artists, different styles, different subjects. I would have to say Renoir's 'Mother and Child' is so gentle and the child so real, so happy and healthy. I equally enjoy Cezanne's 'Mont Sainte-Victoire' and his still life paintings of fruit."

"I would have thought you'd say Van Gogh's 'Postman' was your favorite."

"I enjoy Van Gogh for his aggressive strokes and color combinations he used to depict scenes of everyday life. Renoir is so soft and his colors don't attack me, Cezanne either."

"What painting sticks with you, Amanda?"

"I also thought the Renoirs were top notch. The 'Bather and Maid' or the 'Bathers in the Forest' are so, well, fleshy," chuckled Amanda, "Not that I want to emulate those ladies. Did you like the painting of the tall, thin woman by Mogdelione that was toward the back?"

"You are as beautiful as any of those women, Amanda."

"Thanks, but I'll never look as serene as that one young lady. I also enjoyed the Surat in his pointillistic style. His people were a bit stilted but appeared to be enjoying their day in the park beside the water."

"I also thought the Surat people, although depicted to be walking, really did not convey motion. Van Gogh does a much better job with motion," added David.

“Do you have an idea for lunch?”

“I was thinking of the Crepes’ restaurant near Rittenhouse Square. Sound okay?”

“Let’s just get there, I’m starving.”

CHAPTER THIRTY-SEVEN

Apple Pies

Professor Armitage finished reviewing the sympathetic and parasympathetic nervous systems involved in controlling intestinal and urinary tract function fifteen minutes early. It was the Friday before Thanksgiving and Amanda walked up the stairs in the lecture hall and sat next to David.

"Want to help me make an apple pie?"

"Absolutely," replied David, "My mom taught me how to make pie dough and wrote a great recipe on a 3 by 5 card that I used all through college. Would you be interested in walking to the Reading Market to pick up apples. We could make two or three pies, but I need to buy another pie plate and some spices."

"I've never been to the Reading Market."

"It's in the old Reading railroad station on Broad and Market. Want to pick up a fish and make dinner tonight?"

"I get to pick out the fish," said Amanda. "First, we go home and change. Pick me up at my place in half an hour."

David ran back to his place, dumped the books out of his backpack, grabbed a couple plastic bags and an extra fifty bucks from his stash and high tailed it to Amanda's place. By the time he rounded the corner onto Locust he saw Amanda waiting on the sidewalk in front of her brownstone. She had on blue shorts and a tightfitting pink tee shirt on that left little to David's imagination.

"David you're looking sporty in the black shorts and the teal, collared golf shirt combo."

"I bought them at Wanamaker's the first time we went out shopping, Amanda."

They walked up Eleventh Street to Market hand in hand then to the Reading Market. It was packed with shoppers. David led Amanda into the crowd. On the right was a kiosk with baking supplies. David selected two ten-inch glass pie plates and a pair of eight-inch metal cake pans. Amanda wandered over to the fish while David paid up. He joined her a few minutes later.

"How about Chilean Sea Bass? We could find some green beans and fixings for salad," Amanda said.

"Sea Bass sounds great. Can we throw sliced almonds on the greener beaners?"

"Throw some on the fish as well, David. Does a pound of fish sound like it will be enough for us?"

The couple managed to purchase chocolate covered peanuts and non-pareils while looking for cinnamon, nutmeg, and five-pound bags of sugar and flour.

"Almost forgot the apples, Amanda."

"How about Granny Smith, Braeburn, Honey Crisp, and Pink Ladies, nine of each?"

"That'll be plenty for three pies. I'll grab a couple MacIntosh just for eating."

"We should make the third pie for Mrs. Hopkins."

David loaded the apples into the backpack and hoisted it onto his back. The other purchases were in plastic bags they both carried.

"Next time I'll bring a wagon."

They brought the supplies to Amanda's townhome. Then David

went to his townhouse to pick up his rolling pin and pastry cloth, then re-joined Amanda at her home.

Once back at Amanda's place David set to peeling the apples and placing them in water with lemon juice to keep them from browning. Amanda made the first batch of dough and wrapped it in wax paper and put it into the refrigerator. David was up next and his mom's pie dough recipe differed only slightly. Amanda made the third dough ball and they peeled apples for the next thirty minutes listening to WMMR, waiting for the dough to be ready to roll out.

"Would you like a glass of Bardolino while we make the pies?" offered David.

Amanda said, "The glutens need to hydrate in order that the dough does not crack as we roll it out. An hour later David laid out the rolling cloth which he dusted liberally with flour. Amanda placed her first dough ball down and sliced it in half. David rewrapped the other half in wax paper. He handed the marble rolling pin to Amanda who expressed a great deal of envy. Amanda rolled out the dough in short order, folded it in half and expertly placed it in her pie plate. She rolled out the second half while David mixed the proper assortment of apples with sugar, cinnamon, and a touch of nutmeg. Once the apples were piled, heaping, onto the dough, David dropped a few butter slices on the apples and Amanda placed dough on top, poked a few air holes, and David applied a spritz of water to the dough followed by a sprinkle of sugar.

"One down," said Amanda.

Amanda rolled out the second and third portions of dough while David again prepared the mixture of apples sugar, and spices.

"I like the rolling cloth," said Amanda, "It lets me lift the dough into place without tearing it."

The dough and apples found their way into the next pie plates and Amanda set about pinching the edges and slicing off the excess. She almost made the major faux pas of throwing the excess dough into the trash, but David rescued the dough, balled it up and rolled it out.

"What are you doing?"

"Making snicker doodles. Roll out the dough, add cinnamon, sugar, and butter, then slice off coins and bake."

"Ah, cookies," said Amanda.

"Snicker doodles keep the bakers from diving into and eating the pies," replied David.

"Another gift from your mom?"

"Yep."

"Now bake at 400 for fifteen minutes, then drop the temp to 350 for another thirty minutes."

"I'll read some of the Robert Frost poems I picked up today, many I had never read before, although I'd imagine you know Frost all too well with your English degree."

"Actually, he was not on the reading list, but I do know his more popular poems: 'The Road Less Traveled' and 'Walls Make Good Neighbors.' I studied them in High School."

"Well, let me know if I'm boring you, but I really like his style. Tell you what. I'll put on Dvorak's New World Symphony while I read to you. Here, kick off your shoes and lie on the couch. Eyes closed for better listening. I'll watch the timer."

"It appears kind sir that you are actively wooing this baker. I like it."

David read the book of poems first to last and the pies were done in 50 minutes. He'd already taken the Snicker Doodles out before they burned.

Amanda was asleep when David placed the pies on the stove burners to cool. The top crusts were golden brown, and the house smelled wonderfully of apples and sugar. David wrote a short note thanking Amanda for a wonderful night and said he'd call he in the morning. David realized his feelings for Amanda had become more protective and that he loved every part of her. He felt a warmth when he gazed upon her sleeping form and wanted to lie down and hold her, but knew he'd wake her. She obviously needed some extra sleep. Amanda did not stir when the door clicked shut. He carried that warm feeling back to his place and slept well himself with a smile on his face.

"Is this Love?" Whitesnake

CHAPTER THIRTY-EIGHT

Third Social Committee Meeting

"Hey Don, its Sunday and I want a beer. Can you stop studying soon?"

"Now is as good a time as any, and I really am not enjoying ethics. Seems all too self-evident. The pathology final seems so much more important."

"Maybe you'll be involved in a patient care situation where the family wants one thing, such as prolonging their father's life at all costs, but the patient had already signed a do not resuscitate advance directive."

"Well it's not going to be an issue tonight, so let's go grab a beer with the ladies."

"I'll call and ask Lisa and Cindi," said David dialing the phone.

"We were just saying it's time to grab you guys and head out for a beer," said Lisa.

"Amanda and I made apple pies. I'm bringing one for us,' said David.

"Apple pie and beer can't be beat," said Lisa.

"Don and I will be there in ten minutes"

Once in Watson's Pub Don bought the pitcher, this time Michelob. There were a few other tables with two or three people sipping their beers. David did not recognize any of them so set about slicing into the apple pie. He was smart enough to give a slice to the bartender, who supplied plates and was very impressed with the pie. Cindi poured the Michelob and then raised her glass in a toast to Florence, "That she not be forgotten."

"Let the record show that the members of the 10th Floor Social Committee members miss her terribly."

"Amen to that."

"Apple pie and beer, this is a first," said Don, "I like it."

"So, she was torn up about her failing grade in pharmacology?" asked Cindi.

"She had a real mental block when it came to medications, especially opioids," offered David, "Her brother died of a heroin overdose having been addicted to Oxycodone prescribed for shoulder pain."

"Didn't you tell me he was strung out on black tar heroin but got his hands on some China White," asked Don.

"He did not make allowances for the difference in potency," replied David.

"Such a waste of someone who I hear was a really good athlete," said Lisa.

"To Florence's brother, may he rest in peace and perhaps meet up with his sister in the afterlife." David raised his glass and all chinked together.

"So that's a sad way to start our meeting," said Don, "Anything good happen this past week?"

"Don and I passed our exams," said David.

Lisa asked, "Anyone know Tom Ferrari?"

"Why? I know him from Wednesday group, but not well," replied Don.

"He asked me out yesterday, wants to go to the art museum. I don't know much about him, nor do I know what kind of art he is interested in checking out."

"I would say, Tom's a good guy and the Art Museum will be good, no matter which floor you visit. Of course, I'm all for the Impressionists. I don't know if there is a special exhibit or not. I'd go," said David.

"Okay, I'll take a chance on high art. Not my thing, but a date's a date," Lisa chuckled.

"My CPR class went well, although I don't like practicing on the female manikin," added Cindi, "Now a handsome young male mannikin would stimulate my interest in CPR."

"Cindi, you are a reprobate," said Don.

"I heard the CPR mannikins are all modeled after a young woman named Annie, who actually died, because no one in her group knew CPR. Evidently, Annie had a heart condition and could have been saved with just the basics," said Lisa.

"I think it was her father who started making the CPR practice mannikins," said David.

"That is so sad," said Lisa.

Don raised his glass, "A toast to dear Annie and her father. Many lives have been saved."

CHAPTER THIRTY-NINE

Women's Support Group

Amanda noticed that a number of her women friends were having problems keeping their classwork and their social lives going simultaneously. She decided to start a women's support group, inviting her close friends, but sent word to all women at Jefferson, no matter which class. A dozen women came to that first meeting at Amanda's home, some had heard that Amanda had baked a couple apple pies.

Karen was especially excited that Amanda had taken the initiative to get the women together. "There are so many issues for a group of women like this to discuss. Study habits, social interactions and making new friends, taking time away from Jeff to explore the things Philly has to offer, and learning what it takes to be a successful student while still keeping my identity," said Karen opening up the discussion. "By the way, Amanda, this is a lovely townhome. You were fortunate to land it so close to Jeff."

Most of the women admitted that the sheer volume of material was a huge change from their undergraduate classes and that they worried about keeping their grades up under the huge weight of studying.

Mary said, "The skills I learned in my undergraduate years at U Conn to triage the work have become critical at Jeff. I have learned to rank courses based on how much or how little I know on the subject and spend more or less time reading in the texts or going over lecture notes."

Another issue was that many were concerned that their social lives were being compromised by all the time they needed to study as Karen had mentioned.

"How about I cut some apple pie and we enjoy this one simple pleasure. I bought a few different tea bags and I can put the kettle on to boil," offered Amanda.

"Did you make the pies, Amanda?" asked Joan, "I haven't had a homemade pie in a year."

"David and I spent an evening making three pies. David introduced me to the Reading Market. If you have not been there, it literally has everything you need to make dinner or apple pie," offered Amanda.

"Can I help and get out plates and forks, Amanda?" offered Diane.

"Plates are in the second cabinet on the left of the sink, cups are in the cabinet to the right. Forks are in the drawer to the left of the sink."

Once the pies were sliced and on the plates each woman selected a tea bag and a cup. Karen poured the hot water into each of the cups, so the tea could steep.

"Dig in everyone. Be sure to thank David for the pie when you see him."

"I don't know David," admitted Susan, "I know this will sound silly, but where does he sit in lecture?"

"Middle section, usually tenth row back, and six seats in on the left," replied Amanda. "He is the handsome one that produces the verbatim lecture notes for the note service, so I'm sure you've seen his work."

"His notes are amazing, Amanda, does he just tape record the lectures, then type them up?" asked Sarah.

"He does not use a recorder. As far as I know, David developed his own short hand in grad school and also has a special talent for comprehending what the Professors are going to say next."

"I remember that Japanese Professor. Her accent was so difficult to decipher, but it seemed David was able to accurately get all the lecture points," added Karen.

"It was particularly difficult for me to take notes that day. I believe David went to talk with her. He told me she was very gracious and not all insulted that he had clarifying questions," replied Amanda.

"I'll bet she was thrilled that he took such an interest in getting her lecture points down correctly. She must know that her accent is a bit tough to listen to," said Carol.

"May I request we get back to the matters at hand?" asked Amanda.

"I would like to know from you, Amanda, whether you have found studying with David, or any partner, extremely useful. I know you and David are a thing but is a study partner something we all should pursue?" asked Betty.

"David was the one to offer it and I have found it extremely useful. His take on lecture points is often different from mine and sometimes I have completely missed the ball on an important statement," admitted Amanda.

"I'll bet David would say the same about your contributions, Amanda," said Sara.

"David is good with lists, I am better with the overarching themes and tend to neglect the items in lists."

"Well, I want to try working with a study partner," said Betty. "I live on the fifth floor in Orlowitz. Anyone think I would be a reasonable match for a study mate?"

"Let's give it a try, Betty," replied Karen. "I live on fourth floor, 404 and we could meet at my apartment tomorrow night after dinner and see how we work together."

"Okay. Six o'clock apartment 404."

A number of the other women paired off and set study times.

"I would like Mary to discuss a little about her triage process that she finds so useful," said Diane. "My style is to pile the work and start at the top, usually finding sleep is competing with the next to last assignment, which makes it difficult to say I give the last couple things equal attention."

"I find that if I go through the pile and pick out the ones I'm especially weak on, or that are going to be more important at exam time, let's say pathology versus clinical skills," replied Mary. "I will put the path near the top. For me, physiology is another tough subject that I'm going to spend more time on and will need to be fresh."

"Do we have time for one more item?" asked Martha. "I want to go out with a certain man but find it difficult to allocate time with him as important as another couple chapters in path."

Sara offered, "I had the same concerns, but Amanda suggested I start with a coffee break, then move up to dinner or a movie if all goes well and the time spent seems valuable enough."

"We gotta eat. So maybe designating a date and dinner instead of eating alone may be a reasonable way to accomplish both," added Susan. "Who knows, I may meet someone this way who will match at the same hospital as me a few years down the road. I'd already have someone I know in intern year, regardless of the romantic potential."

"Good point," said Mary. "I hadn't thought about the intern year as a starting over of the loneliness and isolation. I'd like to already know someone, regardless of which Department we ended up in."

"Thanks for the wonderful pie, Amanda."

"Thanks also for organizing this get together."

"Can we plan to do this on a regular basis," asked Karen. "I'm sure other things will come up or have not been covered tonight. I suggest a monthly meeting and I volunteer my apartment in Orlowitz for next month. It'll be cookies. I am not a pie maker."

"Thanks for coming," said Amanda. "Karen, can your place accommodate a larger group in case others hear about it or we chose to invite someone?"

"I'll round up some extra chairs," said Betty, "We will see if we fit. So, its Apartment 404 in Orlowitz at six thirty and bring a guest and bring some burning questions for this august group."

The group stood and a few exchanged promises to try to be study partners as they were leaving Amanda's townhome.

"Well that went very well for a first meeting," thought Amanda. "I did not learn much, but I have my relationship with David and we've somehow managed to get a few things right."

CHAPTER FORTY

Wear a Dress Day

Not all of the calls for general class participation went as planned. David uncharacteristically entered the fray writing 'Wear a Dress Day' on the blackboard, but unfortunately mistakenly dated it for the day of the Pathology Final, a must pass or repeat the year exam. Nevertheless, David dressed up in a long wrap-around brown Hawaiian print, Birkenstocks, and a sleeveless gold colored shirt, both borrowed from Lisa. Simply walking into Jeff Hall and up the escalator drew catcalls from the janitorial staff. The escalator was on the fritz and was nothing more than a metal staircase to climb to the class room floor. David walked over to an empty seat at the lab table that would serve as his test site for the Path final. Dr. Carlos intercepted him and asked David to stand on the table and turn around for all to see his outfit. From where he stood on the lab table David could see he was the only one to wear a dress that day, women or men. David struggled to finish all the 800 questions and was unsure of the accuracy of his answers on quite a few. He wiped his brow with the back of his hand and realized there were quite a few areas of Pathology that he really was not up on, but he was satisfied he gave it his best effort. David did not remember walking back to his row home after the exam. He was mentally shot and physically fatigued. Amanda was probably in the same state and did not offer to eat lunch with him.

The most amazing thing was that after the exam was over David found no one who recalled seeing him standing on the lab table in a dress, such was the intense pressure of the day. This particular exam was extremely challenging, but Professor Carlos had been in the habit for years of placing all of the preceding ten years of tests with answers in the Library for all to study. The trick was that the exam was 800 questions long and many students were still challenged to reach the final question, never mind recalling most of the correct answers.

At least I scored 92%, better than my usual 86%," thought David. "It's taken me a few exams for to realize that my 100% scores at Delaware are a thing of the past. I'm in the 86% group now and that is that."

David made a conscious decision to accept this and not go crazy studying all the time to improve his scores. There were a few students that scored in the high 90's and they were revered or envied. Susan was one such woman who almost never attended lectures, instead opting to work her almost full-time job making twenty dollars per hour as a cashier at an A & P in order to pay for tuition, room and board. She was a charter member of Group C and was able to make excellent use of the note service. Amazing. David learned that not all students needed to follow his trifecta for studying. Some of his classmates like Susan went into the surgical specialties, which involved a different kind of memory, more muscle memory, to succeed. David continued to take copious notes, whether for the note service or for Amanda and himself to review.

A few days after the path exam a story circulated that three students had been caught cheating. According to what was a very tasty rumor, one of David's classmates had struck up a fairly intense relationship with one of the secretaries in the Pathology Department. She supposedly obtained a copy of the pathology final exam the week prior and had given it to her boyfriend. He and his two buddies had spent the next week at the library looking up those questions and their answers. No one seemed to know how the three brought the answers into the test, it seemed unlikely they would have memorized eight hundred answers, otherwise why cheat? Needless to say, they were suspected of cheating, confronted and the truth was revealed by the heartbroken and misused secretary. David never learned what penalty had been imposed but a blue Porsche Boxer was not seen again. Whether the three were forced to repeat the second year or simply expelled did not trickle down to students on David's level.

When David heard the story he thought, "At the end of the day I need to learn, retain, and pass, before moving onto the next challenge," he said, and to reassure himself, "And I want to balance classwork with my love life."

CHAPTER FORTY-ONE

Movies

Amanda and David had studied for the pathology exam all week and were burned out now that the exam was finally behind them.

Amanda put down her notes and said, "David, would you want to see the 'Rocky Horror Picture Show' at the TLA?"

"I've never seen it but know the general plot. Sure, I'd love to see it live. The TLA is just around the corner on South Street."

"People show up to the show in costume and pack water pistols for the rain scene," Amanda said, "You don't have to dress up, but you'd better bring a raincoat or you're likely to get soaked."

"What time does it start? I'll call and reserve seats," said David.

"Seven thirty. I'll run home and change. Be back in half an hour," added Amanda.

Once Amanda returned wearing a long raincoat. They walked the few blocks to the TLC hand in hand in silence. David was still mentally exhausted, but glad to be out with Amanda. He suspected her brain was as fried as his.

"Not much of a line," said David when they got close to the theater.

"Oh, wait until we get inside," replied Amanda, "I hear its always packed."

"I'll go to Will Call, you grab a place in line."

David returned to the line with the tickets. "You we not kidding. Its packed. Just look at the costumes."

“How do you like my outfit?” Amanda said opening her raincoat.

“You’re gorgeous as usual, Amanda. I know that you are wearing an outfit representing the main female character, but I forget the woman’s name.”

“I’m Janet Weiss. You like the dress?”

“Everything about you. Very sexy. I can’t believe all these people in costume. They walked into the theater. “Why are they lining up along the sides?”

“Characters in costume are part of the show. You grab a seat and watch,” said Amanda as she took her place along the side of the theater with the other costumed characters.

David said hello to the couple in the seats adjacent to his.

“I’m Samantha and this is Bob. Have you done this before?”

“No,” replied David, “I heard there’s a lot of singing. Does everyone sing every song? I wish I had brought along a script.”

“You’ll catch on,” Samantha said, “Just go with the flow during the singalongs. Did you bring a water pistol?”

“Amanda, my girlfriend, told me about that. Will this be okay? Who do we spray?”

“Not us. Just shoot up in the air. You’ll know when.”

David pointed Amanda out to Samantha and Bob.

“She’s pretty. Nice Janet costume. Look, she’s even got her Janet moves down.”

“I’ll bet she watched the movie and practiced the moves,” replied David.

“I really like the Time Warp song, can’t wait for it,” said Bob.

“Time Warp,” Rocky Horror

The three of them sang along as best as they could, enjoying the spectacle on stage.

“I can’t believe Amanda, I mean Janet, is really killing it,” said David to Bob.

"She's a quick study, that's for sure, David."

"Here comes the finale," announced Samantha.

After the rocket ship blasted off the curtain closed to loud and long applause. Shortly afterwards Amanda came over to where David, Samantha, and Bob were sitting. "So, how'd you like it?"

"Amanda, or should I say Janet, you were amazing. How long did you practice?"

"I was able to watch the Show once years ago. Took more time than I planned to get Janet's costume together."

"Well, let me introduce you to Samantha and Bob who come here a lot."

"You were great as a Janet understudy, Amanda. Maybe we'll see you again next time," Samantha added as she and Bob walked up the aisle.

"How about we go for a drink?" asked Amanda.

"You pick, I'll pay."

Two weeks later they enjoyed the 'Seven Percent Solution' in the grandeur of the Chestnut Street Theatre. Neither had known that Sherlock was an opium addict.

David was very bothered by the ending of 'Looking for Mr. Goodbar' and confided this to Amanda, "I probably was sucked into Diane Keaton's erotic, but empty relationships."

"You mean that you were aroused during her scenes with Richard Geer, and then shocked as she is brutally murdered while in the throes of sex with another man," answered Amanda. "I bet that's just what Richard Brooks wanted his male moviegoers to experience," she said with a smile.

'Midnight Express' was almost as bothersome, because of the scene in the bathhouse where Billy Haynes defends himself by pithing the guard on a clothes-hook and stealing the guard's uniform to escape. 'The Deer Hunter' scenes where De Niro and Christopher Walken play Russian Roulette until his suicide bothered Amanda more than David. There was a lot of hand holding during those three movies, both in the theatres and during the walks home.

Travolta's 'Saturday Night Fever' was a winner for all, especially listening to the energy of the Brother's Gibb. Not much tension to bother either of them.

For a while they searched out Bogart movies. The Hepburn ones were a bit dated, but the relationship between the characters and the action won them over. Both Amanda and David enjoyed 'African Queen' and of course 'Casablanca.' Amanda recited Ilsa's lines.

David did Rick's classic complaint to Sam, "Of all the gin joints in all the towns in the world, she walks into mine."

They both did Captain Louise's famous 'Round up the usual suspects' without hesitating.

One day after lecture Amanda looked David square in the face and out of the blue announced, "You and I, we need to make a movie someday." She didn't elaborate, and he didn't ask what kind of movie, but filed that idea away. He liked the idea of being with her in the future, no matter what she had plans for.

"Celluloid Heroes," The Kinks

"I think Amanda and I are striking a good balance between studying and doing well on the exams while enjoying the scene in Philly," thought David. "I'm a little anxious about next year's clinical rotations. Amanda and I will be separated for long periods of time, which may prove hard on our relationship. I'll have to be sure to discuss this with Amanda and offer to speak on the phone anytime she wants. I'll find a third year to ask how they dealt with rotations. If I can get most of my clinicals at Delaware Division and survive living at home with my parents, I should be ok. Doing a couple years in Wilmington will be an added bonus. I'll know the attendings, residents, nurses, and lab people. But I don't know what to do about the psych residency. I'd like to get out of Philly for that, but I'm sure

Amanda will match at Jeff. Oh well, this next chunk of time will involve a lot of travel. Wilmington is a short commuter train ride to Philly. It's a plan, but I'll have to make it through the next two years and then hopefully the Match Gods will be kind to us."

CHAPTER FORTY-TWO

Dr. Black and the Dean

David was on note service duty for Dr. Black's lecture dealing with breast resection for malignancy. As in the past Dr. Black's lectures were attended by fewer than twenty students and half left soon after they saw David was the person taking notes. It wasn't that Dr. Black's lectures were boring, it was more the feedback from his performances in the operating room that turned students off.

As the unlucky student in the OR began to sterilize the skin on the woman's chest and breast, Dr. Black's signature oration in the operating room was "Death to the invaders, die, die, die."

Not only did the student applying the betadine solution have to recite these lines, but Dr. Black forced all around the operating table to chant them over and over as the skin was scrubbed. It was more than a little embarrassing for all of the students, but Dr. Black appeared to thrive on the bizarre ritual. David took his surgery rotation in Wilmington and found that his surgeon mentor, Dr. Glass, to be respectful of both the patients and the students, although as a former military surgeon he operated rough and rapidly. His goal was to resect every last cancer cell and his patients required a lot of Demerol for a few days post-op. Most women went home unable to raise her surgical side arm.

David thought it would be a good idea to write a letter to the Dean explaining why attendance at Dr. Black's lectures were so poor. He had some vague notion that a student could make a difference in how the Jefferson machine worked, other than grinding young minds to mush. When the Dean Ollman summoned him to his office on Wednesday at six p.m. David thought it was a kindly invitation to chat. It wasn't.

David had just taken a seat in the chair facing the Dean's desk when Dean Ollman waved his offending letter in David's face, then pulled out David's Jefferson application letter, actually an extended poem, and said, "If WE had known about this you would never have gotten into Jefferson. I have shared your letter with Dr. Black who assured me it was nonsense and that you were not welcome in his operating suite."

David had been under the impression that writing the application letter as a poem served two purposes. One to convey the requested biographical information and second to lend a literary flavor to the extremely dry material. The rhymes were adequate, and few were forced. David had been proud that Professor Yahuda said he'd enjoyed it and had said "Welcome to Jefferson." It wasn't until David had left the Dean in the administration building and was halfway to his apartment that he began to sweat at the realization he had been very naïve and very, very close to being kicked out for challenging a powerful Jefferson surgeon.

If nothing else, this experience remained an active memory as he proceeded through his clinical rotations and through the internship years. He never, but once, challenged the people in power, and that was totally appropriate. He was praised for bringing up that particular issue regarding patient care in a Morbidity and Mortality Conference. David began to pay more attention to hospital politics and power structures. Having been an IV nurse in the past he still was in the habit of developing strong friendships with the nurses and hospital staff from phlebotomists to lab techs, radiology techs, and the men and women who cleaned the rooms. Patients could not move from the emergency room to the floor beds without proper preparation. David made quite a few beds to help the nurses out while on call at night and had no problem pushing patients on their gurneys to their new rooms. He was always there to lift patients up onto their pillows in their beds when it was obvious the micro nurses were going to injure their backs. It was a no brainer that running to the pharmacy for the medications he ordered allowed the nurses to attend to the patient's other needs, especially when they were short staffed on night shift. He developed strong relationships with the floor and charge nurses as a result of just a little extra assistance here and there. His time as an IV nurse while in medical school proved extremely valuable. He knew the IV nurses and they trusted him not to be wasting their time when he called for ASAP assistance. David also learned a lot about giving IV chemotherapy and the nausea it caused in some people. This was all in the days before using ventilator hoods was standard practice.

"I wonder how much exposure I had to Cytoxan, Adriamycin, Mitomycin and the others that I drew up from ampules into syringes," wondered David. Once home he forgot Dr. Black, Dean Ollman, and his anxiety. "I'll go running tonight," he thought. It was a cold night. Snow had piled up on the cars and Eighth Street was barely wide enough for a Volkswagen beetle to pass so he ran in the street instead of on the impassable sidewalks. The footing was a bit of a challenge, but David did not fall despite major slips a couple of times. He was glad he opted to wear gloves as he had to push off snow covered cars a couple times when the tire tracks in the snowy street led him too close to the parked vehicles. Overall, running was the most pleasurable part of his day, other than when he spent time with Amanda. When he was alone with his thoughts and was able to process the events of the day, and despite having the physical challenge of making it through the snowy streets he felt free.

"I guess I really enjoy being alone sometimes, as much as I value my time with Amanda. I can push and challenge myself with a sprint, or slow my pace, take my time and look around at the row houses. Either way I'm not head down in a textbook, reviewing notes, or worrying about the exam tomorrow," he thought.

He could see the Vet ahead and there was a crowd at the Spectrum that night, whether for a game or concert, David didn't know, but the path around the Vet was clear and David was back on Seventh Street in no time.

When David returned to his place he thought, "I wonder what my core temperature is after these runs. I'm covered with snow and ice. How many layers of clothing can I remove before I feel the cold?"

He sat down cross legged on the bricks in front of his townhouse and started peeling off his hat, gloves, coat, and sweatshirt.

"I'm not feeling the cold yet, so off with the shoes, socks, and sweats."

He sat there in his blue shorts, the Stones tee shirt in the pile next to him, his bare chest steaming away.

"I'm not feeling the cold at all. My core temp must be way up tonight. Running all the way to the Vet and back without stopping really got the blood boiling. That's progress," he thought.

He let his mind wander into the sounds of the city. The occasional ambulance siren, cars driving on Walnut Street, people walking by.

"Lord knows what they are thinking about the crazy, half naked man sitting on the bricks,' he mused. After fifteen minutes cross legged on the ice he began to feel cold, so he gathered his clothes, opened his front door, headed for a hot shower, then bed. He listened to Rhymin' Simon for a few minutes before he felt ready to sleep. He was asleep in a few minutes.

"Cold As Ice," Foreigner

CHAPTER FORTY-THREE

Amanda's Summer Plans

"What are you thinking of doing this summer, Amanda?"

"I'd like to work on my HPV project, at least for a month, then travel with my family to Minnesota for our annual weeklong visit to the cabin on the lake. Its lovely there. I hope you and I can someday go there and spend some down time together," Amanda said to David giving him a kiss.

"Sounds great, but that will have to wait for a year, perhaps if we can coordinate a week during our first residency summer. Does your family own the cabin?"

"Oh, heavens no. We've rented from the same people each year for as long as I can remember. It sits right on the water. They have a canoe and a great dock to jump into the somewhat freezing water. Fishing is wonderful and the next cabin over is probably a quarter mile away. Its very secluded, very pristine."

"My family took a week in August every year and traveled to New England, Bar Harbor or Mt. Katahdin, Maine. We often went to the White Mountain range in New Hampshire, climbed all the Presidential peaks, even as young kids. My sister and I did Mt. Washington alone and started in warm weather at the base in shorts and tee shirts, only to get to the summit where a snowstorm was raging. My Mom and Dad drove up and rescued us."

"What are your plans for your summer?"

David smiled and replied, “I am trying to wrangle a position at NIH to work in a research lab. Dr. Taylor suggested his friend in the parathyroid section may need a bottle washer.”

“Where would you live?”

“I have looked into getting an apartment at a place called Turkey Thicket.”

“Oh yes, I remember, right next to Catholic U.”

“I thought living there would give me access to the University’s cultural events and perhaps use of their library. Maybe even join a soccer team and keep in shape.”

“Well it seems you have a great plan. I hope the job at NIH comes through. Will it pay much money?”

“Enough to live on. I plan to ride my Schwinn to and from NIH to save on gas, although there is the Metro stop at Catholic for rainy days. I’ll bet a bus could get me there as well.”

“I did not take the Metro towards Bethesda while I was at Catholic, but going downtown was very easy and safe.”

“I’d like to try to visit you in Philly when you get back from Minnesota. I won’t be able to last an entire summer without seeing you, Amanda.”

“Ditto, and not just to see you, my love.”

“I’ll let you know when my NIH plans firm up.”

CHAPTER FORTY-FOUR

Pharmacology Lecture

Once inside the lecture hall, David took his usual seat and dated the notepad for today's lecture. Dr. Jane was the Pharmacology Department's and perhaps Jefferson's most colorful and humorous Professor. He was able to take dry lists of medications, receptors, interactions, and the resulting drug-drug adverse effects, some potentially lethal, and make them memorable. His favorite quip was "Nothing is irrelevant!" He repeated it more than once some days. David found himself making lists much as he did during the paleontology and mineralogy lectures at Delaware. He had enjoyed mastering the hundreds of fossil and mineral names and being able to spit them out on the exams and usually got 100% correct.

"It took a lot of repetitious studying up until the morning before the exam, but it was worth getting the A," he said to himself, recalling how it was relatively easy to memorize huge lists. He did not remember that during the first couple of his undergraduate years he did little more than study every night. He considered the fact that quite a few of the hard-fought names had been consigned to the cranial-rectal shunt after so many years.

"You have a scientific background, David, unlike me," Amanda had remarked the other night. "I find the concept of receptors and drug detoxification by the hepatic Cytochrome P 450 system mystifying at the least. I have no comparable framework in poetry or music to fall back on to make sense of it. I find myself simply memorizing terms and relationships without a clue of the overall picture. Do you have a visual framework you could give me to make sense of it all?"

"Sure. Here, I'll draw you a picture," replied David, "The liver has hepatocytes capable of binding certain medications, taking them up and detoxifying them using specific enzymes. The resulting compounds are attached to salts and excreted into the bile. The bile and the medications travel out through the GI tract. So, you have to have an intact circulatory system to deliver the medications to the liver, a viable liver with bile ductwork, and functional intestine able to move the compounds out. Anywhere along this pathway problems can arise and the medications and resulting detoxified compounds can back up."

"This must be why Dr. Shep stressed that anatomy was critical in all disciplines. A gall stone could prevent excretion and lead to an accumulation of medications that would cause problems."

"I've never taken more than a few medications my whole life and I've never been really ill," David confided to Amanda one night while they studied together.

"We're lucky to have been so healthy."

"Just fill up the old brain with a few hundred new names," he added, "That's what we need to do now."

"I wish we had some clinical experiences to flesh out the medications. Studying names, effects and adverse interactions may be important, but I want to hear Cephalexin and know what cellulitis looks like," said Amanda.

The sheer weight of the number of medications and their actions threatened to pop their collective fuses. When Dr. Jane told a story about a resident who had not paid proper attention in class it started to make sense. The young physician failed to research the potential for drug-drug actions and clearance through the liver via the Cytochrome P-450 detoxifying system. One medication added to a preexisting regimen of cardiac anti-arrhythmics caused a life-threatening arrhythmia called Torsade de Pointe. Luckily, the third-year resident recognized the problem on the rhythm strip and looked over the medications, identifying the combination at fault. This occurred before five o'clock when the A team was still around. If it had occurred at one A.M. the patient may have coded and perhaps died. Needless to say, that Intern never forgot the lesson of checking out the interactions before adding new medications to the mix. Amanda commented that Dr. Jane's inclusion of the cautionary tale was perhaps more valuable than all the lists of medications, actions, and interactions that had preceded it.

David admitted he felt humbled by the story and that his technique of simply memorizing medication names was not going to be sufficient to rise to the level of being an adequate, nor a wise, physician.

"Come on, David, this is first semester. You've discovered an important flaw in your study technique early on. You'll now move on with a better strategy," reassured Amanda. "I once fretted about making a mistake on a single note in a flute solo, but I learned to move past the errors and make the rest of the song enjoyable. You'll do better the next time."

"Speaking of music, would you be interested in going to hear Southside Johnny Saturday?"

"That's a great idea, but Brad asked me to go to dinner and to a show at the Trocadero Saturday."

"Brad?"

"One of the guys in my dissection group. Nice guy."

"Well, have fun and tell me about the restaurant and the show," said David, "Maybe we can catch a concert later."

"Sure. Sorry about this one."

They finished studying and while David was walking back to his townhouse, he replayed his conversation with Amanda about her date with Brad. "I'm not sure I am all that happy with her going out with anyone else," he thought, "I wonder if I should have expressed my hesitation to her back there? If it comes up again I'll say something. I'm done studying tonight. I'm going to the Vet."

CHAPTER FORTY-FIVE

Gingerbread Men

Christmas was a week away and the last exam was set for the next morning. David and Amanda got through the exam and David had the idea to make Christmas cookies. After the exam David walked over to the Reading Market and picked up flour, brown sugar, molasses, baking soda, eggs, butter, and confectioner's sugar. He almost forgot the large and small gingerbread cutters. David called Amanda and invited her to his townhouse to make the gingerbread men.

"I haven't made gingerbread for years," replied Amanda, "Do you have the red hearts and little silver balls?"

"I even stole food colors, icing tips, and a pastry bag from my mom last weekend to do frosting details," said David.

Amanda brought a very large steel bowl in which to mix the dough. David had forgotten that little item. David laid out the ingredients on the kitchen table and Amanda selected them in order, by memory. She later admitted she did a quick brush up on the ingredients from 'The Joy of Cooking' before coming over.

"I'm always amazed by the wonderful preparation that you do for any project," he told her. "You've bailed me out many times and I appreciate it so much. Another reason I love and respect you immensely."

Amanda sat cross-legged on the chair holding the stainless-steel bowl in her lap as she mixed the thick gingerbread dough. David thought he'd never seen her look more beautiful and content as in that moment. It was a memory David kept for all his life. David rolled out the dough and firmly pushed the gingerbread cutters into the soft, brown dough. He was in no rush to finish as he was especially enjoying being with Amanda that evening. It felt like they were a loving couple. He placed the baking trays on the table, then placed the gingerbread men on well buttered trays side by side, careful not to bend their arms or legs.

"I have part of a bottle of Brunello. Would you care for a glass?"

A little while later the cookies were baked to perfection and when cool the artists began the intricate process of decorating them. David felt more than a little jealous that Amanda was making this a competition, granted she had more artistic skill for the smiling faces. He was relegated to placing the silver buttons in a row on their jackets, and red balls on the sleeves. Amanda pronounced them masterful.

David decided to make pairs of anatomically correct men and women gingerbread people, which made Amanda laugh. Who gets to eat which one?" she inquired, "I know which one I want."

David lifted one unlucky soldier off the cooling tray and offered Amanda the first bite. She kindly nibbled at his boot. Her expression said the gingerbread was delicious. David chunked off an arm from a gingerbread woman and agreed. The only problem was who was worthy to receive the other gingerbread men. They agreed on Professors Carlos, Jansen, Green, and Paul. David was assigned the job of finding the right boxes, wax paper, and Christmas wrapping paper. If Amanda had asked him to jump over the moon, David would have had little difficulty that night as they washed the bowl and cookie cutters. It was past ten o'clock and David asked Amanda, "Do you want to stay the night? I'll make you a breakfast omelet to die for."

Amanda agreed to stay. David said, "You have a lot of gingerbread on your face that needs to be attended to. Let me take care of that spot," he said, kissing Amanda on the forehead, left cheek, nape of neck, throat, then hard on lips. "You are covered with gingerbread flour and really should take a shower. Turns out you're in luck. I have prepared your boudoir upstairs, fresh towel, shampoo, body wash, and a silk robe to wear afterwards.

"Sounds a little less that spontaneous, this invitation to stay the night, sir."

"Let's Spend the Night Together," Rolling Stones

After showering Amanda entered David's bedroom in a silk bathrobe decorated with dragons.

"Where did you find this?" she asked, twirling around.

"Ben picked that up for me on one of his trips to Thailand. How about I blow dry and brush your hair?"

They sat on the rug, David's legs around Amanda's hips as he dried and brushed her long, blond hair. "I enjoy the feel of your hair passing through my fingers," commented David.

"You are doing a great job, but it seems like you have a bit of a tripod going back there."

"Is it going to be a problem?"

"It all depends where it ends up."

"I believe your legs are a bit dry after your shower. I just happen to have some Nivea and will lotion up your feet and legs, just lie back and relax."

David applied the lotion to her feet, then calves and knees. He spent more time with the lotion on her thighs, especially when massaging the upper inner regions. He reached the areas where legs meet groin and buttocks. "I've just got to plant a kiss on your beautiful, flat tummy, Amanda."

"Now I know you got an A in anatomy, David, but you seem to have forgotten the southern abdominal border. Oh my, that feels wonderful!"

David took a sip of wine and next planted a big kiss on Amanda's mouth, then moved down to her breasts, kissing one then the other.

"Do you have a condom?"

"Yes, in my left pants pocket."

"Your pants seem to have fallen off, but I can reach the pocket. Oh, there are two. You are most confident tonight, sir. And KY Jelly as well."

"All for the woman's pleasure. May I suggest a minute of skin on skin, it will be so nice, then the rubber."

"Come on up and in David. Oh, that's really nice. A minute is up. Where's that rubber?"

"I've never experienced a minute go by so rapidly," said a slightly distressed David.

"Can you assist?"

"My pleasure."

"Now I suggest you hop up in the saddle. Our first time, Amanda."

"Shut up, suck my breasts, grab my buttocks and pull me in tight."

Amanda climaxed before David who gently lifted her up and laid her on her back. He entered her, first gently, then arched his back and thrust in more forcibly, again and again. He held her left breast and lifted her buttocks with his right hand. Amanda lifted her pelvis and climaxed again. David moaned softly and collapsed onto Amanda's chest, holding her tightly with both arms around her back. He rolled off and they slept as spoons.

David and Amanda made love twice that night. The next morning David was up first and made coffee and an omelet with toast and marmalade. Amanda then ran home to change. David met her at the entrance to Jeff Hall and they walked in together.

"I feel very warm and comfortable with you, David. I thought I would experience a tremendous ground shift after making love with you, but it just feels right," said Amanda.

"Let me know if that wonderful feeling drifts toward wanting to repeat that loving night," requested David, taking his usual seat.

CHAPTER FORTY-SIX

Macbeth

David nudged Amanda as she walked past him on the way out of the lecture hall that Friday. "You like Shakespeare?"

"Hamlet's one of my favorites. Why?"

"Macbeth is being performed tonight about three blocks from here. The tickets are fifty bucks."

"I'm in," replied Amanda.

They were able to walk over to the tiny theater and take their seats just as the lights dimmed. Amanda said she recalled the general plot. "I like when the witches chant 'Double, double toil and trouble; Fire, burn; and, caldron, bubble.' Then Lady Macbeth delivers the classic line 'Out damned spot!"

They admired the costumes and the quality of the actors delivering their lines.

"I recall doing a term paper on Macbeth in eleventh grade," recalled David, "The Porter said something about drink being responsible for provoking desire but diminishing performance."

"Could be good advice for future fun," Amanda said. "I really enjoyed the plot development."

"That's what English literature majors always say," replied David. "I didn't see the need to kill so many people. I guess being King was not all I thought it was cranked up to be."

"Can we stop by your place and share a whiskey?"

"I will be extra careful to pace myself tonight. I've been warned by the greatest poet ever."

"I prefer to do a shot first, then sip the second one," said Amanda. "How about we climb the wooden hill and test that bed of yours again."

"You don't have to ask me twice, Amanda," he replied. David followed Amanda up the curved staircase but reached out for her waist before they got to the top. "How about a step kiss?" The kiss was long and hot.

"Whew. I need to visit the loo."

"I'll turn down the sheets and prepare the way."

Their love making was hard and fast. Amanda flopped back on the pillow breathing deeply. "That was intense! What got into you?"

David complained, "I thought that one whiskey diminished my performance, as predicted by the Porter, but I guess it was acceptable."

"Oh, don't be so hard on yourself. Pardon the pun. Love making is wonderful, whether soft, intimate and warm, like our first time, or hard and intense like tonight," reassured Amanda.

"How about I invite you up to sit on my chest and face. I can do my best to make up for my short performance. Yes, that's it. Now relax."

Amanda allowed the waves of pleasure to wash over her as she shifted her pelvis against David's mouth. Her legs tightened their grip on his head and she let out a deep moan, arching backwards and thrusting against his nose before sliding down onto his belly, her head falling against David's chest. Her breathing slowed, and she slept for a time on him.

Amanda rolled off David and cuddled up against him. "That was a wonderful sleep. Just hold me, we don't have to rush to get up on Saturday morning."

David woke with the sun in his eyes. "Those curtains are almost threadbare. I'll have to get new ones. How about scrambled eggs with fontina and peppers?"

"Sounds great, but can I have coffee first?"

"You stay in bed and your loyal servant will deliver it piping hot in a few."

David started the coffee while making the omelet. He ran the cup of Joe to Amanda who was lounging with David's recent SciFi choice, 'The Green Hills of Earth' by Heinlein.

Amanda ran her finger across the books of the shelf and said, "You seem to really enjoy Heinlein. How many do you own?"

"Probably more than twenty. Most are back in Wilmington. I've got to get back to the eggs. I'll bring them up with toast and your choice of strawberry preserves or orange marmalade."

"Quite the chef this morning. Marmalade please. I could easily get used to this," smiled Amanda, settling into the overstuffed pillow to read some more.

CHAPTER FORTY-SEVEN

David's Summer at NIH

David looked up from his vascular notes and said, I'm thinking of applying for a summer internship at the NIH in the arthritis research unit."

"Do you just send in a general application for summer work, or do you have to apply to a specific Section for a specific job?" asked Amanda.

"Dr. Taylor gave the name of the head investigator, Dr. Gerald Aurbach of the parathyroid hormone lab in Building Ten in Bethesda. I hope to be doing bench work on the amino acid structure of PTH. I'm not sure which particular aspect of the project, I'll be assigned to, but I'm sure any job would challenge me."

"Where would you live?"

"I found a place in Turkey Thicket. Yeah, I know, I'd be a turkey for the summer. I plan to ride my bike from that apartment complex adjacent to Catholic University, your old stomping grounds, to Bethesda. I checked out the Metro and bus lines, that would take me hours and I think I could do the ride in thirty minutes if I cut through Rock Creek Park, which is near Walter Reed."

"What's the pay?"

"Just enough for rent, food, and some crazy money. I won't need much for the couple months I'll be there."

"I'll miss you."

"What are your summer break plans?"

"I was going to stay in Philly with Mrs. Hopkins and work on my pathology project. I should be able to make real progress if I go at it five days a week. Any chance you could take Amtrak to Philly on the weekends?"

"That was my plan, if you were going to be around. Don and I will continue to pay rent on the townhouse."

"When would you leave?"

"Pretty much as soon as the semester ends, but I'll have to hear back from the PTH lab about the position first."

"Sounds exciting"

A month later David landed the internship and was able to rent a one bedroom in Turkey Thicket over the phone. He took Amtrak to Union station with his Schwinn and gear and was at work by July first. His first job was to drive to a slaughterhouse in Ellicott City each Tuesday and harvest parathyroid glands from the necks of cattle. It was an intense job. The head of the just slaughtered cow was flipped onto one of six spiked platforms and David had only a few minutes before the Health Inspector came down the row with his knife, cutting the parotid glands looking for tuberculosis. In the process he pretty much destroyed the parathyroid glands, David became adept at rapidly locating and removing the glands before the Inspector trashed the surgical site. After the day's batch of cows were slaughtered and the glands placed on dry ice, David could drive to the Ellicott City Bakery for a dozen donuts and head home. A few times a cow was not struck properly on the skull, with what was essentially a jack hammer. The impact it delivered was not enough to kill the poor beast and was able to roll out of the slaughter pen and run around the room. David believed the men working there really enjoyed taking on the terrified two- ton cows with just their very sharp knives. The cow was always cornered and killed, a chain attached to the hoof and it took its place upside down on the circuit as the men sliced open the belly and chest, dropping all the organs onto the killing floor. The cow was decapitated, skinned and the various cuts of meat quickly removed and placed on a conveyer belt for further processing. The entire process took only minutes and the recently terrified cow was reduced to parts and pieces in almost sterile fashion. A fire hose rinsed the cows down as well as the floor. The process was repeated as many times as it took to kill all the cows in the shipment. The men treated David with respect as a newbie as long as David stayed out of their way. Almost all wanted to know why he was interested in the glands and David developed a short description of the research and why it was going to help people with various diseases.

David processed the glands on Wednesday and the material was run down a chromatograph, radiolabeled with cyclic AMP. A few weeks into the work, David was radiolabeling the c-amp when one of the senior fellows asked David why he was wearing a lead apron.

"To protect me from the radiation," David replied.

"You're dealing with an alpha emitter, David. The lead converts the alpha waves into gamma rays. I guess you have not taken radiation physics yet."

"I'm really sorry, Jack," replied David.

"Apologize to your bone marrow and gonads, David. I'm just glad you left the block of Lucite between you and the radiolabeled material. The Lucite may have absorbed most if not all of the alpha particles, preventing them from reaching the lead apron."

"Well that's one good thing I did without knowing what I was doing," replied David.

"I'll enroll you in the next radiation physics course. For the meantime, no more radiolabeling for you. Jonathan will have to take over this particular job. If you didn't know, you didn't know. It was our fault not going through a safety check list with you before you started. Remove the lead apron and finish this batch, then wash up and take the rest of the day off."

CHAPTER FORTY-EIGHT

Soccer Match

Amanda and David went to seven a.m. Sunday Mass at Saint Mary's and returned to David's place for coffee and danish. They studied for an hour, then David went upstairs to dress for his soccer match.

"We have a match with Penn in Fairmont Park at noon. Do you want to come and watch?"

"I'd love to. I'll bring a couple chairs."

"Did you know that Henry was a fullback at A.I. Dupont High School and I was the center back for Concord? We beat them every year." David smiled at the memory. "Today I hope to play center and Henry will likely play right back."

"I recall during your last match. Very few strikers ever got close to taking a shot on your goal. You and Henry seem to be able to read each other's minds. Will you stop by my place on the way to the match, so I can clean up, change clothes and grab a jacket?"

It was a perfect day, cool without wind. Jefferson's squad was playing well. The turf had just been cut and it was dry and fast like a golf fairway. Henry was to David's right, James to his left and no one had been able to penetrate the defense during the first half.

Henry called out, "We three are the Ministry of Defense."

The next play was an exciting run by the Jefferson midfielder, Nicholas, who dropped the ball back to David who then placed it in front of Arthur, the right wing breaking to the center at the top of the eighteen. Arthur let off a powerful blast and the score became two to one.

Soon after kickoff the ball sailed above David's head. He jumped up, chest trapped the ball, then pivoted, landing and twisting on his left foot. What followed was a very loud crack, so loud that all the players hit the pitch thinking someone was shooting at them. Then they noticed David was on the pitch and in pain. They rushed over to assist. Michael, an Ortho Resident, rolled David onto his back, and manipulated his left leg and knee reproducing the click at the medial knee and demonstrating laxity with the anterior Drawer maneuver.

"The anterior cruciate ligament is loose. David, you've probably got the classic medial meniscal tear and cruciate strain, a rupture, if not yet complete."

"Let me try to stand on it," replied David straightening his knee. "It doesn't hurt that much. I think I can play to the end."

"I disagree, David. You could reinjure and pop the cruciate completely loose."

David played another two minutes before a second pop erupted from the left knee. David sheepishly limped off the pitch to watch the end of the match."

"I guess this where having a coach to order me off the pitch before I reinjured myself would have been a good idea," he said to himself.

Amanda ran over and said, "Your knee is already swollen, mister tough, and foolish guy." She had an ice bag ready with an ace bandage to keep it in place. "Couldn't you see this coming?"

"No more than the outcome of the match, Amanda. You know time is linear, of course. Why else would I play the match?"

"Ok, smart boy. That is not an excuse to risk injuring yourself."

"I risk injury every day I cross Ninth Street on my way to class, Amanda."

"Minimizing risk should be number one on your to do list,

David," replied Amanda, "You've survived a gunshot. You should know shit happens."

"I am not going to hold up in my bedroom to avoid scrapes and scratches."

"We should speak of this again later."

After the match finished Michael offered, "I'll drain the blood from your knee in the ER if you want."

"Definitely," replied a depressed David.

Once in the Emergency Room Michael drained 50 cc of fresh blood.

"Sometimes an injection of Medrol can reduce the inflammation," Michael offered," But you're probably looking at a surgical repair. Keep it wrapped in an Ace bandage holding Amanda's ice pack on top. Keep the ice on as long as you can stand it. Keeps the swelling down."

"Thanks Michael. Who would be your choice of surgeons for this?"

"Definitely Jansen. I'll mention it to him tomorrow. I don't know his OR availability, and you'll need some pre-op testing and clearance from the medical boys. You work at getting that done and I'll try to convince Jansen to look at you. He's a good guy. Now get home and put your leg up. It's going to be an uncomfortable night."

"I have a few Lorcet left over from when I got shot."

"That was you? Man, I heard about that. When's the third shoe going to fall?"

David asked the ER nurse, "Can I borrow a pair of crutches? I have a set at my townhouse and will return your set tomorrow."

"No rush. Just do egg shell touchdown and limit weight on the left foot as much as possible."

"Thanks again, Michael."

"Great game David, you set that second goal up perfectly. Too bad it ended like this."

David hobbled out of the ER and back to his home with a very concerned Amanda giving him a gentle push whenever he started to stray off course. Once in his place and on the couch, Amanda changed the ice pack and said she'd be back with some notes to go over. Amanda made dinner with left over chicken and corn salad. She went upstairs and retrieved half a Lorcet for him, then said she had to get home. Thankfully the Eagles had a late game, so David had something to keep his mind off the very uncomfortable throbbing in his left knee, at least until he fell asleep.

The next morning the stiffness, more than the pain was a bear, but David made it to lecture with the help of a second half of the Lorcet and the crutches.

Amanda made a big fuss over him and ran out to buy lunch that they shared in the lecture hall. She walked him home after lectures were done and tucked him in his bed.

"No kiss for the fallen hero?"

"No kiss for what I heard was a very non-compliant center back. Maybe tomorrow if you're repentant."

"Good night and thanks for once again taking care of me."

"Just don't make it a habit, David. Sleep well. I'll make breakfast."

David slept poorly. Getting up to use the head was a real challenge. He fell back into bed and slept until Amanda woke him up with eggs over easy, toast and juice in bed.

"Don't get used to this service, you'll have to start going down the stairs on your own. I'll walk with you to class but have an appointment at twelve thirty. Here are the crutches. I'll carry the other set to return to the ED. Get dressed. Perhaps you can ask Don to walk you home."

Michael arranged for David to consult with Dr. Jansen. After examining David's knee Dr. Jansen said he'd rather wait a few weeks to see if it healed rather than operating now. David thanked Dr. Jansen, then hobbled out.

"Well my racquetball dates with Amanda are scotched for sure," he thought. "Man, it took only a few seconds to wreck my knee, maybe forever. I won't be able to run to the Vet either. That's going to be tough. I've got my notes and books, so might as well make the best use of the time," David thought turning on the bedside lamp and pulling the text and accompanying notes onto his lap while he arranged his pillows on the bed.

CHAPTER FORTY-NINE

Racquetball with Richard

"I'm terribly sorry about your knee pain. You cannot possibly play our racquetball match tonight. I'll go and see if I can pick up a new partner for a match," said Amanda.

"I'll come and watch. Perhaps learn how you consistently beat me," he chuckled, "I really like your new short skirt outfit."

"Thank you, I thought you might."

"Gold and turquoise are good colors on you, sets well with you, being a blondie."

"Thanks again," replied Amanda giving him a kiss.

"You know I played what was called paddleball with a guy in my freshman physical education class. I think his name was Danny. He sported a big Afro, and he was a white guy. Unusual hairdo for U of D at that time. I didn't know a damn thing about strategy for paddleball at first. Danny trashed me mercilessly for weeks until I caught on to the style of playing soft and placing the ball, not just slamming it. By the end of the semester I could beat him, usually twenty-one to five or so."

"Watch and learn, my buggered-up love."

"Amanda was able to find a partner. Richard was a lanky man who gave her a good game. He seemed to know where to place the ball but didn't always make the shot. He lost the match and David suspected he pulled a few shots to make the score go her way.

"Ulterior motive," thought David, "I'll have to keep an eye on him. He may be captivated by her long legs as much as I am and is throwing his game off. Amanda may have chosen her outfit wisely, realizing that added benefit, but she'd never admit to that, so I won't bother asking."

David met Amanda and Richard as they left the court. They were toweling off and David asked, "Can I spring for dinner, somewhere close by?"

"Thanks David, but I must beg off tonight. I promised my wife, Jill, I'd get home and help with the kid's homework. Maybe next week if Amanda here consents to a rematch," said Richard.

Amanda said, "I'd love another match. How about we try to reserve a court for five o'clock next Tuesday?"

"Sounds good," replied Richard. "Nice meeting you David, but I've got to be going."

Amanda and David took a cab to Dante and Luigi's on Tenth Street for a light dinner with a delicious Chainti.

David asked, "Do you feel I monopolize your time, Amanda?"

"Not really. You were my racquetball partner and now you're not. I love studying with you and I like living by myself in Mrs. Hopkins' townhome. I have my circle of friends, the women's support group and the writing salon. I most value the time we spend together, David. Why do you ask? Do you feel encumbered?"

"Certainly not. I value our time together and enjoy my solitary time as well. Best of both worlds. You're my best friend and I want to be the guy you reach for at night."

They held onto each other on the walk to Amanda's home. "Do you want to come up for tea, David?"

"Thanks, but I'd better go home a put this leg up under ice."

"Now you're making good decisions. I'll pick you up at seven thirty and walk with you to class. Sleep well. Watch mixing hydrocodone on top of that wine."

"Duly noted Dr. Jackson."

CHAPTER FIFTY

Second Meeting with Sly

David walked to Twelfth and Bainbridge after classes expecting to see Sly and his crew on the corner. His knee had healed sufficiently, and he felt he could hustle away if things turned sour.

"You don't give up easy do you, David," said Sly.

"You promised to get me a Stone's tee shirt."

"And I did. Let me get it from my pack."

"Any crack dust on my shirt?"

"Man, you don't know nuthin' about my bidness," and tossed the tee shirt to David.

"Sweet. Thanks, Sly. You like the Stones at all?" When Sly failed to answer, David concluded. "I guess not."

"Ok you got your shirt. Anything else? Trying to run a bidness here."

"I guess not. Have you heard from Detective Cermack about your gun?"

"Only he wants me to do his cop-ass class for gun owners."

"Well that's great. Probably means you'll get a permit and your gun back."

"Just let it play out, man."

"I brought you a copy of the picture of you and me when we first met."

"You stuck in in a frame! Nice, but I'm not sure I know what to do wid it."

"Hang it on a wall in your pad, or on a shelf in your crib, whatever. Mine is on my desk and I look at it every day. I really don't have any pain now and my shoulder moves the full range and with full strength. I had a bugger of a time with physical therapy."

"Sorry 'bout that. Just stay off our corner. No threat, just a simple request. You ain't buying and we got expenses. You got your books and classes, we got our corner and sales. They ain't gonna come together."

"Sly, I want you and your friends to stay alive. I don't have to agree with your business. I don't want to know any details of what you guys do. I want you to be safe."

"You sure want a lot of things for a guy I just met and don't know that much about, man."

"That could change, Sly. My phone number is on the back of that photograph. Call me anytime. I don't get to bed until after midnight."

"Right, you got to do your runs."

"Helps to clear my head after packing it with medicines and diseases."

"That's your thing, David, mine is selling product as fast as I can, so if you'll excuse me."

"Of course. Sorry to take you away from that," apologized David.

Sly had already turned to talk with a customer who had just driven up. David turned and walked away with a smile on his face. He did not have to look back over his shoulder this time.

CHAPTER FIFTY-ONE

Dinner with Thomas

Amanda continued to play at the racquetball club.

"As much as I enjoy watching you demolish Richard and most of the others, I notice that one guy is obviously much more experienced. Do you mind losing to him?"

"That's Thomas. I recall you telling me about your paddleball games in college. I'll just plug away until I figure him out and then I'll start winning."

"No complaining or giving up, that's the Amanda I love," replied David giving her a kiss.

Amanda decided to test the depth of David's commitment telling him she had been asked out to dinner by Thomas. "He has until recently been consistently winning, but I think I've got him figured out."

"I'll admit I'm a little jealous, but you let me take Florence out and that went well, so enjoy."

"I just realized we probably have a lot of past and present issues to both uncover and deal with. Nothing for right now, but let's talk about this sort of thing soon," said Amanda.

"Watching you play against Richard and Thomas made me think similar thoughts. Having been a geologist I took it to the physical world. I imagined our relationship could be standing over a sinkhole, or a sewer line excavated under a street covered with four-inch steel plates, so cars could still drive over the hole."

"I'd like to think we could find those holes and work to fill them in with affection and understanding," commented Amanda.

"Well said. I was thinking more along the line of potholes, but the sinkhole allusion is ok. I doubt either of us is overly naïve about how much time and effort this will take. I also worry about the Porcupine Dilemma that Dr. Darla lectured on relative to relationships."

"I don't recall that term, David."

"It has to do with a parable posited by the philosopher Schopenhauer about a group of porcupines trying to survive a winter storm. They were huddled together in a hollow for warmth. The closer they packed themselves, the more they felt the pointed quills. When they pulled back, giving themselves space, the cold crept in. They eventually found an optimum distance apart for comfort and warmth, not perfect, but they survived the winter storm."

"I hope we can do better by reducing the length and number of the quills but again, they will arise from time to time. I will put up with a degree of annoyance using all the patience and affection I can muster, in order to keep the intimacy strong. Can we table this discussion for now? I'd like to consider which issues may be the potholes and what I would do when confronted with one," asked Amanda.

"No potholes here, Amanda. Let me know how the dinner with Thomas goes."

CHAPTER FIFTY-TWO

Amanda Buys a Car

"Do you feel like helping me buy a car?" asked Amanda after Friday's urology lecture. "I'm gonna need wheels to get to my clinicals next semester."

"Sure. What were you thinking of buying, new or used?"

"I've always wanted a convertible, light blue if I had my choice."

"Any particular make?"

"A Saab. I was going to try shopping at one of the larger auto malls, look at the used versus new and the cost. You know I'm not made of money and was not born with a silver spoon in my mouth."

"That makes two of us. I bought the Super beetle we've tooled around in from my dad."

"Well, my parents don't have any extra insects lying around, so I have to go out and catch one on my own," Amanda laughed.

"Should we plan on me driving us around ten o'clock? We could buy the Inquirer at Wawa and check out the cars."

"I'd like to treat you to a sub for dinner. Do you have any Lowenbrau at your place?"

"So now you're a beer gal, huh? Sure, always try to keep a six-pack in the fridge. Don doesn't care for it."

"You've got to promise me you won't try your evil ways on me tonight. We have to get some studying done for next week's exams if we're going to spend Saturday hunting down a car."

"So now they're evil ways, are they? That's not what I thought was going on when last we did the big one, Amanda," David replied with a big smile on his face.

"I know you men are all alike. Well perhaps you are a bit more attractive, thoughtful, and kinder than most, but still always plotting. I'll bet you just ran through the status of your bed sheets and when you last changed them, didn't you? Come clean, lover boy." Amanda was obviously enjoying taunting David, who was naturally at a disadvantage, should the truth be told. He decided to change the subject to which sub sandwich he was thinking about, maybe a pickle, perhaps splurge her money on some chips.

"Good try, changing the subject boy'o, but I can read you like a cheap book. You had designs on me and my svelt-tivity. Well, let me just say I have plenty of designs on your hunk-a-chunksome body most of the time, but not tonight."

The next morning David pulled up in front of 864 Locust to find Amanda waiting on her steps.

"How about we try the Franklin Auto Mall first, I've been by it and its huge," offered David, pulling away from the curb. They drove to the Wawa on Walnut and Ninth Street where David was working part time at night.

"I'll run in and get the paper," said Amanda. She returned having already pulled out the auto sales pages. She sat in the front seat and leafed through the ads. "Now there's a dark blue Saab, a Sonettt II, and it's a convertible!" exclaimed Amanda. "I really wanted a baby-blue one, but this one's good."

"Don't let the salesman see you so excited or you'll be paying more that its worth, which I have no idea about."

"Oh, I bought along a new Blue Book."

"Of course, you did. I should have known you'd come prepared, why was I doubting you?" David drove in silence while Amanda looked at other cars in the paper. Once at Franklin Auto Mall, David parked the VW and got out, ran around the car to open Amanda's door.

"What's your angle, boy. Holding the door, being all helpful today. Setting the ground work for a hot night?"

"Doesn't hurt to try being nice. Let's just stroll by and take a peek at the sticker prices."

Amanda added, "We can walk over to the pickups and act like you are the one in the market for a truck while I look up the Saab in the blue book."

David looked over the fact sheet applied to the rear window of the blue car.

"Looks like it's a '72 with 30,000 miles on it. If it was a Volvo I'd say it was just getting broken in, but I don't know Saabs," admitted David.

"I liked the white leather seats and white rag top."

"I wonder how many horses something like that has under the hood?"

"I've heard they're peppy little things. The book probably has that detail listed. You make eyes at that black Ford pickup and I'll look up the numbers on the Saab."

David did as he was requested and even convinced a salesman to stroll over to proclaim this particular Ford was the sweetest deal on the lot. David had to admit it looked clean and that it would be an upgrade from his VW Bug. The salesman said he'd be back with a quote on trading in the yellow Superbeetle.

"Great," thought David, "I'm a terrible liar with pitiful bargaining skills."

"What do I say to slow this salesman down. I don't want to waste his time on me." David walked over to Amanda and asked her about playing the truck salesman without committing to anything.

"Oh, I'll take care of him. He may just get a sale, but it'll be the Saab, if she checks out ok. Here he comes."

David turned away again as if to study the Ford and was relieved to hear Amanda intercept the salesman with mention of the blue Saab.

"Oh, that car was just detailed this morning. Very nice family of four traded it in for a station wagon. Seems they are expecting a third child and want to go camping. The husband's Saab is not appropriate for the three children. So that is fortunate for you, miss. I am Joey. And may I ask your name? Amanda is a lovely name. Do you think he would go along with the Saab instead of the pickup?

"I am quite sure I will be able to convince him. You see I am buying today," replied Amanda with an uncharacteristic flutter of her eye lashes. David had to walk behind a van to conceal his laughter.

"Here we are. Nice dark blue color, moderately low mileage for a Saab, Amanda. Let me open the driver's door and you see how nicely it will fit you. Ah yes, a perfect fit for you. It comes with power seats, so please adjust it to your comfort. Power windows, seats four adults, and I'll show you the trunk. Plenty of room for two suitcases, even golf clubs. Do you play?"

Amanda said sadly no, but perhaps someday. David again had to wander off to find a hiding place. He'd not seen this side of Amanda and was enjoying it immensely.

"How would you rate the pickup and horsepower for this model, Joey?"

"One hundred and sixty five horses are fine for a vehicle of this size and weight. Plenty of pickup for two adults. 0 to 60 in thirteen seconds. I am assuming you do not yet have children?"

"Quite right, Joey, but we have plans and perhaps will need to return to you in the not so distant future for a slightly larger car."

David had to stifle a guffaw with a coughing fit. He was quite impressed at the quality of Amanda's deception. "Perhaps I'm simply witnessing another side of the woman I am madly in love with," he thought. "This little shopping trip appears to have been a very educational activity for me," he smiled and joined the two as the haggling over a true price began.

"I'll have to speak with my manager to get you the best price. Are there any other vehicles you'd like to see at this time, Amanda?"

"No Joey. Let's focus on this one for now. David and I have to get to my mother's for dinner. I'd hate to be late."

"Quite right, Amanda. The showroom is just over here. Will you be trading in the Volkswagen?"

"No, Joey. David will require it for his commute."

The three made their way into the showroom, Joey excused himself and disappeared into a back office, presumably to determine the best price for Amanda.

"Amanda, I've never witnessed this side of you, the hapless female. And the fluttering eyelashes are a kick."

"Okay, I'm back," said Joey, "I have convinced my manager that since the Saab has been on our lot for only a few hours, it has not cost us much to maintain. So, the bottom line is he is willing to sell it to you for Blue Book value plus tax and registration."

"May I enquire what the Blue Book price would be?"

There followed a good thirty minutes of fairly intense negotiations between Amanda and Joey. David kept out of it, preferring to admire Amanda's performance as he checked out the new cars inside the showroom, while staying within earshot of the two, deep in negotiations.

Amanda called to David, "Honey, I believe Joey and I have reached an agreement. Would you like to see the paperwork?" More fluttering of eyelashes, this time in David's direction.

"I trust your judgement, my love, we can review the numbers after we drive over to your mother's for dinner."

"Oh, I had almost forgotten of that engagement, David, thank you for reminding me. I got all caught up in the negotiations." Amanda hid her huge smile by turning away from Joey, who was probably not paying attention now that the sale had been finalized.

"Amanda, would you accompany me to the cashier where we can complete your purchase?"

The three walked over to pay the bill, Amanda put 50% on her credit card and wrote a check for the remainder. It appeared she had contacted her bank and they had reassured Joey she had the funds.

Joey again disappeared into the back office but returned quickly with two sets of keys and a stack of documents. Amanda signed a few and scanned the others before folding them into her Coach pocketbook. David had never seen that pocketbook before and later learned Amanda borrowed it from Mrs. Hopkins to impress the salesmen. After handshakes all around Amanda and David walked over to her new Saab.

"I'll drive you to your car and you can follow me to Pat's Steaks for lunch, if you can keep up," she said with a smile.

"Little Duce Coup," Jan and Dean

CHAPTER FIFTY-TWO

Sly Shot

When Detective Cermack called, David thought it would be good news that Sly had completed his handgun safety course and was able to license and carry his handgun. However, the Detective told David that Sly and his homey, Gordy, had been shot in a drive by on their corner. Sly was in Jefferson having had a small bowel resection and right thigh muscle repair following two gunshot wounds. Gordy was DOA. Actually, Cermack referred to them as GSWs. Sly's weapon had been linked to the shot fired at the windshield of the car on Twelfth Street, and the bullet in the right front tire of the car carrying the men who ambushed Sly and Gordy. Cermak had returned the Glock to Sly after he completed the gun safety course. Cermack told David he had buried the report on the shoulder GSW for now but was considering a charge of malicious wounding as if Sly had been aiming at David.

"Thanks for telling me about Sly. I'll go up and pay him a visit."

"Still doing the social worker gig with the man who shot you, huh."

"I'm going to see this through, Detective."

David called Amanda and asked if she was interested in visiting Sly, to which she said, "Absolutely, but can you wait until I get there?"

"Sure. Meet you at the surgical nurse's station."

Twenty minutes later Amanda arrived. David had already asked the nurses if it was ok to visit Sly. It was. "You'll be his first visitors. Seems Sly doesn't have a lot of friends, at least not many who would be willing to be seen with a known drug dealer."

Amanda and David knocked on the door and Sly called out, "Come on in." Sly was obviously surprised at seeing Amanda and David instead of his nurse. "What you doing here David and who's the beautiful woman wit you? She must be lost, can't be wit you."

"Humorous Sly. This is Amanda. She knows our back story. Let me say I'm very sorry about Gordy."

"Thanks. I wish I knew where that low life Willie was. He was the backseat shooter who got me in the belly and leg and Gordy in the chest. If I ever find him . . ."

David interrupted Sly at this point. "Hey, violence begets violence. I'm going to bring you that Star Trek, 'Double Helix,' Next Generation video. Going after Willi can only ruin your life. Detective Cermack will take care of Willie ."

"So Sly, my I call you Sly?" asked Amanda.

"You can call me anything you want, just call me," laughed Sly.

"How's your belly and thigh doing?"

"I don't have no problem wit my leg, but my belly's a bitch. I'm taking a lot of my product just to hold it steady."

"Detective Cermack told me you got a shot off and hit the left front tire, causing the car to crash into a telephone pole. His theory is that once the driver bailed out, Gordy got off a chest shot that killed him. The police will track the driver from the Buick registration."

"After Willie kilt Gordy I dumped out all my stash onto his body, so they got nothin on me when the meat wagon showed up."

"What are your plans now, Sly," asked Amanda.

"I got to get out of selling product on the corner before I get kilt my damn self. Somebody put them up to the hit on me and Gordy. Willie's too dumb to think it up himself."

"What about working at the hospital once you heal up?"

"Say what? Do what?"

"You could start as a transporter, food service guy, custodian, anything that gives you medical insurance." replied David.

"Good point. I've already been by wondering how I'm gonna pay for all this." Sly waved his arms around the room.

"Your job now is to heal up and get out of here. They will send Home Health to your place and I can check in on you from time to time," replied David.

"You ain't no social worker and you damn well not gonna wash my butt. Now you, lovely Amanda, can come by and minister to my wounds, both physecal and motional."

Amanda laughed despite trying to hold it in. "We need to get back to the books, Sly. We'll check in on you tomorrow."

"You can come by anytime but leave David back, so we can really talk."

"Ok mister big stuff. Anything you want, pack of cards, a book, a magazine?" asked David.

"I got TV, is fine."

"See you tomorrow then."

"Thanks for coming by Amanda, you too David. And David, I'm really sorry I shot you. Having been shot myself I know it hurts like a bitch, and I just laid in the gutter waiting to be rescued. I look back on you getting shot, then standing up and running away. I just can't believe you did that. You're one tough mother."

"Thanks, Sly, but I was in pretty good physical shape back then, not that I'd ever want to test myself that way again. Rest up, man."

Once out of Sly's room David told Amanda he was going to pay for Sly's hospital care. "The surgeons are on salary, but the OR and room fees will run into thousands of dollars. I can ask Ben for help and if we can land Sly a job with insurance they may be able to retroactively bill Medicaid for at least some of it."

"You're really taking this to heart, aren't you?"

"If it keeps Sly alive, why not. Plus, I work at Wawa slicing meat and cheesecake at night. Sly may pay some of it back to us. I'll call the hospital tomorrow and see how I can pay his bill."

Amanda grabbed David's hand and they started down the hallway, "Come on mister generosity, let's get home and hit the books."

CHAPTER FIFTY-FOUR

My One True Love

David walked over to Mrs. Hopkins' townhome to see where Amanda had parked the blue Saab. He found her cleaning the windshield.

"How are you going to keep the leaves and dirt off your car?"

"First thing I'll do when I have time is to buy a car cover."

"Any idea how much they cost?" asked David.

"Not much when you consider the value of this hot new car."

"Actually, they run about $56.95 for a cheap, lightweight one and $99.99 for one that will make it through a Philly Winter," replied David with a huge smile on his face.

"What are you holding behind your back?"

"Oh, a little something I thought may come in handy for a damsel in distress."

"So now I see you are Sir Walter Raleigh of car covers," laughed Amanda. "Come on let me see what you've got there. What color is it?"

"Blue of course. I hope it fits," replied David holding the package out to Amanda who promptly unzipped the bag and pulled out the blue car cover.

"Wonderful color, David. Can you help me put it on?" she asked.

"Would Sir Walter do anything less?"

"It fits perfectly. Oh, thank you David," she said running around the now covered car to embrace David and deliver a long and firm kiss.

"Do you have time to come in and have a cup of tea? It's a bit early for wine or Jack Daniels, don't you think?"

"Lead the way."

David added a squirt of honey to his Earl Grey, took a sip and put the cup down. "So how did the dinner with Thomas go? Did you have fun and was the meal worthy of a repeat visit?"

"Thomas was the perfect gentleman, although his choice of restaurants was not up our standards. A nice steak and brew place on Thirteenth Street near Walnut. I managed to look interested in a petite filet and a few baby carrots, with a Coors."

"And Thomas?"

"Oh, he's a carnivore. I think he consumed a 20-ounce Delmonico, baked potato with mandatory sour cream and chives, Caesar salad, and then a slice of cheesecake topped with blueberry goo and coffee. I was impressed that he could walk after that performance, but he does move well on the racquetball court."

"What's he do for a living?"

"Midtown stockbroker, divorced, with a couple kids that he did not mention by gender or name."

"That's a bit sad."

"I agree. After dinner, which he generously did pay for, he expressed interest in doing dinner again."

"To which you replied?"

"That I was deeply in love and in a strong relationship with the man, David, that he met courtside."

"Was the walk home uncomfortable after that conversation?"

"Not so much. He opened up about his failed marriage, how work dominated his life to the extent that although he made tons of money, he missed out on seeing his children grow up. Plus, he was not there despite supporting his wife and children for a couple years. Interesting that he made all the right connections for a good marriage but did not seem to be able to recover and try to reinsert himself into their lives."

"You sound like you got into the psychological side of things, just a bit, Amanda."

"It wasn't all that difficult to see the problems, but I was more focused on the pathologic stress between his job and relationship with his family," laughed Amanda, "So I felt more at ease."

"Are you two going to be able to continue playing racquetball with Thomas?"

"I give it a 50-50 chance. I still enjoy playing with Richard, who is happily married and has applied no relationship pressure so far."

"Well know I trust your decisions but miss you terribly when you are out with the boys, racquetball or dinner."

"I know you do, and I appreciated your taking a step back for me to oblige Thomas, which won't happen again, at least with him," she said kissing David hard on the mouth, "You are my one true love and I'd rather be with you than anyone else."

CHAPTER FIFTY-FIVE

Knee Surgery

"You seem to be limping more recently, David, is your knee bothering you?"

"It is swollen, not hot, but the fluid forces the knee into a painful flexion contracture, making it difficult to walk," replied David.

"Are you going to ask Dr. Jansen to drain it?"

"I'm going to ask him to go in and repair the meniscal tear. I don't think its going to heal itself."

Later that day David went to Dr. Jansen's office and was given an appointment for Wednesday. By the time Wednesday came, David was back to using crutches to get around and the knee and now his lower leg were extremely swollen.

"At least I've got something to show Dr. Jansen," thought David.

Dr. Jansen drained David's knee and was able to find a very loud medial meniscal click and a little bit of anterior laxity.

"I agree with you, David. You have not healed the meniscal tear, there is some Drawer sign laxity. You should have an arthrotomy. I will not be able to tell you if the anterior cruciate needs a repair until I get inside. When can you have the surgery?"

"The sooner the better," replied a relieved David.

"I have OR time next Tuesday and an opening for your surgery at ten o'clock. You'll have to have a physical exam, labs, probably another chest radiograph, and an ECG as soon as you can arrange them. Who is your PCP?"

"I don't really have one. I was cared for by the surgeons after my gunshot and have been doing well."

"The TCV service won't do a pre-op for knee surgery. I suggest you go to Student Health and have an Internist do what should be a healthy person check-up and send me a report for the chart."

"I can do that today," replied David. He thanked Dr. Jansen and went out to the secretary to let her know he was having knee surgery the following Tuesday and that he would arrange for the pre-op evaluation and testing to be done today.

"I'll make you a post-op, follow up appointment now as you will likely have a one-night stay in the hospital."

David thanked her and walked out, still using his crutches, heading for Student Health. The physician there took David's history and did a complete physical exam. He wrote the orders for blood work and a chest radiograph, having completed the ECG in the office.

"Good luck with your surgery. Dr. Jansen is a great guy, repaired my right knee three years ago and I've had no problems since."

"That's good to hear. Thanks for probably the best exam I've ever had. Will you be able to get your report to Dr. Jansen by next week?"

"He'll have it tomorrow. The labs should be resulted by Friday, and I don't foresee any problems."

David completed his blood work and chest radiograph, which showed scarring in the right upper lung field, stable compared to his outpatient, post-op films.

"Now I've just got to wait until Tuesday, hobble around, and not fall," thought David, "Thank the lord for nighttime hydrocodone."

CHAPTER FIFTY-SIX

Garden Party

"Hey Don, how about we have a backyard party?"

"That's a pretty dank area, David," answered Don, "Wouldn't you rather have it inside?"

"Nah, we can fix it up," David replied, "I got some ideas from Architectural Digest."

"So, are you going to knock down the brick walls and let some sunshine in?"

"No, but I am going to jazz up the walls with pallets covered in flowers, string lights, and get a table and some chairs. Maybe even get a rattan mat. We can do this, I just need some help schlepping the heavy stuff through the living room. I'll go out and find the table and chairs, the mat and lights, and I hope four clean pallets and some flowers."

"Who do you plan to invite to this garden party?"

"Garden Party," Ricky Nelson

"Well, you and Lillian for starters, Ben, Lisa and Cindi and Cindi's squeeze of the month, and of course Amanda. That makes eight. What night works for you and Lillian?"

"I'd rather do it on Friday. Lillian and I have something for Saturday night."

"That works for me. I'll call Amanda and Ben. If we five can do it, its on. I hope Lisa and Cindi can come as well."

"Let me know when you get the tables and chairs and I'll help carry them. How are you going to use the pallets? Put them on the floor and pile the flower pots on them?"

"Oh no. I'm going to attach them to the walls with lag screws…"

"What's a lag screw?"

"You drill a hole in the mortar around the bricks, ram in a lead cylinder, called a shield, into the hole, then screw through the wood into the lead shield. You'll have to help me hold the pallets up in position. You'll see."

Don went upstairs to call Lillian and David called Amanda and Ben. They were all excited to be invited, so David called Lisa and Cindi who said they'd love to come.

"I'd like to bring something for dessert," offered Lisa.

"Surprise us," replied David, "I'm going to do shish kabob and Sangria."

"It's really nice of you to invite us."

"Please tell Cindi to bring her boyfriend," added David.

"That will make me odd gal out, David."

"I thought you'd say that so I'm inviting my brother, Ben. I have a good feeling you two will hit it off, Lisa."

"You do, huh. Is he a good looking surgeon?"

"No, but he's a great looking Navy man. A gentle hunk-a-hunk."

"Ok, I'll take your word on it, David. If he's half as good looking as you, I'll be a happy gal."

"And he's got a great laugh, Lisa. You'll get on famously. I gotta go and get the patio prepared, big plans for it."

David called Ben to ask for his help in locating the table and chairs and pallets. Of course, Ben knew just the place off South Street.

"How's your knee coming along? Did your Orthopod discharge you to full activity?" asked Ben.

"I'm supposed to refrain from kneeling and probably avoid squatting with weight."

"I'm sure we can get the flowers in the Italian market. I'll come by in my pickup in an hour."

David got out the broom and swept up as much dirt as he could, then threw buckets of water on the walls and patio and swept the muddy water into the drain. It took all of an hour to make it presentable before Ben arrived.

Ben came through the kitchen and looked at the bricks. "One hundred percent better, David. What's with the pallets?"

"I'm going to hang them on the walls to hold the flowers. I saw it in Architectural Digest."

"We'll need to stop by the hardware store to get some lag shields and lag screws," said Ben.

"My thought exactly. Does the Navy base have some clean pallets?"

"A pile of them. I'll ask the Captain if I can have four. I'm sure he'll say yes. He owes me a favor."

"Of course, he does, Ben," smiled David.

The brothers went from the Navy base to the hardware store and then to a flower shop on Eight Street to pick up geraniums, coleus, vincas, and Ben wanted to add a couple basil, oregano, and rosemary plants."

"They'll make the place smell great."

"Can we go to that furniture store you mentioned for the tables and chairs, Ben?"

"I'll bet we find just what you want on South Street."

"Oh, and I want to buy a rattan mat," added David.

"You're really going all out, aren't you, any particular occasion?"

"I kinda want to impress Amanda, if you have to know."

"Well let's get going."

An hour and a half later they had collected the furniture and plants. Don was summoned from his bedroom to help hold the pallets against the walls. The wood looked odd until the plants were inserted between the slats.

"I have to admit the flowers look good and they'll be easy to keep watered," complimented Don.

The mat was spread out and the tables and chairs arranged.

"Just enough room for them," said Ben, "I'm glad we got two of the smaller tables instead of one big one."

"I like the granite tops," said Don, "And the aluminum legs will survive the winter."

"Can I count on you to make a couple small loaves of bread for hors de voirs, Don? I want to get some olive spread and soft cheeses."

"I'm your man, David. I'll make them Friday after class, so they will have a crunchy crust and a soft center. Tell you what, I'll ask Lillian to get or make the spreads. She even has some of the fancy knives, perfect for this."

"Thanks Don."

"Can I bring my signature crab dip and some blue corn chips, David?"

"I was hoping you'd offer, Ben. There should be plenty of food once I get the shish kabobs going. I just may get some lamb and do it up right."

"Let's run over to the Reading Market now before it closes and pick up the crab, lamb, and veggies."

"Don't forget, you'll need some wooden skewers," added Don as he headed up the stairs to call Lillian.

"I hope the ladies will appreciate all the effort we men are putting into this shindig."

Friday evening arrived, and all the tables were set. David had to run out at the last minute to purchase a dozen Sangria glasses and party plates, but everything else was set out and the charcoals were white hot in the hibachi and the shish kabob were ready to go.

"Now we wait for our guests," said Ben, "They'd better bring an appetite. We have a lot of food here"

Amanda was the first to arrive. She had her flute and a bowl of chocolates. “Ben told me you men had thought of everything, so I had to come up with something special. How about some Vivaldi?”

“Great idea Amanda. You going to play from memory?”

“But of course.”

“This is really going to be one for the books.”

Lisa arrived next and put her cheesecake in the fridge. “More for safe keeping,” she said, “Wouldn’t want any fingers sampling it.”

Cindi and Bob brought two bottles of Rose and a bag of oranges, limes, and lemons. “In case the Sangria runs low,” offered Cindi. “Bob, this is David, Don and Lillian are over there. David’s brother Ben is next to Amanda. Everyone, this is Bob.”

“Welcome Bob, I hope you’re hungry. And here’s Don and Lillian.”

Lillian carried a basket and Don brought out his bread, sliced perfectly to accommodate Lillian’s spreads.

Amanda wrapped her arm around David, “What a great idea. You’ve outdone yourself,” and gave him a kiss.

“Give me a second, Amanda.”

“Ben, this is Lisa. She lives across the hall where my Orlowitz apartment was and is a dear friend of mine. She is top in her class of Med Techs. Lisa, this my brother Ben, on loan from the Navy to be your date for this party. I hope you don’t mind me pairing you two up.”

“Glad to meet you Ben, David has told me a lot about you. Now David, you scurry off to your cooking. Ben and I will be just fine. Ben, would you be so kind as to get me a glass of Sangria?”

David smiled and walked back to the grill that he loaded up with skewers of lamb and vegetables.

“Great idea, David, pairing Ben and Lisa,” whispered Amanda, handing David a skewer.

The appetizers were obviously a big hit, and everyone complimented Lillian and Don.

Fifteen minutes later the meat was cooked. Everyone grabbed a plate and chair.

Amanda stood at the doorway, flute in hand. "I'd like to serenade you for a few minutes," she said and started to play the Four Seasons.

"Its beautiful," said Lillian, "What a special talent."

"When Amanda finished everyone stood and clapped their appreciation. David brought Amanda a plate and a glass of Sangria to her chair. "That was amazing. How long did you have to practice that to get it to sound perfect?"

"I was a couple of notes off, but thanks. I practiced that for months before my recital. I guess it stuck. I'm famished. Oh, this meat is really delicious, so juicy. You can cook this for me anytime, David."

The dinner party progressed from quiet and sedate to jovial and when Lisa brought out the cheesecake and drizzled the fresh blueberry compote on top, Ben helped serve the slices as if he'd been teaming up with Lisa for years.

"I think Ben and Lisa have hit it off," Amanda said to David.

"Cindi called for Amanda to play again. Amanda asked what she wanted to hear.

"Isn't there something about a magic flute?"

"Oh, that's a toughie, but I'll give it a try."

After Amanda finished the whirlwind song, David said "You did better than just a try."

"I'll play one more, one that David taught me."

Amanda played 'The Circle Game' and everyone clapped when she finished.

"The Circle Game," Joni Mitchell

David walked over Amanda, placed his arm around her and said, "Isn't she wonderful? I'll get you some cheese cake and a drink." The remainder of the party was quiet as the couples spoke and drank the Sangria until it was late into the night.

CHAPTER FIFTY-SEVEN

Car Crash

A couple weeks after Amanda purchased her car she sat down next to David at the end of the lecture and asked if he'd like to go for a ride.

"Absolutely, I've been patiently waiting for the invite."

"Well then, let's decide where we want to eat dinner and I'll drive us there."

Thirty minutes later Amanda pulled up in front of David's townhome where he'd been sitting on the front stoop. He was able to easily get in the car, because Amanda had the top down.

"I'm surprised by the leg room," he commented, stretching his long legs.

"I'm thinking of going to a place on Fortieth Street above Penn for soup and salad," suggested Amanda, "It got good reviews from Karen, who is not exactly a vegetarian, but has preferences more like yours."

"Fine with me."

Amanda took it slowly getting across the Schuylkill, but then opened it up.

"I believe the speed limit is still 35 here my love," suggested David.

"Oh, let my car breath a bit."

David watched the buildings go by, then started to watch the extraneous things Amanda was doing as she drove. She was running her hand through her hair and throwing hairs out of the car, looking at her teeth in the rearview mirror, changing the radio stations, and looking at the drivers of the cars she was passing.

"She's more than a little distracted, but she's not driven for a long time and it is a sport car. Me, I've got the Super beetle blahs and could floor it for all its worth and never match the pickup of this car," he thought.

They arrived at the restaurant without incident and had a healthy, although lightweight dinner, for David at least. He avoided wine, but Amanda had a glass of house white and took her time enjoying it. The ride home was more sedate as it was moonless and dark. Things were more difficult to see even with headlights.

"Thanks for the ride. Your car is great. The meal was very good, and we've now got some studying to do. I'll walk with you to class tomorrow if you want."

"See you then, David," replied Amanda giving him a peck on the cheek.

A week later Amanda totaled her Saab, crashing into the guardrail on I-95 south. She had been in the passing lane going around a box truck when the aforementioned truck started to drift to the left. Amanda thought she could complete her pass, but the truck suddenly lurched left and hit the front of the light weight Saab. Amanda's car was slammed into the median guardrail at such an angle that her left front wheel was trapped and the car flipped. The roll bar, air bag, and seat belt saved Amanda's life, but she fractured her left thigh. The truck never stopped, and Amanda was rescued by the next car following. She was taken to Chester Crozier, then transferred to Jefferson after she requested the orthopedic care be done there. The Emergency Room physicians stabilized Amanda and later that day she had her femur pinned. She was soon transferred to the orthopedic ward and was asleep when David arrived. He made a phone call to Mrs. Hopkins and to Mrs. Jackson explaining what had happened and that Amanda was doing well. He pulled up a chair and was marveling that Amanda had a few scratches on her face but had suffered no other serious injuries in the crash than the fracture.

"I guess the air bag saved her life, but she'll have raccoon eyes for a while," he thought, shivering at the alternative consequences. Once Amanda woke up he went over to her bed, kissed her and asked if she was in any pain.

"Just stiff and a little nauseous from anesthesia, I suppose. I'm sure you recall the first few hours after your surgery," she replied, trying to muster a smile. "Right now, I'd appreciate it if you would ask my nurse for some mouthwash and a drink of water."

David kissed her again, remarking with a smirk that the mouthwash was a great idea.

"I kissed your sour mouth plenty of times while you were recovering. Off you go for the Scope, pretty please."

The roles of patient and caretaker having been reversed, David brought Amanda her textbooks and rounded up notes from a couple Jeff students on Amanda's rotation.

"My beautiful car is a goner thanks to me," replied Amanda.

"See you tonight for dinner. You get some rest. I remember I was incredibly tired after my little surgical adventure. I saw that you are receiving sub-Q heparin. Good thing. Wouldn't want you to develop a DVT and throw a PE."

"God forbid. Its more than just a textbook concern now that I'm on the patient side of this fracture. Anything in the chart I should know about?"

"Naw, you are healthy as a proverbial horse, a beautiful filly if I may say so. You know I love you, Amanda. I couldn't live without you."

"Come over here. You just earned a big smooch."

David complied without any argument, "But now you really should rest. Anything special I can fetch for you?"

"Please ask Mrs. Hopkins for a couple of clean bras, and tee shirts. I feel like I'm flopping around in this gown. I'll work it out with my nurse. Now I think I will try to get some shut eye. See you tonight. And thank you for making the trip to Philly from Wilmington. I hope you did not have to sell your soul to get permission to leave early."

David was ready to reply but noticed Amanda was already half asleep. He quietly shut the door as he left the room in search of Amanda's nurse. He was a bit shaken after seeing her in the hospital bed. "Despite my eyes telling me she's ok, I can't but think what could have happened to her. For God's sake she flipped the Saab at what was probably well over the speed limit. But she is ok. I've got to focus on that."

"Have I Told You Lately That I Love You?" Rod Stewart

CHAPTER FIFTY-EIGHT

Advice from Brother Ben

"Ben, can you meet me for a beer and to give me some advice?"

"When and where? I'm off Tuesday and Thursday nights this week," replied Ben.

"How about Kyber Pass at five thirty on Tuesday?"

"Five thirty is good. See you then."

While David was walking to Kyber Pass he thought about what he would ask Ben. "I am not so sure my concerns about Amanda are useful, especially without a strategy to deal with my anxieties, perhaps confront Amanda about some of the more significant issues."

When he reached the bar, he ordered cheese fries and a Michelob.

When Ben arrived, the waitress pointed Ben to the table where David was sipping his beer. "Thanks for coming, Ben. What do you want to drink?"

"A Bud would be good. So, what's this about."

"You've met Amanda."

"Nice woman. You two seem to have hit it off," Ben replied, reaching for a forkful of cheese fries.

"True and true. I'd like your advice on what's probably my problem, not hers."

"Shoot."

"I've known Amanda for a little over two years. She's great. Pretty, smart as a whip, and thoughtful. What more can I say? What she sees in me I'll never know."

"But you've got an issue."

"Amanda is buttoned down pretty tight most days while in lectures. Top of her class. Everyone loves her."

"But?"

"But I am worried about a couple of instances where she was not so buttoned down."

"People should not stay, what you call, buttoned down all the time, David. What's really the problem?"

"Okay. First, she crashed her new car on 95, nearly killed herself. Busted her femur. Thank God it wasn't rush hour."

"She got distracted, or what?"

"She can't recall the details, but I've ridden with her and she sometimes does everything except pay attention to driving: hand through her hair, fools with the radio, even reaches under her seat to grab things that have fallen down. She makes me crazy. I'll bet she took her eyes off the car in front of her, popped back up and misread the turn. I know where she crashed, it's a tight turn."

"Good thing she came away with only a busted leg, could've killed herself."

"That too," said David.

"So, she made a big mistake, but something else is bugging you."

"She's a party girl, more than I am."

"That's not saying much, Dave."

"Likes her gin martinis and vodka shots. She can hold her liquor for a while, then just lets loose. I'm afraid she's going to get hurt."

"She a fall down drunk?"

"No, nothing like that, but certainly impaired decision processes."

"So, she lets loose on the weekends after a rough week, and you feel you have to stay on guard for her sake. Is that it? Don't you trust her?"

"I never thought of it in terms of not trusting her, but I couldn't take it if she got really hurt."

"So, this is about you. I'm not mister relationship, but it seems immature on your part," replied Ben.

"I thought I was being the responsible one."

"She's her own person. She's an adult. Perhaps more of a risk taker than you. Maybe she views you as a bit of a nerdy, boring, but nice guy."

David bristled at that. "So, I need to do what? Not worry, not watch out for her?"

"As I see the relationship you and Amanda are building, she may need to tone it down a bit and you loosen up a little. Remember you're the one who got shot. Did Amanda tell you to stop running alone in South Philly?"

"No, she didn't. You're right. She can't feel great about me running to the Vet at midnight," David replied a bit sheepishly.

"Then I think you'll need to look inside your heart for answers to your concerns."

"Also, do either you or Amanda date others? I recall you were strictly a one lady at a time guy in college."

"Still am. Are you saying I'm too intense and controlling?"

"You may try dialing it back a bit, or are you already planning on the townhome together while in residency?"

"It has crossed my mind. On that same tract, I am having the blue Saab repaired. It was not a total loss. Amanda really wanted the car to be baby blue, so I'm gonna have it painted baby blue. It seemed a good time to do that."

"Have you spoken with Amanda about these future plans? Maybe that's where your over blown concern and control issues for her safety are coming from."

"Hopefully she'll appreciate the refinished Saab as a surprise. I haven't discussed my idea of sharing a home during residency. Hell, we're only two thirds through school with no idea where residencies will be. The idea of buying the townhome as an investment seems like a good idea."

"For you, maybe for her as well, but she needs to feel it is right for her. So, you take it a bit slower, tone down your anxiety, give Amanda some space, enjoy her free- spirited weekends. She's worth it."

"Thanks, Ben," said David clinking his glass against Ben's, "I've always appreciated your guidance and trusted your advice."

"I appreciate you saying that, David. An open mind is, of course, a sign of intellectual strength and an embrace of a healthy curiosity."

"I am curious, Ben, what's going on with your plans to retire from the Navy and take that position with the EMT service?"

"I'm going to take my three months of accumulated vacation next month and leave the military for a time. I may want to get back into duty with the naval reserve at some point."

"Have you discussed your plans with your Admiral friend?"

"Actually, I have. He is not happy that I am leaving but supports my desire for more medical training."

The brothers then spoke about their parents and after a couple glasses of beer David said he had to get back to his books.

"By the way, Ben, Don is moving in with his current love interest at the end of the month. Would you be interested in moving in with me?"

"Just like old times."

"There can be a resurgence of Velveeta stuffed meatloaf and crab dip."

"Would your homework allow for some Mash episodes?"

"Could make it happen, Ben. I'll let you know when Don is out."

"That will be great. Can I give you a lift home, Dave?"

"Thanks."

CHAPTER FIFTY-NINE

Pot Holes and Sink Holes

"Amanda, I think we need to talk about pot holes, perhaps even sinkholes. Do you have time and energy for this?"

"Let me guess. You want to know how and why I smashed my new car."

"Well yeah. That and other things," David replied by holding her hands and looking into Amanda's eyes with all the love and affection he could muster.

"I think I'm ready, at least I'll try."

"Yes, I want to talk about your accident. Let me speak first, then you can chime in. Do you recall what you were doing just before the crash, what might have distracted you? Were you thinking about class work? Were you just seeing how well your car managed at high speed and lost it on the curve? Did you reach under the seat for something you'd dropped? I've seen you distracted as you run your fingers through your beautiful blonde hair perhaps taking your eyes off the road for just a second. Ok your turn."

"I probably have a bit of a concussion, so things are a bit fuzzy. I recall a big truck to my right and then I was upside down into the guard rail. You are right about me being less than fully attentive sometimes. Maybe a gentle mention from you would help. I do recall revving the Saab up on the straight away to see her top speed, but I would have slowed it down going into the turn. From what you told me the turn comes up fast and I probably didn't slow down sufficiently, smashed into the guard rail and rolled the car. Is that how you imagined it?"

"Pretty much, but I was not there. I'm just so dammed glad you made it out with only a one broken bone and all your brains still in your lovely head."

"But I sense there is something else you want to discuss, David. Go ahead, this is as good a time as any."

"You're right, Amanda. I want you to know that I had a conversation with Ben a while back on somewhat of a similar topic, not telling stories behind your back, but trying to gain perspective on some of the things that were bothering me about myself."

"Ok, now I am confused. Is this about me or you?"

"You know I love you, respect you and want to always be with you, Amanda."

"But . . . ."

"Do you remember we spoke about encountering potholes, or perhaps traveling over sink holes that needed to be detected and either avoided or filled in?"

"This sounds like more of a sink hole that could overwhelm and swallow us."

"I certainly hope not. I am not naïve that I am overall a bit of a control freak and also tend to be a watcher and protector, rather than a let it loose, hell bent to the wind kind of guy."

"Well said."

"I see you as someone able to keep things bottled up, like studying and test taking, but equally able to cut loose on weekends and just let er' rip sometimes. I believe, and Ben said this about me also, that in those situations, where someone I deeply care about is cutting loose, I tend to hold back and watch for problems. I play the cautious, protector role."

"That would perhaps explain why you play center back on your soccer team and not the go for it as a striker type," added Amanda.

"Not a bad analogy. But there's more at stake sometimes than preventing a goal in a soccer match. You could have killed yourself in that crash and I don't know what I would do without you. I do worry sometimes that you drink to excess and could get into trouble finding your way home alone. I see by the look on your face that I'm straying off course. Ben said I need to loosen up, treat you like the adult you are and let you relax and have fun when you want to. I don't want to hover like the proverbial mother hen. I want to come together as equals of different stripes. Hell, if you had your way, you'd dress me in a completely different wardrobe."

Amanda laughed at that.

David continued, "So, the pothole I've come to realize that I'm always watching for is at once trivial, but very rarely can be serious. And yes, I have not forgotten who jogs at midnight and got shot, causing one beautiful and caring woman much heartache."

"So, your solution is to check out the jogging route in the daytime and be willing to reverse course before the bullets start flying, but not completely doing the hermit in his garret thing?"

"Plus, I want to be with you, the exciting, beautiful, full of life woman that has stolen my heart forever. I don't want to be anything but supportive of your choices and perhaps I can learn to relax and enjoy being around you even more."

"That was quite a pothole, but I don't think it rises to a sinkhole to swallow us up type of dilemma. I will be receptive to your comments about me appearing distracted while driving, that is once my fracture heals and I can drive again," offered Amanda.

"And you find a way to nudge me back on course and I'll think twice before reaching out to hold you back. How's that?" replied David.

"Well, it's a good start. I'll bet very few couples have had this talk this early in their relationship. Yes, I'd like to think we are together on this one, my love. Now come over here and kiss me like you want to eat me up. Then leave me to get some sleep."

"I Want to Kiss You All Over," Exile

CHAPTER SIXTY

Amanda is Discharged

"You will be going downstairs in a wheelchair for an X-Ray of your leg, Amanda," said Gail, Amanda's day nurse, "The transporter should be here any time now."

Just then Amanda heard a familiar voice.

"Hello Doctor Amanda. I'm glad we will have this time together without your third wheel, David, around."

"Sly! How long have you been working here?"

"About a week. They haven't fired me yet and I'm doing my best to not give them any reason to, either," laughed Sly. "Can you transfer to the wheelchair or do I get to pick you up and place you ever so gently in my chariot?"

"I'm quite able to take a few steps, Sly. I appreciate your generous, if not a bit avaricious, offer."

"I know. You afraid if you let me hol' you tight, you ain't never gonna feel right when ol' David tries his moves on you. Am I right or am I right?"

"Ok, Sly. I'm getting into the wheelchair. You have a blanket to cover my legs?"

"Only the best lamb's wool for you Doctor Amanda."

"I am still a student, not a Doctor, Sly. Let's get down to Radiology."

"Your wish, lady is my command. I would like to thank you and David for payin' for my hospitalizations. I want to thank him myself if he'd come over and visit. He probably saved my life. Pushing wheelchairs and stretchers don't pay as well as pushing dope and is boring, but I make my fun talking with patients and I got medical insurance now, which is huge."

"Did the police ever catch Willy and prosecute him for shooting Gordy?"

"Oh yeah, they got him good. He gone upstate now for life, son of a bitch. Sorry Doc, I meant no disrespect."

"None taken, Sly. Did you get you colostomy reversed?"

"Piece of cake. Want to see my scar?"

"That's okay, Sly. And your thigh wound? All good?"

"Never bothers me at all. Well here we are." Sly turned to the clerk and said, "Becky, you call only me for the return ride for Doc Amanda."

"Got it Sly."

"I'll see you then Doc," and Sly left Amanda in her wheelchair at the Radiology waiting area.

He managed a wink without a leer, just a very warm smile for Amanda.

Amanda asked the radiology tech, "How's the femur fracture looking?"

"I'm not supposed to say anything to patients, but as you are a medical student I'll stick my neck out and tell you that the rod in your femur looks to be in good position and your hip joint looks just fine. Of course, Dr. Allen will read it and send a report to the floor. I'll ask your nurse to share that information with you. It'll take about an hour for him to read the morning films. I'll tell transport to come and take you back to your room."

"Please tell them to ask Sly to pick me up," said Amanda with a smile, "He's become somewhat of a friend."

"He is a character, isn't he? I'll push your wheelchair into the hall and you can wait by the secretary's desk for Sly to get here."

Ten minutes later Amanda heard Sly before she saw him. "Your prayers have been answered, Sly has arrived to transport you to your destination."

"You can't just arrive quietly, can you, Sly?" said the radiology secretary.

"This a special job, Maggie, Doctor Amanda is in need of Sly's special care. Now Doc is there anything you need, a blanket, a soda, a shoulder rub from my strong yet sensitive hands?"

"Sylvester, I appreciate the offers, but I'd just like to get back to my room and lay down."

"I can help wit dat. I could lie wit you and read you a story"

"I do not require anyone other than me in my bed, thank you very much."

"Okay, but you don't know what you missin."

"I'm quite sure I'll be just fine, Sly."

Sly pushed Amanda's wheelchair into the hallway and onto the elevator. "You know I only have respect for you Doc Amanda. And I have a mountain of respect for Doc David, you know that. You two go together pretty good. I can see I got no chance to win you over. That man went way out of his way to help me. Now its up to me to do sumpin wit my life to make him proud. There's a bump getting off the elevator, Doc."

"Why Sylvester I believe you are showing your sensitive side."

"Don't you tell him. You know I have a rep to maintain."

"Your secret is safe with me," laughed Amanda as they turned into her room.

"Its good seeing you, Doc. Let me lock the wheels. Do you need a hand to the bed? Anytime you two want to visit you let me know."

After Sly returned Amanda to her room Gail, her nurse, came in to tell her she was being discharged. Amanda called David.

"They are going to discharge me today, David. Can you meet me at Mrs. Hopkins' place at noon?"

"I'll be there. Do you need me to run anything up to you? Is your pain control adequate? Are you having any nausea or constipation issues. You should get them addressed by your nurse before you leave."

"No, I'm feeling okay and the clothes you brought earlier are sufficient. I'll get the typical discharge instructions from Gail and they've provided me with a walker and a cane for later. The drivers will carry me up the stairs into my bedroom," replied Amanda.

"I miss you, Amanda. See you soon." Amanda was discharged using a walker and told not to drive.

CHAPTER SIXTY-ONE

Mrs. Headley's Wine Bar

Where second year classes were mostly about body systems and focused on preparing the students for clinical experiences with patients. Third year would put the didactic together with the clinical experiences using actual patients. The material was anticipated to be much more interesting as it built on the first and second-year didactic material about disease processes and disease states as related to various organ systems. One day after the afternoon lecture about the reproductive systems Amanda approached David with an idea.

"Are you interested in going out for dinner tonight?" asked Amanda. "I read in Philadelphia Magazine about what looks like a cute restaurant on Second Street called Mrs. Headley's Wine Bar. It sits above the Khyber Pass Bar. The magazine had a two for one dinner coupon."

"Sure, what time were you thinking of?"

"I made a reservation for seven thirty, all they had left. We can take a cab down to Second and Chestnut."

"Your leg feels good? There will be stairs."

"I think so. I've been walking for a couple weeks without the walker. I can go with my cane."

"Dress code?"

"I'll wear pants and sweater, black and white."

"I'll come by at seven. I'll wear the new black jeans you picked out. I'll surprise you with the shirt."

David and Amanda passed Washington Square, the Liberty Bell and headed east to Second in the cab. Mrs. Headley's Wine Bar sat above the Khyber Pass Bar, infamous for hosting the two hundred sailors of the Polish Tall Ship crew under the direction of none other than brother Ben. The legend was the crew drained the bar of all things alcohol. A Jefferson legend was that one crew member had a blood alcohol level of four fifty, usually toxic if not lethal. This particular crewmember made it back to his ship after a banana bag and a couple liters of IV fluids.

The stairway upstairs to the restaurant was narrow, but Amanda made it slowly step by step with her cane.

"Whew. I know that was the most work I've done since discharge. This restaurant is quaint, snug, and warm. Well worth the climb."

The hostess found them a table for two right outside the kitchen. Not the most intimate spot, but the smells from the kitchen made up for the commotion at the door.

The waitress blew by and asked what they wanted to drink. Amanda suggested a bottle of burgundy.

"I've tried Valpolicella, which is supposed to be slightly lighter than a burgundy," replied David.

"There are three choices. Two are Volnay-Burgundy blends, the third is a Château Neuf-du-Pape at $60 a bottle. Can I pick a Volnay?"

"Sounds good."

"May we please have a bottle of Clos du Chateau des Ducs?"

"Very good sir."

The wine arrived post haste with menus. Amanda mentioned the two for one coupon and the waitress said it would not pose a problem.

David poured and swirled the wine in the glass. "Good legs, whatever that means."

Amanda took a sip, "I like it. I also like your shirt, so tight fitting, a bit understated, but the colors are good."

"Thanks. So pasta tonight?"

"Sure. Prima Vera for me."

"I've got my eye on the Chicken Picatta."

"Cheers. Great idea, eating here, Amanda."

They shared the wine and waited for a reappearance of the waitress with some bread. It must have been a long wait. David opened his eyes and realized he'd nodded off. Amanda was still snoozing comfortably when the waitress returned.

"Prima Vera and Chicken Picatta please."

Amanda opened her eyes, "Cheers," and took a sip.

The food soon arrived.

"This Prima Vera is very light and tasty," commented Amanda.

"My chicken is great in this lemon sauce. I didn't know I liked capers."

"I'll split you a tiramisu," offered Amanda.

"Coffee?"

"That would be nice."

Dessert demolished, David placed the coupon under his MasterCard.

"Are you a twenty percent tipper, David?"

"When the food and service rates it, I am."

The waitress returned with David's credit card and the bill.

"Now we have to stagger home," David said as he stood up. He reached for Amanda's hand and the slightly tipsy pair managed the stairs into the raucous bar scene below.

"Normally I'd invite you for an aperitif, but I could not handle more than water at this point."

"That makes two of us, my love."

They staggered into the night and hailed down a cab that took them back to Tenth and Pine. The cool night air cleared their heads and David took a chance and asked Amanda if she was feeling sexy.

She wanted to freshen up and David took that time to put on Santana's 'Abraxas' before he went in to brush his teeth and clean up. Amanda was sitting on the edge of the bed with little on but the bed sheet. David had a brief recollection of the time after Macbeth, but chose to follow the lead of Santana's guitar, which turned out to be the best thing to do. He sat on the bed behind Amanda and started brushing her long hair with his right hand while his left reached around and cupped her left breast. Amanda leaned into him and David spread his fingers so his pinkie caressed her left nipple while the thumb massaged her right breast. Santana serenaded them with his music. David asked, "Stay up or reach down?"

"Down would be nice."

David's left hand brushed against her tummy then down to her right and then left inner thighs. His fingers moved onto the mound of love then his tall finger reached out, into her vagina, which was already moist and warm."

"I'll be turning around now," said Amanda, as she arched her pelvis up and over David. "You need to be getting out of those drawers, my lover," she said somewhat hoarsely as David had not ceased to stroke her clitoris. David pulled his pants down and Amanda pulled them off as she mounted him.

"Now we are getting somewhere, but how's the leg?" asked David.

Amanda replied, "You just lie there and be quiet."

Amanda was soft and slow in her lovemaking, which drove David a bit crazy. They climaxed together and rolled over to spoon and fall asleep. Neither moved until the sun shone through the curtains.

"Is it too much to ask to get a coffee in bed?"

"Coming up," said David rolling out and putting on his sweatpants. Amanda took the opportunity to grab a few more minutes of shut eye.

"Bella," Santana

CHAPTER SIXTY-TWO

One AM Party

"It's one A.M. for God's sake. Don't they know we have class tomorrow and an exam first period? Who throws a party on Thursday? Damn those Pharmacy students and their pill parties," David thought.

He'd been next door once to say hello to the three women living there and asked about the big bowl full of different colored capsules and tablets.

"Those are for our pill parties," replied JoLynn, "Anyone can sample one. Many of the students know the Valiums, Barbs, or Ativans by color. We don't put anything dangerous in the bowl but mixing them with alcohol can be problematic."

David was becoming increasingly agitated and sat up and walked out of his bedroom and down the spiral staircase. He forgot to put on shoes or a shirt but was wearing sweatpants. He paused at the front door and wondered what his play would be with the big crowd.

David opened the front door and walked down the three steps to the sidewalk. He requested to borrow the purple straw hat off the head of one woman who was still looking at the half naked man talking to her. David put the hat on and moved closer to the large group of merrymakers on the sidewalk and on Tenth Street.

"Gentlemen and gentle women of JoLynn's pill party. Please disperse and go home. I have an exam at eight a.m. I have not yet called the cops but am willing to do so."

One of the revelers came up behind and to David's right and grabbed both of his shoulders.

David rammed his right elbow into the man's solar plexus, spun around kicked the side of the man's left knee, collapsing the knee then grabbed his left hand and hyperextended the man's left thumb. He applied a pinch to the left carotid sinus, immediately dropping the man's pulse to forty. The attacker collapsed, and David gently lowered his head to the sidewalk with his right foot.

David turned to the remaining crowd and said, "I'd really like for you to leave now. My roommate and I have an exam tomorrow at eight o'clock. We need to sleep."

Just then a police car rolled up and officer not-so-friendly strode over toward David, who admittedly looked like the agitator in his sweats, pink hat, and foot under the man's neck on the sidewalk.

"I'm glad you are here, officers. I requested these revelers to go home and allow me to sleep."

"You need to come with us sir," replied the policeman.

"I certainly will not, officer."

The policeman took out his Taser, pointed it toward David who took off his hat and adjusted his posture. When the policeman fired his Taser, David moved out of the way, grabbed one of the Taser wires with the folded hat, the other wire landed on his bare chest. David pulled it out then pulled wire, pulling the Taser out of the policeman's hand, which both startled the policeman and made him angry.

"Boy you shouldn't have done that," and reached for his gun.

"Stand down officer," commanded Ben, who had been observing the interaction from the doorway. This did cause the policeman to pause.

"Stand down officer," he said again from the townhouse step. "Ben was in his EMT uniform, which bore a resemblance to a police uniform, but Ben's shirt displayed captain's bars.

The officer re-holstered his weapon.

"Oh boy," thought David, "Got to diffuse this and get the crowd away from this mess."

"I will come over to your police car officer, but you need to listen to me, regardless of my appearance."

"Men and women, please disperse and go home, now," commanded the policeman.

The crowd slowly started to move away, many turning to see if David and the police officer would start fighting. David walked to the police car and Ben went up to the doorway. The second policeman shifted his gaze to David.

"I live here and asked the crowd to disperse. The man on the ground attacked me and I subdued him. Yes, he is ok. My brother probably called you and I'm glad you arrived so rapidly. Sorry about the bare chest and pink hat, I thought the crowd would be shocked and pay attention to me."

"I'm not going to charge you, but please don't tell anyone about your little trick with the Taser wire. How'd you avoid the charge?"

"I grounded it on the man's neck, so he got the charge and will be out a while," replied David.

"I'll be heading upstairs to get as much sleep as is left tonight," David said as he walked back into the townhouse. The police drove off after the crowd was fully dispersed.

"Hey Ben," David called out, "Thanks for calling the police and for bailing me out. How'd you know they would stop when you told them the stand down?"

"A strong voice coming from a uniform using a familiar command. They didn't process it as coming from me. At least they holstered their heaters."

"Well thanks for your help, no telling where it all would have gone if they hadn't."

"Good night, Dave, get what sleep you have left," Ben said as he bolted the front door. Ben headed to the kitchen to make a pot of coffee.

“I’m on call tonight,” he explained.

David had seen Ben drink a pot of strong coffee, then sit in the chair and fall asleep, no problem. David, however paid the price of being wide awake all night even after a caffeinated coffee for breakfast. Amazing the difference between the two brothers.

“Good night, Ben,” said David, “And thanks,” over his shoulder as he climbed the stairs.

CHAPTER SIXTY-THREE

David is Chastised

The next day most of his classmates had heard about David's stand-off and adept take down of the attacker who woke up before the police left. He walked away muttering something about being blind-sided, despite the fact that he had attacked David from the rear. The morning lecture was about heart failure and the role of the kidneys. David tried to pay attention but was still fatigued after a short night's sleep and the eight A.M. exam. Luckily, he could count on Amanda's notes should he miss some details. The lectures were now mostly centered on organ systems and disease states, bringing welcome clinical application to the material. David thought the difference was similar to designing a bookcase from boards of mahogany, compared to actually cutting the wood on a table saw, smelling the sawdust, then staining the wood, bringing out another pleasant odor from the brown wood.

Amanda sought him out after the lecture concluded and asked him, "What were you thinking, David?" She was hot and agitated. "Taking on a crowd of forty drunken and drug sedated crazies. And then the cops. Thank God Ben was there to lend a commanding performance. Do you have a death wish?"

David then recalled what Ben had said about his role in the relationship, taking chances that would make Amanda anxious. "You are right, Amanda. I should have handled it differently. I have again caused you pain and I apologize. More than that, I will try to anticipate problems with my head strong actions and take a breath before acting. Again, I'm very sorry."

"I hope you thanked your brother. Now let's head back and grab some lunch. We've got a full afternoon on the gastronomical system with Dr. Lessar."

As they walked to Amanda's for lunch, David asked how her project on HPV was going. "Are you planning to continue the work while you're in residency?"

"I've spoken with Dr. Warren and he thought it would be possible for me to spend some time in the lab. My project does not require supervision and I can work on weekends if I choose to."

"What's your next step?"

"I want to attend the weekly, multi-disciplinary Cancer conferences to hear how they approach oral-pharyngeal cancers, whether using surgery or chemo-radiation as the initial step. I also want to hear how the different otolaryngologists approach the use of biopsy and testing for HPV in planning for treatments."

"I'm sure someday soon you will be participating in the discussions with relevant information for the clinicians about using the sub-types of HPV to guide therapy."

"I don't know about that. I'll still be just a resident pathologist."

"Yes, but you'll have the cutting-edge information. Do you have enough data to write an abstract and present it at a national pathology conference?"

"I'm getting close to being able to write something that will provide new and useful information. What about your work with Dr. Taylor. You guys seem to be pumping out publications all the time."

"He is a publication machine and I'm lucky to be along for the ride. Unfortunately, my moving to residency and focusing on Psych will make working in his lab difficult."

"We'll see. It's a long shot. We'll be busy learning very different things, but you never know."

They had reached Amanda's townhouse. "Come on in. Your standard PB and J? I've even got some Wonder Bread, or do you want to do a salad for me?"

"Gotta go with the standard. Thanks for buying Wonder Bread. It really makes it. Have you got enough milk?"

Amanda got the Smuckers and bread out of the fridge and the Skippy from the cabinet. "I'll make your sandwich while you play sous chef and chop," she said reaching in the fridge for the veggies. "How you can eat that PB and J every day with probably gallons of milk over time, probably since college from what you've told me, I can't fathom. You look healthy enough, so I won't get in your way, David. I wonder what Lessar would say about its nutritional value to the gut."

"I'll ask him," said David between bites. He was making a second sandwich and took a long swig of milk as he finished up the first. Amanda crunched along, adding a bit more vinegar and oil to her greens.

"Next salad, please a few more tomato slices, a couple olives, and some sliced almonds would be nice," she requested.

CHAPTER SIXTY-FOUR

Body Systems: Dermatology

Although skin was probably the most obvious of organ systems, most of the class knew very little about its structure and functions. Dr. Damron exuded his love of the topic, describing skin from the tactile surface we all love to its inner workings.

"I never appreciated the complexity of the various layers of skin and the organelles embedded within it," commented Amanda later that night while they reviewed the notes and photomicrographs in the text.

"Even the lowly pimple makes sense once you know about the follicles and the secretions that feed the bacteria," added David.

"How much truth there is to the old adage that eating junk food promotes acne?" wondered Amanda.

"Dr. Damron seemed to indicate that the change in fatty acids and oils in adolescence is a result of hormonal shifts. Plus, the skin contains its usual cast of suspect skin bacteria responsible for metabolizing the fatty acids and oils creating a mix that alters the bacteria living in the follicles. That's why topical and even some oral antibiotics are really beneficial," answered David.

The next day Dr. Damron was slated to talk about male and female pattern baldness and the hormonal shifts that caused it, but someone had other ideas. Ralph was somewhat of a class clown, bright, but always at the center of things. He wanted everyone to like him as was obvious to anyone who knew him. That morning Ralph strode down to the blackboard and wrote 'Tomorrow, Red Shirt Day."

True to form most of the class wore some version of red shirts the next day. David had only one red Tee shirt from Avalon, New Jersey, in ratty condition but wore it anyway. There were red sweatshirts, red windbreakers, red football jerseys, and Ralph painted his bare chest red. He was easily encouraged to stand and take a bow to the applause of all. Unfortunately, Ralph had selected a red paint that was not easily removed in the shower and took a few days to wear off. He paid special attention to Dr. Damron's comments that day. He was immensely glad he did not color his face red with the same paint. Amanda was the height of fashion in red slacks, red pumps, and a red shirt pin stripped with blue. David told Amanda she was the best-looking woman in the classroom, as always, when she walked up to his seat to grab him for lunch with Rocky and Bullwinkle. Amanda did not chastise David for the ratty tee shirt but did suggest they go shopping at Gimbels in the future, and David took the hint.

"Perhaps I can pick out a couple pairs of sport shorts for racquetball and put some visual pressure on my lovely opponent," he thought.

The trip to Gimbels was a huge success. David purchased two pairs of high-end jeans, one blue the other black, a pair of athletic shorts, and three tee shirts, all lacking any corporate advertisements. Amanda was able to find an outfit she did not already own, which was a stylish and sexy red and yellow blouse and blue pants, very tight at the waist. David was able to convince her not to purchase a new pair of heels. They held hands as they walked back on Market, then down Ninth past the Walnut theatre where the Babies were booked to perform that weekend.

"Amanda, are you interested in going to that concert?"

"I'm always up for live music, David. I don't know The Babies, but if you want to go, we'll go."

They walked to their respective homes feeling very satisfied with their purchases. They made plans to have dinner together before studying.

They reviewed printed notes as well as the information each of them had taken down. As usual, both Amanda and David picked up on details the other had not.

"I wonder if my mind was wandering when Dr. Damron said that," he confided to Amanda, "I don't recall drifting off, but it's obvious you heard it, felt it was significant, and wrote it down. Do you recall ever consciously omitting some things from your notes because you thought them insignificant?"

"I think it's as you mentioned, David. I find it difficult to listen to a lecture, process the information, and take verbatim notes. Usually, I decide to write it all down knowing I can make sense of it later at home."

"It's either that or skip writing comprehensive notes and simply listen and take it in. That's why our hybrid system is useful, Amanda. You may be listening for the central themes while I'm nose down, taking verbatim notes without really hearing what is being discussed.

"One thing I do pay particular attention to is how well you coordinate your clothes. You are a rainbow of colors. Your blouses compliment your slacks and more often than not your shoes whether heels or sneakers enhance your outfits. I imagine you put a tremendous amount of effort into your ensembles.

Amanda looked David up and down. "You are very observant of my outfits, and I guess expend your attire capital on me, knowing you will pass muster with your clothes as long as they are clean, never mind pressed," she chuckled. "Now your attempt to distract us from the issues at hand having worked, its back to the notes."

After another hour of studying, Amanda closed her books, kissed David good night and announced she had to get home to shower and sleep.

"I'll walk you home Amanda," offered David.

"No I'll run home between the raindrops and you stay here."

Despite the pleasant memory he did not enjoy his climb up the wooden hill to his bedroom this night any more than any other. He decided not to run to the Vet tonight, because of the rain. As he lay on his back listening to the street traffic he reviewed the day that had passed and made a mental list of the things he could anticipate for tomorrow. Sleep did not come easily most nights. More and more of David's nights were intruded, quite pleasantly, by visions of making love with Amanda, sometimes causing an hour of insomnia, cutting into his much-needed sleep.

David thought to himself, "I never fantasize about love making with Amanda while running. Probably a good thing, I'd likely wander into traffic and get run over."

"She's a Rainbow," Rolling Stones

CHAPTER SIXTY-FIVE

Follies and Clinical Rotations

There were a lot of talented people in the class. Right across the street from David and Don's house were four men in two townhomes that had hooked up and formed a rock and roll band. Mike was the lead guitar and Manny played rhythm guitar. Roy was on bass and Bruce manned the drums. They practiced every other evening.

"They sound really good," said Don to David.

Mike invited David and Amanda to listen in on the practice sessions and asked David and Amanda to join them with their flutes, but they declined, "For now," they both said. Mike asked them to practice one rock and roll song and then join their group as soon as soon as they felt comfortable. David did start to play his Gemeinhardt again but drifted to the Paul Simon and Jackson Browne songs.

"Perhaps Mike and his guys could learn a couple Jackson Browne songs," he said to Amanda. That weekend Amanda and David played flute together practicing 'Rock Me on The Water' with Amanda listening on the headphones. Once Amanda heard a song she was able to accompany David playing along with the lyrics. On her first go though she had the tune fifty percent down. It was obvious that once she heard Jackson singing the song she was able to play it better than David ever did. David next taught Amanda 'Doctor My Eyes,' which was somewhat monotonal, but again after a run through with the headphones on, she got it and Amanda harmonized with David on that song. She returned the favor and taught David some of the Four Seasons by Vivaldi, which David recognized, but had never tried to play. David played the opening to Stravinsky's 'The Rite of Spring.' Amanda caught on to Stravinsky quickly and they agreed to purchase the flute music for the Vivaldi and Stravinsky pieces and practice them in earnest. The 'Band of Docs' were able to learn 'Rock Me on The Water' and 'Doctor My Eyes' fairly rapidly after David purchased a copy of 'Saturate Before Using' for them. The flutes played the lyrics as Jackson Browne would have sung them and it sounded fairly decent. The Band of Docs played at a couple of parties and were a big hit with their renditions of 'Peggy Sue' and 'Johnny Be Good.' Amanda and David played counterpoint on 'Peggy Sue' but did not perform with them on the 'Johnny be Good' number. The two flutes did join the Band on the Jackson Browne numbers at the Follies and were a big hit with their classmates.

"Amanda, you are truly amazing. You pick up these songs so well, I admit I'm a little bit jealous."

"Well I was a flute major and should be able to learn and hold a tune, David."

Dr. Darla had delivered a hilarious routine at the Follies the prior year, one that Amanda copied on stage with real verve. Amanda came out in a Darla outfit, complete with glasses and heels then proceeded to write her pseudonym as Darla backwards on the chalkboard to the amusement of all. Amanda as Darla then delivered a parody on ethics and bonding with difficult patients.

Dr. Darla routinely was a class favorite and was selected by the Class of '81 to have her portrait painted the next year. David and Amanda managed to survive the Body Systems lectures and soon were given the chance to select rotations at area hospitals in disciplines of their choice. Of course, all locations and topics did not line up as everyone desired, but most were able to select most of their high priority ones. David elected to do all his third-year work in Wilmington and live with his parents. Somewhat reluctantly, he had to travel back to the Jefferson mother ship and attend Dr. Darla's Introduction to Clinical Medicine, which combined sensitivity training, interview skills, some ethics, a lot of non-pathological psychology and was generally well worth the hour-long commutes on Wednesdays. David had a difficult time with role playing because he felt vulnerable in the somewhat unpredictable interactions.

The students were next farmed out to various local hospitals for their third year clinical experiences. Most were able to participate on the rotations they had selected. A few were less fortunate being assigned to rotations they thought would not teach them what they needed. In the end, however, almost all were able to learn valuable lessons either about the technical side of clinical medicine or witness the all-important skills of interacting with people with disease who were anxious and perhaps non-compliant with the treatments the physicians had selected. David reassured Amanda he would be able to drive her to Chester Crozier to continue her cytopathology rotation while on his way to Wilmington, as long as her Orthopedist gave her the green light to get back to school. David said he would rent a larger car, so she would be able to get in and out with her cane or walker as her leg healed.

"The Super beetle would not be so super for you and your Orthopedic equipment, my love." Amanda had a wonderful time in the cytopathology lab while David did a stint on the inpatient neurology floor at the Delaware Division with Dr. Edelson.

The electives were sometimes stressful, other times not. David spent time on an inpatient Oncology unit at the General Hospital in Wilmington with twenty-four fairly stable patients, many had terminal disease and were receiving chemotherapy directed by National Cancer Institute protocols. He learned to perform paracenteses then instill chemotherapy into the abdomen to treat metastatic ovarian cancer. He cared for a twenty-three-year-old woman with uncontrolled cervical cancer who underwent pelvic exoneration and bilateral leg amputations at the hips. David probably spent more time with her husband and daughter than the patient herself and learned a lot about familial stress that malignancy causes. David also got to know the men and women on the floor very well and had the time to get to know them without feeling stressed. The patients appreciated the time he spent with them, often discussing subjects not related to their illness. He let it be known that he was a stamp collector and as he went room to room on his afternoon rounds, he delivered the mail and received stamps from the patients. One woman had been a hair stylist and took it upon herself to teach David how to shape and maintain his beard and control his bushy mop of hair. He did not see Amanda for an entire month and Amanda did not share her stress during their phone calls.

Amanda had quite a different experience working on a pediatric oncology unit at Children's Hospital in Philly. The new admissions were often very ill, and the chemotherapies frequently gave the children nausea, abdominal pain, and headaches. Depression among these children was very common. Amanda stood by and watched as many children died, only to be replaced by another youngster with a terminal leukemia, brain cancer, or other illnesses not amenable to surgical resection. The loss of young lives weighed heavily on Amanda, who had not been exposed to so much death, nor so much suffering, especially in young, innocent children. Most nights she came home and wept for hours, unable to concentrate on studying. She did not enjoy participating in the chemotherapy protocols administered to the children. About halfway through her rotation, she remembered Sallie, her younger sister who died at age three. Sallie's appendix ruptured, and Sallie became septic with kidney and lung failure. Amanda had been very young herself and probably did not comprehend why Sallie became so ill. She had not thought of Sallie for years and now she realized she had issues in her own family to deal with. Amanda also realized she did have the time nor mental energy to tackle such a project just now.

"I wish David was here. He'd know how to handle this, or at least be here to listen to me dump it all out," thought Amanda, "But I'm going to have to handle this alone. Phone calls about this will not be the best way to handle my anxiety, plus David must have his own issues concerning his patients to deal with. Up to this point we communicated very well concerning personal problems when we able to talk face to face. I think we both tried to be responsive and supportive when the other voiced a concern, but it is different with this distance between us and talking over the phone, not seeing his eyes nor feeling his body comforting me is just not the same. Ah well, two more weeks of living hell."

CHAPTER SIXTY-SIX

Jack of Hearts and Jean-Pierre Rampal

When David and Amanda finished up their oncology rotations, they were able to spend a weekend together before starting their next rotations. They went to dinner at The Jack of Hearts, a tiny BYOB bistro on South Street with marble, heart shaped tables. Life sized reproductions of the appropriate playing cards lined the walls and the wait staff all sported red bow ties and aprons. The wrought iron chairs with red, heart shaped seats were not particularly comfortable, but Amanda and David were more interested in each other than the comfort of their seats. David brought a Bordeaux, anticipated paying the uncorking fee, and was pleasantly surprised when the waitress waived it when she saw how excited they were to be together. The meal went well, and the wine was surprisingly tasty for fifteen bucks. Amanda ordered a spinach salad and David the Cobb salad. As they ate, they tried to catch up on the events of the past month. However, it wasn't their typical deep dive into feelings that they both were used to having after been away from each other for so long. They spoke somewhat tangentially about their rotations and what they had learned. David thought Amanda was concealing something but did not confront her.

"So how did you enjoy your rotation at the General?" asked Amanda.

"I had a very rewarding time interacting with the twenty-four adults on the cancer ward. The majority were elderly and had been in the ward before. The attendings were great, took a lot of time with me, included me in their discussions with patients about new treatment options and then allowed me to either be present or to administer the chemotherapy. I had a few favorites, and most were very willing to share stories of their lives with me. I did morning rounds, for which I wrote notes in the chart about their problems and exams. I wrote about plans for that day, whether additional testing or chemotherapy. I also had time to do afternoon rounds, more of a social interaction which allowed me to interact with patients without having to focus on their chemo or symptoms. We could just chat about what interested them. I found out that I enjoyed seeing patients daily in the chronic care setting. It was much more gratifying than the rapid-fire care in the Emergency Department with no follow up.

"Anything especially interesting?"

"I was given the task of buying marijuana on Route 13," replied David with a smile, "Never done that before."

"Why buy grass if you don't smoke it?"

"You know I've never smoked, except hashish the one time in Israel, just to be polite."

"To be polite, of course." Now Amanda was smiling.

"No, really. Anyway Dr. Walker found that his patients benefitted from marijuana. They often had intractable nausea and anorexia and would lose weight. This compromised their ability to continue with their chemotherapy."

"You supervised little old ladies smoking marijuana in their rooms."

"With their windows open if the weather cooperated. It worked."

"So, you were sent out to break the law and purchase marijuana on Route 13."

"I'll tell you I was not at all comfortable, but I did it," replied David. "I drove just past the intersection of 13 and Wrangle Hill Road. I pulled in behind a car on the southbound side. I remember it was a green Datsun B 210. I got out as did the man in the Datsun. I said I was from the hospital and needed the usual."

"Weren't you concerned it could be an undercover policeman?"

"I had been given a description of the dealer and this guy matched it fairly well. Anyway, he handed me a plastic bag and I handed him the money I had been given. I said thanks. He said, 'no problem, next time, dude' and that was that. Just to be extra careful I put the marijuana in my doctor's bag under my ophthalmoscope, some rolls of gauze and my stethoscope. I was thinking if I got stopped by a policeman, I would say I was going to the hospital, which was true."

"How many trips did you make?"

"Three. Each time it went like clockwork and, no, I was not stopped by Officer Friendly. I was very careful not to speed, I'll tell you."

"So now that you've embarked on a life of crime, did you get a rush of excitement with each buy?" Amanda was chuckling. "I'm surprised you and Sylvester haven't become partners."

"I'm out of that business, Amanda."

"So how was your time at Children's."

"Not as pleasant as your rotation, that's for sure, David. My patients came in very ill and some died within days no matter what the attendings did for them. Very often I took a history, did an exam, spoke with the parents, then was present a week later while these poor, young people died. It was rough, but I did learn a lot about childhood leukemia and lymphoma."

"That sounds incredibly stressful, Amanda. Were you able to interact with any of the children long enough to get to know them?"

"I suppose there was one four-year-old girl with acute lymphocytic leukemia. She was so tough, never complained when I had to restart her IV line, almost never cried when she threw up during her chemotherapy."

"How'd she make out?"

"She was still alive when I left. I'll have to call CHOP and find out how she's doing. She was receiving a new regimen and maybe, just maybe it will be a winner for her."

"I'm glad you had that one ray of sunshine in what sounds to have been a terribly sad rotation."

"There was so much suffering and death. It's hard now to look back and recall any other pleasant interactions."

"How did you cope, Amanda? You never called me to let me know you were having such a miserable time."

"I didn't want to burden you with my problems. I figured you were having an equally tough time with your cancer patients, so I tried to bury myself in my books, studying up on the illness of the day. It was difficult to concentrate. I was not trying to focus on the personalities of the children. I was probably doing my best to distance myself from them."

"I can only imagine how difficult that must have been to suppress the personal and sensitive half of the clinical experience, just to survive."

"It certainly was not how I envisioned caring for children, nor learning about diseases."

"I'm so sorry. Should you ever be in a similar situation, just pick up the phone and tell me you need a visit. I'll be there."

"I know you would have come to my rescue, David, but I wanted to try to deal with it all on my own. Looking back now, it's pretty obvious I did not have to cut myself off from the emotional component of caring for those children."

"Anything positive come out of the rotation?"

"I did learn how to speak with family members under extremely trying circumstances. I probably won't be delivering pathological diagnoses to patients and their families as a pathologist, but I will know how to start the conversation."

"Well, this is going to seem a bit awkward, but I have a gift for you, my love," said David handing Amanda a small box. "I also made arrangements for another surprise, Amanda, and we need to finish up here," said David, "I have tickets for a Jean-Pierre Rampal concert at the Academy of Music. I am very interested to hear more about your rotation, but I also want to hear your take on Rampal's skill as he maneuvers through the different pieces of music. Can we skip desert and hustle over to the Academy?"

"This is so thoughtful, David," Amanda said holding the single pearl necklace up to her neck. "You have made this evening very special and have brightened my mood considerably."

David payed the bill then he and Amanda walked to the concert. Amanda especially enjoyed the Bach Flute Sonata. David was struck by Rampal's ability to interpret Scott Joplin's Ragtime as well as a Mozart Flute Sonata with equal genius. They were a bit saddened when Jean-Pierre ended his performance. They both had been able to escape from the stress of their clinical studies into the uplifting music.

While they walked back to David's townhouse, he commented on how well she was walking with her cane. Amanda said the fracture had not been bothering her and that her Orthopedist had advised her to walk as much as was comfortable, but not to do too many stairs, nor jump. The tops of the buildings were outlined by the nearly full moon. A few clouds passed over the moon. The small amount of wind at their backs was not too chilly as they discussed their next set of rotations, Amanda was going on to Labor and Delivery at Lankaneau, David to Nephrology in Wilmington and both were excited at the prospects. Amanda reached out to hold David's hand and gave him a firm squeeze. David squeezed back and held on gently. They were similar in height and holding hands was comfortable. David thought she was holding on to steady herself due to her limp. He did not suspect she was holding on for emotional support.

"Bach Sonata," John Pierre Rampal

CHAPTER SIXTY-SEVEN

David and Amanda's Passionate Hook Up

They walked down Pine to Tenth Street to David's townhome where they shared a Jack and Coke in the living room. Amanda unexpectantly hopped onto David's lap and kissed him hard and long, pressing tightly against him. She reached behind him and pulled his shirttails out of his pants and started to unbutton his shirt. David all but carried her up the stairs to his bedroom then undressed her as she continued her passionate kissing. Amanda pulled his shirt off and barely gave David time to get his pants off when she pressed him back onto the bed. She got on top and started aggressively coupling with him. David had never experienced such forceful lovemaking and soon was lost in his own passion. Amanda climaxed with a loud and long moan, then collapsed onto David's chest. David had already climaxed and wondered what had brought on this passion. She lay quietly without moving for a long time then began to sob, first quietly, then uncontrollably. David stroked her hair and rubbed her back but did not speak for a while.

Eventually, David asked, "Amanda, what's wrong?"

Through her sobs Amanda began to describe her sadness during the past month and mixed in her memories of Sallie and her sister's terrible illness and death. David remained silent, continuing to hold her tightly and kiss her cheeks. After what seemed like hours, Amanda's storm of sadness passed, and she rolled off and went to the bathroom. She returned and sat on the bed stroking David's head.

"You are such a sweet man. I had no idea all of that was going to erupt, but I feel so much better now. Thank you for listening and holding me."

"Of course, my love," replied David, "Are there other things you want to talk about? We've all weekend."

"Not right now. I am a little concerned that we won't be able to get together during this next month."

"I'll see if I can find even one day on the weekends to drive to Philly so we can talk."

"Oh, I'm sure it will not only be talking, mister hotness," Amanda chuckled.

"I'm glad you are obviously feeling a little better. I need to visit the head and clean myself up."

When David returned Amanda was fast asleep. He got under the blanket without disturbing her and rapidly joined her in sleep.

Amanda woke David with a kiss and helped him sit up. She handed him a cup of coffee and sat next to him on the bed. They drank in silence for a few minutes, then David thanked her for allowing him to sleep in. Amanda stood up and went down to the kitchen, reappearing with a couple omelets, cream cheese on everything bagels, and a glass of OJ.

"How about we go to the Art Museum and check out the Degas exhibit?" asked David.

"I would love to spend the day with you, anywhere you want to go is fine with me."

They finished breakfast, then made love, slowly and gently, falling asleep again in each other's arms.

"Night Moves," Bob Seger and The Silver Bullet Band

CHAPTER SIXTY-EIGHT

Engagement Ring

After that passionate night David decided to propose to Amanda.

"No matter where we match, I want Amanda to know how much I love her and that I am in this for the long run. We can support each other as we have done for the past four years. We've done that very well. The possibility of distance between us during residency will need to be discussed once the match comes out."

He wasn't quite sure when or where to ask her, but he knew it was right. He walked to Robbins Eighth and Walnut to look at engagement rings, because their radio commercials appealed to him and were the most frequent on WMMR. Once inside and speaking with the moderately high-pressure salesman, he was overwhelmed by the diversity of choices for quality, color, clarity, cut, and size. David enjoyed looking at the diamonds through the Gemscope, having done mineralogy as an undergrad. He was not all that intimidated by the costs, because he had not yet decided on which stone to select. The prices escalated each time one of the value indicators improved and he knew that eventually he'd have to settle on a diamond of reasonable size and quality. David put clarity above size and had already decided on the classic round style. He knew not to rush into selecting a stone, because there were so many jewelers in that four-block area he had many choices. After shopping around for a couple of weeks he gravitated back to Robbins and made his purchase, a 1.5 carat, color grade E, clarity VS1, and decided to have it set in platinum. The diamond was an excellent, round, brilliant stone as flawless as David could afford. The tricky part was getting Amanda's ring size, but he was able to borrow a set of sizers and tried them on her while she was deeply asleep one night. He imagined the ring on Amanda's finger. It just seemed right, but he was well aware that Amanda may not want to become engaged while in residency, especially if they matched in different cities.

When David went back to pick up the ring, he asked the salesman if he could look at the stone one more time under the Gemscope. The salesman set the ring under the Gemscope and stood back allowing David to take a look.

"This is not the diamond I selected," David said to the salesman, "This one has inclusions that were not present in the stone we looked at last week, the one on which I paid a deposit."

"There must be some mistake, sir. This is the diamond you selected."

David took the diagram from his pocket that was completed when he paid for the diamond. There were no inclusions marked on the diagram of the diamond's table, but the inclusions were obvious under the Gemscope. David refused to pay for the ring and left the store. He went back to his townhome and changed from his blue jeans and tee shirt into his pin striped, three-piece suit and dress shoes. He returned to the store an hour later and requested to speak with Mr. Robbins. He explained that the stone currently in the ring was not the diamond he had partially paid for and showed Mr. Robbins the diagram. Mr. Robbins became very angry. He realized the salesman had not completed the diagram, because almost all diamonds in that price range had some inclusions, which should have been marked on the diagram. Mr. Robbins asked David if he would accept another diamond of better quality and placed it under the Gemscope. It was slightly larger and of better clarity. It did have one inclusion, however, which did not detract from the beauty to the naked eye. David said this would be acceptable and Mr. Robbins completed a new diagram demonstrating the inclusion and listing the carats, clarity, color, cut, and apologized for the mistake. He said the ring would be available tomorrow. David left Robbins Eighth and Walnut feeling vindicated.

"I'm sure wearing the suit made all the difference," he thought.

David returned to the store the next day, looked at the stone under the Gemscope and was pleased to see it was the same diamond he and Mr. Robbins had looked at. David paid the balance for the ring and walked back to his town home. He hid the box containing the ring in his dresser.

"I just made the most expensive purchase of my life, other than for medical school and I am stymied with the ring sitting in my sock drawer," he thought.

David found himself looking at the ring with its flashy diamond each night before going to sleep. He just couldn't decide when to ask her. He debated with himself about asking Mr. Jackson for Amanda's hand in marriage but decided on secrecy because he didn't know Mr. Jackson all that well and wanted to surprise Amanda. So, the ring rested in its velvet-lined gray box in David's sock drawer for the next few weeks.

CHAPTER SIXTY-NINE

Clinical Rotations

The Chief of Medicine at the Wilmington Medical Center was Dr. Robert Flint, who was a nephrologist. David was able to spend time with the third-year resident Dr. Benson, rotating on nephrology and attended morning report with the medical residents, hosted by Dr. Flint. David was learning so much so rapidly. He read each night in his text on a topic applicable to one of the interesting patients he met during rounds on the floors or in the medical ICU. He also accompanied Dr. Benson when he rounded at Saint Francis Hospital across town and was amazed at the difference in the levels of sophistication between the two hospitals. Dr. Benson and David transferred a few patients to the Delaware Division for in house dialysis and advanced care on the medical service. David was often the first person the nurses called and had opportunities to answer their questions within his scope of expertise. He had Dr. Benson's permission to call him should David feel he was not able to solve the problems himself and Dr. Benson never rebuked him. One patient was extremely challenging. The young man was a chronic alcoholic and for whatever reason had resorted to drinking a pint of methanol chased with a pint of isopropyl alcohol. The man was complaining of severe abdominal pains, but the ER resident noted the man was blind. Toxicology screen demonstrated the methanol and isopropyl. Dialysis was not going to benefit his methanol poisoning, so he was hydrated, and his urine alkalized, but to no avail. He went into renal failure and was totally blind in a day. David found himself spending much of his time counseling the man about blindness and the support systems available to him. Otherwise, patient care was very pleasant, and David enjoyed learning about diseases of the kidney and how it affected cardiac and pulmonary function. He recalled the lectures by Dr. Carlos, Dr. Green, and Dr. Jane about pathology, physiology, and pharmacology dealing with combinations of organ dysfunction and realized he had received excellent preparation for the work he was now doing. He also had to read the Jefferson core curriculum materials but enjoyed interacting with actual patients and to be able to relate to the real clinical information so much more enjoyably. David worked diligently, and Dr. Benson was very glad to oblige David when he asked to leave a bit early to pick up Amanda to drive her home. David lost a lot of time driving back to his townhouse each night instead of staying in Wilmington. He just had to get up extra early to drive Amanda to Lankaneau. He was glad to be able to spend the travel time with Amanda, who was becoming stronger each day. The problem was now that she no longer had car, even if she could drive herself. David already had a plan in place for that.

Thankfully, Amanda was able to get around without her walker on her obstetrics rotation. She had some difficulty with her first delivery, but she did well with the second one. She found delivering healthy babies and seeing the joy in the faces of the mothers and fathers really restored her interest in medicine. The depression and sadness from the pediatric oncology unit was still in the back of her mind, but as she followed her deliveries to discharge she was able to balance the wonders of childhood life with the undeniable sadness of childhood cancer. She was sleeping more soundly and had more energy to study. When Amanda rode with David to her townhome she described one delivery where the chief resident announced, "and here comes the placenta." Ms. Jones, the mother, named her daughter Placenta, because she thought that name was so pretty. The little baby girl went home as Placenta Jones. Amanda was able to review most if not all of her cases with David without the anxiety she had felt when doing Oncology. Amanda's fracture healed rapidly and by the end of the rotation Amanda was able to walk with a cane everywhere she went. She and David were able to eat dinner together and it seemed to David they both were more relaxed and able to talk about their lives without any tension. The year was rapidly ending, and their conversations often turned to The Match, looming the near future. Neither Amanda nor David broached the topic of moving in together should they both match in Philly nor about marriage, but the topic was always on David's mind. He rarely forgot about the ring.

CHAPTER SEVENTY

Dinner at Tres-Chimeneas

"I've got a great idea for dinner," said David, looking up from his Nephrology textbook, "How about we eat at the Cordon Blue restaurant over near Eleventh and Quince Street? Dr. Holloway, my ID professor while I was on Infectious Disease rotation in Wilmington, took a group of us to dinner and paid for the whole thing. It was a magnificent Five Star night. The chef had been a student of Holloway's back in the day. The restaurant itself was fairly intimidating. As you walked up the stairs to enter, the menus were affixed to the wall, no prices mind you. When we entered the restaurant, we were each handed a tall-stemmed glass of white Bordeaux. Pricey was all I could think of. Dinner was to die for, and dessert was a freshly baked Plum and Thyme Galette. What do you think? My treat of course."

"That sounds delicious, David. Tonight? Sounds like we need to dress up."

"Great. I'll call now and see if they have a reservation. This will be no Mrs. Headley's Wine Bar dinner, I promise."

"Oh, that was fun in its own right, but this sounds like a big step up."

"I wonder if the chef will remember our dinner party if I drop Dr. Holloway's name. I recall the chef came out in his white, puff hat and sat with us at the end of the night. He was very personable, but he and Doc Holloway had cooked up a stunt to embarrass me."

"What did they do? Were they angry with you?" asked Amanda with real concern in her voice.

"Nah. I know Bill Holloway really liked me. I worked long hours to enlist patients into his antibiotic protocols," David replied, smiling at the memories. "What they did was have the Chef, and I forget his name, come out and hand me the bill for the meal. We were a party of sixteen and the amount was a doozy. Dr. Holloway announced it was customary that the person who sat at the head of the table, and he was very clear that he was at the tail end, had the honor to pick up the tab."

"And I suppose you were sitting in the chair of honor."

"Correct. I took one look at the bill, thought about the fifty dollars in my wallet and that the only credit card I owned was from Sears and Roebuck. Well, my face probably said it all to everyone. While I was anticipating spending the next month washing Cordon blue off plates in the kitchen, the rest of the table were laughing their asses off. The Chef kindly bailed me out after what seemed an eternity and handed the bill to Dr. Holloway, who shot me a special you're welcome look that made it all okay. I'll probably never forget that dinner and will always check ahead on the prices and likely total cost."

David and Amanda decided to dress up. David wore his suit with the new tie Amanda had purchased during their last foray to the Wanamaker men's store. Amanda wore a shimmering blue dress, the pearl pendant David had given her, and three-inch heels. David could have sworn Amanda was an inch taller than he was that night. They walked up the narrow staircase and as David had mentioned the menus without prices lined the wall. Amanda entered first and was handed a tall-stemmed glass of white wine by the waitress. Amanda turned to David and said, "You certainly were not exaggerating."

They were shown to their seats and handed menus. On the white tablecloth were placed blue and white bread plates. The pattern on the handle of the butter knife matched the plates. The waitress set French bread on the table with whipped, honey butter in a blue bowl, which David sampled immediately having missed lunch. Amanda looked around and was impressed at the diversity of people. Couples and tables of up to six filled the intimate restaurant. French art and wine posters added charm to the walls. The waitress returned and asked if they were doing well so far.

"Couldn't be any better."

"May I take your order?"

Amanda ordered the Chicken Cordon-Blu as did David. Amanda asked for the beet salad and David the wedge of lettuce with, of course, blue cheese dressing.

"When in Rome," he said.

"Very good," she replied and left David and Amanda to converse about their plans once the Match came out. They both avoided the topic of moving in together should they both match in Philly, but the conversations were lighthearted.

David became serious only once when he described his feelings for Amanda. "Over the past six years I've lived in Newark, Orono, Elat, and now in Philly, but I never considered any of them as my home. At least not until now. And its not the city that is my home, it is you, Amanda. My home is where you are. You are the love of my life and I want to live in this home forever. I suppose this sounds like a marriage proposal and maybe soon it will be, but I just wanted to say it to you, so you could hear it."

"Amanda leaned over the table and held David's hand. "That is the nicest thing anyone has ever said to me, David. You are the first and last thing, person, I think of each day. Without stealing your metaphor, you are my home and I want to live here with you as well."

David stood up and walked around the table to kiss Amanda. The woman at the next table had overheard their conversation and held her hand to her heart and looked at her husband who wondered what her passionate expression was all about. His wife smiled and blew him a kiss.

Amanda and David sat quietly for a moment then Amanda picked up her fork. The delicious food did not dampen their subsequent discussions, either. Amanda reached into her purse and brought out a small, thin, and nicely wrapped item.

"A present for you, David."

What is it?" asked David as he unwrapped the gift. "It's a painting! Thank you, Amanda. I don't know the artist but it calls to mind thc painting we saw together the day we visited the Pennsylvania School of Fine Arts. Is this the one that reminded me of Van Gogh? I believe it is. What a lovely surprise and all for a buck and a half!"

"You're welcome even though you are making fun of me. Very good, David. I went back there a few weeks ago and spoke with the proprietor who suggested this one painted by a local Philly artist was an exceptional find. The artist fancies himself an aficionado of Van Gogh."

"I love it. Now I won't have to stare at the blank, white wall every night as I am studying. This is so very thoughtful, Amanda."

"And thank you for what has been a wonderful night out, my love," she said, leaning over to give him a tender kiss.

"I'm not sure this will be our go-to restaurant in Philly, but one can hope."

"Maybe I can learn a few things about Chicken Cordon-Blu and try it out on you in my new apartment, where ever that will be."

"Just a few more days before match day, then we'll know."

The waitress returned with their meals, which were, as promised, out of this world delicious.

"My mom makes really good chicken, but nothing on this level," exclaimed Amanda.

"My mom is a great cook, but mostly in the pot roast and potatoes arena," replied David, "She does make great bread."

The waitress returned when every last morsel of their dinner had been consumed and asked about their choices for dessert.

"I was here a while back and the kitchen made a wicked puff pastry, is there such a thing as a Thyme Galette," asked David, "What are your choices tonight?"

"We have the Plum Thyme Galette you recalled as well as Palmiers, which are French pastry cookies, and of course the Mille-Feuille Napoleon."

"May I have the Thyme Galette," asked Amanda.

"I would very much like the Mille-Feuille," said David.

"Excellent choices. May I refresh your wine, or bring a wine list?"

"I really am enjoying this wine," said Amanda, "I would like another pour. Is this white a Bordeux?"

The waitress replied that it was.

"I will follow my most wise friend," said David.

"Most wise friend? I believe you are either half toasted, or setting the lure for the big fish tonight," smiled Amanda.

"A little of the first and always the second."

The desserts arrived and were both visually a big hit and delicious.

"I admit I am biting my tongue not to order seconds on dessert, Amanda."

"I'll put Napoleons on my 'learn to do' list after the Cordon-Blu," laughed Amanda.

The bill was astronomically expensive as expected, but David had no problem paying it with a twenty percent tip.

"This has got to be the best dinner and time out with my lovely lady I've ever experienced."

They thanked the waitress.

"My thanks also to the Cordon-Blu and pastry chefs," said David, handing the waitress two twenty-dollar bills for them. He did not even recall his hope that the chef would come out to say hello. The two walked carefully down the staircase and out into the night air.

It was a short walk home and once at her town house Amanda said, “I’m exhausted. I’d rather sleep here tonight”.

“Pick you up at six-thirty for mass?” asked David.

“I’ll be waiting.” David helped her up the stairs and opened the wooden door to the townhome for her.

“Hope you sleep well tonight, my love,” he called out as the door closed.

CHAPTER SEVENTY-ONE

Missed Period

At the end of the month, Amanda received some very disconcerting news from her own womb. She had missed her period. When she back calculated her use of her birth control pills, she found she had four extra pills. She thought back to the prior month and realized she had likely skipped the pills during the depths of her depression. Unfortunately, she also did not take one when she and David made passionate love the night after she completed the oncology rotation. She did not have to think twice to know David had not worn protection either, so aggressive had she been, initiating the encounter.

"Shit," she thought to herself, "I've got to get a pregnancy test first thing tomorrow."

Amanda did not share her thoughts with David, even after the pregnancy test returned positive.

"I thought my breasts were a bit tender," thought Amanda, "So now the big decision, or actually two decisions. First do I carry this pregnancy and have a child or get an abortion ASAP. Secondly, do I tell David now, after the abortion, or never. That's the tougher problem. Will he want me to carry the baby, get married, the whole thing. I want to do a Path residency now and not put it off for a couple years. After David told me he's thinking of Psych, which he could probably do at Jeff, I wonder if he wants to take on a wife and child, bigger apartment, new car," she chuckled at the irony of wrecking her Saab and David puttering around in the yellow Beetle.

"I'll get the abortion now and confide in David later, who I pray will see my logic and not be too hurt. Hell. We've never talked about that part of our future. Well, there's nothing I can do today but get some sleep. No chance of arranging an abortion on Sunday, so this will have to wait until we start our next rotations. Damn! I did not know I was fertile Myrtle. Now I know David and I both are, but that five-day window without my pills was really tight. This is one hell of an ethical situation, nothing I ever dreamed of when Dr. Darla was teaching us ethics."

David and Amanda got together at Amanda's townhome to study around noon. Amanda did her level best not to let on anything was bothering her, but David picked up on something and Amanda told him she did not sleep well because of aching in her thigh.

"I did a lot of standing, delivering the babies, which I loved doing, by the way."

David did not question her again. He told her he'd drive her to Chester Crozier Monday morning for the new burn unit rotation and pick her up that evening.

"Will you be ok? What if a child comes in with severe burns?"

"I think I will be able to handle it. If it gets dicey, I will speak with the resident about my reaction to the children on oncology and maybe I will be able to care for some of the patients closer to discharge."

"Sounds good, but please talk with me as soon as that dark depression creeps in."

Amanda arranged to have the abortion on Saturday morning back in Philly. She took a taxi and David never suspected anything. Amanda realized she had crossed a line in her relationship with David. She was not sure if it was only the trust issue by not confiding with David to reach a shared decision. She thought long and hard about her commitment to David. She had been almost glib when she told him their relationship would survive residency in different cities and different disciplines. Now she realized David was coming in second and she was looking out for Amanda first and foremost. She thought of her one dinner with her racquetball partner, Thomas. "That was fun, relaxing even though he wasn't my style. Studying, tests, all those medical school stresses had been completely absent during dinner. Maybe that was more the attraction and not Thomas, as nice a man as he is," she thought. "I enjoy my time with Richard, but it is unlikely we two will have a dinner date. He seems happily married. Would a few more dates outside my relationship with David answer the question? I just don't know," she told herself. I never had a serious boyfriend during my undergraduate days. David is a deadly serious fellow. Maybe he is pushing me too hard, too fast. Maybe I am holding back, because I am not sure I want to continue this intense relationship, possibly moving to marriage. I think he'd have wanted to be in on the discussion even if he supported me getting the abortion. I must talk with him next weekend. Why do I feel frightened to talk with David? I don't know. Perhaps I could speak with Father Joseph before confronting David," she said to herself.

CHAPTER SEVENTY-TWO

Amanda in the Confessional Booth

Amanda decided to talk with Father Joseph before telling David about her abortion. She went to Saint Mary's that afternoon. It was a cool and blustery day. Amanda was glad she had chosen to wear her light blue jacket. There were only a couple people in line at the confessional waiting for Father Joseph.

"Bless me Father for I have sinned, really sinned."

"I recognize you as a regular at the seven a.m. masses, my child. You have recently been accompanied by a young man. Are you close?"

"Yes, Father we are. I love and trust him very much. I became pregnant last month after a very passionate night. I had been very stressed during my clinical rotation and had forgotten to take my birth control pills."

"And I assume the young man got caught up in passion as well and did not use protection either. Does he know?"

"Correct and no he does not, but I want to tell him. I'm afraid he will be angry with me for not sharing in the decision."

"The bigger issue at hand is that you aborted a life. You know the Holy Father and Catholic Church doctrine absolutely prohibit abortion except in very special situations."

"I am aware of that, Father. I wish to be granted absolution for taking the life of a fetus and be given penance."

"What will be your next medical school assignment?" asked Father Joseph.

"I am now rotating on labor and delivery, Father, but will be starting a burn unit rotation soon."

"First you should consider the young man's feelings, despite him having no choice at this point. Second, I assign you fifty Hail Mary's, as she was mother to Jesus. Third I hope you will be able to spend considerable time in the newborn nursery and consider that you could have had a child yourself to love and care for."

"Thank you, Father."

"I would also request you return to the confessional and tell me how you and your young man are doing as you handle this crisis of faith. I suspect you will have much to do to repair the damage to your relationship, that is if you choose to maintain your love. Please continue to attend Mass and to bring your young man with you. That little bit of structure will prove very useful."

"I will be glad to do that as well, Father."

"May you go in the love and peace of our Lord, Jesus Christ," said Father Joseph making the sign of the cross in the confessional window. Amanda blessed herself and went to the communion railing to begin her prayers.

On her walk home it started to sprinkle, a warm rain, but still annoying as her jacket did not have a hood. Amanda imagined an iceberg calving off an Antarctica glacier, "This is not a fissure between David and me," she thought, "It is between my prior self and my present self. What do I want? I love David and want to be with him, but do I want to take on marriage now? How will residency change us? Will it support our stressful times or create new stress? I had a near melt down during the oncology rotation, mostly due to losing contact with my touchstone, David. Should I learn to confront and overcome my problems by myself? Will David encounter problems and need my support, perhaps overwhelming my own stress tolerance? I will need more time to sort these many questions out."

Chapter Seventy-Three: Informing David

Amanda did not tell David about her priest's request for her to spend as much time as possible with newborns and holding them. She could do that at Jeff in her spare time, especially the babies born to drug addicted mothers. Amanda wondered if she could continue to withhold the truth from David, knowing she had ended her own fetus' life. She was up in the air about when and where to tell David about her abortion. She felt the tension building and wondered how long she could keep it bottled up without giving clues that David would pick up on. She wondered how marriage would work in this type of situation, but certainly one as significant as an abortion would never occur again.

Amanda tried to select the perfect time and place to tell David about her abortion, but in the end, she told him while they studied. Amanda was sitting cross legged in the corner of the couch with a blanket over her legs. David was sitting in the middle facing her with his feet under a wooden tray table on which he had been writing.

"Of course, it was your decision to make, Amanda, but I would have appreciated being told about it to be able to share my thoughts. I can only imagine the stress the pregnancy put on you. But remember I was one half of that crazy night. I should have put on a condom but was swept away by your passion. No excuse, just the truth. Do you recall way back to Kyle's Friday night party? You asked me to do something?"

"It was 'be honest with me.' I remember, David, and I'm sorry I did not include you up front in the decision."

"Does this change our relationship, Amanda? I mean do you think you and I can be honest in all things going forward? Are you having second thoughts about staying a couple now and during residency. That will no doubt be more time consuming and difficult than these monthly clinical rotations, even if we were to both match at the same hospital. I know you want to stay at Jeff and pursue pathology. Dr. Paul told me he could write me a strong letter and get me an interview at Harvard, where he trained. I suspect he could also make an argument for me to remain at Jeff if I try to match here."

"I just don't know what I am thinking, David. I love you, I really do. I care for you and want to be with you. This pregnancy, as short as it was, has really started me thinking about a lot of things. Do you remember when Dr. Darla discussed Maslow's hierarchy of needs? I think you and I are reaching the 'self-actualization summit.' I need to continue to grow with you in our relationship, yet still maintain a degree of self-autonomy, which I want to continue to develop. You are confronting your own changes, developing a more spontaneous side of yourself. All this in a relationship boxed in by our medical education at Jeff and soon by our residencies. Can you give me a little time to sort things out?"

"Absolutely, Amanda. All the time you need. I remember Dr. Darla discussing the Michelangelo effect in relationships. I believe you have sculpted some portion of who I now am. I have probably pushed for adjustments in your, let's face it, almost perfect personality and behaviors. I just want to continue to spend time with you. It's a big piece of my heart that's at risk here. Of all the things that have happened recently, I would do it all over again. I love you. You are the most important person in my life and I'm sure time will pass quickly for us, no matter where we end up in residency. I'll talk with Dr. Paul about the quality of the pysch residencies at Jeff, maybe even Penn or Temple. I know he favors his alma mater, Harvard, but it's a long way from Jeff, where it seems you will end up. I am willing to make it work if it's what you want. I love you more every day. That's corny but true."

David reached over to hold Amanda and she responded with her head on his chest and her breathing slowed. David picked up her feet and stretched her out on the couch. He covered her with the blanket and arranged the pillow under her head. He decided to make a bed with a blanket on the rug, so he would not disturb her. The sunlight woke Amanda first and she climbed next to David on the floor and fell back to sleep until the alarm went off and it was time to get ready for the clinicals. Amanda still felt a bit uneasy despite sharing the truth about her abortion with David. She asked David how he felt. "I must admit I am a bit unsettled but will work on understanding my feelings and the origins of the stress and possible solutions."

"I really admire how you are able to move to define the issues and look forward to solutions," admitted Amanda.

"I'm doing it for me and I'm doing it for us," replied David, reaching for Amanda and holding her close.

CHAPTER SEVENTY-FOUR

Match Day

Although there was a general excitement in the lecture hall as friends exchanged their news about matching, Amanda and David were not so fortunate. Most of the Jefferson students were selected at the institutions of their choice, such was the quality of their education and performances. Amanda matched for pathology at Jeff, while David matched for psych at Harvard.

Amanda tried to bolster David's spirits after class, "The Brigham is not too shabby a residency to land, my love. We'll just have to work harder to minimize the impact of the distance. The phones work well and the train travels both ways. I will do what I can to see you each weekend as I'm sure you will. Boston is a great place to live, I was there a few times during my undergrad days. Think of it as having two world class cities to call our own."

"Thanks Amanda, but it won't be the same not coming home to see you each evening. I know there are phones and mail service, trains, and planes, but we will both need to invest in our own residency programs in order to maximize our residency experiences."

"I know that but allow me a little slack to be somewhat unrealistic right now. Do you want to join another couple for dinner? That may help distract us a bit. Is Ben around tonight?"

"He's working EMT today and tonight. He's moved into Don's room and keeps crazy hours. We used to eat dinner or breakfast together on a regular basis. After he took the promotion, he seems to be working all the time."

"What about the woman who had the apartment in Orlowitz across the hall from you? I think her name was Lisa, she was in the Med Tech program. Do you want to give her a call?"

"Lisa graduated and got a job at the hospital in Lancaster. She'll do well, probably end up running the lab in a couple years. Who else do you have in mind?"

"How about Don and his number one squeeze, Lillian. I hear they are going to WVU for Internal Medicine."

"I'll give Don a call. Ok if I let them select the restaurant if they want double up with us? I haven't spoken to Don much since he moved into Lillian's apartment."

"Let me know where and when. Pip-pip, stiff upper lip and all that."

"Where are the boys of Monty Python when you need them?"

"Let's get home and clean up for dinner. A shower always does me good."

"Do you want to start looking at housing for next year, now you've got your assignment?"

"I've done some preliminary investigations. Remember that quaint Quince Street? There may be some turnover. I called a relator and she thought she had a couple of leads. Can we make time to look with her?"

"Absolutely. Quince Street was where I wanted to go after leaving Orlowitz, but there were no vacancies," said David, "You would be close to Jeff and I recall it being a very safe neighborhood. What time did you and the realtor agree upon?"

"Ten tomorrow. Will that work for you?"

"Of course. I'll be your silent partner, just looking for the types of problems that I encountered in that Tenth and Pine hovel."

David called Don who said he and Lillian would be happy to double date for dinner. David told Don he could make the choice of which restaurant and what time would be good for Lillian. Don asked if David had heard of Bookbinders on the waterfront. David said that would be a good choice, not wanting to tell Don he and Ben had eaten there and found it to be okay, but a bit touristy. They agreed on meeting at the restaurant at six thirty. Don said he would call David if he could not get a table for seven o'clock, which he was able to do. Amanda had not met Lillian and took time to get to know her over a glass of wine. While at the bar, Don caught David up on his opportunity to do internal medicine in Morgantown. When their table was ready, the couples walked into the dining room for dinner and the conversations focused again on Don's plans to move to Morgantown for his residency.

"I'm hoping to get into a pulmonary fellowship and WVU has a very strong program."

"I would imagine the black lung patients make up a lot of the population," said Amanda.

"And probably a lot of the research as well," added David.

"Lillian, will you be able to find work in the Clinic or the hospital now that you've earned your RN?" asked Amanda.

"Actually, I earned a BSN while at Jeff," replied Lillian, "It was a bit more work, but I was told it was a better degree in the long run."

"Impressive, Lillian," said David. "It seems your relationship is pretty solid for Lillian to just pick up and move to the hills of West Virginia with my roommate."

Don smiled and said that he and Lillian were engaged.

"Congratulations you two," exclaimed Amanda, "That's a big step."

Don turned to David and before he could ask, David said, "Amanda and I have not dipped our toes into that conversation yet, Don."

Amanda smiled at Lillian and said, "You will have to tell me all the things you will be learning about the time leading up to actually getting married, Lillian."

"Like scouting the lay of the land for you, Amanda?"

"Only if you want, but I'm sure I know nothing about it," laughed Amanda.

Don looked at David. "Why so quiet roomie?"

"I'm just enjoying seeing you and Lillian so happy," said David, trying to hide his discomfort about the subject.

The remainder of the dinner went well, and the food was not as mundane as David had recalled.

"Good fish and chips and I liked the microbrew," he said to Amanda.

The couples finished up with dessert and then exchanged handshakes and embraces before driving home.

"I must admit I've not seen Don that happy and confident, Amanda."

"Lillian seems nice, I hope the move to Morgantown and a new job will not be too stressful with a marriage on the horizon."

The conversation turned to plans for graduation and did not return to marriage.

CHAPTER SEVENTY-FIVE

Home Hunting

David and Amanda walked over to Quince Street and admired the street lined with quaint town homes.

"I love the flowers in window boxes. The street is immaculate and feels safe," observed Amanda.

"They are real flowers, not like the plastic ones along Eight Street," noted David.

"That speaks to the resident's investing time in appearances," replied Amanda.

"There's the sign for the rental. Have you met your realtor? I suppose it will be obvious who she is when she shows up." asked David.

"Any time now. There she is. Hello Diana. This is David."

"Hello David. Amanda are you ready to look at the apartment?"

"I have a question, Diana," said David, "Any chance the entire townhouse would be up for sale?"

Amanda shot David a look.

"Interesting," said Diana, "I'll discreetly investigate that. For now, let's look at what's available."

Diana opened the front door and the three entered the foyer.

"The apartment is on the third floor."

"Pretty wide foyer, but steep steps," said Amanda.

David observed, "The wood has been well preserved, almost as if there was a staircase runner on it at one time. Yes, look at these tiny screw holes at the side of each riser, I wish I could've seen the rug they chose."

"The staircase is attractive with the natural wood," replied Amanda.

"The third-floor window is tall enough to allow for moving bed and dressers into the apartment, you'll just need a crane."

They climbed the stairs and peered into the galley kitchen with stainless steel appliances.

"The stove, fridge, and dishwasher are two years old," said Diana anticipating their question. "You can see the stove is gas, so perhaps the unit is heated by gas as well."

"The cabinets appear to be adequate, but the sink is a little small," observed Amanda.

"The hinges are top quality," added David. "What do you think of the dining area and the living room, Amanda?"

"There is a good flow from the kitchen, the walls are in good shape and I like the cream color. This is a single floor apartment and you'd not expect much different." They checked out the tiled bathroom with new showerhead and faucets, the fairly spacious closet, and the bedroom with oak floor. The three windows were tall and well-sealed, not like the ones in David's place where he could put his fingers between the window and the brick casing, which is why he had plastic across his entire window wall. The windowsills and baseboards appeared to have been given a fresh coat of paint.

"Are the tenants quiet on the second floor?" asked Amanda.

"I did not ask, but will enquire," answered Diana.

"So how much are they asking for this apartment?"

"$950 a month with a security deposit of $950 up front. I'll tell you this unit will be gone in a few days."

"I like the apartment, love the street, and hope the other tenants are quiet," said Amanda.

"How are the unit and water heated and how much do the utilities run a month?" asked David.

"I believe gas for both, but I'll check. I wish we could get to the basement, but access is through the first-floor apartment. Good questions. I can find out by calling the office about the listing."

"Barring problems with the heat and utility costs, I'd like to put the $950 down today," said Amanda.

"And I'd really like to know if the entire townhouse is coming up someday soon. Can you get us a floor plan of the entire building?" asked David.

Amanda shot David another look that said, "I will talk with you about this."

Diana said, "I'll call my office now and get some answers for you, Amanda." Diana was trying mightily to address herself to Amanda, without ignoring David's questions.

Diana went downstairs and Amanda asked, "What's this about buying the building?"

"Number one, it would be a great investment. You'll be in residency, maybe a fellowship for four to six years at Jeff. Number two, this townhouse will appreciate and be easy to sell when you are ready. Number three, as the landlord you'd receive monthly income from the second and third floor tenants to pay for the mortgage."

"You're assuming I'd be on the first floor. This place is likely to cost big money. My mom and dad are not loaded."

"I know my contributing would be complicated, but if you're interested in a financial partnership we could talk more once we get details from Diana."

Diana came back into the bedroom and said, "The other two occupants are tenants, neither are the owners. The woman on the first floor is a Jeff student due to move on to her match in Cincinnati July first. The others are a long term, older couple who probably would elect to stay if Amanda elected to buy the building. I'll get the floor plan and the average utility costs tomorrow."

"Okay. May I write a $950 check now with the request to move into the first floor apartment and make a written agreement that the deposit would be applied to the purchase of the entire townhouse, should that be possible?"

"I don't see why I couldn't write it up that way," replied Diana.

Amanda wrote out the check and handed it to Diana. They shook hands and walked down the stairs.

"Thank you, Diana, for your help. I'll be waiting for your call about the first-floor apartment and if the owner could consider selling the building. Would be nice not to have to climb three flights when I move in and then every day after work."

"Let's grab some lunch. Are you up for pizza?"

"Sure. There's a place next to Jeff Hall that's not bad. How about we try out a white pizza?"

They enjoyed the lunch. David had never had white, four cheese pizza before. They chatted about Amanda finding a roommate versus living alone on Quince Street, neither mentioning the option to purchase the entire building. Amanda was excited about continuing her after research and thought it might be rolled into credit for her residency.

"I will have to see if my new Psych Professors would be in favor of my continuing to do some work with Dr. Taylor, albeit long distance research could be a bit difficult. I could do background research, check citations if and when Dr. Taylor writes his next publication," offered David. "Here I am planning long distance immunology research when I don't even have an apartment in Boston to call home. I've got to make the mental shift to be a psychiatry resident and bone up on all the things I'll need to know when I am called to do consults."

"Would you and your parents be interested in going out to a restaurant after graduation ceremonies?" Amanda and David agreed not to try to combine the families for the meal to keep it intimate.

"Plenty of time for getting together later," thought David.

David did not ask Amanda if she wanted to spend the night with him at his townhouse. Neither did Amanda mention being together that night. She did tell David her parents were spending the night in a hotel. She wanted to go over and spend some time with them. Ben was driving David's parents to Philly on graduation morning, so David had the night to himself.

"First time in a long time that I don't have anything to study for," he thought. I should try to find a place in Boston. I'll call Phil and Karen. I think they still live in Brighton. Man, I haven't seen them in years. I wonder if they made Aliyah. They were talking about it."

"Then I'll see you at the Academy tomorrow," said David trying to sound upbeat.

"You bet," replied Amanda, "I'll be the one in the cap and gown," she smiled.

CHAPTER SEVENTY-SIX

Graduation Day

David put on a sport coat and tie. "I'm sure Mom and Dad will want to go to a restaurant after the ceremony. I hope they like Ralph's," he thought, "I'm glad I made a reservation."

He carried his gown and tam in a plastic bag to be less conspicuous on the walk to the Academy of Music on Broad Street.

"I'll put it on once I get there," he said to himself.

David had already said goodbye to Don. His parents and sisters came up to see the apartment last night and had made plans to go to brunch together at the Crepes place on Walnut Street. David had already said goodbye to Lisa and Cindi last week. Their semesters ended earlier than the Medical School did, so they were likely already at work. David had taken down the twenty-foot-long banner he and Don made, attaching paper cutouts representing their time at Jefferson. David thought back to the night he and Amanda made gingerbread men as he walked through the kitchen. Ben was going to stay in the townhouse another month. His time in the Navy was almost up. He had a pretty good job lined up with the EMT service. He was also looking at a promotion once he moved to full time. Ben had shown David the new extension baton that he was going to carry for that job. It was about six inches long with a metal ball at the end. When extended with a flick of Ben's wrist it became a foot-long weapon.

"I'll have to disarm the knuckleheads who want to hassle us while we try to save lives," Ben explained.

David took another look around the living room and kitchen where he and Amanda had studied.

"Might as well get over to the Academy," he said out loud to no one there. He opened the front door and stepped out for perhaps one of the last times.

The morning was clear and warm, but not enough to raise a sweat as he walked the five blocks. He passed the Wawa on Broad Street where he had been a stock boy at lunchtime during his freshman year. David recalled having to take a lie detector test. He, of course passed it and only then would the man administering the test explain to David how the belt across his chest and the electrodes on his wrists were able to detect subtle changes in respirations and pulse. Initially, David had been insulted that he, a medical student, would not be implicitly trusted, but then realized it was not personal and probably a good policy for as large an outfit as Wawa. He crossed Broad and walked the block to the entrance of the Academy, which was bustling with men and women in gowns conversing with their families.

"There's Ben, Mom, and Dad," he thought as he waved to them.

"Where is your cap and gown, David," asked his mom.

"In the bag. I'll put in on now, didn't want to get it all sweaty."

"Where will we sit, David?" asked his father, getting right down to the business at hand.

"I've got your tickets, Dad. You are in the center section, row twenty. You should have no problem seeing the stage. I just hope this doesn't go on too long. I know we will be reciting the Hippocratic Oath, singing the Jefferson School Song. God, I hope they pass out the words. The class is about two hundred and we all will march across the stage, shake the Dean's hand and sit back down. That will take some time."

"We'll be ok, David," answered his mom, "After all it took four years and a lot of work to reach today, so enjoy and don't worry about us."

Ben rejoined them saying, "I checked out the restrooms, up and to the right. I suggest we go now as they're not crowded."

"I'll find my seat," said David, "Here are your seat tickets. By the time you get back it'll be close to starting."

David walked down the aisle and spotted Mr. and Mrs. Jackson. Amanda was not with them, so David took the opportunity to go over and greet them.

"Hello Mrs. and Mr. Jackson. Where's your lovely daughter?"

"She went to freshen up," replied Mrs. Jackson.

"Big day for you, David," said Mr. Jackson, "Are your parents here?"

"Also in the freshen up rooms," replied David. "I'm glad I caught you two. I have a favor to ask."

"Please ask us David," replied Mrs. Jackson.

"I repaired and repainted baby blue," said David. "I wanted to surprise Amanda, so I parked it across the street. Here are the keys." David handed the set of car keys to Mr. Jackson. "The favor is that you give the keys to Amanda, then ask her to play the tape in the radio."

"That is an amazing gesture David," said Mrs. Jackson, "What a surprise for Amanda. May I ask what is on the tape?"

"The song is by the group named Orleans. The song is "You're Still The One."

"That really says it all, doesn't it, David," said Mr. Jackson. "I'll be glad to give her the keys and ask her to play that song. What an extremely generous and loving gift, David. I'm impressed."

"You're Still The One," Orleans

"David," said Mrs. Jackson, "You'd better get to your seat, I think they are about to start."

The graduation went as planned. David's attention was on the J row. Amanda flashed a smile when David looked back and caught her eye, but she didn't indicate she wanted to talk.

"Maybe later," thought David. He made small talk with his classmates to the left and right. They had been partners in the cadaver dissection classes but otherwise hadn't spent time together.

Before the class of '81 walked across the stage to receive their diplomas, Dean Ollman took time to eulogize Dr. Carlos who had suffered a heart attack and died last year. David had heard that Dr. Carlos signed himself out of the hospital against the advice of his Cardiologist. Dr. Carlos must have known just how seriously the infarction had damaged his heart.

"I wonder if he just wanted to control his final few days and not become a cardiac cripple," David wondered.

The Dean also mentioned Dr. Asher's death from lung cancer. David was especially touched that Ollman said some very nice things about Florence and did not make a big thing of her suicide, just that she was a hard-working student, a founding member of the woman's support group, and a real credit to the Jefferson community.

When his row stood and lined up to walk across the stage, David recalled the last time he had seen Dean Ollman. "I wonder if he will remember me," thought David.

Dean Ollman did remember his meeting with David and as they shook hands said "I see that you did well here at Jefferson and on your clinical rotations. Good luck in Boston," he added handing David the rolled up, faux graduation degree.

The next Doctoral student's name was already being announced and David walked off the stage and sat down in his seat.

"Well, that's over," he said to the woman to his left who was already deep in excited conversation with the new physician to her left.

After the Y's and Z's were off the stage everyone stood and recited the Hippocratic Oath. David like most of the new physicians present referred to the program where he read half of it. The Jefferson song was not the most inspiring, but it marked the end of the ceremony. Tams were tossed into the air. Handshakes and embraces were shared. David felt a minor twinge of sadness that the four years were over and a little regret that he'd not made more friends.

"Amanda is the one friend I wanted and the one love of my life," he thought, "I wonder what will happen tomorrow? She's being a little distant today."

Mom and Dad were waiting for him in the lobby. Ben had already left to get the car.

Dad asked about Ralph's, "An unusual name for an Italian restaurant, don't you think? Will I be able to get a good steak?"

"I can vouch for the steaks, Amanda and I have eaten there many times. The wine selection is very good as well."

"Where is Amanda?" asked Vera, "I was hoping to see her again, but I suppose her parents have spirited her away."

"It's a madhouse now, Mom. Ben's probably waiting for us out front. Let me have your hand and we can walk out."

As always, Ben was prepared. Mom's Lincoln town car was front and center. They had no problem getting to or parking near Ralph's. The reservations turned out to be an excellent idea, as Ralph's was packed with graduates and their families. The linen table clothes and place settings, the wait staff in black ties and red and white checked aprons bustled about taking orders and delivering trays heaped with delicious smelling food. Their waitress took their orders and David suggested the Brunello, "Amanda and I drank this one the last meal we had here."

The meal was a success. Dave got his steak and pronounced it satisfactory, which coming from him would have been the equivalent of a rave review from anyone else. Vera had the four-cheese ravioli and said it was the best she'd ever tasted, "So light and fresh."

"Made fresh daily," replied David.

"You know I like Zinfandels," said Dave, "But this one, what was the name, is good."

"Brunello di Montalcino. Mom, Ben, do you like the wine?"

"A lovely choice Doctor Coleman. Oh, I love the sound of that. Do you remember I told you that you should be a doctor when you were studying Geology?"

"Yes mom. I took the long way around through graduate school to reach the medical school decision."

Ben chuckled at the understatement of the year. "When do you start at The Brigham?"

"July first. That will not be the best day to get sick and be admitted to the hospital. The third years will be gone and all the admissions will be by guys like me, as green as they get."

"I'm sure you'll be fine," said his mom, "You know Ariel, my college roommate who is your godmother, lives in Boston."

"I've been to her house just off Boston Commons, stayed a night there while I was in Maine."

"Well Ariel would love another visit from you once you find an apartment and are settled. Take Ariel and Joe out to dinner. They'd appreciate it and they will be a good resource for you once you're there."

"I'll be sure to look Ariel and Joe up when I get to Boston in July, Mom."

David was glad when the conversation moved onto Ben's upcoming move from the Navy to the job with the Philadelphia EMT squad. Ben was always so cool under questioning. He offered to drive his parents home having seen the second bottle of red wine emptied. Dave apparently enjoyed it as much as his beloved Zinfandel.

"See you tomorrow, David," he said.

David moved closer to Ben and whispered in his ear, "I'm going to confession after you leave, then I'm going back to the townhouse. Do you think you'll be coming back to Philly tonight?"

"If you want me to I will," replied Ben.

"I'd really appreciate the opportunity to talk with you, Ben. A lot's been happening."

David asked the waiter for the check, but his dad had already spoken with the waitress and said, "You paid for four years at Jefferson, David. I can get this check. Thanks for selecting a very nice restaurant. I have a new wine to look forward to as well."

"Thanks for a lovely meal, David," said Vera, "So, will we see you tomorrow afternoon. Do you think Amanda could come with you?"

"I believe Amanda's parents have their own plans for her, Mom."

"The car's out back," offered Ben, saving David from having to commit to a Sunday trip to Wilmington.

"Let me use the ladies' room. Please wait for me, Doctor Coleman, I want to give you one more hug."

CHAPTER SEVENTY-SEVEN

David in the Confessional

David walked from Ralph's to Saint Mary's. It was close to five o'clock and David recalled Saturday confessions started at five thirty. He was not a little bit anxious about what he would share with the priest. "I hope Father Joseph will be here to hear my confession," thought David. Old Saint Mary's still radiated the familiar warmth David had come to relish on Sunday. David waited in line until it was his turn. He entered the confessional booth, knelt down, made the sign of the cross, then said, "Bless me Father for I have sinned."

"What are your sins, my son," said Father Joseph.

"I'm so relieved that it is you, Father Joseph, you make me feel so comfortable. I have committed the sin of pride, perhaps hubris and for that I am truly sorry."

"Please tell me more about this act of pride, David. Yes, I recognize you, my son."

"Well, it is not just one instance, but perhaps the most serious was when I suggested my girlfriend Amanda think about purchasing an entire townhome instead of simply renting one apartment. I kinda sprang it on her and it was obvious it made her uncomfortable and that she needed time to think about it. I made the argument that it would be a great investment, and after her residency, and perhaps fellowship at Jefferson, she could easily sell it. The property is on a safe and very cute street, close to Jefferson."

"How did she leave it with the realtor?"

"Amanda did ask the realtor to write the contract to rent the third floor with the contingency to apply the rental deposit towards possibly purchasing the property if the owner agrees."

"So, Amanda did not outright reject the idea," replied Father Joseph. "Was there another instance of a prideful action, David?"

"I came off so sure that we could continue our relationship, despite me being in Boston in my residency while Amanda was here in Philly. She may want the option to meet other men. I'll be so far away and we'll both be so busy in our residencies. I guess I just hoped things would continue as now, despite the distances."

"That is understandable, but perhaps naïve, David. Have you and Amanda made specific promises to be together, to be married some day in the future?"

"We have not proposed marriage to each other. We have both said we would work to keep our relationship going despite living in different cities."

"That sounds like you both are not ready to commit to taking that step to holy matrimony, which is a very big and difficult step. Is there more?"

"Well, I took it upon myself to have Amanda's Saab repaired, which she wrecked on I-95. She broke her leg you know, but otherwise come out ok. Anyway, I had it rebuilt and repainted in the color she had really wanted, baby blue. I intended it to be a surprise but had not considered that she may have some pretty scary memories attached to it now. I guess I just don't know when I've overreached. I don't want to cause her any pain, whether over the apartment or town home, continuing our relationship during residency, or with the Saab."

"These three examples of making assumptions, perhaps out of pride, certainly seem to be made with the best of intentions. I do not believe they rise to the level of overweening pride, or hubris as you mentioned. I also do not believe they by themselves are relationship ending mistakes David. I assign you ten Our Father's and three Hail Mary's, but also to meditate on three statements from the Bible. I hope I can remember these. The first is from 1 Corinthians 13:4 and often used in marriage ceremonies. 'Love is patient and kind, love does not envy or boast; it isn't arrogant.'

The second is from Romans 12:16. 'Live in harmony with one another. Do not be haughty, but associated with the lowly. Never be wise in your own sight.'

My favorite is from Ecclesiastes 7:8. 'Better is the end of a thing, than its beginning, and the patient in spirit is better than the proud in spirit.'

Another way of saying these things is "You cannot find what you deny yourself. What does that make you think about?"

David thought for a moment, then spoke through the confessional's wooden screen, "I cannot find love from others if I do not love or accept myself."

"I believe you've hit upon a very profound truth, David."

"Thank you for all your guidance, Father Joseph."

"Now go in the spirit and love of our Lord, Jesus Christ. Perform your penance with a positive attitude. Aspire to do better in your dealings with Amanda. Please attend Sunday Mass together.

David felt a great weight lift from his shoulders having spoken with Father Joseph.

"I'll have to connect with a church in Boston and keep this Sunday Mass thing going, especially if Amanda ever visits. I know she'll continue to go the Saint Mary's. God, I hope she and I will be able to keep things moving forward, even if more slowly, with me in Boston. I suppose I should be somewhat concerned Amanda may find another guy," David thought, "Oh well, can't do anything about that now except be my loveable and supportive self. So, I'm going back to my lonely townhome and wait for Ben to show. How much am I willing to share with him about what's going on between Amanda and me? Certainly not the abortion, that is a very private matter between Amanda, especially Amanda, and I. But in for a penny, in for a pound with the other things such as moving to Boston, finding a place, being able to find the time to speak with Amanda, and Ben, perhaps take the train to Philly once in a while. A lot to consider. I mostly wish I could know what is going on in Amanda's head."

"Baby Blue," Bad Finger

CHAPTER SEVENTY-EIGHT

Ending

Amanda had already packed her clothes and books before the graduation ceremony. David waited until Amanda and her parents left for the Academy of Music, then went over to Amanda's townhome to speak with Mrs. Hopkins. David asked her to hide a 45 rpm record in Amanda's luggage where she was not likely to find it until she arrived home. The record was "You're Still The One," by Orleans. David had not played it for Amanda but hoped it would convey his feelings. David knew he was doubling down on the song, once on the cassette tape in the car, and now this one in her luggage. Mrs. Hopkins said she would be glad to keep it secret.

After Saturday's ceremony Amanda's parents took her out to dinner, then went home, promising to pick her up sometime on Sunday. Unbeknownst to David, Amanda called her mother Saturday night and asked if she could come to Philly as soon as she could on Sunday morning to bring her home. She didn't answer when her mother asked why so early or why she did not want to spend some time with David before leaving Sunday morning. Amanda was up at five o'clock, stripped her bed and vacuumed the room. She was ready when her mother came to pick her up. Mrs. Jackson did not ask too many questions during the drive home after it became obvious Amanda was deep in her thoughts.

David decided he would go to seven o'clock Mass by himself. He needed time to think in a safe place and perhaps was holding onto a tiny crumb of hope that Amanda would be there. She was not. Father Joseph made his usual eye contact with all present, including David. He did not indicate with a special look that he recognized Amanda was not with David. After Mass David placed the crisp twenty-dollar bill in the orphan's box, which made him smile at the memory of his first Mass at Saint Mary's. Then he slowly walked home, taking the way past Amanda's town home on Locust.

"I guess it was a bit of a stretch to think Amanda would tell me she'd not be going to Mass then show up anyway," he thought, "More magical thinking on my part."

Amanda had asked David on Friday if they could skip Mass on Sunday due to packing and getting home. David thought it a bit odd that Amanda would skip seven a.m. Mass when there was plenty of time on Sunday to pack up and get ready to leave but didn't argue.

"Perhaps her time to herself is starting now. I did agree to give her all the time she needed, but I guess I wasn't prepared for it to start so soon," thought David. "I have to admit I don't feel so upbeat knowing Amanda's left Philly. Just a few hours without her and I'm approaching basket case status. Not good."

"Ain't No Sunshine When She's Gone," Bill Withers.

After packing his own belongings, he walked to Amanda's townhouse and met Mrs. Hopkins at the door, who said, "Amanda left a little after seven thirty a.m. She said to tell you she was sorry to miss you, her mother had to get home. Something about Amanda's sister. Call her tonight."

She did not say Amanda had not asked that David call her that night.

"Normally I'd ask you in for a cup of tea, David, but I must meet with friends to do some shopping. Have a good summer Doctor Coleman and congratulations on achieving your four-year goal. You know I miss Amanda already."

"So do I, Mrs. Hopkins. Thanks for all you did for Amanda. Thank you for being so kind to me. I know she enjoyed your company and always felt safe living here. It is a very nice location and you keep a lovely home."

David climbed down the eight steps to the sidewalk then turned left toward his apartment on Tenth Street south of Pine. The rain fell against his face, mixing with his tears. David could not get past the idea that Amanda was taking the easy way out. He did not like that the word coward had popped into his head.

"I thought we communicated better than this," thought David, "And I believe I was responsive to Amanda's complaints and provided emotional support on top of answering her concerns."

He really cared, even felt that he loved Amanda more now, realizing the difficult time ahead. To have her essentially run away from him was devastating.

"I'm starting to feel myself closing off," he said to himself, "Like I used to do when I was getting the goodbye-and-thanks-for-the-fun vibes while at Delaware. I really don't want to go there, at least so quickly. I hope Ben is able to come here tonight. I'm gonna have to lean on him and run this by him to be sure I'm not making too much about it."

David turned the key and entered his townhome a much different fellow than he had been just hours ago. He put on the James Gang Three tape and sprawled out on the couch. He found himself replaying the times he spent with Amanda and how he grew from being infatuated to valuing their friendship, to building a relationship of trust and love. What was the basis of their love? She was there for him after he got shot and he took care of her after she fractured her femur. They shared intimate moments and had felt confident about that. The pregnancy had not derailed their affection, or had it? That was something David needed to think about and someday soon confront Amanda about. Hell, they had made tentative plans to buy a townhome together! Or had they? Amanda had not shared any more details about the rental vs purchase options with David and David decided not to press the issue quite yet. Maybe things had moved too fast, and Amanda had recognized it first. David admitted he tended to jump into things, then work like hell to do a good job accomplishing what he had promised to do. Magical thinking was one way Ben used to describe the process. David eventually slipped into a troubled sleep. He awoke an hour later with a crook in his neck and not able to recall any of the dreams he had experienced. He put in another call to Ben asking to meet him for dinner. David was not ready to travel to Wilmington and confront his parents and their questions just yet.

"I came to Jeff alone, not knowing anyone. I made quite a few friends and was so very fortunate to meet Amanda, the love of my life. Going home alone, at least for the short term is not the end of the world. I will likely miss having Ben close by. Ben will probably advise me to try to be patient and give Amanda the time she'll need. He'll probably even comment that Amanda will likely be answering any number of difficult questions from her parents about me and our relationship going forward. Ben will tell me she and I have the rest of June to make contact before I go to Harvard, which is true. Ben's a smart man."

David went up to his room, changed into shorts, his new Stone's shirt, and sneakers. He opened his dresser drawer, snapped open the gray box and looked at the engagement ring with a broad smile. He snapped the box shut, tucked it in under his socks and closed the drawer. David went down to the kitchen and drank a glass of apple juice, stepped out into the bright sunshine with a smile on his face, then went for a run to Veteran's Stadium.

Ending song. "Walk Away," James Gang

Songs

Anticipation. Carly Simon
Requim for a Friend. Elton John
Amerita, Sense of Direction. Climax Blues Band
Boy Blue. ELO
Thirty Days in the Hole. Humble Pie
Cold as Ice. Foreigner
Someone Shot Me in my Shoulder. John Legend
I Can't Write with my Left Hand. Bill Withers
Sister Morphine. The Rolling Stones
Lets Stay Together. Al Green
For a Dancer. Jackson Browne
Sitting on the Dock of the Bay. Otis Redding
Twisted. Joni Mitchell
She's a Rainbow. The Rolling Stones
Is This Love. White Snake
Time Warp. The Rocky Horror Picture Show
Celluloid Hero. The Kinks
Let's Spend the Night Together. The Rolling Stones
Little Duce Coup. Jan and Dean
Garden Party. Rick Nelson
The Circle Game. Joni Mitchell
Have I Told You Lately I Love You? Rod Stewart
Kiss You All Over. Exile
Bella. Santana

Rock Me on the Water. Jackson Browne
Bach Sonata. Jean Pierre Rampal
Night Moves. Bob Seger and the Silver Bullet Band
You're Still the One. Orleans
Baby Blue. Bad Finger
Ain't No Sunshine When She's Gone. Bill Withers
Walk Away. The James Gang